AROUND THE SUN

AROUND THE SUN

A NOVEL

ERIC MICHAEL BOVIM

Epigraph Books
Rhinebeck, New York

Paperback ISBN 978-1-951937-38-6
eBook ISBN 978-1-951937-39-3

Library of Congress Control Number 2020908664

Book and cover design by Colin Rolfe
Cover photo by Lucas Neves

Epigraph Books
22 East Market Street, Suite 304
Rhinebeck, NY 12572
(845) 876-4861
epigraphPS.com

To Virginia Bailey, who loved her words and loved me too
and to Mila, Cami, and Alex.

acknowledgments

To write this book, I relied heavily upon encouragement and reviews from several gracious people: Christopher Merrill; Karen Thompson Walker; Daniel Burgess; David Busis; Mickey Rapkin. Of course, I want to especially thank Claudia Herr for her edits to the manuscript, which, bloated as it was, became a more tapered and lucid text after she cut seventy pages.

Time was my enemy for much of the writing process. There was simply never enough of it, for varying reasons, so I found myself writing the novel in bursts—*out of or away from my home or country*, in coffee shops, hotel rooms, long-haul flights abroad, or wherever I could steal the uninterrupted time necessary to express a few hundred words at a time.

Some of the places I have visited—San Francisco, Barbados, Copenhagen, and Spain—absolutely inform the novel's mood and itinerant nature. Some seep into the novel, others do not.

Apart from travel, music had a heavy influence on the atmosphere of the prose. After reading Teju Cole's "Open City" in 2013, I became aware of Mahler's Ninth Symphony, which became a kind of soundtrack while writing the first section of the book. In 2016, while seated onstage during a live performance of Bruckner's Seventh Symphony in Vienna, I listened to the second movement endlessly while rewriting the second half of the book. There were other pieces of music that captured my imagination during the writing process, but these figure most prominently and even impacted some of the novel's tone.

Some falsely regard writing as a glamourous act, even though it demands absolute solitude. There is certainly nothing glamourous about rewriting and refining and rewriting sentences, even if may occur, at times, at a corner table in a café, say, in Copenhagen. Solitude feeds fiction, and I wish to thank my family for granting me the access to it over the years.

"These fragments I have shored against my ruins."

The Waste Land, **T.S. Eliot**

PART 1

chapter one

I T WAS a quiet line that stretched across the threshold from the airbridge into the fuselage world, business travelers, mainly, eyes fixed into screens and sipping away their liters of glacial water, an idling American engine.

Further ahead, in the first-class cabin, I glimpsed the Steve Jobs biographer, Walter Isaacson, blocking the aisle, straining to hoist an overnight bag into an overhead bin. Mid-thirties men unpacked carry-ons monastically, a whisper of directives into their earpieces, virtual meetings stretched to the brink. You got double miles for first class. Champagne fizzed in plastic flutes and the silent flight attendants stood with dim smiles. Behind the economy class partition, an old woman in the window seat, wrapped in a silk shawl, bit an irradiated white peach, chin glassy with nectar. Overhead, dirty plastic TV boxes. Scalded Arabica and microwaved sausage. Predeparture trickle of Sunday brunch piano, faint Gershwin.

Once the plane was taxiing, the CEO of United, spray-tanned and flanked by subordinates in a hangar, waved an onscreen "Hello." The new global fleet of today burns less fuel than the fleet of yesterday—emphasis on today. He spoke in the same suit, on different days, from major landmarks in different hubs—the Pantheon, Big Ben, sunset Buddhist temples, the Taj Mahal at dawn—narrating to a brassy version of the score to "An American in Paris" in nearly a full minute of flare-gun promotion. Then he navigated around the new website, swiped screens of the companion app. The next shot was of a Spanish celebrity chef chiffonading basil to make a vinaigrette. The menus on the transatlantic route all bore his name.

When it ended, I calculated the production costs at more than $200,000—come to think of it, the rights to the music alone were definitely over seven figures. I tried to quantify the corn in the fuel, the tonnage of Iowa crop yields incinerating in the engines. This was Tuesday morning.

Soon the captain broke in: we would be landing thirty to forty minutes late. The only choice was patience. He was static omniscience, armed and barricaded behind a terror-proof door. Surveying all the passengers I wondered who else like me had randomly been chosen for pre-screened security check-in—I had simply slipped through the scanner like a mist. Now a safety video played. I started to contemplate my free drink. Cabin life had its preordained rhythms. The goal was not to think.

I had been woken that morning when my vibrating cell phone rattled the water glass on the nightstand with emails coming in from Tokyo. What if I had awoken in the middle of the night, glanced at the alarm, saw that the time was close, and, rather than waking, had pushed in the pin on the clock and fallen back asleep? What if, instead of sitting up with night sweats and drinking the glass empty, showering, rubbing my chin and debating whether to shave, then walking downstairs into the kitchen and making Colin pancakes with chocolate chips sprinkled into the patch of batter, and cellophane-wrapping them for later, the dreaded pale headlights of the sedan waiting in the rain—what if, instead of sinking into the backseat for another trek to Dulles, I had climbed back up the stairs to wake him, hitting the dormant parkway in the Maserati by eight, glazed alpine white, off to one of his tournaments, a good two-hour morning drive? I would have taken the empty roads through the Sunday city, the decaying bridge over the bay to the tallgrass peninsula deep in autumn, to Easton, while he was swaddled in wool in the backseat.

Rising steam from the mug in the cup holder. A satellite broadcast of NHL banter and trade speculation. The only driver for many miles. I headquartered my company in a Leed-certified building where the toilets halfflushed, and my drive in was always a highlight. Weekdays I would take the scenic byway that paralleled the Potomac, blaring music—usually Oasis, especially where Noel Gallagher sings, or R.E.M. or Pearl Jam—or playing YouTube poetry readings by T.S. Eliot or less fortunate poets, or holding myself captive to trade speculation on the radio, and when I saw the spires of Georgetown University across the river, I would decide amongst the three bridges that fed Northern Virginia into the District of Columbia. I took conference calls via Bluetooth, hands at ten and two, and when I skipped the calls or killed the music and the readings, I drove in pleasant catatonic silence, marking the seasons by whether the leaves had turned lemon or garnet, had crisped then fallen, or had come again, tiny green stars on their weary limbs.

This daydream Sunday I would have slowed near the known speed traps, then blown open the engine on the straightaway, passing under wet arches of garnet leaves, their phantom smell entering the car. He would have been asleep, right there with me.

But this was Tuesday and the corn-fed engines roared and flushed the sanitized Gershwin and my plane lifted off, a streaking human lyric in the sky.

It was a steep ascent through silvery clouds, and soon we passed over the Shenandoah, the ink of the Mississippi, the heartland patchwork plains, then the anonymous canyons and camel hump mountain range and the creosote rail ties across it all, and somewhere below there is a rusted Model-T, a cactus grown into the fender, some shotgun shell ghost town, and to the north, in Council Bluffs, Iowa, deer are grazing near the electrified fence surrounding a Google server farm, all those thickets of tendril wires gripping the national privacy. Death Valley. Apache, Cherokee, Hopi, Navajo. Then some stunted green fringe, Silicon Valley. The usual approach: right over San Francisco Bay and out into the Pacific, banking eastward and over the polyglot city, the vital edge of America.

My seatmate wore a blue suit with chalky pinstripes and was completely middle-aged, like me. There were still raindrops on his jacket and he smelled like mildewy wool. I declined the champagne, ordered English tea, milk and two sugars, for no apparent reason. He turned to me and asked if I was from the east, a question that I thought was simply déclassé. Usually, I slip-noosed all potential airline comradery with one-word tugs—"yesses"— and if necessary I pretended to speak no English. But he kept at it.

"Politics?" he asked, pinky-stirring his Bloody Mary. He had his laptop open and was sifting through time-sensitive legal briefs, red pen hand-scribbled notes, flipping through timesheets and invoices.

"I'm agnostic," I said.

"I meant are you on the Hill? I think we've met before; you look familiar. I think you're with Senator Gonzalez, am I right? I think so, right? You were his chief of staff?"

"I'm just a consultant."

"Consultant," he said with his head raised, swirling the ice cubes in his now empty glass, as if appraising some ancient scroll. He had a voice full of paver stones. "Litigator. Securities. Nice to meet you." He held out his hand. "But then you worked for Senator Rogers, I think. What kind of consultant?"

"I, in fact, never worked on Capitol Hill. I'm an agnostic."

"That's very funny. Clever. How does that work in principle? I mean, you need to pick a side. Where are you now?"

"A P.R. firm."

"Democrat or Republican?"

"We do corporate work, so no." I tried to emphasize my disinterest by rummaging in my bag for a bag of seedless grapes.

"We always need a P.R. guy for our cases. I represent a guy accused of fraud. You think you can get him an interview in the *Journal* or the *Times*? We've tried and it's been a battle. We just need a piece, something to sway the jury. His trial is in three months. The jury is mostly multiracial—no offense."

I covered my hands on my lap, as if it mattered.

He watched me doing this and said, "I may try to get involved myself, maybe go on TV and speak in his defense. What do you think? And I am sure I have seen you somewhere."

"I'm afraid we're oversubscribed at the moment." I stuffed some grapes in my mouth and tried to reclaim some savor of solitude by turning towards the window and feigning interest in the view—green earth in between the gauzy clouds, car specks marching off to nowhere. He went on speaking about his plaintiff while I initiated my breathing exercises and imagined Catskill light over the whoosh of the jet stream.

Then there was a shrill loudspeaker interruption, a pitch to apply for the airline Visa card—bonus miles for debt—and my seatmate took one of the applications that were being distributed without looking up, placed it over his invoices, and started checking the tidy boxes with trance intensity. I pretended to look across at the other window and glanced at his sheet. Divorced. New dependents. New address. The "Other" income box, the one that says, "over $750,000." I finished my breathing exercises and thought about the unanswered emails, texts, voicemails. Gold prices. The indeterminate distance past the clouds.

"Then I must have seen you on television," he said to me, checking the hours on his timesheet with a cell calculator.

There was a woman across the aisle in the window seat. She was smiling at me. The resemblance to Monica was uncanny.

"These drinks. It's like flying in a convenience store now. I'm serious. Try flying to Paris or Seoul or Buenos Aires—same food, different direction. They don't give you much of anything anywhere anymore. You're expected to be self-sufficient. You're probably not old enough to remember what it was like to fly to London on the Concorde. They'd set up a caviar buffet right in aisle—right there. Petrossian. It was vodka and caviar and Marlboros and zip—New York to Europe in three hours tops."

He looked me up and down and said, "Maybe you've made those trips too. Well, if you haven't, they are truly exceptional and I am talking about the whole gamut—the glitzy hotels, the clients, the chauffeured cars—all that aristocracy. We need it over here, I'll tell you that. I don't know your politics, but mine are whatever is paying the hourly fees, you know? The aristocracy. You know they have people over there whose father's father went to Cambridge or Oxford or wherever—and they basically carry the causes of their ancestors, this is their vocation, it's this mission or value system passed down through the lineage. They're not as free thinking as we are, but at least it's more civil; they are honoring tradition. I need another one." He signaled for a refill.

The stewardess, Brenda, per her nametag, came back and snapped open a can of Motts and poured out the Smirnoff nip without blinking and stabbed at a lemon cube and poked it into the drink. She wore too much rouge and had parchment hands.

"Twenty years ago, they'd leave the goddamn bottle and the captain would come out and have one with us. Who knows if they flew intoxicated back then, just like in that movie. So, what do you think?"

"I think there are rules against that."

"You're funny. No, I meant the case, my case, the jury."

"Do you know what I think of the *Times* and the *Journal?*"

"I'm desperate to know," he said, chugging the drink.

"Your case is fairly hopeless and there's nothing the media will want to write about it because your story likely has too many nuances. There's too many stories and too few journalists. That's my assessment, *Lorem Ipsum Dolorem.*"

"Coffee too, dear. Thank you," he said, not as shocked as I had hoped.

Brenda poured the coffee a little too theatrically, as if the pot were a carafe of Margaux. Would I like the chicken or the beef or we have ravioli, she asked us. I waved her off and ordered vodka-cranberry.

"Well," he said, "I guess we should have hired you a few years ago before we loaded up on bad firms. It's nice to get a fucking straight answer now and then."

The woman across the aisle smiled again. She was maybe forty, most certainly private sector. She wore a peak lapel white suit. Although, Monica would have worn it differently; she would have lent it some insouciance, projected some mild defiance with that way she fluffed her hair from her shoulders with the back of her hands, jettisoning that raven sheen behind her. She would have perforated the monotony by pulling on the pink gloves with the fox fur cuffs that she used to break out this time of year.

This was the month she always left for Mexico. I am like a monarch butterfly, she would say. I fly south after the first frost. Then she would migrate for a month to that red clay town with a bell tower up in the hills, had a hunched studio right off the Calle San Miguel, near the poorly lit bodega with no labels on their tequila bottles and the bartender with the Fu Manchu. She said the town had the right light for her work, air that nursed her imagination.

We are never where we are.

It was something she said whenever she saw me on the phone making dinner or reading an email if we were already in a conversation, when my attention was subdivided among apps and browsers and inboxes and people. This was my fifth business trip in two months. If I was not on the phone I was in a meeting and if I was not in a meeting or on the phone I was on a business trip. Whatever was left I called home.

★

LAST WEEK, I'd flown to Copenhagen to meet a new client, my journey marked by the clang of saucers at the Segafredo coffee kiosk in the arrivals terminal at Tegel. A man with an Ayatollah beard was stretched out asleep on a bank of leather chairs, an empty orange Fanta bottle on the table beside his head, everywhere the punishing density of German, the sky lunar gray with morning and later the October sea already frozen as I rode out to the old Grand Bretagne, now the country's finest hotel, where I even saw the Danish Queen sleigh-riding by, votives flickering on all the breakfast tables when I arrived and an oversized staircase spiraling up through the center of the refurbished building. They had kept the original façade, but now it was called d'Angleterre.

I waited for Lars, my client, in the hotel bar, long enough for a croissant and two macchiatos. I'd been hired by the private equity firm that backed him and his lover, Fung. Lars was a Dutch hacker, something to do with bitcoin and the Mt. Gox scandal, and now he and Fung were co-founders of a startup that translated spoken Mandarin into English and vice versa. The IPO was the week after Thanksgiving.

"You look so tired," he said when he arrived. He sat down, hand tremoring. "I'm not going to have something. Are you going to have something? Maybe it's better if we go walking. It's better maybe."

"We can walk if you like, Lars. Why don't we go to the Café Norden? It's nice there—and it's nice to finally meet you."

He had disappointing splotches of facial hair that gave a sense of "almost" growing on his face, and his head was shaved to a near shine. We left the hotel and walked down streets with unpronounceable names, diphthongs and exotic letter pairings—like Catalan blended with German. He was nearly six foot three, all his bulk stuffed in a crimson blazer and spandex denim. The shops were just opening. People were riding bicycles to work. It was not clear to me yet if I would invite Lars to dinner; I had been instructed by Alan to try Noma, what the lists considered the world's best restaurant. You sucked live ants served on bark through a straw or bit into a nest of veal fibers, slurped parsley jelly and razor clams—Viking primitivism. My job demanded I sometimes consume things against my will. Looking at Lars, fiddling with his phone while he walked, I did not sense he would care if we skipped Noma altogether.

When we arrived in Amagertov Square, the pigeons and the students and the bicycles were amassed at the fountain and the water was turned off but all the heat lamps were on, glowing orange above the tables at all the cafés. We went inside and found seats near the corner by the news-papers. The waitress spoke brittle Scandinavian English and stood a little impatiently at our table. We ordered little sandwiches of smoked fish with turnips and tiny pickles and clear yellow beer to wash it down. I watched the barman sweep the foam from the glass after he poured it. He handed it to me and I licked the remaining foam from the sides of the glass and tasted the cold beer and watched life outside. It was mostly small talk until the beer kicked in.

"So, what is it that you are you thinking we should do?" His hand was still shaking and beer foam was sliding down the side of his glass.

I said, "Can you repeat your version of events again please. One last time."

He recounted everything from the night of the hackathon, elucidated the nature of his relationship with Fung, and when he was finished I ordered us another round. I deliberately asked him to repeat the story again to see if he resisted further embellishment.

"We do not want any more sensation, Lars. The articles last week were enough. Now we need to project facts, eclipse bad news with new news. Do you understand?"

He was massaging his temples. "It's less about the criminal possibility and more that what I have built may be diminished by this scandal. This is the thing."

I sipped the beer and waited for him to go on.

"If Morgan Stanley wants to end the IPO then I guess this was for nothing. I will never get such a shot like this again. Everything, all of it—it all would have been a waste. I don't want to change the world, I just want it to know who I am."

He reached into his breast pocket and handed me his phone. "I have all the settings right. Do you want to try it, see for yourself?"

The surface was sticky and the home screen was a photograph of the Fibonacci sequence inside a conch shell.

"Do you know Chinese? Well I guess it doesn't matter. Just say something into it in English, anything. It will come out in Mandarin. Hold down the zero key, just like this, and then speak a few words at a time, then listen for the Chinese to come out of the speaker. Just talk regular about anything and OneSpeak will do the rest."

I spoke a few words, and the screen froze. Then the app crashed.

We did not go to Noma. I rebooked myself on an earlier 6:00 a.m. flight to Berlin the next morning. There were no directs to Portugal. I had a speech later in the morning, a confab of robotics engineers who had built a hitchhiking humanoid robot—hitchBOT—that they were about to let loose. Toronto to Los Angeles. I could go home after that.

When I landed back in Tegel for my connection, I thought about calling Alan to tell him what had happened with OneSpeak. I sat down in a café beneath the enormous departures board and began to draft an email to him, but once I read over it I deleted it. The menu noted, in footnotes, the items containing quinine. There were only forty minutes until boarding for my connection. I ordered a "vital" breakfast of muesli. My waiter said he was from Portugal, but he looked like Hugo Chavez.

"How long you stay Lisbon? Three days? Wow. Okay. They have a touristic center. You go there. Largest aquarium in the world, sharks! Museum of coaches. How you say. Ehhh, cars with wood. Cowboy times? Stagecoaches, yes! You go there. Oh, Lisbon…you walk around, so much there."

Muesli came with some tart plain yogurt. There was a miniscule container of wildflower honey tucked amid the silverware.

On the TV a woman wearing turquoise eyeshadow was reporting live in front of the Bundestag, some story involving the words "spy" and "U.S." I sat and typed an email to Hawthorne back at the office to see where we were with the Ugandans as "Ride Like the Wind" played over loudspeakers. I rode a people-mover to my gate, where there was a stand that sold frankfurters and steins of Schultheiss. I went into the Lufthansa business lounge and there were men in three-piece suits eating gummi bears and drinking cava. I rewrote the email about the malfunction to Alan and deleted it again.

★

MY PANIC attacks began the morning of her funeral and a month later full depression set in. Dr. Weller put me on a trial regimen. Stick to a routine. Hire a nanny. Take a leave of absence. Take flowers to the cemetery but don't take Colin yet. Take him to the cemetery more often. Consider selling the house. So, I hired a live-in nanny, a Filipina with grown children who bleach-washed the bathrooms mid-week, neatened his trophies, tucked paired socks into the drawers—kept Colin's room as immaculate as Monica had, always tight hospital corners on the bed.

My goal was to try not to think. When I was away, I was a good enough father through texts. I would wait to hit send once the wheels left the tarmac.

I don't know why I would procrastinate until a single column of cell signal remained. By the end of the year, though, I was taking seven pills a day just to freeze the frame of my decline. Grief can bleed you into white nothing. Colin soon became symptomatic: tying and untying his shoes three times before school, looking for dirt in the house, insisting on new toothbrushes every night, drinking from the same sippy cup.

I simultaneously heeded everyone's advice—returned to work too soon, took Colin to the amusement park, brought him out for pizza twice a week, sang to him, administered his pills, watched him fall asleep.

When he was six I told him the partial truth.

She won't come home. She was so very sick. She is in a better place. I never mentioned the police.

I would wake up remembering little details, like that she quit law when she sold her first piece, oil on canvas, a long-range buffalo herd gnawing the Colorado plains, or what she thought such a sight might have looked like before they were all cold-blood slaughtered. Her exact words. By then, White & Partners was more or less a success. I was half Mexican and so my complete re-enfranchisement became her *cause célèbre*. I had found this amusing. She was a realist without the saccharine Norman Rockwell patina, her landscapes imbued with some bitter-end prehistoric gloom. Her father disapproved—of me and the painting, precisely which was most offensive to him I was never sure. He had an ulcer and a membership at Augusta, owed his wealth to sugar beets, and once sucker punched the bartender at the Savoy for smiling at his paramour, caught him with a martini shaker to the head. The poor Serb never stood a chance, he'd say. He told that story within the first ten minutes of meeting someone, up until his second heart attack. After that he was an invalid. He and Monica were not on speaking terms since she had become a working artist. Her mother faded away in a facility in the Berkshires for schizophrenics, where she had been remanded since the eighties. We saw her twice a year until she died months before Colin was born.

Monica had a vendetta against big commercial institutions. She purged the Virginia house of anything prefab, even flavored dental floss. She brought me to upstart salad chains with mission statements. She resented Starbucks—all the condescending flavor permutations—honey maples and winter mint mochas and spiced chai pumpkin, and so on. The year she died, for my thirty-seventh birthday, she bought a Breville burr grinder, eager that I dedicate myself to outperforming Big Coffee. I bought Rwandan beans online from a co-op. They came in vacuum-sealed silvery bags, hallmark sweetness and cocoa notes, none of the pitch-black aftertaste. Grind size twelve and 17.8 seconds to produce a double-shot. It took four months of trial and error to get the tamp down right—anywhere between twenty to thirty pounds of pressure, all in the wrist—any more and it's over-extracted and tarry, any less it's under-extracted and watery. Nothing less than 195 degrees for a good pull. The provenance of the beans, the digitally calibrated grind, human compression—there was no improvisation. Bad coffee agitated me. It was the product of human error, and it bothered me in the same way they filled the wine glass too full in bad restaurants. All avocational endeavors should be undertaken with the aim of mastery.

She had died shortly after I finally got it down, and since then every morning I used a butter knife to pry out the basket and break up the grinds with my fingers and sprinkle the grounds on random perennials, depositing the export from an impoverished nation into my yard, low-wage labor enriching the rose beds. She would have approved.

Colin and I still lived in the house, less than a mile from the CIA, where cell calls dropped at all hours without notice. We could hear the boom of jet engines echoing from the sky, flights in takeoff paths or final approaches, who knew which, just too high for contrails, and sometimes I stood at the window or the balcony and watched the red blinking wings vanish into the heights. A Baptist church stood across the street, and a bell rang on Sundays and the congregation of slacks and hats and pink dresses and little boat shoes filed in. Black crows perched on the crucifix atop the steeple every morning. I would see her painting in the backyard, the sycamores shedding their bark like English poplars do, the flaky bits nestling into the paint, and her blowing into the cobalt dollop like it was a dandelion and the bark just sinking deeper. The backyard was a total sanctuary—almost. Even with the birdsong and the vaulted trees blotting the traffic noise and the neighbors, which gave the space the feel of some distant artists' colony, I could never forget we were less than ten miles from Washington.

Last night I came in from the balcony and went to Colin's room to tuck him in.

"Hey," I said, turning on the white noise machine. "Daddy is going to California tomorrow morning."

I waited.

"It's not even two days. You'll be in school. You won't even notice it." I lifted his chin and said, "You won't."

He rolled over and turned away. I walked out and into the hallway, Atticus, our Maltese, in tow.

"Will you sit here with me?" he said.

Sit down with him, Mark, I heard Monica say, and I answered her back, sometimes, my lips moving.

*

MIDFLIGHT, I felt faint and short of breath. I opened another button on my shirt and finished my drink and sucked the ice cubes. No one was watching. I placed the white pill beneath my tongue, chewed it down with ice. They kept their heads bowed, load-bearing fixation, sci-fi paperbacks and Sudoku pads and rainbow scatter plots and power point graphics, and I imagined their interior monologues, pieced together the unspoken commotion. There was just a collective hush and a jet-stream hum._

As the plane tilted north some of that syrupy, high-altitude light poured onto my lap.

When I opened my laptop, there were nearly a hundred unread emails. There were unread texts. "Guns, whiskey, and envelopes for at-risk Congressmen," wrote Hank, referring to the National Rifle Association and Distilled Spirits Council, and the fundraising checks he was handing out to various chiefs of staff.

Condensation was spreading across the window. I saw what I thought was the Mississippi below. I had no written speech, only something from memory that I would unfurl at our meeting at the Four Seasons San Francisco. I looked up, put the paper down on my lap, finished the grapes, stacked the plastic cocktail cup into the Styrofoam tea cup. I pushed the call light button to order another tea and I tried not to think.

*

I FIGURED I would do what I could with Lars and Fung. I contemplated how all of this might play out, which journalists to call for major interviews, and I devised a comprehensive mental list in under three seconds: which hypothetical piece would publish online, fungible content, how it would catalyze reprints and me-too pieces by other bloggers and print reporters who did not want to let a racing story get too far down the track without them pulling up alongside it, and all of that healthy content would surface instantaneously on Google, enliven the brand and recirculate around OneSpeak like a digital blood transfusion.

I ordered a Vodka drink and watched the ticker symbols on my seat screen march west, my shares climbing higher every forty-five seconds, and so on.

We were somewhere around Nevada, and I browsed the airline magazine, a collection of sponsored stories under three pages, all in blue-eyed prose, a Chicago steakhouse menu, poetically-named cocktails alongside an advertorial for a beige office park city in wherever North Carolina. Then I whipped up a throwaway sermon, something of a riff. We would talk to press, not avoid them. Control what was seen, a brand being just a consensus of perceptions. We would refrain from social media, for now. We would switch wardrobes. We would speak in new voices. We would instigate this metamorphosis with an in-depth feature, preferably with someone wan and bewitched by money, a tech blogger, probably.

I had this experimental idea that they could write an open letter to the investment community on Twitter. I could buy my own coffee plantation in Rwanda. The per capita income was $250 per year. The fee OneSpeak had agreed to pay my firm—$3 million just to think—would supply a year's worth of income to 12,000 Rwandans. After overhead and taxes, given that I was the sole shareholder of White & Partners, I stood to clear $750,000 personally.

I glanced back at the advertorial. When Googled, you saw that it was really a dim pulse city along that corridor of I-95 where seventy-five is the speed limit and every mile or so ekes out new billboards for discount fireworks or cigar and perfume outlets or roadside motels with HBO for $32.50 per night. You could smell the hot tar of shredded tires in the breakdown lane, the cable technician shouting "Hello" through the screen door, and almost spot that trace of life within the mobile home, even at highway speed, hear his footsteps crunching the grass, see an old man's face vanish from the screen door into a shadow and into a TV dinner and a flickering gameshow. The t-shirts are cardboard stiff, and you shake them out into that highway wind beneath the billboard, clothing pins twisting on the line like demonic sparrows. A mile away someone like you is pulling over at a gas station convenience store for diapers and screwcap wine, skinny latchkey kids chugging liters of Mountain Dew and smoking by the haul-away propane tanks locked up by the dumpster. Rows of household goods in bright packages, vacuum sealed bags containing things not ordinarily fried, energy drinks in violent colors. Oily men of all ages on parole, on the prowl, probation.

You walk out with your scratch-away ticket and see a rusty Buick with a duct-taped rear light, a man in a bandana chastising his woman for being on the pipe. *That's private shit, that's private fucking shit we do out alone bitch. These children is in harm's way now bitch.*

I turned the page to busts of four chemotherapy patients. A man in his fifties, shirtless, lying on a complicated machine. A phone number in the lower left corner, below the website and QR code.

I knew Colin was at the kitchen table, demanding that Mae let him FaceTime me and I could hear her explaining that FaceTime does not work when someone was miles above Nevada. I resisted the urge to log on.

Brenda swung by with the drink cart, pouring more Margaux carafes of tepid coffee, sugar packets crammed into Styrofoam cups.

Where did the sugar come from, Colin would have asked.

A plantation outside of Sao Paulo, and maybe the baron had a small warehouse on site for the unhung art, and maybe he had someone to do his clothes and sipped Drambuie and stalked his own art collection afterhours. I saw the patchy byways bisecting the jungle, the sea voyages, the names of all the ports of call, expressionless customs officials, the sugar on the docks. There was an import quota allocated to Brazil.

He would giggle through missing front baby teeth as I described those eighteen-wheelers long-hauling all that sugar from the ports into cities like Charlotte and Raleigh, the minor notes of America.

Where are those, he would say.

All around us.

At the last radiant edge of America, Lars and Fung were waiting for me, their lone counsel, retained to translate them out of the headlines. I wanted to barge into the cockpit and steer the plane backward, walk back into the house, recite all the facts of her to Colin. This is how she sketched you when you were just a week old. Or maybe I would have shut off the phone last night and missed this flight altogether. We would drive into the tallgrass peninsula. I made a note to myself to show him more pictures of her. I saw the desert below, empty and scathing. The border of Nevada looks like the border of California. We are never where we are. She loved these kinds of flowers, hyacinth. One time I called her the hyacinth girl and she made me purple cupcakes. He giggled. When you arrived, you had a full head of bloody black hair, not even crying, not a whimper. You are a good boy, don't cry. Please try not to cry. Mommy held you this way. Put your hand there. Think of her. You will hear her when you pray. Just close your eyes.

So I flew.

chapter two

L ONG BRIDGE Management was headquartered two blocks south of Central Park in a high rise beside the Harry Winston store at the corner of West Fifty Sixth and Fifth Avenue, a city block without beggars clotted with Medici wealth.

It was the precise spot in Manhattan certain to inflame international NGOs, envious Greenwich hedge funds, anyone who did anything altruistic at all in the past decade for the heavily-indebted countries of equatorial Africa; Argentina analysts and think-tank types; a Reagan vs. Mondale majority of the media—and this even included British press, particularly *The Guardian,* although *The Economist* published, on cue, each winter, its restrained, frigid diatribe about the "vulture fund," a deceptive phrase meant to describe their business practice of buying up the distressed debt of poor countries and rapaciously litigating their way towards full payment on the bonds, plus accrued interest, of course. Their coverage was lopsided— never mind that the brutal despots of these countries and their even more brutal sons had siphoned off large quantities of the national patrimony, oil, diamonds, precious metals, had left their country to rot, ruling afar from their Mayfair mansions or their St. Germain *pieds-à-terre.*

The Peninsula hotel was right there on Long Bridge's block, or, if you preferred—which I did—you could stroll across Fifth Avenue to the St. Regis.

Despite myself, I found that I liked Alan Newman right away, his Old Testament omniscience, although I would still put him through the standard rigmarole for the fun of it.

We had met in late October of that year, a phone call that had been rescheduled repeatedly after belligerent volleys of emails between assistants that spanned too many days. He was an unnaturally calm man, smooth baritone, one of those perpetually unwrinkled gentlemen who stay pristine whatever the weather, his mind alive, in dialectic with itself, a distance runner's physique verging on enfeebled.

During the OneSpeak crisis Alan hovered above it all, King Solomon, a man who had gracefully exiled all forms of stress from his life. Those at my firm who met him universally said he would excel at delivering a terminal cancer diagnosis to a small child's mother.

"As you well know, Long Bridge specializes in assessing and adjudicating risk," he said. "We make bets on our judgments. We get right up to the line and back away when we sense a death blow. We are not wrong very often. Often we are spectacularly right. Evidently, this is why so many people hate us."

Miraculously, the Long Bridge partners had managed to stay out of public view for much of the past decade, a hermetically sealed outfit, infallible Mandarins ruling from behind the high walls of the Forbidden City; that I was even on the phone with Alan was, in itself, a remarkable rarity, something worthy of Georgetown cocktail circuit chatter.

I had known how this conversation would play out ever since Alan's ambiguous first email to me, a correspondence so purposefully elliptical it seemed crafted as sport by law professors. I knew where the note would lead but was anyway prepared to steer the call towards a formal engagement.

Those who resist specifying the precise nature of their media quandary are usually mired in a slow-motion saga, their ambiguity a tell-tale sign, and I had some sense that he would be calling with a crisis. Invoking crisis, you shed accountability, ensured self-preservation: to endow a crisis with artificial mystery was to inflate it beyond manageable dimensions, a mess demanding professional oversight. Thus, for having recognized the need for a P.R. firm, you could even win some credit.

My firm was a clean-up crew, albeit white collar and excessively expensive. Unlike their legal counsel, we were never cosseted, and for that inequity I had decided after Monica died to charge a "Fuck You" price, enough to force a reappraisal of our pedigree, but mostly because I didn't care if they turned us away; the less I cared, the more I charged, and, to my surprise, the more they paid us to handle the live grenade of the news media.

"When it was unfashionable to do so, my firm invested $390 million in a tech startup," said Alan. "We made over $4 billion five months later. The market snatches up mythology. There was no product per se, just an algorithm. We gamble but tell investors we are 'taking calculated risks.'"

"And you are looking to my firm to handle your reputational challenges?" I interrupted.

The trick was to throw underhand pitches—warm them up a little before the heat, and, if you could, try and seem a little naïve. The trick was Hawthorne's, who I had been working with now for almost fifteen years. After I interviewed him the first time for the job, he sent along a thank you note the next day on personalized stationary, initials embossed in a Roman font, and, in his final sentence, had said that he deemed me a "fine fellow," which endeared him to me permanently.

I made him an equity partner almost five years ago, a supreme supervisor of all my supervisors. He was an outright icon in the firm, a self-styled Victorian. The women revered his chivalrous charm and the young upstarts lapped up his frothy tales, as he was prone to vague and sententious proclamations, such as that his father invented Earth Day. He could, if asked, unhesitatingly spew the names of the four presidents who preceded Theodore Roosevelt, knew all the good Cantonese restaurants in Hong Kong that served bird's nest soup, said *pamplemousse* when he meant anything Sunkist orange, had master sommeliers who would offer him samples of the Grand Premier Crus stashed in any city with a direct flight from London. He liked his dirty martinis so dirty that they arrived the squalid opacity of soapy bath water; he deployed spectacle as a device in his own personal myth-making. One Halloween he hosted a Hawaiian-themed party for the office—all the staff's kids came; he had carved floral patterns into his pumpkins, but they ended up profane—a dozen candlelit Georgia O'Keefe vaginas glowing on his porch, which, to everyone's amusement, coaxed grimaces from the prim chaperones of the little trick-or-treaters. For me— apart from being a confidante of sorts—he was, professionally-speaking, an indispensable wind-up aristocrat, a dervish to unleash on new clients; invariably, after their first exposure to his lightning knowledge of the world, they would emerge a touch giddy, desperate for more interactions with the man who governed, but never managed, over twenty million dollars of my business. He was leagues more complex than he seemed, knew instinctively how to sell things, anything, to anybody, whether they had the resources or not. This once got us into some trouble with Raphael Correa's Ecuador: They agreed to pay us $2.5 million to eradicate a tariff on their apparel exports, but, conveniently, stopped paying three months into the engagement—that's what we called them, engagements. It was something Hawthorne and I had contrived to put a bit of polish on a dull metal: all clients were engagements, of course, but most of our competitors in town referred to their clients as clients, which to us both, sounded unnecessarily quaint. I knew that Alan would enjoy Hawthorne, and I was already thinking up ways to introduce them to each other.

"We like our cryptic reputation very much," Alan had said on the phone, and I imagined him running the tip of his index finger around the rim of a porcelain teacup as he said this, gazing across Central Park. "We are the white blood cells of capitalism. We buy distressed things, refurbish them back to health and release them, reinvigorated, back into the economy. The banks are closed. We speculate and rain money into ventures where banks would give sterile funding. I am calling about something different. One of our bets has veered off course."

"Who referred us?" I said, interrupting his monologue—another copyrighted skill co-forged with Hawthorne, a very necessary intervention that curtailed the confessional meanderings of prospects, kept things at a crisp clip, which is where I liked things in general.

I had the previous night's hockey game scores up on my computer screen.

"I'd like to send over a non-disclosure agreement before we proceed any further. I have asked Manuel to email it over just now. Sign it. Send it back. Then we can keep going. Generally speaking, we stand to lose quite a lot of money if things aren't put back in place."

When the document arrived, Margaret swept in with a pen and, after I signed it, whisked the sheet away wordlessly, without eye contact, leaving in her wake a fresh espresso with a lemon rind beside the dainty spoon on the saucer. She was always doing things like this, unsolicited gestures meant to bring me comfort, restore my chi, as she called it.

With the NDA signed, Alan began to recount the story of one of their most recent investments, a startup selling a technology that translated Mandarin into English, vice versa, and could be embedded into smartphones.

"Chinese is just the gateway, the base code for what we can eventually use to translate other major languages. There would be no need to learn another language besides your own, which, if you are an American today, is quite important."

He explained how it would not take much to envision how this technology could spring to life with a clever companion app, translating live, spoken languages into reconfigured sound waves, streaming into the ear, meaning fed direct to the brain, like sound through a pipe, nanoseconds of translation, languages without borders.

"This sounds familiar. I suspect there is competing technology in the market—or soon to be?" I had the ball ready to go.

"Kleiner Perkins pumped $65 million of Series A money into something similar three years ago. That is probably what you are recollecting. It was a small-minded venture that sought to put English into other languages, starting with Spanish. That had no potential. Who in the English-speaking world needs to speak Spanish today? Nobody. We came upon something last April. We found out about it from a hacker. We own an exceedingly large sum of bitcoin and, in one of our transactions, we encountered a glitch. Bitcoin is code after all. The code we purchased, in essence, was broken, some obviously corrupted code from a Silk Road reprobate masquerading as a legit seller. We fired the guy internally when it happened. It never should have happened. We didn't want it to come out that we bought bitcoin from an online hit man—or God knows who. So we searched for the most sublimely gifted hacker we could hire. We got to Lars VandenBruck. We hired him to fix the code, redeem our purchase for our investors. He was in Amsterdam but he performed his work with amazing swiftness, but the point is that we learned during the engagement that Lars was working on something special—OneSpeak—which is what we sunk our money into."

I had the phone on mute and was typing an email to Colin's hockey coach about a missing elbow pad. I did not feel the need to speak. I tried not to talk much in meetings either. I knew that by saying very little, others would ascribe to you a vast, unwarranted intelligence.

"Someone from Google had flown them all in for the party. Wait…let me back up. Lars is dating Fung. The two had met at a hackathon in Big Sur six months ago. At a silent rave, I believe, somewhere amidst the Redwoods."

"Hold on—these are the people—bald guy and the Chinese girl, from the photo in the *Times* two weeks ago? The wireless headphones—the Serbian DJ?"

"Bosnian, yes. And, yes, *Vanity Fair* covered the party as part of a series on young entrepreneurs. Google underwrote the hackathon because Yahoo! was planning to do it, and, as a middle finger to Yahoo!, some witty Google C-Suiter hired the Bosnian DJ known for mixing Rachmaninov with German techno."

"Right, those kids in the photo with the Ewok Village trees—and that blonde actress who divorced her British rock band husband?"

"Gwyneth Paltrow, yes, the Ewok Village trees, yes, a little campfire in the clear, then a little weed, then a little other stuff and then a tweet, and now an investigation by the state attorney general for possible statutory rape of Fung by Lars and distribution of methamphetamine to a minor. That is not public yet. It will be in about three days."

I was actually surprised by the downward progression of these events, however entertaining, and let out an audible, "Jesus," for good measure.

"It was consensual, of course, but she was seventeen. We have an IPO in six weeks and this is a real problem," said Alan, with no particular irony. "These guys are oblivious to their predicament. We are not dealing with grownups, Mark. Lars is a renegade; three sheets and an overdose from a blackout. Fung just turned eighteen. I don't really know. The P.R. girl— Fung's sister, Li, I think she is called—she has a law degree from Stanford, speaks four languages, has to be the smartest person in the room, but I want some adult supervision to see us through the IPO."

"What about the state AG stuff?" I asked.

"Absolutely mum, well, wait—and one of our partners knows the Governor well, so we are going through that channel."

Despite his detectable anger, the tone of Alan's voice did not fluctuate during the entire call.

"At first we thought the investigation was a rumor floated by a rival technology, some chaff to derail the IPO. But it's legit. Not at all a rumor.

We've got no response from Sacramento and we have a roadshow about to start in three weeks. Fung has committed several press atrocities, generally speaking, about OneSpeak, and I cannot imagine what she will say or do when the questions come about all this. By the way, you should know that she is part of the open source crowd, so she has an antipathy to 'no comment.' She argues it's a 'withholding of the truth.'"

Hawthorne's head peered around my now cracked door, a thumbs up, then a thumbs down, then a neutral expression, which I quickly knocked back to thumbs up with a brisk head nod, then he made that greasy gesture bouncers make when demanding a little tip, the rapid sandpapering of thumb over forefinger.

He moved fully into the office now and closed the door, stood somewhat appraisingly, arms crossed and legs wide, just to spectate and take in the sale.

I instinctively raised my voice as if he were joining in the conversation, but, when I noticed it, I lowered it just as quickly.

"Listen: sharing the truth in the press is rarely helpful. Perhaps you can get her just to say, 'I don't know, can I get back to you?' and hope she flakes out and forgets." I winced a little at this, feeling like I had too carelessly revealed a frank opinion.

Hawthorne sat down on the sofa and opened *The New Yorker* and a canister of marcona almonds from Dean & Deluca.

Alan was too wound up to notice my carelessness, his anger manifesting as a slight shift in cadence.

"Look, Mark, this is why we called you. We want a pro to spearhead things for a while. Last week, after the employees lobbied for it, they installed Braille newspapers over the urinals in the men's room. Well, that's in the press now. I think Mashable ran the headline, 'The Blind Translating to the Blind.' Lars thought it was funny. Fung is an amateur ornithologist, spends her afternoons taking auspices. They need to hear from an outsider that the situation is grave. They need to commit to a program, stop speaking *ad hoc* to the press on their cell phones from Cozumel or Kauai, or wherever it is they go scuba diving. Did I mention that Lars got Fung into that last month? She ended up in a hyperbaric chamber after her first dive—too deep too quickly—and spent twelve hours in a three-bed Mexican hospital. Lars sat vigil, doing blog posts from her bedside and posting recovery updates on Twitter. Motherfucking incredible."

I had had the phone on speaker by the time he got to scuba diving and Hawthorne was in stitches, spilling almonds on the sofa, the magazine folded in his lap, his shoulders bouncing with silent laughter.

There was a long pause, and, next, a query for a contract and a price.

I knew how this would all transpire, the flights to the west coast away from Colin, the trains up the east coast, wrinkled suits; I looked out the window at the rain, registered a microburst of depression; it was not even ten thirty in the morning; my next pill wasn't until two.

Alan was breathing into the phone. I closed the laptop, conjuring up all ways that Lars and Fung would obliterate my solitude, impose an absence on Colin. When I evaluated what all of that was worth, and calculated the value of what my experience and knowhow would bring to the IPO, purported by Alan to haul in around $4 billion in new capital, and considered how a bad press run for an IPO could shear a good $1.5 billion off that opening day valuation, a shit blog here, a shit CNBC interview there, I arrived at a radical price I felt was worth it for renting out my expertise (even if this triage could be done easily enough). I felt all the internal gusts blowing, couldn't stop myself from getting right to it.

"This is an unusual case, we provide an exceptional service, and there is no number." Hawthorne looked up.

"I'm sorry?"

"You are obviously familiar with the notion of goodwill?"

"Obviously."

"Then you know our service is an intangible, akin to goodwill."

"Yes."

"To enable OneSpeak to get, hitch free, to IPO, raise $4 billion, hold that value and expand it—that holds a value that cannot be expressed through a retainer, which is how we work with most clients, but not in the case of IPOs."

"Alright…"

"The price is going to need to be shares of the IPO, at a strike price of $12.50 per share."

"That's four dollars beneath the IPO price."

"I am aware. And we will need a substantial tranche of shares, of course, exercisable immediately and fully vested." The ball was now entering the strike zone.

"And precisely how many shares do we need to pay to get P.R.?" Alan's voice had turned snarky. At that moment, an NHL alert materialized across the top edge of my iPhone: the Boston Bruins had just extended an important left winger through the 2020–21 season.

"We'd take on OneSpeak in exchange for one million shares in the company."

There was a pause, a split second passed, and Alan had done the math. "I really...I mean that is offensively insane. Absolutely ridiculous."

I held the silence. I smiled at the rain that was now heavier, drumming the window panes. Hawthorne had put down the magazine completely.

"This is truly offensive." Alan was chuckling now. "The IPO price is fourteen dollars per share. Under normal circumstances the stock will double in less than six months. I really cannot believe you are asking for tens of millions of dollars to do press releases and interviews. This conversation is unbelievably disappointing."

"I understand. I wish you luck, then," I said, and hung up.

There was a brief pause, then Hawthorne and I debated the pros and cons of promoting one of the firm's plucky vice presidents, Joel James, largely disliked by his peers for his coveted blue badge on his Twitter handle that certified his identity as the real Joel James, an artifact of his previous stint as an editor at a Silicon Valley website.

Margaret drifted in, quiet as a feather, removed the empty espresso cup, left a cup of lemon verbena tea in its place, three gag-sized multivitamins, a shot glass of soda water.

I tried to imagine the kind of debris left behind by hackers in the forest: gold foil condom wrappers strewn around the base of the redwoods; I made a mental note to dig out my Rachmaninov CDs. I told Hawthorne to hold on, wait here, I have to piss, and I walked deliberately fast, trying as best I could to avoid all forms of incidental social interactions with subordinates, slipping my gaze just beneath the rays of eye contact coming from the bank of interns along the corridor that ran from my wing of the office to the bathrooms. Inside, two of our senior executives were swapping stories about a fishing trip in which one of the senior executives had caught eight small sharks with his son, eating one grilled, Cajun style, for lunch, while the other marveled at it all as some out of reach pursuit, although I was paying him more than twice what I was paying Margaret and right then and there I remembered that he ate microwaved scrambled eggs in the office each morning in bad suits; I also recalled telling Hawthorne we couldn't bring him along anymore to client pitches. I came back and relayed to Hawthorne the shark story. He was reading another Paul Theroux *New Yorker* short story, snacking on the almonds left on the sofa.

"Mark, I thought about it," said Hawthorne. "The Joel James situation. It will ignite the passionate haters from the European accounts, forcing some of them to start looking elsewhere, thin the herd a bit, and it will fatten up Joel's already swollen ego to the point of insufferability, which will—you mark my words—within the next six months, instigate some kind of personal crisis and this will humble him enough that he might start listening to Oscar, who, I have it on good authority, got slanderously drunk at his sister's wedding in Nevada and committed an extramarital indiscretion. He was already not very well-liked by the Panamanians or the Bahrainis, who are paying on time and taking their cues these days from Heather, who—thank God—we promoted last year yet, of course, now she's going to pop out a bambino and go out on maternity leave, which would leave us saddled with Oscar and the Panamanians and a recalcitrant Joel James, who, also on good authority, told the New Zealanders that Oscar was on his last legs here and that they needn't work too closely with him anymore, that it was okay for them to just call him up direct, that he was their man in Havana, so to speak. What kind of sharks were they?"

"Lemon sharks, I think. Heather is pregnant? Isn't she divorced?"

"In vitro. April. Did I mention Francois was coming to lunch? Flew down from Teterboro on the corporate jet to discuss the rebrand. It's been moved to a private room. I read the article about him you sent me. I've never worked with a former hairstylist. They are the most disorganized client I have ever worked with. They would not thrive in a Germanic society."

"We live in a Germanic society. Do you think we can get away with referencing this in our introductory remarks? The hairstylist part?"

"Don't see why not. Probably a terrible idea, too. I like it. There's another thing." Hawthorne sounded giddy. "Earlier this morning, I got off the phone with Gloria and she finally got it all set up. We will be having a special audience tomorrow with Yoweri Museveni, after his speech at the Library of Congress. Noon, or shortly thereafter, you know the Africans. Location TBD, you know, security. Well, what do you think? Another kill tomorrow for the wall?"

"Is that Ghana? I think Gloria is an outstanding referral source. We should be paying her more. What are we paying her for all of this?"

"Whatever it is, we should pay her more."

Gloria's long service as a trade negotiator meant she knew the heads of every regime on the continent, and had befriended a smattering of key advisors like the Nigerian Finance Minister. Whenever Gloria was about to introduce me to a head of state, it was always with the proviso that "they were grossly misunderstood right now" by the likes of *Foreign Affairs* magazine and Fareed Zakaria, code for saying what they really wanted was for us to book them on Charlie Rose for a long, truth-packed, one-sided format to proselytize over the misunderstanding, which is not at all the Charlie Rose format—or really anyone's format—though it did not preclude us from accepting these assignments on condition of our own proviso (explained always to the exceedingly polite and frail aide tasked by his president as our liaison); Charlie Rose, we told them, might actually ask very direct questions, but we, of course, would cheerfully and earnestly preview with the president the anticipated interview.

"By the way, Gerard was pleasingly appreciative of the raise you approved yesterday, Mark. Mentioned something about now being able to buy an engagement ring for a girl he has been dating for several years. Can you believe that? We live in a day and age when making a previous salary of $110,000 leaves you unable to buy an engagement ring. Tragic times, really. Museveni is an anti-homosexual and won't lift a presidential finger to overturn a law that bans gays from being gay and doing gay acts, which the law makes punishable by death; but don't worry, Mark, according to Laura and Marcus—yes, I pulled them into this—no one legitimately believes they would actually execute any of them. But petitions are floating around from gay groups and celebrities to the State Department. This will be tricky. We'll need to pay for a few opinion articles. I've already called Gary. We'll need to assemble a chorus of Museveni supporters. It's a big misunderstanding, Mark. The Africans, Gloria says, confuse homosexuality with pedophilia, which is justifiably abhorrent, but they do not distinguish between the two and so this whole mess is being misreported by the press as a bounty hunt by Museveni against the gays."

"Right. Don't we have the lunch tomorrow with Francois and the team? I don't suppose we can cancel that." I waited for a confirmation but got none. "Well, I suppose we will just spend the day hustling around then. How long is the audience?"

"He's giving us fifteen minutes. Fifteen minutes for $2 million. I'm thinking we should charge that just because we should."

"It seems absurd."

"It is for sure absurd."

"Not the money but that we have to have a special meeting at all."

"Precisely. They've got the balls to hypothetically execute their gay pedophiles but the president cannot hire a firm recommended by a trusted American advisor without meeting its principals."

"It's a lopsided pool of attention, and we are going to experience a strange, surreal, absurd fifteen minutes tomorrow after lunch with Francois that is all of those things too," I said, envisioning myself saying many times in the meeting, *Loren Ipsem Dolorum.*

Sally McGee walked in, my head of HR. She had a nervous affliction, could have been mild Tourette's, her face would twitch every few seconds or so and her lips would purse into a kiss followed by rapid blinking. She began as my assistant, came in on her first day eight years ago with what appeared to be a tackle box for her lunch box and a wardrobe scoured from one of those Georgetown consignment shops that recirculated the Ralph Lauren suits of embassy row wives. Coco Chanel gone fishin'. She knew about my condition and protected it.

Hawthorne was smirking.

"So," she said, standing in the doorway. She typically could anticipate whatever I was about to say and thus she began nearly every conversation we had with "so."

"Whatever on the Joel James idea, Hawthorne. You decide." I turned to Sally. "We might be promoting Joel James. If so, twenty percent seems fair."

I said, "The Elliot guy was quite fascinating. In about seventy-two hours, after their investment gets tarred and feathered in *The Wall Street Journal*, he should be calling us waving the white flag."

"It will be a pointless and obscene fee," said Hawthorne.

The truth was that White & Partners did not need any new clients; we were brimming with engagements already, and we couldn't find people fast enough to keep up with all the work.

The firm was twelve years old, employed 150 people, had performed some personal work for President Clinton (we would have happily done work for President George W. Bush but his crowd was famously insular to the point of professional incest). We represented seventeen foreign governments, the uncorrupted countries who grotesquely overpaid, and took on clients the way an Ivy League school scrutinized prospective fresh- men. After the Ecuador fiasco three years ago, I insisted that all potential clients submit an *Application of Consideration*. Once a particular engage- ment was determined a "good fit," there was the matter of the cost, a set fee normally in the low millions, to be paid up front upon execution of the contract. If the wire was not received within twenty-four hours of the signed contract, the agreement was null: we would not commence an iota of work until payment was received.

Since this process had been put in place four years ago, there had been only one botched new client: Wal-Mart. They had wanted a firm to reengi- neer their reputation, something around their corporate refrain of "Save Money, Live Better," a perfect Demi-glace of messaging, the base for their state and national media defense of their importation of goods manufac- tured in China. They ended up hiring a firm on K Street staffed with dia- betic-looking men in double-breasted suits. When their work with this firm went awry—and it only took a month for them to get caught paying think tank scholars five thousand dollars each for writing opinion articles—the story of Wal-Mart, a Fortune 1 behemoth, hiring a "back-up firm" had spilled into *The Wall Street Journal* (we leaked it), and the article named us as the firm that had demanded Wal-Mart submit an application to be considered as a client. Our legend inflated to such proportions that every Upper East-side rentier was calling to retain our counsel for his wife's food allergy awareness foundation or former college roommate's S.E.C. mess, their brother's doomed proxy battle with Carl Icahn.

After the Wal-Mart saga, we received twenty Applications for Consideration from Fortune 250 companies the following Friday. We accepted only half of those applications from this batch, but added seven- teen million in new revenue that month alone. We hired thirty more pro- fessionals and talked about opening a fifth office, Berlin, mostly because Hawthorne had a fetish for East Berlin art galleries, among other fetishes; maybe Mexico City, mostly because I had harbored delusions of retiring to its Pacific coast, deteriorating pleasantly in an adobe home bushy with Bougainvillea, Manny, my gardener-confidante, pruning the vines on the pergola, dispensing trans-generational wisdom. I had postponed the discus- sion. We had so much excess cash on hand that I had instructed our CFO to buy two million dollars' worth of gold when it was $500 an ounce. So, at the start of last year, we had six years of operating capital, securitized as gold bars in a vault somewhere.

I preferred to be a behind-the-scenes leader, a presence but not a force. I feigned some token humilities: avoided Italian loafers; wrote with pens lifted from the local hospice; eschewed public speaking invitations; hung Colin's art on my office walls. Outwardly, I kept an even keel, for Colin's sake, but, inwardly, all of this was as meaningless to me as discarded ribbon. I knew that everyone who worked for me—even those who were jealous—genuinely admired what had been accomplished at the firm, but I could fathom how they didn't see right through to the bone of it. Simplicity eludes us all.

The Capitol Hill papers wrote fretfully about White & Partners, unable to explain the nucleus of our explosive growth. At The Palm, industry competitors flung their dagger glances my way as my lunch guests observed the buzzing room in glee. Around this time, I had stopped wearing ties altogether, which pissed off detractors even more. People I had never met tweeted about me. I had grown very secure in my seraphic standing in town, and I acquired a few theatrical eccentricities: when gravitas was called for, I somberly deployed the meaningless Latin filler text for websites under construction—*Lorem Ipsum Dolorem*; no one ever seemed to notice. In my condition, this emboldened me to clamp down on the serial abuse of adverbs in all written correspondence with engagements, which led to the ousting of a longtime employee, Barbara Hiller, who I knew had been speculating about the origins of my success for a while and whom Hawthorne had pegged as the source of media leaks, the mole for *The Washington Post's* story on the "Adverb Mandate," written as straight-faced as if it was the Watergate scandal, dilating every innuendo about anything to do with White & Partners, all harvested from unnamed sources, dispatched as an alert on all subscribing mobile phones.

I didn't care: a scandal in Washington was as evanescent as it was inevitable, rarely triggering a complete excommunication. Even if there were more professional missteps, White & Partners had adamantine bona fides.

We shared a building with the bureaucrats of the GSA. In the underground garage, there were lots of Honda Pilots and rusted out Corollas comingled with my staff's gleaming fleet of European cars. I had technicians from Bang & Olufsen install 300-watt speakers with adaptive bass linearization in the hallway, the reception, the bathrooms, the kitchen, zone-controlled, staff-curated playlists, usually a mix of classic rock, gang-sta rap, and Hollywoodized hip-hop. It was the music of an invading army running rampant through eleven thousand square feet of class A office space on the top floor of a trophy building in the commercial district of DC, $125,000 a month, views of the Capitol, the kind of sonic rabble deployed in '89 against Noriega. There was not an immediate uprising. Given that White & Partners was a despotic nation, the criticisms and vituperations of those who felt victimized by the profane lyrics or the noise levels—or both—took their opposition underground. Soon—maybe three days later—*The Hill* ran a tabloid story on White & Partners' "new fascination with misogynistic and oppressive hip-hop music that had sharply divided the DC-based consulting behemoth."

"So, you wanna do this?" Sally said. She was looking right at me.

"Joel is deserving. Let's do this please, if you don't mind."

Margaret peeked in and frowned; it was her signal for a critical interruption.

"It's Hanna. She says she must speak with you."

Sally rolled her eyes and got up and left.

"Alright."

Hanna Nelson was a friend, sort of, and she was an important jour-nalist, even if *THE BEACON* was a supernova nearing its demise and she didn't know it.

"Hanna?"

"Mark, hey, listen can you meet me in a bit for a story?"

"Uh, maybe. Today?"

"Like, now?"

"Today's tough. What's so urgent? Can't we speak by phone?

"One of your competitors. Their CEO is leaving. The place is a zoo. Come. I'm at The Jefferson at eleven thirty."

"Is this off the record?"

"Absolutely. Always."

I knew what this was, she was drafting an obituary on Lincoln Strategic and needed someone to shed a little confirmatory light on rumored events. It was a game, anyway, roulette without money. You put in your bets and out came someone, or many people, scandalized because of your intel. I played because everyone else played against me, and if I didn't play the stakes would be higher and higher each day.

The Jefferson was my favorite hotel in the city. It was small and had an excellent, snug bar, like something out of the thirteenth arrondissement.

Hanna had a table in the corner by the patio doors. She wore jeans and no makeup. Her laptop was out and she was already typing.

"Are you drafting my bio?" I said.

We ordered coffees and she began to gush about her promotion.

"They are making me bureau chief. Next year. Can you believe it? It's almost confirmed. I need to keep up with the scoops, you know, mega impress the Daltons, who are fucking assholes, shit people, Mark. It's nearly done. I need more scoops. They need to be convinced. That's what Harrison says. He promised me he would nominate me but he says I'm young and they have concerns."

"Youth is a dirty word, but since when in journalism?"

"I'd be on the Sunday shows, own the circuit, Mark."

"And then you've arrived." I took an unusually long sip of coffee and feigned impatience, observing the people in the room.

"Mark it's a big deal, maybe not for you and your fancy firm, but the rest of us have a right to rise too."

"Just be careful how you rise."

She tore open two packs of sugar and dumped them in her coffee. I looked around and realized other people were glancing at us, two banking lobbyists I recognized, the ranking member of the Senate Foreign Relations Committee. I thought they probably recognized Hanna first.

"Shall we drink something stronger, to celebrate?" I said.

"It's not even noon, or maybe it is."

"Maybe it is." I signaled the waiter and ordered a bottle of champagne. He was Indian and gave a small bow at the request.

The champagne bucket came filled with shaved ice and he displayed the Bollinger. After my approval he poured two flutes midway and plunged the bottle deep into the ice. It turned out to be rosé, which I thought might further pique the enmity of our onlookers. I saw someone texting and looking over. He also handed us a plate of jumbo strawberries, stems still on.

"Mark it's amazing. Amazing. But it's so early! You are so bad!"

She was swallowing the strawberries whole, stem on.

"To the princess of political media."

"And you are a prince," she said, putting down the flute of champagne and reaching in her purse for her tape recorder. The green light came on.

She straightened her sitting posture and did a little thing with her shoulders and said, "I assume the rumors are true?"

"Lincoln?"

"Lincoln."

"They are all true," I said, lying.

A smile broke out on her face. "And no names," I said.

"No names, as always."

She swallowed a third strawberry, finished her glass, and stood up. "The piece hits in two hours."

She leaned over and kissed my check and then she was gone. I sat and typed a few emails to the Japanese about their pizzas and drank the rosé and the texts continued.

★

MONICA WOULD have thought much of this was frivolous, and would have cautioned me against taking so many video game risks with the business. If I couldn't always see her perfectly anymore, I could hear her all throughout the day, a whisper that ripped a hole in time. Stay in balance, keep the dog—take Colin to an island. Her dresses still hung in our closet. Her makeup was still in the drawers. It was a way to preserve her scent.

We had broken up once in college but it was for two days. Otherwise she had been with me since I was eighteen. She had tiny hands and bewitching eyes, as if drawn by hand and darkly shaded. We would study together late in the library, only the turning of pages breaking the chapel silence. One of her earliest sketches—of that library façade—hangs in Colin's room.

Many nights, after studying, I took her on walks off campus to a stream that cut through a grove of white birch and this is where she first discovered the forsythias. In the spring, once they had blossomed, she would cut some branches and place them in a mason jar on the desk in her dorm room; sometimes their little blooms fell, and there would be a stray blossom near the framed pictures of her sisters, arranged decoratively beside the hardbacks of Dutch old masters, Pointillists and Fauvists and Impressionists, but she did not care for Cézanne. At night, she kept a jasmine-scented candle burning that cast a glow on the frames and the books, and sometimes, depending on how she arranged things that week, the visage of Van Gogh would flicker in the light.

There were nights when we said nothing. It was not like silence but something else.

All four years of college, before we were engaged, she wore the horse-shoe nail forged into a ring that I had sourced at the checkout line of a strip mall CD store in the nearby town. I proposed to her in Madrid, 1999, after we graduated, at Kilometre Zero, the geographic center of the country in *La Puerta del Sol*. She insisted it serve as her wedding band. We flew my mother to Barcelona a month before I returned to America for good, and we had a small service on the beach by that copper Frank Gehry whale. The whole affair cost us less than $5,000.

Sometimes, while I hear her, I find I have forgotten the pitch of her voice, and I must will into existence the facts of her being—that she made her own jewelry, that she detangled her wet hair with her fingertips; and when I try and recall her most endearing aspects, sometimes nothing comes through. I see her but cannot hear her; or I hear her but cannot see her. But usually at the peak of busy periods in my work day or on my own walks, some castaway recollection flashes in my mind, and I take solace in the fact that these fragments are still there—that you can lose a memory and still forget nothing.

She loved the sound of the water.

When we walked far enough down the hill, past the taller grass and a little into the woods, we found our place, a clearing by the birches covered in moss. It was dark enough there, and afterwards we always quickly fell asleep and I would awake, the middle of the spring night, cold, and always turn to her and reach to stroke her hair and wish for more moonlight, if only to watch her breathe.

★

I SOURCED my late morning espressos from a nearby shop in Chinatown that served cheap Australian wine and three varieties of absinthe, chatty baristas in jeans like wet suits and wearing à la mode lumberjack beards; there were youngish women with statement haircuts two-handing their steaming cups like a rice bowl, cross-legged, text books heaped on the empty chair; the sense that most of the clientele cared deeply for civics, microfinance, climate change; the invariable feeling that in my three thousand dollar bespoke suit, I was an outlier among this co-ed, unshaven pseudo-intelligentsia, pickled in their solipsism.

The customers existed in one of three modes: intense post-breakup discourse, headphone wires on the table like excess yarn; solitary and postmodern ruminative—wannabe Bodhisattvas—usually wearing headphones; crossword puzzle introverts, sometimes with headphones, sometimes an almond-milk chai tea, which I could not abide.

My time in the coffee shop rarely exceeded fifteen minutes. The truth was that I did not stay longer because I came alone and, seated for any extended period, savoring my cortado, I felt hi-wattage stares from the patrons. I was a reminder of what they had turned from or would fail to become or the father they had fled, a stone monument in the town square demanding graffiti. I also disliked reading newspapers in public, so I had no prop to shield me from the gawkers.

The truth was that I did not read the newspapers at all anymore, did not consume a regular diet of news media—from any source. The news came to me through hearsay, tweets, the colleague playing Paul Revere down the hallway trumpeting a plane crash or a stock crash, or both. The news was an omnipresent negative space: it found you wherever you were; it came during my walks, a near siren alert on my iPhone from the *Associated Press*; at the gym or in airports, peripheral silent images on a bank of televisions seeped into consciousness, a glimpse of onscreen captions, ticker text half-insinuating the story, a reel of raw cold facts one could splice into any story of their choosing. The "news" was less an amalgam of facts and more the image fashioned by how those fragments were pieced together. The facts enabled a mosaic of stories to be told, but the newsprint font or the studio glamour or the polish of a radio broadcast enameled them in objective truth. Even a stolid maternal voice from the BBC—the only brand from which I occasionally took the news—stirred the subjective dust.

My phone was ringing.

"Where are you? Are you at the Sculpture Garden? I can send a car."

"I'm drinking absinthe, Margaret. I'm about to slice off my left ear. Send an ambulance."

"Mark how far away is that place? You only have ninety minutes until your meeting with everyone."

"This is the meeting about bonuses?"

"This is the meeting about Turkmenistan."

I hung up, ordered a macchiato to go, studied the absinthe placard on the brick wall, and recalled the time early in Barcelona when I had posed as a *Rolling Stone* correspondent to score an interview with Andy, the reclusive American barman at Bar Marsella, where real absinthe was sold, deep in the destitution of the Barrio Xines, graffiti spray-painted satanically in its sunless alleys, the Guardia Civil on patrol, semi-automatics slung across their bodies, finger near the trigger even in the daytime.

Their absinthe was made offsite, somewhere near Andorra in a slanted barn on a goat farm in the Pyrenees, Andy said, in small batches using wormwood, the hallucinogen with cannabic properties. I remember traipsing there on Tuesday night with my writer's group, a scattering of expatriate souls that met once a week to discuss what we had produced. If you ever wish to write anything abroad, it's best to flee anything resembling a writer's group. In mine, no one had written much of anything and these colloquies would soon become nothing more than a pretext to scour the city late on weeknights, kindred spirits reveling in Barcelona long after the tourist wave had receded. My group trekked deep into the Xines, past the range of the Guardia Civil. When we reached the Bar Marsella, there was a haze of brightly lit cigarette smoke; the interior had that orange glow of Toulouse-Lautrec canvases of *Pigalle* dancers, and the Edith Piaf recordings evoked *Belle Époque* charm. We did not light any sugar cube and drop it into the anise-flavored liquor like *gauche* German backpackers—what was left of them, at least. Andy exhorted us to drink it straight so that it would take effect more quickly.

We each had two absinthe that night, and as I felt my body warming and gliding into a state of numb paralysis, I saw all of the young, clean faces of the American backpackers, the dazed-out permanent dropouts, mostly American, despotic-looking men with five o'clock shadows in corners furiously smoking, their driftwood companions dropping the straps of their cheap dresses below the shoulders in defiance of the heat, and I knew I wanted to live like this, among these Trotsky-faced expats, gently poisoning myself and subjugating my superego, a free radical in American life, not of it, but still of it, enough toe-hold in the sheer culture to climb above it all to question all that I had seen, a soul in its chrysalis burning with words. Eventually, any bona fides will get you cast out of the expat garden.

The barista handed me my cortado. They were a holdover from my years in Spain.

I had lived a brief walk downhill from Calle de la Magdalena from the Antón Martín metro stop in a heavily trafficked area of narrow streets that had a sour and wicked smell in the summer, and by the metro stairs there were always the gypsies moaning their pathetic adagios and there were also the blind who sold the daily lottery tickets—some kind of government program—who shouted out their refrain, *la suerte para hoy*, for all to hear, hollering into the rain or into the wind and, when the seasons changed, they just hollered into lower temperatures because in Madrid it never snowed.

When I had the early shift, I woke well before the sun and walked in total dark down the Calle del Dios and made my way to the Calle del Prado to catch one of the cabs that idled outside the Palace Hotel, waiting for the hibernating tourists to spring and make for museums within walking distance. Everything in Madrid, truly, was always within walking distance, if you could acclimate yourself to the idea that walking forty-five minutes to somewhere was normal. When I walked in the total early darkness, I saw the overnight fish deliveries from Galicia being unloaded, the aluminum door pulled down at night to cover the storefront partially raised, the light inside partially illuminating the fish in the coolers on the sidewalk, the *bacalao* on ice, that until yesterday had swum happily in the Atlantic, maybe having made its way north from Portugal. Not much else stirred so early anywhere in Spain. You gained nothing from rising early. Often, when it rained and I was walking to the taxis, the fluorescence of the street lamps, the red streaks of the odd taxi tearing a wet sound on the sprinkled streets, they all conspired to make this place feel even more foreign to a young, ambitious American, only capable of textbook Spanish, who, at the market recently, confused the word *pollo* with *polla*—chicken and dick—much to the pleasure of the stunted old ladies giggling behind the counter.

I heard the man in line behind me say to the barista, "Kim Jong Dong"—referring to North Korea's mysterious dictator for life—"is said to be a demi-God. The Korean press prints silly shit, like that he got four holes-in-one the first time he played golf. That is a true fact! He's been up in the mountains now for forty-three days, stretching, twirling his baton, meditating, but now he's come down and everything is back to normal in Pyongyang."

The barista with a birth mark on his forearm shaped like Singapore tilted the full cup of espresso and proceeded to pour the hot milk, and, this way, at an angle, he made a little *fleur de lis* design atop the dairy foam.

As I sipped the cortado, the design would keep changing, massing together, its borders eroding with each sip like a barrier island ravaged by coastal storms. I had already received a solicitation that morning, an email with the header "Nature in the Balance" from the president of the Fire Island Preservation Association. Climate change was shrinking and morphing their island, inches each year, she wrote, and they wanted a campaign to "raise awareness and to secure feature pieces in major national news outlets."

I imagined overhead shots of Fire Island by helicopter, maybe footage from an overhead drone, fed to a cable news network for a "hard-hitting" feature, saw the middle-aged housewife straining to decipher the story as she sweated on the treadmill, but the captions that exclaimed the yearly diminution of the local habitat and wildlife would cipher the image. I sipped away the last foamy borders of my latté design until it had vanished and walked for a while.

I texted Margaret: be there soon…have a quick appt.

She texted back: Mark!

The coffee shop was not far from the National Gallery of Art, and often I would slip out mid-morning like this, texting Margaret then muting my cell phone, dreading the inevitable intrusions from work. To reach the museum, I had to pass through Chinatown, a route that brought me past Verizon Center and over to Ninth Street, a long walk downhill over the sidewalk grates where the Metro squealed below, its musk discernable from a block away.

Today was the painful overcast of a Robert Frost poem, and by the time I had crossed Constitution Avenue into the park, it had started to rain hard, puddles pooling at the curb. I bought a five-dollar umbrella from a street vendor selling popsicles in various neons and the predictable DC iconography: FBI t-shirts, campaign pins, beer mugs with presidential seals, commemorative front-page election results. The weather had driven at least one hundred startled tourists to shelter under the canopy of a gnarled oak. Others crowded beneath the lone Metro Bus stop or the roofline of a ticket kiosk by the outdoor skating rink in the Sculpture Garden or the steel awning of a hot dog cart.

I plunged ahead in the rain, dry except for my socks. I felt the mood sag return, and I knew what was coming.

Dr. Weller said her death had triggered depression. He would stare blankly, as he was fond of doing, an apparition in the conversation. In such moments he would remove his rimless glasses and wipe them with a Kleenex from a box he kept beside his chair with the footstool, rest his hands on his Buddha belly and recline so far in his La-Z-Boy that it looked as if he might inadvertently doze off. Behind the flea market lamp in the corner, I noticed his small pharmacy of anti-depressant samples.

When I reached the gallery, there was a monumental replica of a John Singer Sargent portrait—a dainty girl posing with a parasol the shade of pink frosting. I had not realized there was a new exhibition, even though I was a member here and I guessed at whether these were on the loan from the Museum of Fine Arts in Boston and if they had also procured some Winslow Homer landscapes, and I registered the feeling that I would rather stare into Homer's watercolors, always meticulously overcast and a little menacing, than linger amidst Singer Sargent's epicurean oils; I would rather have spent the morning at the National Gallery with El Greco, Goya, and all of the hazel Monets and preternatural blue Chagalls than discuss the antics of Lars and Fung—whatever their names, whatever they were doing.

It began to rain harder and I went inside. The interior was too large for echoes.

I had first encountered art through my mother but had my first profound experience at the Pompidou's retrospective of Francis Bacon twenty summers ago, in between my sophomore and junior years at Easton University—where there were no art electives, or any art department to speak of—and thus I became enamored with abstract painting; if they resembled reality it hardly mattered—the more postmodern-something the better.

Although I did not care deeply for the American Romantics, I asked the guard where to find the Singer Sargent exhibit.

He stood, wiped his mouth, put something in tinfoil onto his chair—I smelled the tang of lamb, some kind of gyro—he pointed towards the pamphlets on the wall, motioned to the second floor, and then sat down and resumed his lunch, the crumpled front page of *The Washington Post* serving as an unfolded napkin on his lap.

Walking the long, smooth stairs felt like ascending a slope of polished stone. The museum's layout was monotonously labyrinthine and it led you to wander through overlooked galleries. It was my usual day to visit but I had the idea that today I would also find the Cézannes. I wanted to see them through her eyes to see why she was never affected by them. At first I mistook her tastes for Spartan, but then again she loved Gauguin, Basquiat, Chagall, Kandinsky, even Vermeer. She said great art operated on two planes, seen and unseen. All artists must compress and eliminate as much of their material as possible to make the remaining material vibrate. She said a version of this at each of the three gallery openings she did the year she died: one in Florence, two in Madrid. Too much of art was made in common cloth. They nodded, as if the English filtered through the Italian. They smoked and nodded. We can know more of something through its absence, for the omissions written into stories or painted into settings all command our imagination. They even clapped. This line was in a brochure that I had made for her final opening: Galleria Cervantes, Calle Serrano, 43, Madrid.

I sauntered through the museum, Monica everywhere.

I walked into the room with the Botticellis, searching for an absence and finding nothing, but there was no unintended negative space in Renaissance art. Then, I heard a shriek of childish laughter; two small girls were racing, running to the brink of collapse down the giant hallway, their mother floating like a feather behind them, diaper bags in each hand. There were no windows and I wondered if it had stopped raining because she seemed pristine. As she came closer she sauntered like a regent fanned by palm fronds; she was pretty, in a different way than Monica.

Some women are defined by their beauty while others seem to make it an accessory to their personalities. Whereas Monica was beautiful because she was smart, kind, and humble, this woman had a beauty derived from some blithe prescience about the good future ahead of her. She becalmed everyone in the room save for her two girls, but, I thought, maybe boundless joy in kids is an expression of calm in the parents.

I wondered what good fortune had allowed this carefree woman to enjoy a rainy day at a museum with her daughters. Just then, I felt a shame at the pills I took and I experienced an all-at-once vision of being married to this woman and then disappointing her as a husband when she found out about my drug regimen and all the rest of me that, even deep into adulthood, was still covered in scaffolding. Should I marry this woman, a woman like this, or remarry at all? The requisite time had passed, Dr. Weller had said. Don't you think it's disrespectful to Monica, I said, noticing all the of the full

Kleenex boxes on all the tables in his office. I had not dated anyone since Monica and it had been over twenty years since I started dating Monica. There were websites for these things, others if you just wanted sex, he said without sounding seedy. Because she was an absence, she was also a presence, and I could not consider being with another woman without it feeling like adultery, I said, though I knew instinctively Monica would want me to restage my life and to fall in love again.

I followed them into the Goya gallery. I wondered if I could ever walk like this woman while I was professionally bound to extinguishing front-page anxiety for clients. I thought about my quoted fee for the OneSpeak engagement and wondered if it would even be worth it.

The woman smiled at me.

Besides time committed, there would be quite a bit of travel, hours of remedial explanation, large setbacks, and when Lars and Fung would fail to heed good counsel—which, undoubtedly, they would (they all did)— perhaps, given the stakes, I would be then forced into heated exchanges with Alan and his persnickety Long Bridge colleagues, and I would undoubtedly find myself disgruntled, exhausted, traversing the continent on United's weary fleet, playing at the fringes of influence. Texting Colin from some air bridge, returning home from Seattle, the airline dinner no dinner at all, I would have bought chips and hummus, consumed enough coffee that I would find myself pissing every thirty minutes; with the plane tilting in the night, I would be pissing on a smear of leftover excrement; this would be what my life had become, pondering everything in an airline bathroom, $2 million a year to play the solitary man at the diner counter in a real life Edward Hopper painting.

She smiled at me again.

I considered acting on her smiles—there was a third as she turned the corner towards the giant stairs. She reminded me of her. Maybe the first woman you date should be like her, maybe that would be easier for Colin. I envisioned she would handle Colin like her girls, a warm May breeze after the years of winter. For about ten more seconds I followed her, determining if I should initiate a conversation, keeping a respectful distance. She could fix Colin and maybe she could fix me.

Certain people make us better. Monica had this power.

It was Monica's idea for me to go to Spain. I was editor of my college newspaper. I loved David Foster Wallace, mostly his essays, and she encouraged me to take a year off after school, maybe even write.

"I'll be in law school. So boring. My father is giving me a thirty-thousand-dollar allowance for getting into Harvard. I'll split it with you."

That I had taken to journalism at all was because I had flunked organic chemistry my freshman year. The first semester of my sophomore year, I dropped my pre-med status and took a class in poetry.

Professor Shelley was somewhat a figure of speculation amongst the class. When she read poems aloud, she had the intense gaze of someone practicing voodoo. She mustered a tenuous connection to the Lannan Foundation, and such money meant writers and poets of renown came to give readings at our regional university, the audience a mix of students, amateur poets on the open mic circuit, always a few very well-dressed couples in their sixties who had driven down from Baltimore.

I owned a paperback of one of the few published copies of Professor Shelley's short story collection; I had borrowed it to lift her spirits. When I asked for it, Professor Shelley had gone straight to the shelf to where an entire row of her books sat like unopened instruction manuals, un-creased, and handed one to me, the cover art more akin to something you'd see on the front of a book by Spinoza or Heidegger, mostly shapes and oddly paired colors. It was the sort of book where the narrator of all the stories is a young girl making whimsical small talk with imaginary friends from her tree house, indirectly relaying domestic strife between her parents.

Our class was comprised of students who had failed organic chemistry: the football linebackers only capable of half-memorized sonnets to impress exchange student girlfriends; the "Hannas" and the "Prestons" with multiple piercings whose poetic muse spoke only in doggerel.

When we were reading "God's Grandeur," a poem by an obscure Jesuit (whose work received its due acclaim posthumously, when it was promoted by T.S. Eliot) one of these—Zoe, when it was her turn to comment on the poem's unique prosody of sprung rhythm—proclaimed her atheism and embrace of "a female deity, a Priestess." She proclaimed the poem sexist and offensive. Professor Shelley, visibly annoyed, asked her which stanza gave offense. Was it the famously declarative opening, "The world is charged the grandeur of God/It will flame out like shining from shook foil"? Did she not enjoy the lovely notion that "there lives the dearest freshness deep down things"? All of it was offensive, she said, all of it. I memorized that poem after that. It took me an hour until I could recite every stanza verbatim, all the iambs on the appropriate syllables.

I sprang it upon Monica over pizza that night on the floor of her room, some screwcap cab and plastic cups.

She looked at me, laughing through her dimple, like I was speaking in tongues. Read the one about the happy grass, she said. I then read her "Fern Hill" by Dylan Thomas, which she said was nonsensical except for the final stanzas, which she asked me to repeat over and over: "As I was young and in the mercy of his means/time held me green and dying/though I sang in my chains like the sea." She had fallen asleep during the seventh reading, the wine bottle half empty and the candle light flickering.

Professor Shelley made sure to invite me to all the literary "afterparties" that followed the Lannan readings. In my Junior year, the poet W.S. Merwin came to campus. His reading spanned almost ninety minutes, a somber, hushed, and dramatic affair. The well-dressed couples in the front row, the entire English Department—as this was a major poet, you see— let out audible gasps at every arresting stanza, and when his deep voice dropped off to conclude each poem, an affected crescendo of murmuring amongst the regional literati ensued, as if they had just been made privy to the meaning of life itself.

I met him after at Professor Shelley's party; it was nearly spring, and I recall exactly what he told me. Her bungalow was but ten minutes from the school's front gates, nearby the lake where some of us smoked weed on Wednesday nights and during exam week. Monica and I were the only students invited to the party. She made me wear a jacket but she herself wore jeans and a tight-fitting t-shirt and she looked amazing. I was underage but Professor Shelley put a glass of red in my hand and told me to, "just mingle around, try and soak up the conversation, gather useful bits."

Her house was full of tribal masks, Navajo exotica, and Santa Fe pottery. There were very few remnants of her son save for a portrait of him in uniform over the fireplace. Monica and I sipped our wine fugitively. I stood exceedingly close to her to lean down occasionally and pick up her scent; I contemplated luring her into the bathroom to make out, as was our habit at parties.

She giggled. "Mark, not now. We're here for this poet, for you to meet him. You said you loved his poems. Later."

"Now and later. Poets are timeless. If he departs I can speak to him through my muse."

"Look, he's right over there. Go talk to him. Tell your muse he or she can come along too."

She had my hand and led me over to his orbit, where a retinue of tenured professors clustered and the one with the Hemingway beard was going on about the etymology of the word "enchant," which he said was rooted in the Latin "*incantare*," literally "in sing," as if to lull someone into a spell through song alone. I felt the stares of the older men admiring Monica and intuited their interpretations about how she came to be mine. The bearded professor was perfectly delighted with himself when the story concluded and Merwin played along. Merwin's wife was a formal woman who seemed to find such flagrant erudition low and obsequious, and she was raising her saucer to shoulder level, looking around for a server to come by and offer a refill, but there was no staff. She noticed us, lowered her saucer, and said to her husband, "I think you have some young admirers."

Monica squeezed my hand, a signal: say something monumental, Mark. But I did not know what to say. My sudden paralysis was Prufrockian: should I quote one of his poems; recite something from Dylan Thomas; refer to my own published poem, or would my pride be tarnished when he asked me to repeat the name of the literary journal that had published it? Monica had waded into small talk with his wife, talking up the college's virtues and why it was ideal for law school aspirants. I was blinking nervously and taking copious sips of the wine, and then wondered if this coterie of professors, which did not include Professor Shelley, knew that I was underage, and then when I felt the wine give me a little lift, finally, I said, "I am just starting out as a poet and I wondered if you had any particular advice for someone like me."

He was standing with his shoulders still facing the professors; only his face was turned towards me. "Someone like you?" he said. His wife gave him a look and an elbow.

"Yes, well, I had a poem published last year in the *South River Bend Review* and want to keep at it." The other professors seemed bemused by me announcing myself as a young poet to the future Poet Laureate of the United States.

"And what precisely was your poem about?"

"Time, I guess. How we simultaneously yearn for the future and the

past in the present, how our yearning never stops, and how our humanity will not permit us to be released from the past." Professor Shelley was
walking over and I noticed that several of the nearby professors were eavesdropping on this conversation between tutor and tyro, Monica issuing little
hand squeezes of encouragement, urging me to go on.

"Well, it's something I'd like to keep at, poetry, I mean. Your own work
seems to be preoccupied with searches, with nature, things which I'd like
to take on in my own work." The one with the Hemingway beard was now
taking this all in deliciously, smiling in admiration of my bravura or senten-
tiousness, of which I would never be sure.

Merwin, who had stayed facing his adult colleagues the entire dialogue,
finally handed his empty wine glass to his wife, cleared his throat, turned to
me and, pausing, as if to invite an audience for the oracular pronouncement
to come, said, as if lines of his own verse, "Listen. Listen. And listen to what
you are listening for."

He turned his body away back to the group, a signal that this was all
he would be giving me tonight, and of his mystical utterance I have been
struggling to decode it ever since.

But now, standing among the Titians, age forty-one, a little gray streaked
into my temples, diminishment was my only expectation. The list of things
I could no longer attain, or reasonably attempt to become, expanded every
quarter and quite disturbed me. Had the days of the future already passed?
I was young enough still that I had a window of potential, but it was a short,
unpaved airstrip crammed between two mountains, shrouded in fog. Was I
landing or was I taking off?

I wandered the museum, resisting the urge to check my phone for messages. The phone vibrated again, only once though. I remembered Dr.
Weller's advice to try and extinguish impulsive behaviors, that obsessively
checking emails and text was one of those. But my phone was my work, my
altar. Being a consultant mandated a constant state of battle readiness. At
any moment, counsel needed to be dispensed, orders given to junior staff,
calls received from disgruntled clients—the media, who were lurking to pry
into the scope of our engagements. The phone was my instrument and I
wanted to banish it from my life but couldn't. I had started buying the gold
as my insurance policy should this all flutter away: the clients, the staff, the
false legend for all this success. Victor would be calling soon from New York
because we were being paid $75,000 a month by his law firm on behalf of

the president of Guinea but had not achieved a single media placement. We were paid through the law firm, instead of by the sovereign, to establish attorney-client privilege, a maneuver that shielded all our emails and memos from discovery in the event of a lawsuit. Although losing the money would have meant nothing to me or to the firm, and even though the work was being done by others below me, still, such a call represented a sense of personal failure. The phone was vibrating now; a text from Colin: *Dad. Hi. It's Colin. That man that kills the bulls what is his name again?*

To ward off acute separation anxiety, I'd bought him a phone. It took a written diagnosis from Dr. Weller of "moderate to severe mood disorder" for Colin to even be permitted to bring the phone to school. For a while, when the panic attacks began, we tried liquid Xanax. They sometimes said he was found whimpering in the bathroom stall about natural disasters, usually tsunamis. The school consented with the proviso that he leave it with the school nurse each morning, and use it only if he had been appropriately excused from class when the teacher recognized the prodromal symptoms of an episode. As I read his text, I imagined him in the nurse's office, laboring over the keystrokes, straining to spell all the words correctly to please me, struggling with all his psychic burdens; I imagined him asking the nurse to review his text for grammar. His precocity sometimes made me think I should enroll him in a private school, but tearing him from childhood friends and throwing him in with the sharp-elbowed boys he would assuredly meet soon enough in life was cruel. I imagined, as he typed, that he assumed I was off at work doing important adult things, and I envisioned his squinting face trying to make sense of why his father had eloped to a museum for the late morning and why he was trailing a beautiful woman and her two daughters gallery to gallery.

Matadors, I texted, guiltily.

Almost instantaneously, he replied: *thankyou I just needed to know that ok thankyou thankyou daddy.*

I was about his age when my mother announced one Sunday that we were going downtown to this museum to see the Degas collection, *la ciudad* as she called it, stepping into maroon high heels and draping herself in a shawl, dressed, I thought even then, a little too flamboyantly for the occasion, too Latina. She had an Aztec face and was a Yucatan woman, as she called it; her agrarian genetics were programmed to always keep us moving in all circumstances. I had only enough time with Monet to learn that if

I squinted, the image would sharpen. We had moved four times since my father was sentenced. Put him to work, Lucia, he would have said, wadding up a brochure in his fist, tossing it at some marble nude. His father was a Spaniard, mother from Iowa. He should be cutting lawns and pruning hedges not looking at pictures of them. I envisioned him creeping up to the canvases as if he was about to slice a tree from the scene.

At night, he would shovel microwaved corn kernels into his mouth from the TV dinner on his lap. I would take his cracked boots beside the recliner and hand them to my mother when he asked.

You'll teach him nothing. All my carpenters speak like that, all day, squealing at each other with that party music playing, drinking orange sodas and they squeal their Española. The niggers can barely speak at all. Monkeys, that's all. One tenth Hispanic. Do you want him to hammer nails all day and be around all of them and that?

She hung her head, rinsing empty beer bottles in the sink. Do you not know that there is a revolt underway to slaughter America?

He did not know that she stowed away her recycling money in an ivory box with a plastic Virgin Mary fixed on the lid. He will think my bible is inside, she said. He will not want that it is opened.

Colin would have fit easily on her lap. I was now in a circular gallery off the Impressionist wing, surrounded by four pastorals, *The Voyage of Life*: masterpiece depictions the Hudson River Valley, Catskills, and Adirondacks, where Cole had staged an entire movement around landscape painting. They are as much a study in the painting of religious light as they are an allegory for the stages of life. I stood up and walked so close to the paintings that the guard stood up too, hoping my physical proximity to the first painting would reflect that I was moved and wanted to linger. I took in the angels on the river banks, pointing the boat forward, and then, as the boy in the boat aged into manhood by the third painting, the sky had darkened and the voyage became an ordeal.

The last canvas depicted a luminescent afterlife on the horizon and the small boy in the boat has become an old man. Standing before these paintings I did not have a profound experience of art so much as I had a profound experience of light, Cole's brilliant chiaroscuro, the way his paintings seemed to be dominated by luminosity. The phone rang-vibrated. I pulled it from the breast pocket in my suit and saw that there were two voicemails. I guessed at whether they related to any internal crises or if this was about our new African client or the upcoming Turkmenistan pitch, the Fire Island people, or all the wants and needs of the staff awaiting just blocks away.

I tried to hook my thumbs through my belt and let out a little sigh and realized that I had forgotten my belt and then I realized that I had also forgotten that today was picture day at school.

Reaching into my pocket, I found another pill and chewed it for good measure and I felt the lifting come, and soon I had some certitude of a stable mood manifest, a muted mirth come through like light off dull brass.

I walked through the lobby staring into the phone and the mix of soaked umbrellas and wet tourists gave the exit area the smell of air-conditioned rain.

Outside a chill bit the nose. The rain had ended but it was still overcast and unseasonably cold. I pulled up the collar on my suit. I was staring into the phone, scrolling through emails; far too many required a long, typed response, and there were other business complexities that merited phone calls or meetings. One email to everyone in the office consecrated a new client win, a $95,000-a-month engagement for the Guggenheim Foundation; another email just to me from Jacob said that a biotech giant in San Diego was firing us after one month because I had not been attending their weekly phone calls, and, yes, the note continued, I should not have to staff weekly calls considering we had an executive staff of nineteen professionals, they could handle it, although perhaps we were selling my involvement a little too carelessly.

I tapped another text to Colin, hoping he was still in the bathroom but no longer whimpering: *tonight is hockey night. Be ready! We can have pasta afterwards!!* I had been too anxious to look at the paintings clear-eyed and had left unsatisfied. The tourists were scattering again down the sidewalks, forming lines at entrances, huddling at the vendor carts, licking mustard from their fingertips. I found some pocket change, enough to buy a foot long and sauerkraut. When the Pakistani vendor opened the container lid, steam soared out and water dripped from the tongs holding the sausage onto the bun.

I sat right there on the bench, a quick lunch, sniping at each email that was addressed only to me. I had tried to build this business, I thought, according to the MBA maxim: it should survive if you don't. But I had not succeeded in doing this at all; somehow this entire business had coiled around me.

I saw a black sedan pull up to the curb and the serene woman and her daughters stepped in, the familiar sticker for Uber on the back window. I had wanted her to turn and see me, a thought that was eclipsed almost immediately by the phone ringing. I watched the car drive away.

"Mark, if this is urgent, and you said it was, we should be meeting in person and you should stop pussyfooting around with these offers. We need to put this thing up for auction like I counseled you seven months ago. You need to start listening to me. You need to come to New York. We need to do this now."

Harry Golucci had represented every public relations and lobbying firm of import that had been involved with any transaction of note in the past ten years. He was not even five foot four but in person he came across as six foot eight. His unabashed New Jersey accent would have reduced him to cliché were it not for the fact that he was every bit as bright as he was mercenary. I'd had him on retainer since last year, when a large law firm made a tepid acquisition overture.

"It happened again," I said.

"Yes, I know, they called me too."

"That's gauche of them. And I don't like them to begin with. What did they say?"

"Well, they asked me if you are as difficult as people say you are—and they asked me about your status."

"Does it matter?"

"Does what matter?"

"My 'mental status.' And that's none of their business."

"They care. Buy a car and you want to be sure the engine works. Tell me how much this time."

"Five times earnings. What did you say about me?"

"Against?"

"The multiple is against four million in net profit. And?"

"And what?"

"What did you tell them about me?"

"I told them the truth. I told them Mark's beautiful wife passed several years ago and he is doing his best now. I told them to wake the fuck up and stop fucking around, that Mark White owns and operates the country's premier strategic communications firm and he is doing it whether or not the economy tanks like it did in 2007, and that he's doing it even with his own troubles and that those, by the way—and I told them this—were none of their goddamn business, is what I told them."

"And?"

"Mark, sell."

"Why now?"

"You have achieved peak mystique. But one bad decision, Mark, just one, and the mystique is shattered. I tell all my clients to sell when the party is at its raging zenith and that's where you are today, so sell."

"That's very lyrical."

"Jesus, Mark, are you listening to me? What about the payout? They wouldn't tell me over how many years."

"Three years—half up front." It was a generous arrangement.

"Really?"

"Yes. Really."

"Take it. Take it yesterday. Twenty million dollars, Mark. Ten million tomorrow, $5 million at the end of each subsequent year. You could do whatever you damn well please after that kind of money, even after taxes, which—and I think you will recall—is taxed at capital gains rates of twenty percent, not the forty plus percent you pay now to be a rich son of a bitch. You'll net $16 million. It's the greatest offer you will ever receive for your mystique, which, I will remind you again, has a shelf life like anything. You are at the absolute top, the absolute top where everyone you are not paying or counseling absolutely hates you. Now it's time to go."

Reaching no decision, I told Harry I would call him back in a week, and hung up.

My hotdog had grown cold but I finished it. I thought about taking a vacation with Colin, someplace unchained from seasonal cycles. It was a good offer and Harry was right.

I sat down on a bench. I had no pen and paper or iPad so instead I wrote an email to myself, something to capture my *esprit de corps* in the moment to share later with Dr. Weller, the kind of thing that, if emailed to the press, would light my reputation on fire:

Dear Mark,

The only things now that bring pleasure are eating, watching Colin play hockey and cheering alongside all the parents—and, surprisingly, socializing with those parents—reading my old books, which I am consuming at a dangerous pace, and listening to my favorite music in the car to work or in the study after work, after Colin has fallen into sleep. Apart from these activities, I am dangerously irritable, prone to cynicism and post-ironic snark, chronically exasperated with the anodyne small talk of acquaintances, colleagues, anyone breaching my solitude; am disappointed and shamed by the condition of my psyche and physical body, an estuary of pharmaceuticals; a life that—admittedly, tragically, insuperably—is pretty fucked up. All day I play vigilante, on the watch for dangerous thoughts and patterns, readily, quickly and a little desperately lowering the hammer on the pinions that hold the lid on me, a watchdog sniffing out the pathology concealed within each impulse. And it's true: I hear a loud inaudible voice in my head that tells me what I need to say.

Perhaps this too shall pass? But I sense a too-soon cosmic slackening. I sense the pinions loosening, see the clouds gathering far distant, the crows over the wheat field, the total darkness of a permanent eclipse. I holster my spirit in apathy. Ahead, I can see the tall hills, far and dry, lit in a private light: I want to live in a Jubilee year of solitude, but solitude summons enemies and demons. I am nearly out of time. After such knowledge, what decisions?

I reread the email twice, made a few edits to the final paragraph, admired the apathy metaphor, double-checked that this was indeed being sent only to me, and hit send.

I walked back up Seventh Street, passed by the Verizon Center, veering around the battalion of restless Black Panthers with their megaphones patrolling the corner at Metro Center; I stopped for another *cortado*, then I rode the elevator of my building to our floor and avoiding eye contact snuck into my office where I was reminded of lemon sharks, kept seeing the Catskill light but hearing Harry.

chapter three

I HAD very little décor in my office, a few family photos and a framed
clipping of the last story I had ever filed as a journalist: a piece after
September 11 in the *Wall Street Journal*. My mother's gift to me for
Christmas that year. I had decided to come home.

That entire week following the attacks, Spaniards would pluck me from
the populace, sought me out not to extend condolences but to vent. That
Bush of America should not bomb the civilians of Afghanistan, that he
should not make a war that is unjust. Or that it was Los Mooros, who did it,
said the shoeshine man on Calle Serrano, referring to the Moroccans who
sought to chronically penetrate Spain with their flotillas.

I had premier access to what was happening, worldwide, the day of the
attacks because I was in the newsroom. I called friends back home, woke
my mother, who was still sleeping, to tell her the towers had fallen, and
they all called me for days to find more information in real time. The cable
networks installed a ticker feature on their newscasts; those have been in
place ever since.

Three days after the attacks, a memo was quickly circulated inside the
Reuters European bureaus: We were not to refer to the 9/11 attacks as
terrorism, it read, or to call the hijackers terrorists; one man's terrorist is

another man's freedom fighter, it read. It was an unprincipled decision, the attempted neutrality less impartial than it was cowardly.

In defiance, I filed a few stories, inconsequential pieces about what Spanish officials were saying about the attacks, that included the word "terrorists."

My editor in London quickly chastised me, changed the offending verbiage, and filed the altered story to the wire. I monkeyed like this with London for a week until my bureau chief called me in.

"You are not making a good name for yourself." His hands were on his hips while he leaned back in his chair.

"Neither are the terrorists. I'm sorry—the Taliban."

"Listen, we all have people back home. I get what you're doing, Mark, but you must be careful. The Brits remember this stuff. This kind of shit gets you transferred to Bogota or Mexico City. You wanna get kidnapped?"

When I got home at two o'clock, I watched the live post-terror coverage on CNN International, the dust and debris drift through lower Manhattan, and I waited a while for America to wake up and then I called Monica in her dorm and relayed the situation.

"You are both right," she said. "You can keep writing stuff you hate or you can come home."

"What would I even do?"

"Can't they transfer you here?"

"To Boston? That bureau has, like, four people."

"What about Washington?"

"I've asked about it. Matt says someone has to die for a good slot to open."

"Maybe it's time to make a change."

"Maybe."

"Perhaps you're not a wire reporter."

"I am not a wire reporter. However, I am good at it. I respect deadlines."

"You do. You've had a good run, two years. But come home. I graduate in May. We can settle here in Boston. Francesca's brother is at a marketing agency in New York. She says he can help you with a position in Boston. Lots of journalists take non-writing jobs starting out. Why should you be special?"

"I am special now. I can call anyone in the world. Hello, this is Mark White from Reuters. They will take the call. I called William Safire the other day. We discussed his piece on Ehud Barak and the Camp David peace talks. We spoke for fifteen minutes. He's a charming man."

"Did you mention your situation?"

"Sure did. And you know what? He said I could move back home—and maybe get a gig as a 'copy boy' at the *New York Times*. Ridiculous. He gave it to me straight. He was sympathetic. I said, 'I interviewed the Bashar Assad last week with Aznar. But in America I'm a copy boy?' He wasn't being derogatory. Just giving it to me straight. But now it all makes sense. Journalism is not a meritocracy."

"I get it, but it's no reason to stay marooned somewhere if you are unhappy."

"And, if I ever want to cause Word War III, I can make up some whacky headlines, like Bush to invade Iraq, Putin to Take the Oil, Nuclear Arsenal Deployed Against China—and hit the F11 key—and zip the stories directly to the wire. Bypass the editors altogether. There is no protective mechanism against such a thing, can you believe it? I often wonder what mix of headlines it would take to cause a military situation. We joke about it at the bureau, at least the Americans. At least we did until they destroyed the twin towers."

"That's sick."

"The news is a weapon."

"That's really sick, Mark. Don't tell other people that."

"Well, the news is a weapon too—of mass information."

"Of mass destruction."

"Mostly to those who read the news. I don't know who reads my stories, unless they have a Reuters terminal or are standing at NYSE and troll the big board. No one can get them online. Seems I am writing for a washed-out wire hack named Lionel, or something, based in London, or some suit in City of London, day trading. It's still a rush to see them flash on the screen. But I have to cut and paste my copy to get it to my mom."

"She misses you."

"I know. The money here helps. I can live on half of what I earn and send her the rest."

"I have class soon. Why don't you call me later tonight?"

"The cell charges are astronomical. Has to be during my shift here."

"Maybe that payphone?"

"Gypsies vandalized it. Last week. There's none anymore now in Santa

Ana. I'd have to walk all the way to Puerta del Sol. By the way, they are say-ing there might be an anthrax attack. Vapor form, sprayed down the middle of Times Square."

"I saw that too. Okay, so...."

"Someday they will invent a way to call people on your phone and you can talk to them face to face, like on Star Trek."

"That would be nice."

"And you could touch them."

"That would be nice too."

"And you could watch them on a camera, their every move."

"That is creepy."

"I interviewed the CEO of a porn company last week. Women in stalls with cameras pretending to love someone behind the lens. All in a ware-house. Wildly profitable. He sells magazines. He says the future is mobile; that we will all watch porn movies on phones at airports, on buses, play-grounds, wherever. That is nuts, eh?"

"OMG."

"I know. We're gonna watch porn on the shitty little calculator screen on my Nokia. Really? It is something, though, to be connected. I feel lonely here for so much of the day. I eat lunch alone at places that honor my Sodexo coupon. Civil servant types. They draw out the lunch for hours. I'm out in thirty. Then what? Outside the bureau, I am cut off. Back into Spanish and stretching my mind to formulate grammar all day. It's tiring. Here at work I am tethered to the world. I can use slang. The phones work. I have American channels. The email isn't slow. It's just endless Spanish all day otherwise and my head hurts and I get tired living outside my own language. I can't find real writers here, just a lot of expat women named Phoebe who are always 'working on something.' Hemingway used up all the expat writers, I think. But not the wine. I've had so much wine. All day long. You cannot drink enough water in Spain to stay hydrated. I've been thirsty for two years."

"Stop drinking. Those poor girls."

"They seemed fine with it, actually. Being out of your country, your lan-guage. It makes you seek out those like you. Like attracts like. You get in a bubble, a world within a world. You end up cauterizing your connection to the culture. It's funny, I came here to escape my identity, to bloom as a writer. I'm faintly Spanish, even less of a writer. I wear baseball caps everywhere now in town, even inside until it's completely awkward for everyone. All that's happened living abroad is I have become more American."

"Come home, Mark. We'll figure it out."

★

MARGARET DIDN'T knock, just came in, an open palm gesture an Italian might make to getting their shoes scuffed. I apologized but she seemed genuinely upset.

"People were looking for you, Mark. And Hanna called again."

"Give me five minutes," I said. I dialed Hanna's cell.

"So I see you are amassing a cache of warlords and despots," she said.

"I thought this piece was on Lincoln."

"Standard story about a firm signing new clients, Mark, you know the drill."

"How many words?"

"You know the answer to that too: they only give me one thousand words."

Editors were ruthless about pieces pushing past this arbitrary boundary; they'd hack out whole swaths of fertile narrative in favor of a few Crayola sentences and multiple quotes from scattershot *sources* and *experts* and *persons familiar with the situation*. If I was lucky, I would be quoted once and have about fifty words all my own.

"Why don't I just email you my quote?"

"You could. Or I can try and trick some info from you. P.S., I heard you finished the rosé."

"You could try, but I doubt you are so cynical, Hanna."

I had simply given her too many headlines, so many unreported tidbits, her unofficial career builder, that I knew she would never empty the round on me.

"Send me the quote, I'll read you the best bits of the piece in a few hours and you can revise as you see fit, okay? Everything good otherwise, business, life, your son?"

"Everything is perfect."

Margaret came in again, angrier than before. Her eyes were sallow and she was kneading her fingers together. "They are all waiting and giving me hell!"

"Alright, alright!"

I walked in and felt embarrassed for being so late; they were all around the conference table with a plate of six-hundred calorie pumpkin muffins and a tray of unripe honeydew. No one seemed to mind that we were thirty minutes past our start. Hawthorne was peeling a clementine and gave a little nod to start the meeting.

Wendy Morgan, one of my executive vice presidents of media relations, was speaking: "Today I left my building pass at home and only realized it after coming here from the dentist where I got two cavities filled, an impromptu flu shot at CVS, and an overdue mammogram—performed twice because the technician screwed up. Hell, if you are going to let a man mash your breasts twice at least wear your lipstick, but I forgot that at home too. Now I am going to shove some bamboo under my fingernails and go and write this goddamn op-ed for the Saudis that Joel James fucked up."

The muffins were slowly being eaten as she spoke but the melon would go untouched for the entire forty-five-minute meeting; we would leave the tray in the kitchen by the coffee maker for the impoverished interns and junior associates who ate leftovers of any kind.

"I understand that this is a major opportunity for us, major. Bill, the one who brought it to us and who was former governor of one of those flyover states, he says it's major so I really think we need our best ideas right now," said Hawthorne.

We were all seated in Velázquez, the room named after the Spanish painter of *Las Meninas*. It hung in the Prado and was notable for the way the painter inserted himself into the portrait, looking out at you from behind his own canvas, the young Princess Margaret Theresa being tended to by her handmaidens; King Philip IV and Queen Mariana are looking at you too from their reflections in the mirror set against the back wall— but they are really looking at the painting from the vantage of where you stand, accounting for their reflection, you and the ghosts looking at the same painting. It was the portraiture of irony, I thought, seeing it the first time, standing in the Prado in jeans and sandals; it was a double perspective that transfixed me in the sense that referent scenes, relationships, life could be rendered and perceived in simultaneous vantages.

"What is major?" I asked.

"Like $250 million major," he said.

"In fees?" Sally said.

"No, that's all in. Bill tells me these people have grand notions. Parades. Fireworks. Bono. Rockets. That sort of thing," Hawthorne said. "I suspect we would get about ten percent of it all—max."

"So what's the net on that?" I asked.

Hawthorne stopped peeling and looked up at Sally. "Well, first, if we even get paid—and let's assume we do since we will demand the funds in escrow—we'd see about $20 million of it."

"Is Turkmenistan the country where the president has the slopey Mongolian eyes and killed those Iranian women in the 1970s?" said Wendy.

I sat and tuned out. I didn't like to run meetings, preferred to hover in the room, a heavy presence. I thought about tonight's dinner for Colin. There was no practice. I'd need to cook something. Or maybe we would go out to Makimoto's for sushi. I thought about this year's Christmas card and how to handle that, and figured I would ask Margaret to get a harmless card of a snowy sylvan scene, warm yellow light in someone's mountain hermitage, fierce Christian words concerning Christ's birth. I imagined that if we won this business, that if we had to travel to Turkmenistan, that I would be the last man in the office willing to go. I did not know where it was and flipped open my iPad, reread last night's message to Monica along with the others. With such an extravagant fee in hand, I would likely buy more bullion from Fred, my Easton roommate who had made it all the way to Lloyds in London; I had neglected to tell Harry about White & Partners' gold reserves, which undoubtedly would spike the purchase price if I decided to sell. I looked around the room at this collection of grown-ups playing with the reputations of large multinationals who had failed to assimilate into the digital era and knew nothing about how to manipulate Google search results or how to lure former U.S. Officials to shill for them in the newspaper as spokespersons or opinion article authors.

"I think that's Azerbaijan," said Hank. He had a headmaster's face, a pillar of a nose, the chiseled cheeks and chin of a Roman Senator. As he spoke he grimaced, shut his eyes as if in desperate prayer, and massaged his face with his right hand; then he spooled out a monologue about the last Russian Czar with his face resting in the cradle of his left palm, elbow on the table, his eyewear waving in the air with his free right hand, making desultory statements about the decline of the news media. He possessed an array of mannerisms that were deployed in rapid succession when the conversation gathered speed, meant to call attention to his level of engagement.

"No, wait, you know, perhaps it's Kazakhstan," he said, savoring every phrase like the wine of a last supper. "You know, once I saw the Almaty Symphony Orchestra. Carnegie Hall. It was at the world premiere of some sprawling piece, musicians in traditional garb, that sort of thing. Karl Jenkins was the composer. The playbill said he was one of the only living top ten composers of the past twenty years."

I started to read the RFP. It was in a small font and single-spaced.

I am afflicted with implacable distractedness and have to read things at least twice if I hope to adequately understand them. For this reason, I remain intimidated by the act of reading; my cognitive limitations are re-exposed to me.

It's not that I wasn't Ivy material. I felt smart but tested dumb. When I called the admissions hotline for Yale that April morning, the rejection was dealt swiftly, quick and good. Better this way, I told myself. At least the woman said, "I'm very sorry dear."

I had been sitting in our living room, the early light angling through the window onto the pine floor and onto my father's tools. My mother was waiting in the kitchen. When I appeared she was sitting with her hands folded in front of her, clasping the rosary, elbows resting on the table, the tea cup drained. I didn't even have to say anything. She pushed out a smile, then started to cry. My father stayed outside, washing and waxing the cars, as usual. Was that special call at least free, he asked? Was that hotline free? He asked me to wax his truck. He inspected my work twice, I guess looking for smudges. Then he told me to rip up all the geraniums in the pots that were crispy from winter. After I did that I ate a plate of scrambled eggs and took a three-mile run.

Easton didn't have a hotline. They were a regular mailbox college. They offered me a $5,000 scholarship. My mother cried. That means you owe them $120,000 total, my father said, dip wadded fat into in his lower lip.

The man he first-degree stabbed in the ribs died four months later. Life sentence, made all the local papers, including *The Washington Post*. A black man refusing to pay my father's price, or so he thought. Then reaching into his jacket for a smoke, not a weapon. So he rushed him. Fourteen stab wounds. He had four kids. His wife was in a halfway house. My father had torn down a wall in his condo to make a large bedroom for all the kids.

My mother took a job cleaning rooms at the Holiday Inn, waiting tables on the weekend at Friendly's. She was too old to earn large tips and usually came home with around fifty dollars. She took large vitamin pills from CVS all day, nothing she had been prescribed by any doctor. She moved into an apartment soon, and I slept on the couch.

I mowed and mulched the neighbors' yards, chicken scratch money, he called it, but something for books, clothes, a dented, rusted-out Oldsmobile. They gave me loans and ten years to pay them at moderately aggressive rates.

He was lucky he didn't get the chair, his lawyer said.

On our Thanksgiving visit, he slapped my mother for feeling sorry for that nigger who wanted to kill him, and the guards rushed him and pulled him back from her. Her dress was torn and he was laughing. I grabbed her under her arms and lifted her off the floor and pushed her into the rusted car and drove her home and we returned to our life without him. We never visited again and he never wrote.

I learned last year from a website that he hung himself. He was only fifty-two. Franklin R. Belmond. She let me change my name before my freshman year. White. Fuck you, I thought. Fuck you, Frank. I'm half Mexican but I will dilute your perfect white race with my Mexican filth.

"I believe that the president of Turkmenistan is a benevolent dictator," Hawthorne said, fiddling with his peels.

He had been with me when we first met with Prime Minister Hatoyama in Kyoto, when White & Partners was handling all their trade work. Ahead of the audience with Hatoyama, we had what seemed an unnecessary number of preparatory meetings. At each one, a fidgety staffer would ask me if I would recommend to the Prime Minister that the press release we were drafting on the state of negotiation use the word "complex" in the headline, followed by a vigorous head nod, and head nods from the colony of underlings. I thought it strange. A press release should be simple, I said to Hawthorne. Why are they making this complicated? Each meeting the same thing. "It might be one of those words that jumped the border long ago," Hawthorne said, "you know, a word that feels different in Tokyo just like the sushi here tastes different than the sushi at home. Maybe it symbolizes more than it infers."

I asked the U.S. Ambassador, a querulous academic type, the purpose behind using this word, "complex," when it, in fact, violated every tenet of public relations, reductive clarity being the prevailing ideal. You don't state your mind clearly in Japan in political matters, he said, already

uncomfortable with my visit and my breach of protocols at the official dinner the evening before (I was caught whispering to Hawthorne while the
Hatoyama was giving his toast). He went on to explain that the Japanese
prize ambiguity, linguistic iridescence, *tamamushi-iro*: a way of expressing
things that, from certain angles, as with the wings of the jewel beetle from
which the concept draws its inspiration, enables various perspectives and
meanings.

"President—and I cannot pronounce his name so won't even try—is a
reformed Marxist," Hawthorne said. "But that was when we were all kids
in the backseat of our parents' car, waiting in line for gas during the Carter
embargo. He's cleaned up his act since. Sent all his kids to Princeton; their
English is perfect. He's pushing eighty, is contemplating his legacy, which,
even being charitable, Bill says it's shabby, not much to speak of really:
erected some new buildings, moved the capital of the country on a whim,
may have had his fourth wife kidnapped, ruthlessly repressed some pro-De-
mocracy rioters in the early Reagan years, disallowed actual voting in elec-
tions in the sense that his prime opponents where jailed or maimed or
killed, always by meddlesome neighbors, he would say."

"My father has been there before, when he was stationed in Moscow.
The women shave," Wendy said.

"Well, it's not too bad, we have an air base there, and they had 4.3%
GDP last year. Coca-Cola has a bottling facility there," Hank said.
"Wonderful place if you like bomb shelter chic," Hank said. "Perhaps it's a
locale from which to source new interns." They all laughed. I recalled that
the oil on canvas replica of *Las Meninas* now hanging beside the conference room door had been procured by an intern, at my direction, from a
Bulgarian concern that specialized in replicas and—I suspected—forgeries
of all varieties.

"All in all," Hawthorne said, "President Whoeverthefuck has kept the
whole rickety place together, humming along quasi-Democratically. Bill
says without him they'd all still be plowing fields with oxen and drinking
homemade wine if it weren't for his good sense to construct a vast pipe-
line to ship oil through the former Soviet states into the nether regions of
Eastern Europe, parts between Moldova and Serbia."

"What are they looking for in a firm and is there competition?" said
Tomas Toren—everyone used his surname in conjunction with his first
name. He had a Swedish heartthrob face and he earned $350,000 per year.

I paid him that for three reasons: I found it endearing that he ordered patterned bespoke shirts from Borelli in Rome; he wrote fantastic opinion articles in anyone's voice in under three hours; he was unapologetically ambitious and would accept any task dutifully.

"Well there's this extensive Request for Qualifications. You should read it Tomas Toren. You'd enjoy it. At least twenty grammatical errors the first ten words. But Bill says to ignore it. He's in good now with the president and thinks we can short circuit the whole process with a delegation-style visit there."

"When would we go?" said Tomas Toren, lifting his bangs away from his face.

"Whenever we want, I suppose," Hawthorne said.

"Is there extreme weather in Turkmenistan?" asked Hank.

"What is the difference between a cyclone and a monsoon?" said Wendy.

"Do you suppose we might get gifts. My father said when you go to places like these they bestow signs of friendship, shit like Patek Philippe watches," said Hank.

"I think, Hank, you can expect a knock on your door at two in the morning from Anna and Svetlana. They would be your local gifts," said Wendy.

"Is this one of those countries Putin wants?" asked Sally.

"This is one of those countries no one wants. That's why they are spending over $1 billion on this thing. Considering that they pump one million barrels per day, they could be spending more. Surprisingly, there is a Michelin star restaurant in Ashgabat, mostly offal, mutton, and the sinewy cuts, but I'm told by my Svetlana there that it's quite fantastic so we should pretty much plan on eating there every night. God only knows what is being served elsewhere in the city. National dish is *manti*—dumplings filled with ground pumpkin. Lots of pies and soupy goulashes, too. My gosh, that reminds me I'm all out of smoked Hungarian paprika at home. They love chai tea and the drink of the nation is fermented camel's milk, *chal*, surprisingly served as a sparkling beverage. Local wine made from muscatel grapes, which would make for overly sweet white. I'll have to have some cases shipped, which raises another question. Our contract. Should President Whoeverthefuck be flying us over on private, in which case I bring some jeroboams I purchased at auction last September. Left Bank Bordeaux '89. We should think about proper storage but Bill says every hotel there is over-the-top Ottoman excessive, Vegas but bigger and more gold, caviar on the omelets and gold on the ceilings. I suppose there'd be a local gallery but one never knows about post-Soviet societies. They are usually incapable of producing any great art because there is nothing they are permitted to say without fear of the gulag. Yes, their security apparatus is fully intact and expect your room to be bugged and to be followed. When Anna and Svetlana come knocking, Hank, plunge head first into their Snow White embrace knowing you will be on YouTube if you slip up. It's a hunter-gatherer society so expect lots of animal firs and throws all over the place in your room so you may be able to obscure the private bits in mink," said Hawthorne.

"Are we thinking we might second someone to be on the ground there for the year prior?" Hank asked.

"Joel James," I said.

"Is he ready?" asked Sally.

"Is anyone ever ready?" said Hawthorne.

Finally, looking up from my iPad, annoyed, I said, "Listen, I'm not sure why we need a big meeting on this. These guys are not going to read our proposal. They are going to buy the ribbon and the packaging. That's all. We need to be thinking of it that way. Ask former Governor Richardson to be the lead on the delegation, invite that prestigious economist with the monocle, bundle up a few execs here in the office, fly over there and tell the president what he needs to do. Get on the front pages of their measly national newspaper with grandiose statements. Jesus, it's not so hard. Send a two-page memo ahead of time that uses words they cannot translate."

"Right! That's tits and the ass, Mark!"

"Hawthorne please," said Sally.

"Mark is on to something. Why waste all this time constructing an opus? This is like selling a car; they want gloss and shine. They don't particularly wish to lift the hood and inspect the engine," said Tomas Toren.

"What are our big ideas?" I said.

"We were thinking of sending bloggers there, you know, a kind of fresh look at the country through the eyes of the new media, pictures of the president doing presidential things, locals making honey, showing a general sense of order," said Wendy, breaking a muffin in half and swallowing part of it whole.

"It would be better if we just send a photographer for that. What will these bloggers write? Even if we pay them they must put an edge on their pieces so they don't come across as shills. Let's hire Annie Leibowitz," I said. "Have her go over there for a week and take photos of all the tribal dwellings and enough of whatever looks modern and do a coffee table book. We can parade her around with the book on a world tour—Paris, Rome, LA, New York, London, of course."

"Brilliant. Tomas Toren, write that down. It says here, Mark, we also need to produce two parades per day for fifteen days, fireworks each night, an opening ceremony for the EXPO, concerts, and our theme should be focused on 'new energy future'—note I intentionally dropped a 'the' because they did not insert it into the text. I suppose that one did not go to Princeton. State school," said Hawthorne.

They all laughed.

"Space," I said. "We should do trips into space. We represent Virgin. Call Sir Richard and ask if we can do a co-branded thing with Virgin Galactic. We can shuttle people into space from a location inside Turkmenistan."

"I love that," said Sally.

"Virgin Galactic launches from New Mexico," said Wendy.

"So we'll pay them to launch from Turkmenistan," said Tomas Toren.

"We should call the Louvre," I said. "The Museé d'Orsay, The Hermitage, Guggenheim, MOMA. Call them all. Get their Van Goghs or their Rembrandts, old masters—a Vermeer if we can. Yes, a temporary exhibition in their new museum. World class art in a second-tier country. That's a story. It would put them on the map. *New York Times Magazine,* or one of those Teju Cole essays in *The New Yorker.* If they won't loan a piece, we can get them virtually rendered—digital reproductions on LED screens. I saw it at the Consumer Electronics Show last year. You could not tell them from the real thing. Yes, that's it, a retrospective—both digital and actual—of works culled from the great museums of the world."

Hank was holding a muffin and said, "But how will we do that? We don't know anyone at any of these museums."

"The insurance alone," said Sally.

"If they are talking about the future, why are we using paintings from a hundred years ago?" said Wendy. Hank was still holding his muffin. Even Hawthorne was quiet.

"Because," I said, "you have to travel backward in time to move ahead."

As I said this, I saw Joel James pass by the conference room, a Burberry tie and a checkered shirt, and give me a little nod, a gesture I assumed meant that he appreciated the raise and de facto promotion.

Everyone else in the room noticed it too. By their silence, I detected that it had been an unpopular decision, heaping so much responsibility onto an upstart who had been with the firm for less than two years.

Wendy glanced back at her notes and began reciting the list of to-do's that she would delegate to her team after this meeting. It wouldn't take long: they were pacing the hallways back and forth, awaiting their commands, and while I didn't necessarily think that delegating basic logistical tasks to junior staff was a bad idea, I regretted that I had, somehow encouraged a culture here of non-doing on the part of senior staff, that the bespoke intent of the firm and the notion of an engagement running through the hands of expert professionals was at risk or already partially extinct. What did this junior staff know of me in my office picking Hawthorne's marcona almonds from between the cushions? Or did they know that nearly every day I was chauffeured to a perfunctory lunch to troll for business, today an airline CEO who had nothing to do with bitcoin, China, startups, or metham-phetamines, an old economy cuff-linked colossus who hired us before the Caesar salads had even been served, something about unions and a thorny amendment to a defense spending bill, but the whole time I was counting down the remaining hours of the day until I could respectfully slip out and go home to my son?

What would the long-term engagements think if they knew we ran accounts this way, I thought, and I considered what grand visions the junior staffers imagined was taking shape in the Velázquez conference room, this hunched college of cardinals plotting ruination for some pit stop nation, or, better yet, engineering it's resurrection by YouTube, the white smoke that announced our clever plot being the bawdy laughter that seeped through the glass and gave everyone within earshot the sensorial reassurance that this was a marvelous business filled with marvelous people doing wondrous things with their lives and talents.

Sally was lurking outside my office after the meeting.

Margaret left out and I downed my espresso like a whiskey shot, slammed the cute little cup down on the glass table so hard the handle cracked off and said, aloud, "Presto!"

Sally then came in with a broad grin and closed the door and said: "So."

As her one lone word arced through the silence, she sat down, placing my empty espresso cup on top of its saucer. She wore a smile that had trust, disapproval, love, respect, and piercing disappointment.

"You are worrying me."

"Don't worry about me."

"I always worry about you. That call you had the other day, the one with the guy in New York about the start-up, Hawthorne relayed it to me, that you asked for tens of millions of dollars-worth of stock when you knew a couple million would do. It's like you are playing kamikaze with the business. It's unsettling, Mark. I am worried."

"I don't worry about me; so you shouldn't worry about me. I employ over one hundred people, pay my taxes, upstanding citizen—all that. All our clients are happy, as far as I know. They continue to pay on time. We have six years of operating capital stashed away. We could lose everything tomorrow and stay in business for six more years! We are fine. Me is fine."

"You need to take a break, Mark. Maybe see someone new? I don't think this is healthy anymore."

"Well, I've never felt better," I said.

She looked at me like Dr. Weller; this made me very angry.

So, I said: "You know, while we are having this little heart to heart, I need to share something with you, something disturbing. I have been loath to share it because it concerns someone we both love, but fiduciary duty and all, well, here it is: I am pretty much sure I saw Evgeny in the bathroom yesterday wiping cocaine from his nose. Maybe Ketamine. I can't be certain."

"What is Ketamine?

"Like OxyContin but derivative of cat tranquilizer. You run it through a sifter until it's a fine powder and snort it. I wouldn't try it, though. Fucked up. Stick with cocaine or Oxy. It's the new thing. The Russians are pushing it into this country via Baltimore. Fucking Putin."

"You're serious?"

"One hundred percent."

"Well, if this is true, we should examine the company policy on office substance abuse," she said. "And if it's true and it affects his work and this introduces client risk—from a retention side or due to exposure of their sensitive information—we will need to reconsider the levels of D&O insurance we have."

"Precisely. I think a memo is warranted."

"And maybe introduce randomized drug testing. And maybe conduct a sweeping study on the NFL's drug policy, get that in your hands as soon as possible, meaning a memo to you by tomorrow."

Now I knew where she was going.

"It was a good attempt, no?" I said without emoting anything.

"And I could get someone to work all night on the memo for you too. Maybe we will even resign working for Russia, not that they don't pay the rent and more each month. We could have constructed an elaborate new intra-office memo on cracking down on substance abuse, sent a little shock of fear into the staff. It would have been a nice way to shut everyone up."

She tilted her head and suddenly altered her demeanor and grew maternal. "Mark..."

"Isn't it pretty to think so?"

★

IT WOULD be another thirty minutes until Colin was home from school. I undressed, put on jeans, flip-flops, a black t-shirt, poured a Corona into a thermos without a lime, and leashed the dog.

I took my usual route around the block, passing the plots of miniaturized manor homes comingled with mid-century bungalows, the sort of house once considered luxurious in 1963 because it featured an attached one-car garage and a broad bay window in the living room.

Our home was once a farm house. The previous owners, taken with their travels to Southern France and Tuscany, had renovated every corner of the place in the style of the villas and country homes that had enchanted them abroad. Monica was drawn to the little Evita balconies off the French doors of the master suite that faced the backyard. I paid just under $4 million for it but no one would ever guess this from the neighborhood.

When I got back, Mae was hurriedly feeding Colin a snack of graham crackers and peanut butter. The hockey bag is not packed, she said. Daddy, where is my jersey I cannot find it, Colin said. I went upstairs, rummaged through his laundry and found the jersey wadded up inside his bath towel. I grabbed a pair of hockey socks, went into the garage, double-checked that all his equipment was accounted for, loaded his bag and sticks into the car, started the car, and turned on the seat-warmers.

The rink was a twenty-minute drive on the same highway that led to

Dulles airport, and during these drives I switched off my phone. I wanted to be a father, completely and fully. Colin deserved that; I had a solemn duty to be better for him than I was, but sometimes I found it so difficult to muster the enthusiasm to comport myself as a dedicated father should. Against Dr. Weller's orders, I popped another pill fifteen minutes before we hit the toll road so that by the time we were at highway speed and the phone was off and Colin had begun cross-examining me about life, as little boys do when they have their fathers captive, I was mirthful again, lifted into a chemical state that enabled me to be effortlessly caring, effortlessly attentive, to answer questions about infinity and the horsepower of a Ferrari versus a Bugatti.

The entire facility was permeated with the stench of sweaty hockey pads, a wet sour smell that extended from the locker rooms to the lobby. But it did nothing to foul the comradery of the kids and the parents and the coaches and the staff. It was another home.

The worst and best part of my day was fitting Colin into his pads and skates; easing a seven-year-old boy into hockey gear is an ordeal like wriggling your grandmother into medieval body armor. I found it stressful, sweaty, physically taxing, and fun, amusing, exciting, leaving me with a sense of fatherly accomplishment.

Had you walked into the locker room twenty minutes before practice you would have seen an entire row of mothers and fathers kneeling before their sons, adjusting Velcro shin guards, fastening helmets, lacing skates, the heel of the boot resting on a parent's knee, just below the thigh, the sharp blade menacing nothing. The boys all wore the raw masks of purity; in their faces I could only see wide potential, none of the legible stasis that would appear on that same face twenty years later, the phantom of things that might have been; that story, at ten, even by twelve, is not yet written into their faces, but sometime after thirteen, when their adult features begin to emerge, you can already see their lives' faint trajectory starting to impose its sharp cruel limits; whiff the potential that has curdled into false expectations, a beating story, year by year, of swift diminishment. I figured I had a season and a half left as locker room valet before he would be capable of handling these tasks himself, would no longer want me or need me in the locker room. I sensed that this window with Colin was soon going to close, shut for good, and he would be off in an orbit all his own, me inevitably a dim moon in his life. I always took my time suiting him up.

Sometimes I laced up myself, skated with the kids in an ad hoc assistant coach capacity. I still skated well, could fire the puck hard enough to elicit a proud smile from Colin, ring it hard off the glass to make the other kids take notice.

The air in a hockey rink smells like cold wet sugar. Gliding on the ice at a speed of, say, fifteen to twenty miles per hour, taking the smooth turns tightly, feeling the blade gnaw into the ice and all your body weight lightened with centripetal force, smelling the ice and feeling the cold in your nostrils, I began to see hockey as my refuge, an escape from the ironic, loud, sniping adult world. To focus on staying balanced on a thin edge of steel, atop a sheet of ice—to not fall—was meditation for me. You could fall in hockey and, with all the pads, it did not hurt you, but, as an assistant coach, I wore only sweatpants and a helmet and there were certain risks for me in falling, but when I was out there with the kids, skating around and fooling with the puck, I never thought I would fall and forgot sometimes that I was even on ice. It was, in its own way, easier than walking.

I considered playing in an adult league but most of the games ended well past midnight, and I was already throttling Mae's hours into the red zone of excessive. She was in bed by the time we arrived home, around a quarter after nine. There was some limp lasagna left out in a tray, which I heated for Colin as he flitted around the house burning off the leftover little boy energy. I set the kitchen island and poured two waters, played R.E.M. on shuffle on my phone, and made a small salad for Colin. I realized then that I had hardly touched my Niçoise salad at lunch; I recalled that I had black coffee for breakfast, caffeine all day, extra tranquilizer around dinner. If I could eat it, this would be my first proper meal of the day. Then I poured myself a heaping glass of Cabernet, which I inhaled quickly and which was justifiably necessary if I was to descend enough for any kind of satiating sleep.

We sat together at the bar stools at the kitchen island, eating in the low halogen light, not a sound. I was on my second plate and second glass and Colin had inhaled his square of lasagna; I served him another. The eponymous song from their most maligned album, *Around the Sun*, (the one whose cover placed their Martian, apparitional figures in the foreground of what appears to be a canted aqueduct) began to play: *Hold on boy, you don't know what's comin'*. His legs dangled from the stool. The counter nearly reached his chin. His napkin was sodden with sauce and gooey mozzarella.

He was a small boy for his age, lean and sinewy, as if birthed from stone. At soccer, he could outrun everyone—and the older boys, too—and had a slightly unhealthy fascination with sharks. A chess grandmaster, a Chinese graduate student at Georgetown University, came each Sunday to coach Colin at the game, and he was already playing at an Elo rating of 1500. I watched him eat; he was forgetting the world with each bite. He had perfectly shaped ears and skin the color of light honey. This entire scene, I thought, and this moment and the two of us in this house are straight from Norman Rockwell—almost.

Bedtime at a quarter to ten.

It began the year she died, and I can no longer remember what it was like for him to fall asleep easily. Do we ever understand completely the origins of things like this? Me in the tartan chaise in the corner of his room, the dark, the waiting for his breathing to turn nocturnal. I sit vigil with my iPad, reading or writing in the dark, the only period of my day when I can indulge in these things in peace. Colin knows that I do this, doesn't care.

I am there, and it is enough. *Hold on to this boy a little longer/Take another trip—around the sun.*

From the bed, under the dark, he dispatches a small bundle of questions to me that reveal his view of the world as a damn fine place worth fighting for: How much does a Ferrari cost and how many sharks are there in the world and which one is the strongest and how many years old do you need to be to play in the NHL and can I bring my chess set to hockey so I can teach Tommy Gregg to play it and what is your favorite color?

When he is finally asleep, I tiptoe downstairs, stepping over a box of math flash cards and plastic nunchucks, careful to sidestep the known creaks in the old floor so as not to rouse Atticus.

I flip on all the lights of my study, pour a puritanical thumb of Macallan 18, neat, dash of spring water.

I survey a few emails from work and then switch to my personal account. Most of it is spam: solicitations for me to wire money abroad, to buy experimental pharmaceuticals from Eastern Europe, explore shocking pornography. There is a group email by a college friend exclaiming that she is with child and that she and her husband, an actuary, will be relocating from their condo in the city to a four bedroom in Bethesda. I imagine the aluminum siding, massive garage, the mote of grass, their neighbor's breath not fifteen feet across the "lawn."

I emptied the highball, got up, grabbed the pile and sat back down. I reached for the stack of mail by the door. I had been mailed almost three pounds of catalogues that day alone; there were glossy envelopes from credit card companies that promised instant cash—$20,000—if I were only to borrow a vault of money at a ridiculous APR; an unpaid parking ticket that I would forget to bring to Margaret tomorrow; a vicious mailing from the Republican National Committee imploring another donation; two post-card-sized invitations from new local competing dentists, stuck together, offering discount teeth bleaching; nothing but bills and sales pitches and small businesses and big businesses trying to jackboot my money; there were no handwritten letters nor thank you notes nor actual postcards from European capitals from the college offspring of first, second, or third cous-ins, nor layered notes from old lovers, or wayward and newly-religious Midwestern relatives; that day—or any day in the recent past and into the recent future—there was not, is not, nor will be, any real mail at all; there are no real songs on the radio anymore or real programs on the television or any real time, no present tenses, anytime, anywhere, to speak of anymore.

Another track now plays from *Chronic Town*, R.E.M.'s debut EP, only five tracks, released in 1982, the year that she was born.

We were dishwashers together at the campus cafeteria, earning mini-mum wage and wearing ridiculous uniforms.

The first time she spoke to me, the first thing I noticed was her Southern accent. She maybe reached my shoulders and, beneath her apron, she was wearing a loose V-neck white t-shirt. Her hair was in a ponytail. She had high cheekbones and hazel eyes with such depth that I felt embarrassed for staring at them so much as we sprayed spaghetti off the plates and scraped the uneaten portions into the bin.

We made our way gingerly through the rocky terrain of small talk and mutual suspicion, that predictable awkwardness between members of the opposite sex, thrust into proximity as freshmen, co-workers, unspoken attraction. She was shy back then. But you could see her trying to read the ticker tape on me. Over all the detergents and sour leftovers, I would still be able to smell her. She smelled the same way for seventeen years.

I wanted to kiss her, instantaneously, right in the cafeteria, this little thing, this modest full-lipped Southern thing.

"My favorite band was R.E.M. too."

"You're kidding, right?" I said.

"They're from my town—Athens. You know they're playing in Boston soon, right?"

"Yes," I said, noticing a tattoo of a crescent moon the size of a dime on her right wrist. I kept trying to bump her hand underneath the soapy water

She smelled amazing.

"Are you going to go out tonight? It's just for freshmen."

"Maybe. Sure. What dorm are you?"

"Newton. My roommate has a pet tarantula, I'm doubtful about that relationship."

She was laughing. She had perfect teeth.

"My roommate, Lila, is a Communist." And I laughed so hard I dropped the spray hose.

"What's your favorite song?" I said.

"Ever?"

"No, silly," I said, tapping the back of my left hand against her right shoulder. "R.E.M."

"That's tough. When I was thirteen I heard them play for the first time in Athens, this real small club. I think they played at least ten songs from *Murmur* and *Chronic Town*."

I told her *Chronic Town* was my favorite catalogue of songs in the entire R.E.M. canon; I explained how it is mystically beautiful and chthonic, a haunting arpeggio of guitar that feels gothic but hopeful, and all the murmured lyrics are vague and strange and Michael Stipe's voice is ghostly and shy, a bard who disintegrates often into babble; Mike Mills sings across the refrain in a thin treble of call-and-response harmony; Peter Buck in rebel laconic drift over his guitar, thinking, "fuck the world."

"What do you think the album means, I mean the lyrics?" I said. There were no clear lyrics; the sounds seemed to matter more than the words, leaving one to wonder if the lyrics carried any great import at all, or were instead an afterthought meant to accompany the chorus, bridge and refrain.

"Gosh, no idea. Even when they played it some of the words were tough to hear over the guitars. You would have loved it."

"Do you think we should set up our roommates—the tarantula guy and the Communist?"

"You think they'd hit it off?"

"I have a sixth sense."

Atticus barked. Someone—a man—was walking down the street in view from the floodlights of the church across the street.

I lifted my phone and put on "Gardening at Night," and recalled that it was playing when I picked her up that night at her dorm, her roommate already sizing me up, as if she expected I would be sleeping over often and soon, occupying her space. She was very pretty too; she knew it, played it hard, weaponizing her beauty by keeping aloof.

Monica was wearing the same shirt and these corduroy pants of violent green but she had brushed out her hair and had sprayed on something and, even without makeup and detergents, she looked and smelled even more wonderfully that she had hours earlier.

"Ready?" she said. Lila looked on, bunched in her bed like a bitter convalescent writing postcards home, somewhere north of the Adirondacks.

"You know you can relax, right?" Monica said. "It's just your first college party and there will be a lot of beer and plenty of pretty girls."

I stared out the window into the empty street. The dog was curled by the transom at the front door; I finished the Macallan's and then poured another.

After their drummer suffered a near-fatal brain aneurysm in 1995, he left the band to become a peanut farmer in Georgia—and the band played on, a three-legged dog, as Stipe told *Rolling Stone*, producing five more albums until their surprise amicable breakup in 2011—a week before she died. All their work post Bill Berry's departure bears a critical smudge, and, it's true, some of their experimentation in electronica resulted in songs that sounded creepily extraterrestrial. I didn't care. A three-legged dog is still a dog. I embraced the defects, the degradation, the pitches in the dirt, fuck the critics.

What in this world that we truly love doesn't degrade over time?

I want the sun to shine on me. I want the truth to set me free.

I toggled through a few songs until I found their experimental album, *New Adventures in Hi-Fi*, a mix of in-studio and live concert recordings. We were there in the audience to hear the fourth track, "Undertow," recorded live in Boston; she had bought the tickets from a scalper as a surprise for me weeks after we met.

I took out my iPad, finished my drink, and looked at the steeple, turned on the notes function and began to finger peck a letter to her:

Dear Monica,

I want you to hear me. You are somewhere amidst the crowd noise at the end of an R.E.M. song, album 10, track 4, "Undertow," recorded live at the Fleet Center's first concert ever, Boston, October 2, 1995, the resumption of ordinary time after the Jubilee year of 1994. I can hear you, but I cannot hear you. The roar of the crowd, underneath the static, indecipherable, a faint whistling in the hiss of expiring guitar chords, a sonic nod to the fans. We are both of us there in it, canonized in the track, together. We were there in a joyous uproar and you were there and I can hear you: we are somewhere together, digitized for all of time.

chapter four

Y OU FELT the movement of the high-speed train as a kind of steady progress that rushed you through the industrial belt between Union Station and Baltimore and within forty minutes, out the east window, you could see marshlands, spot the various waterfowl standing in the tall bay grass at the edge of the water. Further on was a segment of that north-bound route where the train would pass through Havre de Grace, where the Susquehanna River meets with the Chesapeake Bay. The sunrise cast an hourglass blaze of copper light across the lake as you traversed a bridge so low to water it felt like floating over the river; in the rising hills on each bank of the river, on swathes of bright grass, stood Victorian mansions and their Adirondack chairs, mere white specks from this distance, awaiting the sunrise over the bay, the bittersweet segment of the journey to New York.

I was reviewing an entire folder of research on Alan, drinking my coffee, chewing a bag of granola, flipping the pages of biography and ingesting the views. In less than twelve hours, Margaret had assembled a compendium of Alan Newman history: where he went to high school, when he first divorced, the title of his Harvard thesis, Forbes estimates of net worth.

The train kept its smooth pace all the way through to New Jersey. I heard my favorite couplet from "The Wasteland": *Sweet Thames run softly while I sing my song/Sweet Thames run softly for I speak not loud or long.*

I had received his unexpected call a week after we had first spoken, but when he called I had been readying my briefcase so that I could escape traffic in time to drive Colin to a late afternoon hockey practice.

"Goddammit," I said as Margaret gave me the look.

"Do you want me to buy you some time? You could speak to him from the car," she said.

I frowned, put down my briefcase, slumped in my chair and waved her on to transfer the call. I was irritable at getting this call unannounced; I had instructed Margaret to keep my schedule as tightly controlled as she could so that I could plan for when I might braid some spontaneity and absence into the day.

It wasn't her fault. I smiled at her and she seemed to feel better. My irritability though was reaching some kind of unexpected zenith. All week I had had the numinous experience that the caffeine and the benzodiazepines and Valproic acid had alchemized into impulsivity; I was having difficulty concentrating, everything occurring more rapidly than usual with unexpected consequences: The night before, I had shattered the stem off a Bordeaux glass, miscalculating the distance of the counter and rushing it at too steep an angle. I felt all three tenses of time conflating into one single streamlined experience, time in arabesque, where the past and future coiled so tightly to suffocate any sense of now.

I took a deep breath, sighed, pushed the speakerphone button, visualized the rink and tying Colin's laces and knew, before I even heard his offer, that I would take it simply to be able hang up the phone, push the elevator button, descend nine floors, and drive home.

Of course, I had not seen the reports that Goldman Sachs, the underwriter of the IPO, was considering withdrawing the stock offering on account of the investigation, which, as expected, had been leaked, and the response by OneSpeak, as expected, even from a cursory Google search this morning, had been comically bungled, Fung managing to come across simultaneously as combative and voluble, even wading into the metaphysical as when *The Wall Street Journal* made a front-page pull quote of her attempt at obfuscation by explaining the powder keg tweet that launched the investigation: "Can a tweet truly depict a fragment of time whose essence, to the twitterer, is obscured?"

"Our situation has changed," Alan said, "and we know now that we need help. Long Bridge Management is prepared to pay an advance of $1 million—up front—to take the engagement. With respect to your request for shares of stock; we will award your firm 500,000 shares of OneSpeak stock—but at the eighteen dollars per share strike price, if you succeed in averting this crisis, and I will let you define 'averted' in your scope of work. I cannot offer you what you were asking for, which, still…but whatever. Let's move past that. I know you can help us. I need you to fly to Copenhagen tomorrow to meet Lars. When can we get this papered?" The way he had structured things, if the stock rose to a modest twenty dollars per share on the first day of trading, White & Partners would earn $2 million—for doing nothing.

"Mark, I personally hope that you dig deep and decide to take it," he said, though he halted before saying this was a take it or leave it offer, and I could smell more truffles of money in his voice. If the IPO were withdrawn, the hedge fund, aside from failing to recoup its original several-hundred-million-dollar investment, stood to lose over $1 billion in forgone stock value.

Impersonating a calmer, more effusive version of me—sounding nearly vacant—I played a pause, then said, "Alan, it's an eminently fair offer and I accept." Then there was a moment of silence on his end, as if he were stricken by my sudden acquiescence.

"That's good news—that's very good news, Mark. We are very excited for this new chapter. Lars and Fung are even keen to get some 'third party' perspective seeing as a criminal investigation is now formally proceeding."

"I understand the need for haste; I'll book the flight, I need to be in Lisbon later in the week anyway," I said, envisioning myself handling this over Bluetooth on the ride into work.

"Excellent. Just excellent. When you return, why don't you train up here next week and we can have lunch and run through everything. There isn't much time."

I just wanted to get off the phone. I had zero interest in going up to New York, let alone dreary Copenhagen. I momentarily considered bringing Colin, but he was already missing too much school and if I could confine this to a day trip, the angst on both our parts would be minimized. I also considered sending Hawthorne, Wendy, even Joel James, but I knew that whatever their talents or charms, they alone could not enchant Alan: the person who has hired you will always want you, and no attempt at outsourcing that relationship to subordinates would survive a month—most of the time, the account would not survive at all.

It was Monday. Leaving for Europe tomorrow, I would be home by Friday. Lunch next Monday in Manhattan would be fine, I said.

I hung up, downed the cup of greenish-yellow tea that Margaret had slipped before me, sucked on the two lemon wedges resting on the saucer, said viperously, "Goddammit!" Margaret slipped out with the empty cup.

When I kissed him goodnight and told him I would be going away for the week, Colin began to cry but I waved Mae off and gave him his pills.

I sat in the dark, quiet and waiting. Then his voice, a near whisper.

Don't you know her middle name?

Is it something about a flower? Purple?

She loved a special purple flower, that's right.

But don't you know her middle name?

I forget it. I forget it daddy. Daddy is that bad

That is not bad, buddy. sometimes I forget important things.

Do you forget my name?

Never.

But you forgot picture day.

This is true, yes.

So what if you did forget me, how would you remember

I won't forget.

But it can happen, like me forgetting mommy's name. so how can you not forget

I will glue it to my brain. it's Caitlin. her middle name.

Is she a ghost? does the glue hurt?

What?

A ghost, in our house now?

Colin she is in heaven. heaven, not here on earth. she is an angel now.

So she is an angel but she comes here to watch me, like a ghost? is she scary? do you think she is scary or even scared?

I think she loves you so much she is protecting you and whispering to you and kissing you at night.

Can you give me a kiss?

Like this?

Yes!

Or like this?

Yes, hehehehehe.
Is she here on the earth, for real?
For real, she is here on earth, still.
Does she move around
You mean in a car?
On planes
Angels go anywhere
I thought so

On the train, I had situated myself in the single-rider seat by the left window.

The first-class cabin was moderately full and all the women seemed to be wearing Pucci scarves, their tame husbands handling the corners of the newspaper as one lifts the wings of an injured butterfly. The attendant handed me a newspaper that I waved off, instead ordering coffee and cantaloupe, which, when it arrived, was unripe.

I put on my headphones and eagerly waited for the train to roll into motion. Once we were moving, I had to hold onto my coffee to keep it from sloshing onto my scattered pages that outlined the long wondrous life of Alan Newman.

I had imagined that he rose each morning at a military hour, night ink still in the sky, and descended the stairs of his Washington Square brownstone in Stubbs & Wootton slippers. I had him for a man who ground his own beans, procured from a noted roaster in Antwerp. I imagined him ironically referring to it as *"jus de chaussette"*—sock juice—the pejorative term in France for drip coffee, although the pages before me bore no evidence that Alan spoke any French.

As I imagined it, this sock juice, he would sit in the coffee maker, untouched for much of the morning, while he read his *Times* in a paisley robe, some burnt toast and local butter, softened overnight in a ramekin, a sprinkle of kosher salt. I imagined him the kind of man who used a shave brush to massage cream into his whiskers, taking pleasure in bringing the down the blade against the growth, afterwards, rubbing the alum salt stone over his clean face, the even keel of the BBC emanating from the iPhone in the soap dish on the sink.

His biography mentioned Harvard, a degree in comparative literature, and so I imagined that he was exceedingly skinny in the days when he hand-wrote wrote his thesis, and I saw him at a table far back in the Wursthaus in Harvard Square, always a half-eaten Reuben, endless glasses of lemon water. I gave him a robust epistolary life: his sons, Joshua and Jacob, were the beneficiaries of Alan's sagacity, notes penned from the quiet light of the breakfast table, pithy, amusingly digressive and aphoristic, maybe a few hundred words max. Highlights would include: lyrical passages on the changing of the seasons, a précis of political deteriorations in all hot jungle countries with unbearable debt burdens, the laudatory aspects of V.S. Naipaul, a lament for elephant poaching in Zimbabwe and a looming Guggenheim fundraiser to do something about it, the happenings in Tribeca, writing of it as exotically as one panegyrizes Gauguin's Fiji. I guessed that Alan was not a religious Jew but would bet he was a fierce Zionist, and he authenticated my speculation when he told me he had moved to Israel after Harvard for a two-year military stint, night patrols near the border camps, cagey about if he ever used his piece.

I went on like this, passing time, letting calls go to voicemail, until Clive called.

The managing director of my New York office, he wanted me to stop in and say hello.

"Mark, so lovely to have you in the city. I dare say you are sneaking up on us again. Word has it you are here for the day."

"Just the day," I said, hand cupping my mouth to try and blot out the train noise.

"Well perhaps there's some time to swoop in and rouse the troops. I know it's not the House of Lords. But it's been a good year, as you know, and I think anytime we can be in the presence of Mark White it's a fine thing. And you're paying ninety-five dollars per square foot for this place.

"You are too gracious, Clive. I am hoping this is in and out, that kind of thing. I am afraid I must pass. Next time. And you should come down soon, let's meet up, grab a game, the works."

"I understand. I understand. Well then, if you have a moment free otherwise, do give us a shout. There are some staffing matters that need your blessing and I cannot get ahold of Sally. When I do she always sends me your way regardless."

"What are the issues?"

He sounded surprised I had asked.

"Wow, okay then, it's the matter of succession planning for George, due to retire end of this year."

"And?"

"And I was thinking Nina."

"Nina."

"Yes, Nina. I know, she's not ideal but the clients love her."

"And the staff does not."

"Yes, well, I considered the alternative, Preston, and I just don't see the logic; he's so slow."

"Whatever you think, Clive, works for me."

"You're sure. Cause if you have uncertainties we can discuss at another time."

"I am fine. It's a good decision. Well done. *Loren Ipsum Dolorem.*"

Once at Penn Station, I stepped onto the dark urine-smelling platform, amid the crowds herding into the lone escalator up to the swarm and rush of the main floor, my personal sense of value depreciated almost instantly. Whereas I was a somebody in the sixty-eight square miles of swampland that was our nation's capital, I was of no consequence in the 305 square miles of five boroughs that formed the front gate of New York city.

In Washington, something akin to an Ivy League gravitas was the product of my notoriety and mixed race, and being Hispanic was an advantage, sort of.

The perception of prestige became a kind of currency: inflating proportionately to the expanding mythology around White & Partners. Why feel guilty about this obvious chasm between fact and fantasy? The success of others around me in Washington, as best I could glean, was unwarranted, even criminal in the chicanerous way it had been achieved. You could make a fabulous living marrying former presidential chiefs of staff and splashing the lurid details of your third divorce in *The Washington Post.* Those most devoid of intellect rose; the intellectual center of the town, anywhere else, would have been considered dullards, the strata of professionals who never make partner in London, Paris, or New York. Yet, these parvenus were the *crema* of "official Washington." It's all they had—their contacts, and they laundered them into money. Washington was a town of people filled with opinions but very few ideas, and I did not consider myself a fiber in its cheap weave.

My clients said they enjoyed the fresh thinking represented by my firm, the clean take on old problems, the desire to embrace risk—it was the reason we were hired to handle the OneSpeak crisis. Here again was a chasm: White & Partners was not inventing anything and we were not even in the same category of critical thinking as management consultants like McKinsey & Co., although we purported to be similar. If we did embrace anything truly unique, it was our disdain for official Washington, its curdled upper class. We got our reputation, I suppose, because of this loathing, this antipathy towards whoring out your Rolodex. In being the opposite of good-old-boy consulting, White & Partners forged something from skill, attracted talent through an emphasis on meritocracy, and it was the presence of these two qualities—skill and meritocracy—that clients subliminally perceived, but they sensed them not because we emitted them so brightly but because against the shrouded consulting environs of DC they were so starkly lit.

This perceptual currency, hidebound to Washington, was inherently sectarian, a ruble quickly deflated and nearly worthless as I traveled north on the Acela into the very den of America. I left Penn Station and got the first taxi in the line, and wondered if Alan would find me disappointing.

My driver amused himself by driving over each pothole without decelerating. Why I was in a taxi and not a chauffeured car was because the Uber app was inexplicably down. He was not from here, North African, it seemed, and his wild native music came off like victory songs in the aftermath of a bloody revolution. I took a pill and noticed him peering at me repeatedly in the rearview mirror. The cable news program broadcasting from the backseat of the taxi said Obama had "sternly" rebuked Putin for Crimea; they played a clip in which he talked about destroying ISIS.

I got out at Fifth Avenue in front of Harry Winston, windows sparkling with canary diamond engagement rings the size of hail and seasonally colored jewels, broaches, and pendants; behind them was a scaled replica of Fifth Avenue itself, light snow dusting the street, miniature humans with handbags and briefcases in conversation, sauntering to lunches, easy meetings where smaller plastic humans from outer boroughs would merely take notes.

It was unseasonably chilly and I walked across the street and bought a hot dog from the vendor by the Disney Store, asking for ketchup, relish, the works. I ate it in three bites. I twisted the cap off an unhealthily large bottle of grape soda, took a few swigs, and threw it in the garbage.

Although I had done this line of work for so long and to such acclaim, Dr. Weller told me that getting nervous made me human, but, as I often retorted, I didn't want to be human, I wanted to be infallible, to forget certain things but to remember them too. I ordered another grape soda, washed down another small white pill and threw away the bottle again. I couldn't remember how many pills I had taken this morning.

I had time to kill, almost two hours. I walked a few blocks north to The Plaza, the horseshit smell strong from Central Park. I viewed New York as this vague vast terrain. I needed totems: Gramercy Tavern, The Plaza, the shoeshine stands at the Public Library, the Guggenheim. The Plaza was across from FAO Schwarz, but when I arrived, the store awning had that expired look, lights out in the store, nothing inside. THANK YOU, NEW YORK! The banner spanned the width of the building.

"What's the deal?" I asked the hotel doorman.

"Out of business. Last month. Sad."

Tourists were standing in front, taking selfies.

"But why? It was always busy, always so many people."

"Yeah but were they buying anything? Maybe not. I heard the landlord wanted to double the rent, too. You looking to get a gift, something for the kids, then Disney is down Fifth and you can get something too over there."

He pointed to the glass pyramid to the left. It was the Apple Store.

I walked south down Fifth, past the Disney Store, then slowed as I passed the old Scribner Building, and then meandered down the residential side streets until I found myself lost among the idling stretch limousines on Park Avenue. I didn't mind willfully getting lost in a big city to kill time. It was easier than sitting down and taking calls. Your feet will find what your heart is looking for, I heard Monica say.

After Madrid, Monica said she never cared for New York the same way.

"Too monochromatic, monotheistic," she said.

I was holding a bucket of broken seashells, stepping on her shadow on the sand, keeping pace.

"It's like everyone decided to goose step to money, you know, never knowing the full flavor of their own city. Madrid had customs, common dishes, everyone knew a stray verse by Lorca. In New York, it's win or get out. No room for self-iteration."

She stopped suddenly, grabbing her toe. I picked up the jagged shell and tossed it out toward Nantucket Sound.

"No blood," I said, "baby is all safe."

"I think he will look like you, but I can tell he will be shy, shy and gentle. You won't browbeat him if he doesn't play hockey?"

"Never."

"Or be one of those fathers who doesn't read to their sons?"

"Hardly."

"He will need me more at first, then more of you than me. Boys require their fathers to map themselves."

"That's a lovely notion." We stopped walking. Just the rush of the water against the jetty rocks. We let the silence magnify the previous statement, and then the church bells began to toll from town.

"Why do you never paint the sea?"

"It's one of the few things that cannot be improved. I paint what I think I can justify as an improvement. Otherwise I am just adulterating nature. Who can improve the sea? Maybe Winslow Homer. But he merely caught a glimpse of it. It's too easy to modify anything and call it better."

We lingered in our silence a little longer until I said, "Can you believe the business is taking off?"

"Can you believe it?" She seemed immune to the question. Redirecting my questions was her way of telling me to explore things more deeply.

"I'm proud the plan worked, that we have a tide of clients rushing in."

"Validating. Yes, that's very validating."

She buried her toes in the sand and looked at the sea.

"I know that the reporting made you very happy, Mark. What do you think all of this money will do for you?"

"It's a creative endeavor, like painting, like—"

"Mark you don't really think that. Do you? Please tell me you don't. Please."

I didn't believe it at all, of course, but it's what I told myself to machete through the fear.

"I'm just saying I am enjoying this, all of it."

"Well if it inspires you then I am all for it." She held her gaze out at the ferry boat coming into the harbor, hands on her belly. Now, neither of us was telling each other the truth.

The truth changes colors on us, sometimes daily.

I took out my phone to check for any messages from Colin. There were none. I crossed Fifth and passed The Peninsula and saw Nobu, Alan too, standing at the door reading a *Financial Times* folded width-wise.

"Mark?"

"Alan," I said, extending my hand a little too eagerly.

He was not wearing a tie; he had a checkered shirt under a lilac cashmere sweater, thrown over his shoulders like a Swiss banker on holiday; he was tall, arched eyebrows that gave him a perpetual look of active listening and he had fine, long strands of parted gray hair.

We sat down and made small talk first, Alan ordering several specialty sushi plates and too many nigiri rolls. I had a Sapporo and nervously watched Alan drink club soda and ask for a saucer of lime wedges. Soon, a bowl of steaming edamame pods arrived, sprinkled with salt crystals that looked like tiny bits of oyster shell.

Many wealthy clients want to either pump you for information, a test of your worthiness, or expound upon their experiences, as if their companion might receive some of it as useful, holy wisdom.

Alan seemed to want to tell his life story in a manner that tested my patience to endure it and therefore my ability to extract lessons from it.

I learned that he rose quickly to the bond desk, selling T-Bills to mostly German brokers on his black rotary phone. After selling millions of dollars of American debt to Europeans, Alan said, he would walk up Broadway and spend his evening hours at an indie bookstore that sold first editions behind locked cases, where he read the first pages of most of the books in the classic section, neatening the spines of the *Aeneid* or the *Iliad* in some recess of the store, the non-regulars taking him for staff.

"I remarried on condition—to myself—that it would be a long-term marriage." He was still chewing a piece of salmon nigiri. "My ex was a misery, always on a cleanse, and those were the days when a cleanse meant you had done a stint in a Swiss sanitarium. By the end, her entire physiognomy suggested biblical-grade adversity, a Daryl Hannah weightlessness, and I considered having her committed but it was much too irksome a thing to effect, and there were all kinds of histories to consider. We were married fewer than six years; it took me that long to find the right lawyer and I was still relatively upper middle class, by Manhattan standards, helming the bond practice at Lehman Brothers."

Alan used expletives freely, when diction mandated, the sub-adjectival form of "Fuck." The only holiday he acknowledged was Thanksgiving—this only infused the holiday with greater import; the boys instinctively knew their friends or girlfriends were not welcome to take the Amtrak down from Boston for the Holy Thursday meal, which Alan and Melinda prepared with surgical perfection and wartime deliberation. "Everything covered in white hydrangea blossoms that she had miraculously sourced from Fenton's on Park (she tucked the cuttings into mint julep cups scored from a flea market in Montmartre)."

Living for so long in the Northeast, he had, as if by osmosis, acquired Puritan sensibilities: he carried himself like a proper Boston Brahmin, a wry smile checked by a mask of perpetual restraint, someone who would express irritability with only a soft clearing of the throat. As he spoke, I imagined Alan's letters to his sons ringing out with an unspoken fear of the annihilation of American values. Hard work. Dedication. Perfectionism. Trustworthiness. Superiority. But that world of the easy past, the four years at Harvard that so effortlessly paved a pathway to fortune, was no longer accessible; I sensed that Alan, all along, had been presciently awaiting a drastic cultural reorientation, a swell that would wipe out these venerated American tenets. Now the detritus of the storm had washed up on his doorstop; he saw himself as the white knight-errant of the realm, squeezing the balls of third world strongmen whose graft impoverished their people. For once, he had invested in New America—OneSpeak— and it was America that was about to lance him fatally.

"Your ex sounds like a teachable moment," I said, immediately regretting it.

But he didn't slow down. "Who knows why we do what we do? I met her in the bookstore. She asked me where to find something by Alan Watts. She wore white tights, green pumps, a black lace dress, probably Dior, a naughty school girl look even by Village standards. Did I marry her because I had only known nurses at Harvard, because I too was in that phase where I was sampling all of the well-published mystics and sages, where the guests of the Wall Street dinner parties who were not high or stoned or on a pill— and, I assure you, I was not among them—would all wind up discussing the Zapruder film, whether communism was our times' Bubonic plague, and, after I uncorked a little Derrida obscurantism, and all of the women had that too-eager glazed-over look, right, like they wanted to arrange an Ash Wednesday Midtown tryst? I would walk home, smoking when I didn't smoke, despondent, pretty sure I would never find a suitable woman in New York City until I thought I did."

I wanted to discuss OneSpeak but I mentally heard Hawthorne telling me just to let him go on, that he would reveal himself and all his hidden meanings by the light of my silence.

A tray arrived: hamachi fanned out in a windmill, each translucent sliver topped with a shaving of jalapeño.

"I did believe in predestination, still do, in fact, and so I figured this silly girl with the Robert Plant hair was my fated Sibyl—and she rode horses. After Andrea threw one of her fits at the Alfred Dunhill mansion in Mayfair—some imagined infidelity with a chambermaid—I asked myself amid this barrage, as the straight edge was shaking in the poor barber's hands, 'Why did I do it?' Why do we do what we do? 'Is Ahab, Ahab? Is it I, God, or who, that lifts this arm?' I often think that quote is about the concept of immanence. Do you read much, Mark?"

I felt my phone vibrate against my chest.

"Yes. And you are much happier now?" I said.

After he related a story about his Japanese butler at the St. Regis in Rome, Akiko, who cheerfully offered to unpack his suitcase and his corresponding enchantment upon his return, after a good morning stroll through the Villa Borghese, to find his shirts had been miraculously pressed, folded, and stacked, tucked away in the Umbrian oak *cassettone*, I reimaged his epistolary life as one extended *ars poetica* of fine living. Maybe he would describe the quirks of a certain foreign airport terminal, the quality of the brioche at a Sartre haunt on the Boulevard Saint-Germain, render a montage of his trip to Rome with his new wife, everything planned with wartime deliberation. Maybe men like Alan knew life only in pink and green, only the fragrance of warm oranges and English tea rose in their hotel rooms with perfectly intelligent and balanced second wives, a lit Hermes candle on the credenza, maybe an "Oh, what the hell" cigarette in the window seat while the church bells tolled noon.

I played the pauses.

It struck me that OneSpeak was a massive distraction for this man, a Gordian media crisis that he wanted farmed out, at any cost, so that he and his coterie of lawyers could resume their harassment of despots in the US court system. He explained with a broad smile how Elliot had attached the hundreds of millions of Argentine deposits into the Federal Reserve, seized the presidential aircraft when it landed at Teterboro, ran a humiliating full-page color ad in the *Wall Street Journal* that read, "Welcome President Bad Apple to the Big Apple," the day that Néstor Kirchner was to ring the opening bell of the NYSE; they dug up old hotel bills from the Waldorf Astoria for the delegation from Congo-Brazzaville, when the entourage, in town for the UN General Assembly, racked up an astounding (never paid) $250,000 tab for: hairdressers, a case of 1959 Cheval Blanc, the most opulent suites, room damage and other costs pertaining to spa treatments and perpetual room service, etc. These were the dregs, the dead skin cells that must be sloughed off society, Alan explained, but OneSpeak, Lars and Fung, they were something else altogether.

"Melinda thinks they are the future. I know she's right but I love her and hate her for it. I can't relate to them. When you cannot relate to someone you cannot do real business with them. But she is my best friend and when we met I thought she smelled like flowering trees," said Alan, referring to his first encounter with his happy new wife in the hospital.

"She was an intoxicant, a counterpoint to my arid bachelorhood after Andrea, after my sad drift into stale routines: chess in the park with homeless savants, impromptu shoe shines near the Public Library whenever there was no wait, dinner at the delis filled with people likely taking expired antibiotics. Sometimes I did Carnegie Hall. In a winter of three blizzards I read all of Dostoyevsky, grew bored by the spring, hitched a plane to London, got sick of warm beer and Indian food, toured the English countryside of Wordsworth, which looks very much like certain places in western Vermont, and then I thought about abandoning all of it—New York, banking—and opening a cheese or pie shop somewhere upstate, starting over, farm animals grazing in the overgrown fields. I was a tourist in my own life."

Here, now, arrived the infamous black miso cod, glazed and sweet.

"I like that line," I said.

"Well it was true, Mark. I was watching myself living my life but feeling like I was not really living it. New York numbs you to yourself. You only see other people, never yourself. I suppose this is why so many jaunt down to the Hamptons or take their puddle-hoppers to Nantucket. Something about the water. Something about being out from under skyscrapers and noise, the quiet and the space are palliatives. We have a place on Nantucket, near Brant Point. You can stroll right into town without fear of being run over by a Moslem taxi driver. It's Mayberry. It's absolute peace and calm for us."

My phone kept buzzing and the pills were wearing thin.

I excused myself, stood up rather quickly, nudging the table, and walked to the back of the restaurant. Monica was everywhere. She was here at this lunch, looming now in Alan in one of those perfect waterfront homes we had coveted together. I pictured Colin eating alone at the table while Mae cleaned up the dishes, expecting me home after school for hockey practice, a little boy already taking his father's medicine. Our faults span bloodlines.

I went inside the bathroom stall, swallowed two of the yellow pills and added a little white one too, sat there, still, for at least seven minutes, until something of an analgesic calm overcame me and I could resume the lunch with Alan. When I came out I must have looked flushed.

"Everything okay, Mark?"

"It's fine. Perfectly fine. I'm a diabetic." The lie unfazed me.

"Of course. My father. Type 2. But you seem in relatively good shape. I'm sure you are thriving despite it. Anyway, I don't always go one like this—"

"Not at all, Alan. I enjoy your stories. They're enchanting, really."

"Well, you seem like you can handle being put on the spot. Thank you again for coming. We are really excited to have you on board. So, one thing to ask. Thanks for meeting with Lars in Copenhagen"

"You got my email?"

"Yes I did."

"Well is that an issue? I mean if it doesn't' work—"

"Certainly not."

Well, if it didn't work and they wanted an IPO then I wouldn't stand in the way.

"Very well. So, meanwhile, I'll raise you one: Who said, 'Buy on the sound of the canons, sell on the sound of the trumpets'?"

"Nathan Rothschild."

Alan sat back and smiled, wiping his mouth with his napkin, taking a sip of green tea. "Amazing. Marvelous, truly!"

There was no good excuse to cry foul, not when you were paid this well. Most White & Partner clients paid us handsomely to—on the spot— hack the inner sanctum of the media metropolis: *The New York Times, Wall Street Journal*, sometimes magazines like *Time*, gleaming upstarts like *Vox*, venerable old brownstones like *The New Yorker*. A congregation of publications held sway over the vast plains of opinion and decision-makers in America. There was a code to entry; certain preconditions conferred a worthiness to be fit to be in their print. We knew the secret skull and bones handshake could find a way to beam a client's perspective into those pages; sneak into a feature story here and there; score a pure 800 words of unadulterated point of view in the opinion pages now and then. But our key was not cast from tight relationships with editors: we entered by deconstruction. A news story was the sum of an inviolable mix: something external happening (the "event"), someone saying something (the "reaction"), someone disagreeing ("counterpoint"), the specter of the unexpected (a looming IPO, an interview with the new CEO). It was an immutable equation.

Understanding the variables was a foothold into the story, and we hacked the press because we knew the formula, got how to prefabricate an irresistible variable—a statement, quote, interview, study, opinion article—so that it was slipped easily and unknowingly by the journalist himself into their brew, eventually bottled and labeled a front-page story in *The New York Times*, on a date of the client's choosing. This took some time and guile to perfect, admittedly, but it was formulaic in the end. But what Alan wanted was something altogether different. It was rare for us to be retained by a client to produce an absence, to reverse the equation and render all the variables a zero, to keep a client off the front pages, the cable news, the networks, the internet itself. Burglarizing the media was one thing, slipping from their confines undetected was another.

I said: "And you must know that the scion of Europe's greatest banking dynasty engineered one of history's greatest short sales in history using a bird."

"Rothschild again?"

"A horseback courier is dispatched from Waterloo to Paris, three o'clock, June of 1815. The battle outcome is still uncertain, but Napoleon is confident. Overconfident, in fact. By nightfall his army was decimated; Prussian forces had, alas, broken through Bonaparte's flank to bring about defeat."

Alan was loving this.

"The French army devolved into chaos, the retreating army scattering into the moonlit hills. By then, a carrier pigeon had left Waterloo for London, bearing the news. I guess you could say that it was what we today would call, 'Breaking News.' By the time the Duke of Wellington had arrived victorious in London—to the sound of the trumpets—Nathan Rothschild had already minted a fresh fortune: with news of Waterloo in hand an hour earlier from his pigeon, he had rushed to the London Stock Exchange and engineered a colossal short sale of bonds."

"That's absolutely marvelous, Mark. History major?"

"Literature."

"Do you find it ironic that our friends at OneSpeak may be felled by a virtual bird?" he said.

"You mean their tweets?" I said. "Sixty million messages are flown daily, a tidy 140 characters. It was birds, too, that launched newswire journalism. Reuters spawned from a fleet of carrier pigeons in the mid-1800s."

Alan was finishing his sorbet. "Many fortunes have been made from birds. I read recently that the *Associated Press* has rendered curious *ex cathedra* commandments to reporters, best summed up as, 'Thou shall not tweet!' Reporters, hypothetically, who observe a major accident or come across explosive political news, are instructed to run these bits through the AP's editorial apparatchik, and press them onto the wire. That would be like, I guess, Nathan Rothschild dispatching the news of Waterloo to himself by stage coach instead of by bird."

Alan was pausing now, smiling, sipping his tea, my cue to unveil my grand plans.

I really had nothing prepared. So I ran him through the general formula of how to hack the media and said that for this circumstance we would need to do something experimental and that I wasn't sure what that was yet.

He looked at me askance. "Is that it?"

For a second, I considered saying yes, there was a problem, you see, I am a widower and my eight-year-old son expects me to be home more often than I am and now you are hauling me all over the globe without any notice. I had the shares to consider, so many of them vesting in two weeks.

I smiled and said, "It's just a start."

"How old is your son, Mark?"

I was surprised he knew about Colin and then I remembered, as a trader, his job was to acquire information, and I wondered what else he knew about me.

"Eight."

Alan looked at me appraisingly. "Family is all we have, Mark."

He had stopped drinking his tea, and for a moment we were like old friends, not in New York, not in the throes of a media crisis of two kids' making; there was no Attorney General, no Goldman Sachs to pull out the carpet.

★

WHEN I left, it was raining at a sharp angle and all the leaves looked like sodden rags blowing in the wind.

I walked along the southern rim of the park towards Columbus Circle. There was an exoskeleton of scaffolding at the base of the nearby buildings, rubbish stalls on the street corners. Pedestrians jostled for their space. I watched an older man, worn black Samsonite briefcase, stand still, waiting for the crowd to flow past him until he could move at his preferred gait.

In the faint drizzle, at the corner of West Sixty-First Street and Central Park West, two women in pantsuits were hollering at each other over a taxi.

The phone rang. "Mark, it's Joel. Joel James." He sounded a little giddy.

"Yes, Joel," I said, slowing to a saunter, halting at the crosswalk.

"Well, I've got some good news, I think. MSNBC wants you on tonight, live. Nine p.m. You'd be discussing Museveni."

"Museveni? What the fuck, we barely work for him…like as of six days ago. Anyway, I must get home now, I'm on the Acela at four p.m."

"Yeah, the other thing is that Skadden Arps isn't happy. Hawthorne just informed me he got a call."

"What?"

"Our contract is up for renewal in two months. They just called. They were harsh with Hawthorne and asked for you. We thought since…"

"Jesus Christ, Joel. Jesus. Well, why are you calling me, tell Hawthorne to set up a call. And as for TV, I cannot do it. I have a train. Then, apparently, a fucking plane tomorrow." It began to rain harder and I moved under some scaffolding where they were jackhammering the sidewalk.

"The Ambassador called this morning and requested that you appear instead of him, Mark. I'm sorry." His voice slackened.

"Of course he did."

"Well, yes, so, look it's top of the hour. It's a new anchor, so I think she might be a bit combative, trying to make a name for herself, you know. Mark, as you yourself would indicate, this is a tremendous op to market the firm for Africa work. Isabella and I have built an extensive embassy row list.

When this spot runs, we zip it out. Set up some meetings. They're all busy having teas with Tony Podesta and his red loafers."

"Why does Skadden have to be today?"

"It's when Victor is in town, I suppose. You're the only one there."

"Well, can't we deploy someone else? I mean I am supposed to be coming home tonight."

"He requested you, Mark."

"Fuck!" A few people far down the sidewalk turned and looked back at me, the proverbial Tourette's case.

"So..." Joel was holding the vowel.

The rain softened and the light changed again and a herd of coffee-walkers streamed around me like I was a pebble. This would put me in New York overnight.

"Joel, lemme call you back in five minutes, okay?"

"Mark, that's fine but they need to confirm ASAP. She said Robert Zoellick would be on along with you."

"Five minutes," I said and hung up.

I dialed Mae and when she answered there was an echo.

"I am cleaning the shower, Mr. White. Is everything good? Are you home for dinner?"

"Mae what time is hockey tonight?"

"Tonight, there is no hockey."

"Oh. Good. Well, something for work has come up. I think I am gonna need to be home around midnight. Yeah, I mean that's probably the earliest."

There was the expected pause and then, "Okay, Mr. White. I will tell Colin."

"Tell Colin pancakes in the morning and that I will take him to see the pandas again. Tell him to call me when he gets home, too."

"Okay, Mr. White, I will tell him this."

I called Joel back and consented to the meeting with Skadden Arps at a quarter past four. and a live spot on MSNBC at nine p.m.

"I'm sorry Mark, really."

"Joel, it's fine. Not your fault. Send me some notes, if you would, on Uganda, what to say, alright?"

"Sure thing, boss." We hung up.

I walked straight to the St. Regis, booked a room—the only one left, a Grand Deluxe King, for $2,400 per night. Staff descended upon me from nowhere, although I had no bags—opening doors, issuing greetings, offering bottled water—and walking through the swivel doors I felt a sudden shift from the brutal exterior world into the stately realm of the hotel, its frescoed ceilings, lit display cases from Chopard.

The polyglot staff had been dialed past polite to pre-Industrial subservience. I went to my Grand Deluxe King. Soon, the doorbell rang. Champagne and strawberries. I handed him the suit and asked that it be cleaned within the hour. I tipped the butler twenty dollars and he bowed, somewhat hurriedly, left. I opened the top dresser drawer, and felt it slither along its silken hinges. Smoked almonds and champagne. I undressed, put on a robe, showered, shaved, drank more champagne, took a pill, and readied to meet them.

The meeting was in a trophy high rise across the street from *The New York Times* headquarters on the forty-sixth floor.

When the doors opened, there was beige everywhere, the hardwood, the couches, the chairs, even the rugs. The views were magnificent. It was possible to see whatever landmark you desired from the floor to ceiling windows, clear across the river. There was a Lucian Freud over the urinal.

A woman in an elegant, crème skirt, escorted me to the corner conference room and offered tea and espresso.

Pixels of rain tapped against the floor to ceiling glass; it was soundproof, but, peering down at Eighth Avenue, the taxis darting all over the streets, I could seemingly hear their tires sloshing, men in their moist suits shouting at the fates, and I sensed that umbrellas would snag on the labyrinth of scaffolding so many rushed through, the *faux* colonnade, screaming into their phones to be heard over the traffic and the rain. Someone would be selling roasted chestnuts this time of year, that acrid burnt smell staking out a couple city blocks.

Now, I heard his familiar bass from inside the conference room. His hair had thinned some since college, his face, handsome still, had only slightly aged, little pock marks at the sides of the chin. I had last seen him at a classmate's wedding in Greenwich, the gaudy bunches of lilies in vases on all the cocktail tables on what, hours before, was the third fairway. Linda, his wife, was an investment banker. She had an apian aspect to her face, a recessive chin. Monica never liked her.

Monica and I last visited them eight years ago, the fall, at their penthouse in the East Village, a day wet and cold, much like this one. The residence—as Linda kept referring to it—was a mausoleum of sparseness and fragile quietude. There were orchids everywhere, jacquard linens in the guest room, fruits out of season in a jade bowl on the nightstand. Their neighbor downstairs was a Flemish Zoroastrian who had just made a biopic about Nabokov and had something to do with the Tribeca Film Festival, Linda said, one of many *sui generis* utterances she would make while Vic and I were engrossed in workplace stagecraft.

"Mark, my gosh, Mark!" Vic said magnanimously, arms outstretched.

"It's good to see you again, Vic." The others looked impatient to begin but I figured to drag this on as long as possible. "How is Linda, the girls?"

"Fine. Wonderful. Everyone is fine. You know Linda is doing some teaching now at Columbia—guest lecturer. Ella is in swimming, of course, Tessa just turned four. They are all great. We just spent the weekend in sailing...I have a first-time boat, a schooner, used, of course, but like new."

Vic held a pause until it began to curdle with awkwardness, and, then, "Mark, are you here for just today?"

"I've been here since this morning. When I got your call I had to make arrangements last minute."

"Yes, well, we appreciate that."

The others were watching this, a female peer whose name I did not know, dressed in an unmistakable Ralph Lauren suit, tired as any human could look, which even the gunmetal pinstripes could not conceal. There was another: doughy face, bald around the crown, vaguely British. The other, Rich, with whom I had spoken before by phone—and who ran things for the client day to day—was habitually bemused by the kind of work we performed. He merely acknowledged its occurrence, never actually admitting to any of its substance.

"Well, here I am. I appreciate the invitation," I said. "Are you still working on your Japanese, Little Vic?"

A small recoil: "That was a long while ago, Mr. White. I never travel much anymore to Asia. Only through Narita to Hong Kong for partner meetings. What about you? Lots of travel I suppose, not just for this client, of course."

"I get around. Sao Paulo last month. We had to take a helicopter to the city from the airport for security reasons," I said, wincing—hopefully not noticeably—as I said this last part.

"Well, that sounds ominous," Vic said, his colleagues smiling and laughing nervously. "I'd be very worried if I were Mrs. White."

Curiosity is the first virtue to go when you acquire money.

"I thought I was here to discuss new terms, Little Vic."

"Well, you are. We will." He was smiling and knew what he was doing.

The tension lingered, seconds passed, and then an intern-looking woman, squeamish to be interrupting, stepped in and said, "Mr. Adams, your call from Geneva is on the line."

"Rich," Vic said, facing a very slender, tall colleague in Benjamin Franklin spectacles, "I will need to take this. It's the matter on the Luxembourg bonds, I'm afraid. Cannot be moved. I'm sure you can handle things for a while."

Vic avoided eye contact with me as he spoke; I wasn't sure if he even knew that I was aware of this sophisticated ruse to escape our meeting.

I took a Coke from the silver bucket in the center of the table filled with ice and sodas as the champagne was starting to wear off. They began to enumerate a litany of concerns about our performance by the client, the Government of Guinea. With Victor gone, Rich was eager to start in.

"We were really expecting some media by now, Mark. Your firm has been on retainer now for at least—what is it, Mary, five months?—and we don't have anything to show for it."

I couldn't tell if this was chastisement or a plea for me to vow to redouble our efforts and to do better. The best formula was contrition and appeasement.

"I absolutely understand what you're saying, Rick, absolutely, and I want to assuage your concerns, which are not only valid but also addressable."

"It's Rich, his name is Rich," said Katrin, who suddenly wore that countenance of revulsion I had seen lawyers use so many times to kick us off their pedestal.

"And we appreciate that you have enjoyed a long relationship with Mr. Adams, Mr. White, but you have not enjoyed a positive relationship with Skadden Arps these past five months. In fact, let me just speak for those in this room: We feel fleeced. You have received over $250,000—up front— from the Guinea and we have to report to the president that we have nothing to show for it. How do you think this makes us look, Mr. White? You are not the only one with longstanding ties. This firm earns over $10 million per year from Guinea and your underperformance—no, your non-performance—puts us all in a bad spot."

I was staring at the Coke can too long.

"We haven't even received a phone call, Mark, nothing," said Rich.

"You've not received a phone call this week?" I said.

"Ever," he said.

"Only three emails promising a report," said Katrin, motioning to the balding one, who pulled out a file and handed it to me. The emails were each about three sentences long, grammatical errors. They were from Joel James, copying Hawthorne.

I had done this enough times before, and I said, "I have to tell you how unacceptable this is to me—and I cannot apologize to you enough."

I watched their faces for trace evidence of emotional change but there was nothing. The bald one folded his arms. Katrin sat back, beckoning for more.

"This is really a disgrace and not at all what we stand for or how we work for our clients."

"Mr. White, what are you going to do about it?"

I had considered this question on the elevator ride up. I was prepared to comp them the next two months' retainer, but I knew she would not have this, and the way she was looking at me, that Upper East Side smugness, I wanted her to know that I was not some mixed race chieftain from some outpost on the southbound Acela.

I folded my hands, and leaned into the table, ready to unleash a slew of fastballs.

"I am going to refund you all your money. We are going to work for free these next two months, and if you are not satisfied we will part ways as friends. As you say, Katrin, there are long histories to consider."

They sat there, partially unfazed, or maybe shocked. Katrin leaned in to the table.

"You are refunding $250,000?"

"I am going to have it wired to you tomorrow, if you would be so kind as to handle the administrative aspects with Margaret, my assistant," I said, facing Rich.

Rich looked at Katrin and then they all looked at me, saying nothing. I could hear Victor talking in the hallway. "Now, if there is nothing else, I will excuse myself."

When I walked out he was gone. His assistant sat up and said my name tersely, seemingly apprised of me and why I was here. "Do you know the way out?"

I rode the elevator down fifty-six floors, feeling my ears pop. Once in the lobby you could see the night had come; the building was nearly empty and the nightshift security personnel had taken over. I sat down beneath an oversized canvas of off-white acrylic with rocks dried in, high rise apocalyptic art.

I called Sally and explained what had happened. I could hear her kids in the bathtub.

"I need to know how this went down, how we work for someone for five months and produce zero. Zilch!" The security guard looked up. I paced. "This promotion cost me a lot of fucking money."

"You promoted Joel, not me. Well we have the money but, yes, I agree. Why did you refund it? It was really unnecessary. You could have simply resigned."

"It felt worse not to give it back than to give it back."

"When do we refund it?"

"Tomorrow."

"Tomorrow! Tomorrow, Mark!"

"Well, we have it, there's not an issue. We'll wire it and that's that."

"We have rent due on four offices and payroll due in two weeks. That's about $1.85 million in total. Yes, we can afford it on paper, but clients must pay, there's a thing called cash flow and this outgoing wire will throw everything off."

"Listen, you're worked up. Put Oscar to bed and we can discuss in the morning."

"Cancel your TV appearance. You sound completely destroyed."

"It's only TV," I said and hung up.

I walked for nearly an hour, south to the bottom of the city. Coming down Fifth Avenue I heard something my mother had said before she died. You are wherever you are, and don't forget the settings. They were final words. I walked farther along, passing Bryant Park, stopping to watch the leaves of a giant sycamore drift in the wind to the earth. The settings matter. Her skin, in the end, was fibrous, cracked lips; when I kissed her goodbye, she was murmuring in Spanish, which I did not speak well, *la cabeza, la cabeza,* and my mind immediately went to her father who was killed by a

gunshot to the head, one fine spring morning, walking his dog in a neighborhood where the sprinklers came on early and there were always tulips
cropping up at the base of mailboxes, but she went on like this for almost an
hour about *la cabeza* and then she said it, in English, said it clearly, the *don't
forget the settings* part, and, soon, by Broadway and Fifth, I was recalling the
time we had the harp with our tea cakes together in New York, my birthday,
the lobby bar of the Plaza, surrounded by so much finery, cashmere and the
skins of unknown, mispronounced winter animals, killed by Slavic-looking
men, and all of the secrets hidden in these sounds of the servility, foreign
staff: *Yes ma'am, certainly ma'am, a pleasure sir, precisely sir, excellent of course,
certainly, certainly, certainly.* The grandeur of that hotel possessed me, the
ceilings painted to Vatican perfection, the milk and the cookies, gold leaf
paint on the Corinthian order, all the drinking around us, swaddled amid
jacquard, silk cornice, leopard prints, rust velvet love seats, glass tables
hoisting mini Zen moss gardens, French tongues, English patois, the zebra
rug underfoot, perfectly titrated bourbon cocktails and that almost derailed
the disorder of the outside world.

I took another pill.

I had always imagined it was like underage sex; the way he forced himself on her, how she became the setting for me, germinating inside her,
neither truly Mexican or American, a byproduct of parking lot sex between
two people, strangers a week prior, fused into marriage by duty. The ship-
out date loomed four months ahead on the calendar, and she was clearly
showing at the wedding, a perceptible rounding of the lower abdomen, the
painful cinching of her wedding gown, to unround it, my heritage of lust,
provenance of Andrew Harold White and Margarita Maria Sanchez, the
water breaking on the lawn, the frantic calls to a naval destroyer patrolling
somewhere in the Indian Ocean, my physical setting, wombed in panic and
cortisone. I went on like this, practically sleepwalking, wandering in a luxury Italian food court in a transitional neighborhood of lower Manhattan,
smelling the ripeness of the *salumis* that hung and the dried, nutty cheeses
that lay split open on wooden tables, finally settling into the vegetarian
counter where I was served icy, acidic white wine and grilled artichoke
hearts and an empty bowl for the leaves.

I tried calling Colin but got no answer. Mae said he was showering.

"Before hockey?"

"He didn't want to tonight. He was tired. He is missing you I think and he had much homework."

"Alright then," I said, and I sipped more wine and ordered some *fritto misto*.

I looked around. Beside me was a middle-aged woman in a tan raincoat, a silvery flock of curls. A few scattered couples on dates at the bar. The kitchen staff wore bandanas, spoke Central American Spanish.

I devoured the sugar snap peas noisily and ordered a *café torinese*, equal parts espresso, milk foam, and hot chocolate. The coffee tasted even better than it looked, savoring first, with a spoon, the rich crema, and soon after, I went for the peach *panna cotta*, in two bites, inhaling the custardy, orange cream in the little cup, so reminiscent of the cold, saccharine shock of my mother's *tres leches* cake.

She said to be mindful of where you are, Mark. The settings matter.

I stepped back onto Fifth Avenue and the night was cold. The moon glowed white over the square across the street.

I checked my watch. It was time. I took an Uber to NBC studios. You feel like you can say anything on live television, anything that you can conjure on your feet, heat-stricken under those lights. You are talking to yourself, it seems, when the voice across the table from you, lost in the bright haze or sputtering in your ear, seems to rev up the survival instincts. Time takes on a rallentando effect, and you hear things that you might say to let loose, even before a second has passed you know the myriad declarations that would get you disinvited from the network. The light is its own anesthesia. Eventually, success breaks everyone down until their integrity acquires a cubist aspect.

You need to come to the stage armed and loaded, ready with cotton-candy wisdom and soundbites, every sentence stripped to its five second nucleus, Twitter-grade concision. The kinds of people who excel at this, the splaying of the pseudo-intellect for adulation, are the ones who like to micromanage the climate of their reputations on a daily, almost hourly, basis. I did TV because this is what I was supposed to be doing as a CEO, a crisis communications expert, as the anchors always dubbed me. I once thought you could slip easily into self-made myths and identities as you rose, but I soon realized the world foisted its own wardrobe upon you, that a title demanded you inhabit a role, speak a certain way in public, adopt a skin-care regimen, become pop culture literate, be ready to pop a few tantric moves when needed.

The makeup girl finished dusting me off. A cameraman came and walked me over to my spot.

They put me in a dark room without windows and told me to stare straight at the magic marker smiley face taped to the wall. A gorilla-shaped man manipulated the camera out of the light and smacked gum bubbles, adjusting the tripod, twisting the lens. He had a hacking smoker's cough. I sat, squirmed, heard Bob Zoellick and Susan Samson, the anchor, chatting through the earpiece; he was in studio, of course, in DC. I reached in my pocket and swallowed a few pills, and felt an immediate halo of sedation.

He coughed again, asked me to sit up, and said, "Thirty seconds." Then back to his camera, such a solemn devotion to his camera. I was feeling blood anger towards Joel James for not warning me I would be off-location. I could have been in studio for this session, easily accommodating my nighttime routine with Colin. I kept stoking the rage but it kept getting slowed and softened in the pharmaceutical cloud.

The cameraman coughed, flicked the switch, and the LED light hit me. I tried not to make a sour face, sat on my hands and suit tail to give a taut, attentive onscreen appearance. Never touch your face. Only talk when the pause is loud in the room. Just like I told clients. I heard their voices on the poly con a few feet in front of me.

Cable news producers wanted TV programming to unfold in the carefree manner of a beer commercial. Talk in statements that quickly shuttle the viewer to your perspective, no ambiguity. Smile, however vacant, shouting, lots of shouting, enough to draw eyeballs from waiting room viewers and marooned airport lounge refugees. You had to be unique enough so that they could brandish an impressive onscreen caption below your image: "Mark White, Media Expert."

I heard their voices but was faithfully devoted to my hazy blunted anger.

The lights were very strong. I stared ahead but felt liked yawning, blinking, coughing, eating, talking; I felt like storming out of this interview altogether and going home, but I remained on my chair.

The smiley face was getting blurry.

Ten seconds.

Blurrier.

And that's precisely why so many are outraged. It's this sense that Africa is beyond repair, hopeless, when in fact it's not. Africa, Uganda in particular, can prosper and take a bigger seat on the global stage, but it has to reject this kind of despicable political grandstanding shown by Museveni. He's not a warlord, true, but he's persecuting, essentially condoning the murder of those in the LGBT community in Uganda.

The smiley face was swaying and blurry.

Thank you, Ambassador Zoellick, for that perspective. All right, let's get a reaction from our next guest, Mark White. Mr. White is Chairman and CEO of White & Partners, one of the top media consulting firms in the world, and he represents President Museveni on this matter. Mr. White, how do you respond to these charges that your client is encouraging the murder of gays in Uganda?

The smiley face was blurry and moving.

I thought I saw the cameraman cough; his fist was plugging his mouth. My phone was buzzing in my breast pocket, and I knew it was Colin, hopefully not watching this.

John, I don't think you can make these kinds of allegations. They're completely baseless and overwrought.

Okay, well, this is Susan Samson, sir. But what do you mean by baseless? The president, your client, is supporting a law that makes sodomy illegal and punishable by death.

The phone kept ringing and ringing.

Well, Harry, the president doesn't make laws in Uganda, just like in this country. And you should know that the word gay, in Ugandan, means the same as pedophile. And I—it's because the words are similar that—I really think the president is just misspeaking, mistranslating.

There was an unusually long pause in my earpiece. I felt myself sweating, ringing and sweating, such an urge to yawn and lay down.

I heard next Ambassador Zoellick express his outrage at my comments.

They were both talking together now, seemingly over one another, and it sounded like their ire was focused on me.

I heard the words pedophile and insulting and homophobic and pathetic and…then I don't remember what I heard until I felt the hacking cough man shaking my shoulder and telling me to wake up.

"Dude, you passed out on air," he said, not disguising his amusement.

"I did?"

"Dude," he coughed again and pulled out his Marlboros, "it wasn't pretty, they had to cut to commercial. Harold—his name is Harold—is on the line and wants to speak to you. You want one of these?"

I took four cigarettes and placed them in my breast pocket. "How long was I out for?"

"Thirty, maybe thirty-five seconds," he said. "It was actually kind of cool, rebellious, man. You were telling that guy off about the gays and then bam."

I had foolishly taken too many pills. My phone was ringing incessantly now but this time I knew that it was not Colin. I should have refrained from the booze and sedatives, the hubris of appearing alongside Zoellick, should have been home in my bed. I should have been panicked but was Zen tranquil about the whole affair.

I reached into my wallet and found some twenties. "Here," I said, handing the money to the cameraman, "for the cigarettes, whatever else. If they ask, tell them I am clean. Also, tell Harry to go fuck herself."

"Dude!" He laughed, nodded in assent, opened the studio door and I stepped into the bright shock of the hallway, walked past the writers and late-night producers and news infantry who displayed their disgust with head nods and murmurs.

*

I WALKED into the Armageddon neon of Times Square, felt nothing and walked past one of those Bangladeshi joints, the ones that sold power cords and VCRs and gadgets of the past under white ice halogen, and I should have felt something but felt very little, and maybe that was the point of all the light.

I wandered around Broadway, by a strip club, bouncers solemn at the red velvet ropes, and walked into McFadden's, had a shot of whiskey, surveyed the November city through the window, its illuminated blocks of sports bars, wig shops, and suitcase wholesalers, the illicit red signs, OPEN, at all the nameless fluorescence where pizza was sold by the oily slice. I left. Maybe if I lived here I would go home to Colin under the wrath of a Midtown moon, pedestrian hoards at every cross walk. I found no sanctuary. I wanted to evade the soundtrack of squealing braking subways. I wanted to avoid all the Midtown riders in all that underworld slave ship gloom; maybe living here I would become immune to the manic street preachers and their megaphone prophesies on Seventh Avenue, the side streets and the fellating alley shadows, something under cardboard evoking a human shiver.

How to news-varnish the lewd?

How to news-varnish all these random high school rapes and Ponzi scheme suicides, the need to correlate such events with a parabolic direction—hope or fear, of money or of death, all the sins that are fit to print.

I stopped short of fully inhaling it all, because it repulsed me as much as it enchanted me. I am not of this piss reek and throbbing neon and bloodlust honking in this human storm in Times Square.

And I could not smell Monica anymore. I longed for the days when she made me Mexican coffee and I read all my unread college novels in the early morning, in the herringbone chair, the small acts intended to prolong time.

But tonight, I had nowhere to go, was no one in this city, had no one. I hewed to the neon.

I rode an Uber back to the St. Regis. Their heat lamps were on over the entrance and I lingered there and smoked for a while. My head was already spinning. I went inside to the bar. I ordered an old-fashioned with Woodford Reserve. I swirled my glass and inhaled my first and savored my second, until I realized I was way too drunk so I added another just to put me out.

The ice in the highball was like a fist of blood diamonds. They didn't have any cable television playing at this fine bar. There was just me, some older man of European descent reading the *Wall Street Journal,* and an assortment of women in their late thirties, flaunting their suggestive elegance in the way only escorts can do. The barman said there was one last round before closing. One of them made eye contact with me. She looked Chinese. I had considered this transaction for some time, as these sorts of displays were common on all my trips, though I had never partaken in any extramarital sexual activity while Monica was alive, or since she'd passed. She ran her finger along the rim of her martini, smiling at me. I didn't have any cash. There was an "intimacy kit" in the bathroom drawer—there always were at a place like this. She had Monica's hair, a decent face caked with rouge and eyeliner, and she wore a silk red dress that cut across the neckline and gold bangles on her wrist. I signaled for one more. Melvin made it much stronger than the previous two, sensing I needed it or something more sinister.

I was looking at her and that was all it took for her to feel welcome to walk over and introduce herself to me as "Mimi." The obvious fake name was a sort of psychic lubricant, a way to invite me to produce a false name of my own, as if a consensual falsehood was a bridge to "yes."

Even at the St. Regis, an escort wears cheap perfume. It was something overly saccharine like a little girl's body spray. She smelled appealing anyway. Her teeth were perfect, very western. I pegged her at mid-thirties, and she seemed to be at total ease in the old squat elevator, didn't mind the absence of small talk as we rode up together silently and kept delivering bursts of eye contact and smiles, feeding into the hunger I felt swelling inside me.

I had no plans for how things would proceed. While I had not sensually touched a woman since Monica died, I was less nervous than I was perplexed at the protocols that would take effect once we were inside the room. For a moment, I considered that she was an undercover cop; there were no outward signs that she was, although I had no concept of what those signs were anyway. Was there a gun and badge in her purse? Too small. At the door, she took the key card from me, coming in close, looking up at my eyes and sharing breath. Whether this was for my comfort or to give the appearance of intimacy to other stray guests walking the halls I didn't know. I could smell liquor on her breath. When we entered the room, I asked her if she wanted a drink.

Talking seemed to crack the intimacy, so I wordlessly passed her the glass of scotch and sat down on the end of the bed. She downed the scotch and walked over, placed her hands on my shoulders and lured me to stand and face her. She was kissing my neck. I still held the scotch glass. We would have appeared like lovers now, were this a film. Was this a sting? I felt a sudden affection for her now. Was this dissimulation what men paid so avidly for, I wondered. She ran her hands along my chest for a few minutes and then she kissed my neck and when she was done I fell asleep with her in my arms, and when it was morning I was entirely naked and alone, the traffic noise loud in the room because she had left the window slightly open.

★

I GLANCED at my phone on the nightstand and there were three missed calls from Colin. I searched the bathroom for Advil, found none, and instead found the intimacy kit was unopened. That fact stunned me, mostly because I had no rationale for why "Mimi" would take such a risk with a total stranger. I started to pace the room, trying to reassemble the time with her. I remembered nothing. The phone was ringing and it was Colin.

"Daddy? Where are you?"

"Hi, pal. Daddy misses you. I'm in New York."

It was Thursday morning and I suddenly realized my flight to San Francisco would leave Dulles in less than twenty-four hours.

He didn't say anything.

I took a swig of what remained in the scotch glass.

"So you know my math test? Well, I didn't do so well."

"What does that mean, Colin?"

"Well, like a fifteen out of twenty. That's technically a C+."

"That is a C+, Colin. Didn't you study?"

"I totally forgot we had a test."

"Listen, Colin, school is more important than sports right now, okay? Understand?"

There was silence and then I knew what was coming. "But you don't help me! Never, ever, ever, ever! You don't daddy!"

"Colin!" I shouted into the phone but got nothing back. It was Mae now, telling me she had it handled.

"Alright, listen, I pull into Union Station around six thirty. I should be home past seven. I head out tomorrow for San Francisco. Unfortunate, I know."

She paused, seemingly to hold her tongue. "We will see you then, Mr. White."

I hung up, heard the honking sounds, and it was a jolt to consider the events of the prior night. My wallet was accounted for, as was my Rolex. I could never tolerate silence in a hotel room, even nice ones; I put back on the TV and refugees were exiting Syria. My phone began to buzz. The door knocked and a younger man with eyes cast to my feet handed me a clean white envelope with my name in cursive on the front. I sat on the bed next to the liquor stain and opened the letter. The note read: "You fell asleep. Went back to my room. Don't worry, I'm married. Mimi." There was an East Village address.

I replayed the events again from the previous night, my libido rising unsuspiciously while at the same time I felt a sudden panic, then nausea. My forehead began to bead up with sweat. I felt seized by the same grief I had felt the night Monica died, and now I was ashamed that someone had seen me like this. This is your legacy, Mark? This is how you treat our son?

I ran to the bathroom and vomited.

I was sweating profusely.

The phone began to ring and it was not Colin. I stripped off my underwear and hunched over the toilet, waiting. There was a used condom in the bin beside me. Her arsenal, I thought. Briefly, I felt relieved, even mildly euphoric until I realized the core of my sins was intact. The call went to voicemail. I grabbed an indiscriminate combination of my pills and threw them in the toilet. I stood up in front of the mirror and looked disgusting, devoutly middle-aged, hairy. I looked so alien to who I was when we first met in the cafeteria. I was reminded of the extremes pursued with Mimi, and I felt ashamed.

I showered, shaved, texted Harry for an update, texted Hawthorne for an update, called Sally about my dissatisfaction with Joel James and quickly investigated gold prices.

★

I LOOKED in my closet; I had only packed for a day trip. There were two more meetings, a lunch, then a train-ride home. The hotel laundry service could not return a garment in less than two hours. It was seven in the morning and my first meeting was a quarter past nine. I rummaged in the closet for the iron and ironing board and haphazardly tried to renew my white shirt, wiping away the trace of lipstick on the collar. I sprayed on some cologne and had to call downstairs again, this time for a razor and shaving cream.

When I finally sat down in the breakfast room, they brought me coffee, poured fresh squeezed orange juice, left a basket of pastry, all without asking. Someone came to offer me a *Wall Street Journal, New York Times* or *Financial Times*. I waved them away. It wasn't until I had ordered breakfast that I realized, standing across from me, smiling sheepishly, was Hawthorne.

"Sleep well?" I heard the familiar voice say, as he sat down.

"Hawthorne…" I squinted at him and then began to smirk. I thought for a minute he had arranged the tryst with Mimi.

"Quite the appearance last evening," he said. "Excuse me, garçon, I'll have a mimosa."

"You saw?"

"Mark, everybody saw."

"I suppose."

"Well, it was live television. You weren't on PBS."

"Any clients see?"

The waiter came and placed two mimosas in tiffany crystal beside our waters.

"Yes, all the banks saw. They called. That's why I came, Mark. We got axed. Goldman, JP Morgan, the ratings agencies, two VC funds. About $3 million."

I tried to appear nonchalant and took one of the flutes and sipped the mimosa. "These pastries are absolutely fabulous, Hawthorne. Would you care for one?"

"Oh, come on, Mark. This is very serious. The team is spooked. I don't think you should be going to San Francisco. I will go for you."

"The hell you won't!" The other guests turned and looked at me; I had accidentally shouted at Hawthorne, the first time I had raised my voice at him, ever.

"Mark, it's not the money. I know we're stable. Long term is great. But we have a lot of prospects, and it's too early to know if they will run for the hills or not. Also, a faction involving Wendy is talking about resigning *en masse*, something about going to Fleishman Hillard."

"Jesus, why would they want to go there?"

"Same thought I had, Mark. But we cannot afford revenue *and* staff attrition. Not so much, so quickly."

I stared at the leftover macchiato froth. Hawthorne didn't have to lecture me. I already knew what had been done.

"What did you tell me when you first hired me? That this was all pretend. Bubbles and air and pretense. We don't make widgets, Mark. There is no inventory, no factory. The demand is entirely capricious. We have an inventory of talent, then there is demand, then we hope to God they pay their bills on time. Any bad press will scare all the pretty birds away, and they won't come back. At this stage in our careers, I'd rather do unmitigated success than play Sisyphus and fuck around at rehab. Right, Mark? Come on, look, everyone adores you, respects you. You're allowed a few foul balls, right?"

I was still staring into the macchiato and decided just to blurt it out.

"I had sex last night with a married woman. I don't know her real name. We did it three times. I don't know why it happened."

Hawthorne reclined in his chair appraisingly. It was the first time I had ever noticed a dash of paternity in his manner, nothing judgmental, just a highly paid colleague trying to determine how to respond to his boss confessing random hotel sex.

"I suppose you needed that," he said, as lovingly as possible.

"I was obliterated. I met her right over there at the bar. I remember very little. I feel like a pig."

"Were you taking those pills you take?" he asked, carefully.

"What?"

He just looked back at me.

"Who else knows about the pills?"

"Pretty much everybody. Jesus, Mark, you don't particularly try to conceal them, do you?"

I started to feel nauseous again, wanted to take a pill but obviously couldn't with Hawthorne across from me.

"Do you like Brioni ties?" I asked.

"What?"

"You heard me."

"We have a meeting in one hour."

"So you're checking my schedule now?"

"Sally gave it to me. And I don't think we need to go tie shopping now."

"Well, I don't have a tie."

"Where is your tie?"

"Mimi used it and now it's destroyed."

"How far away is Brioni?"

"Five minutes by foot."

When we got outside, something like winter had set in. Hawthorne called an Uber and we arrived at the store, picked out two different ties, and I put mine on in the dressing room.

"They are the best ties in the world," I proclaimed to Hawthorne and the store staff, who beamed at the recognition. I put them on my corporate card.

We still had an hour. We should walk up to Central Park, I said, or maybe find a diner, something to get out of the cold. Hawthorne seemed aloof, it looked like micro-epiphanies going on in his mind, about what, I could only assume. A New York sidewalk is no place for sauntering; Hawthorne had bumped into a man talking on the phone with a mega Starbucks cup. *Christ watch it!* He never stopped moving. These hysterics, this separation from civility, reminded me of the game Monica and I sometimes played in Madrid while walking: find the American. You tried to find the person walking faster than all the others, the one who failed to obey traffic signals, stampeded through crowds and crosswalks. To most Madrileños, a city stroll was a leisurely pursuit; an American wore shorts and a t-shirt and kept his head down and rarely looked up, walking alone. The Spanish seemed to fear solitude and that psychic aversion meant a sea of Spanish walking in a kind of collective, the tectonic plates shifting in unison, pedestrian defiance against fascism—or perhaps it was the other way around.

You walked up to your mark and said, in Spanish, "Are you American?"

"They are bombing hospitals now," said Hawthorne.

"What?"

"Jamaat-ul-Ahrar, the breakaway faction of the Pakistani Taliban. We will need to resign that account." He was reading a news alert on his iPhone. I tried to slow our gait to Madrid speed, and Hawthorne unknowingly assented to the new pace.

"Hawthorne who are you talking about? We don't work for terrorists."

"You would be correct, although I don't think the media will discern between them and the Egyptians. We are getting a lot of calls now, Mark. Hanna's little piece ran. An epistle to our greatness now overshadowed by MSNBC."

"What do they pay?"

"Ninety a month. And yes, they paid half up front. We are now in month eight."

I was trying to discern if Hawthorne's souring mood was related to my cable performance entirely or also because of this occurrence. We walked up Fifth Avenue past Cipriani's and the Metropolitan Club, and I saw the green book stalls against the Central Park wall, reminiscent of the Left Bank outside of Paris. I wanted to touch the books, absorb their essence.

122 / ERIC MICHAEL BOVIM

"I just emailed Sally and it's actually $100,000 a month," he said. He was happy now it seemed, as if he had reached a critical conclusion.

"So, we shall endure in our poverty, as my late father said from his deathbed in Taormina. These are the moments that form the distinctions between rich and poor. I think the lottery is rigged to give the poor some hope. You never see a poor person remade because of a winning ticket. There is an art to changing stations and the secret is that it has nothing to do with acquiring more money, but learning instead how to live as if you don't have it."

"Well said," I quipped, deep into the lager-yellow pages of an early edition of *Portrait of the Artist as a Young Man*. You should tweet that."

"Haven't we produced enough notoriety for the month?" he said, looking at me a little menacingly. He produced reading glasses out of nowhere and picked up *Hamlet*.

I exhaled a cold cloud of smoke, closed the book, stood up, buttoned my blazer and ran my fingertips through the hair of my temples and exhaled again. Hawthorne seemed primed for some kind of response. I Madrid-sauntered to the next stall and grabbed a random stack of poetry off the shelf: Shakespeare, Milton, Dickinson, Frost, Eliot. I felt like a cigarette, but let the idea flutter away as I imagined how my sudden smoking habit, combined with my tryst and my cable TV humiliation might play—even to my consigliere. People will believe a lie until the bitter end, so long as the fiction is colorless and consistent.

There was a bench by the wall and we sat down in between the bird shit spots.

We sat and I broke the silence. "I see everything too clearly. The gradations are abolished."

"The distinctions are required," he said. "They help us to forget ourselves"

"You mean self-delusion."

"No. We need to forget ourselves."

I realized my fingers were numb from the cold, my nose dripping. "I guess...I guess it's that there are about ten authentic minutes in my whole fucking day. Every day. After that, life becomes too easy. At lunch with Alan, he said so many things that made sense. Even if there was bullshit artistic sushi, it was an actual, real conversation."

"Mark—"

"And I don't understand why I can't just take a break from this all now and then, you know? I'm tired. I am wiped. I just can't pitch fastballs all day, Hawthorne. I can't pitch like this!"

"Mark, do you need some of your medicines?"

"Fuck you!"

I stood up and hurled my books at the vendor and marched off towards The Plaza, thinking I could get a drink there. Hawthorne was behind me calling my name. He grabbed my elbow and turned me around and held me by the shoulders with both hands.

"Mark! Mark!" He was shaking me.

My nose was dripping, snot running into my mouth.

"Mark enough! This is unseemly!"

I was breathing heavily.

"We have a statement to get out. A statement. About last night. Sally sent me a draft and we have to issue it before noon."

People were looking now, some even stopping, becoming bystanders. I noticed an unshaven homeless man looking up at me from his feral crouch; I heard Monica telling me to stop, sit down, read something, anything, Mark; I felt my pocket vibrating, maybe Colin or a client or Harry or who the fuck cares; I heard the honking and the traffic slush from the twentieth floor through an open window, alone with my lust and grief.

"We need to issue your statement. That's why I'm here." He was enunciating each word as if I was an invalid, or worse.

The bystanders had dispersed, for the most part. It was good that this had occurred in Manhattan and not DC, I thought.

"Are we done here?" he said in a way that signaled he had moved on from this episode, even though it had been uploaded permanently into his memory.

We walked down Fifth past The Peninsula and then turned towards the MoMa and came all the way to Radio City Music Hall, near our meeting. We walked saying very little, stray comments about this and that client, meaningless remarks intended to ward away discomfort.

There is common cause in joyless things.

I wanted desperately a footlong and a grape soda.

I heard loose change in the Salvation Army bucket. We sat down at a bench nearby.

"Here is the statement," he said in a distinctive legal register. "Sally asked me to show this to you. We need you to approve it. Approve it please so we can dispatch it pronto."

He pulled out a piece of paper, unfolded it, and handed it to me:

STATEMENT BY WHITE & PARTNERS ON THE MSNBC APPEARANCE OF CHAIRMAN AND CEO, MARK WHITE, AT 9 P.M. EST, NOVEMBER 13, 2016

Last night, White & Partners Chairman and CEO, Mark White, made an unscheduled appearance on Susan Samson LIVE. Mr. White, who had been traveling abroad just the week prior, had been taking some prescription medication for an illness contracted while in Europe. The jetlag and combination of medicines clearly were problematic, and Mr. White suffered a brief lapse of concentration during the live broadcast. Although regrettable, Mr. White is feeling completely healthy today and has returned to work and looks forward to appearing on-air again to support the over one hundred clients that make up our great firm.

PART 2

chapter five

THE SUBURBAN carried me recklessly fast from the arrivals terminal through morning fog along the Pacific all the way to Nob Hill.
Margaret deliberately put me in an out of the way hotel across from
Huntington Park, a flat city block of green, lined with meticulously pruned
cherry and plane trees, same pale scaling bark you can find in the long formal columns of the Luxembourg Gardens. Maybe she was trying to reju-
venate me.

I had been upgraded. I rode all the way up to the eleventh floor. My
room had an expansive view of the city and the park below. I stood still for
a few moments, gazing across at the fountain in the center of the park. A
Chinese woman in a red sweat suit, standing on one leg, was doing Tai Chi
exercises near one of the cherry trees.

I unpacked, hung the suit, the extra white shirts, thought I smelled
Mimi in my clothes, unloaded the toiletries by the sink and unzipped the
travel kit, but there were no pills: I remembered I had flushed the whole
stash down the toilet at the St. Regis. It's only one night, I thought.

I brushed my teeth twice, flipped on the bathroom television, which was
built into the mirror, and watched FOX News while I shaved. Rebel fight-
ers were advancing. Everywhere. Turkey shot down a Russian jet. There
was a tired-looking retired General on, pushing for NATO involvement.

I towel-dried my face; they'd moved on to the story of a five-year-old girl found suffocated in her mother's trunk.

I rode the elevator to the lobby, grabbed a copy of the *San Francisco Chronicle*, and walked outside. The doorman made easy small talk, but I kept my head down and muttered something and walked on. An alert rang out from my phone: Lars was now following me on Twitter, something he said he would be doing after our meeting in Copenhagen. This led me to scroll down my feed: a crisp image of the new Apple Watch—a computer-phone you could wear on your wrist—tweeted by an East Coast intellectual magazine, a prophesy in less than 140 characters trembling on the screen: "The future isn't even here yet, and it's already exhausted us in advance."

I felt the *Chronicle* in my hand, exceptionally light; the layoffs indeed had not only shorn the newsroom but had withered the paper: it's dimensions resembled a community newspaper's—over-sized headlines in childish fonts, stories ridiculously double-spaced about city life, local tragedies, as if there were no life beyond the city, no tragedies unfolding beyond this bay, beyond these hills.

I tried to forget the news and the tweet and walked down the steep wet sidewalk. It felt like an autumn morning and I decided to go to the only café I knew.

I walked down the sharp slope of Mason and turned onto Pine Street, passing brick hotels with rickety fire escapes, Oriental saunas with drawn curtains beside a bodega that announced "ATM inside," a dirty Starbucks fifty yards away at the bottom of the hill at the corner of Grant and Bush and the Dragon Gates of Chinatown.

The heat had not sprung yet; Monica had loved this about the Mediterranean climate of this city, so much like Barcelona, she said. Were you to travel north sixty miles to Napa it was possible, even in the summer, to experience the occurrence of all four seasons in the span of a day. There was the icy Alpine early morning air that warmed into the wet leaves of fall and that, by noon, had morphed into a fragrance of spring, all rosemary and thyme and rose scents; that blossomed, by mid-day, into a hot vellum of sulfur.

At Café de la Presse, I ordered an espresso and croissant.

The café bar looked overstocked. The television was flashing imagery of a cracked desert floor, or someplace in southern California rendered arid by the drought. The story ran for what seemed like five minutes, until they ran the same tired general talking about NATO and Turkey.

The waiter brought a warm, perfect croissant, shiny from its baked egg wash, that, once bit, would flake into sawdust pieces, a crisping like dried November leaves. The coffee tasted delicious and I hastily buttered the croissant while it was warm and ate it in three bites.

I opened my laptop to catch up on personal emails. There were very few of them, maybe twenty, the oldest from three months ago; there was one from Colin's school yesterday. It was his report card: D's in all his subjects except for math—where he had a C+.

This is only third grade, I said aloud, as if to Monica. The waiter turned.

But I knew what this meant almost immediately—and all the remedies involved. It was too much to even contemplate and now I was feeling short of breath and the sweats were coming next.

Another email from his teacher asked if we could meet today.

I finished the coffee and drank down the ice water, doing my breathing and envisioning Catskill light. I closed the laptop and looked outside.

The phone was ringing. By now, there was a prodromal sign of withdrawal, a dull itchy ache in the eye sockets, jumpiness.

The waiter had been visiting me multiple times in the past few minutes, inquiring if I needed anything else and placing the check on the table. I was starting to feel miserable without the pills. A question loomed on the plasma: "Should the US pay ransom to terrorists?" The distracted feeling was there, the gnawing at my jaw and eye sockets, a half aggravated, half anticipatory humming, like being unable to think from hunger.

The waiter came and refilled the water glass and I drank that one down too.

I paid the check and left hurriedly.

Outside, there was a girl in her twenties in a green bomber jacket walking two German Shepherds and an array of miniature white dogs, a fistful of leashes rising to her hand like the suspension cables of a bridge. I noticed more dog walkers; it was ten o'clock, the hour when this underclass doubled as for-hire dog walker for the twenty-something executive who shuttled off to Silicon Valley before sunrise to code.

How could he be nearly flunking every course, I asked myself, partially aloud.

I walked through the Dragon Gates, but I still wasn't quite all the way into Chinatown. A block up on the right was a narrow coffee shop, roughly the size of an Amtrak bathroom with a line out the door.

I figured one more espresso would halt the agitation, that scatteredness that prohibited normal thought. A college-aged boy, catwalk thin, manned the counter.

The menu was overhead on a flat screen, ticker symbols were racing right to left, a lottery of letters, the rolling march of capitalism. QQQ was up 1.4%.

In addition to the espresso, I asked for an orange juice. Gosh, we, like, don't have that, he said, just cold pressed vegetables, elixirs.

Maybe I'd want a cold pressed kale juice instead?

Maybe not, I said.

There was no grapefruit either—or any citrus; only vegetable transmuted into juice form, fashionably spiced with things like turmeric.

I asked him for tomato juice but they didn't have that and he didn't seem to think it was very funny.

I drank the espresso right there at the counter as soon as he handed it to me and said, "Presto!" and walked out.

An Asian girl in a black t-shirt, midway through a cigarette, was arguing bilingually with her boyfriend on the phone, alleging multiple infidelities. I asked her for a cigarette.

She looked at me appraisingly and handed me one.

We smoked, mere feet from each other, observing the dog walkers.

I tried to remember if I owned QQQ.

Last quarter he got all B's. What the fuck happened, and how the fuck can Lars and Fung be billionaires, pregnant with—if they wished—political influence; it wasn't a question of whether they would eventually spike the political punch with their notions of America. You had to contemplate the degree to which their involvement in politics would be septic, but then I remembered that it was all invariably toxic and one more pollutant in that cesspool made little difference. Maybe each side nullified the others' noise so that the resultant PH was neutral? But last quarter he had B's.

San Francisco had been a place of iconoclasts until it had become gentrified with very wealthy Internet industrialists. It was true that they were also iconoclasts in their own right, but their quest was commercial, not cultural, and now, by all accounts, despite their claims that technology was enabling greater interconnectedness, the bastion from which these revolutionary technologies sprung was a city at war with itself, its creative and corporate factions pitted against each other and the number of outcasts who could no longer afford to live in its heart or eat in its cafés was rapidly growing.

I thought about gritty Beatnik San Francisco, the schizophrenic hysterical on the street corner in flannel and a dirty baseball cap, pushing a shopping cart. I thought about the underclass of outcasts stashed throughout the city: the wannabe Beat poets who sang their angry doggerel in shabby book shops; theta healers who existed mainly on Yelp, out of plain view from the pedestrian public; émigré acupuncturists with devotees capable of evoking sudden transformations; shamans who had done time with ancient tribes in Peru; yogis named Indigo who led their little classes on second floor studios above those shops that hawked superannuated communications gadgetry; blocked novelists, failed and miserable, destitute jazz pianists and confused painters who still believed that they were one masterful triptych away from a retrospective at the Pompidou; well-mannered documentarians based out of their houses in Oakland; well-to-do web coders who took their out of town guests to Alcatraz; the moon-eyed Tarot card readers and the grisly guitarist and the borderline flamenco dancers who worked late into the night for many different men, for very little money, and I though Colin's going to fail, he's going to miss out on private school and fumble through college, and, who knows, he might end up out here someday, living under a borrowed name in a squalid flat with a girl name Vicky.

Then Monica telling me it's my fault, I travel too much, I am not there, and me telling her she is mostly to blame—she didn't need to walk Atticus so late at night on a busy street, didn't need to leave for Mexico like a monarch butterfly to paint her ridiculous canvases.

I ordered an Uber and when it came the girl beside me was now on her third cigarette and my eyes ached and my fingers were tingly; I was untalkative, slightly nauseous from the nicotine or caffeine, or both. Without the pills, I wasn't sure what was happening with my nervous system. I was in full-blown withdrawal, an alarm clock ringing inside my body.

I knew I needed to be at the Four Seasons soon. I called a car and sat doubled-over, dizzy from too much coffee and nicotine, the window slightly rolled down just in case. When we arrived, I tried to compose myself and did my breathing, and the lobby smelled like cinnamon and clove, like a proper house should where the parents do the homework at night with their only son.

There were doppelgänger Mirós and Chagalls on the lacquered walls. I sat down on the lobby sofa. I felt the nervous stares of the staff on my back. My head was pounding.

I sank into a plush chair beside a mini yellow orchid, a neat stack of *New York Times* on the coffee table. I smelled the clove again, saw the coffee and tea service set up by the reception. I was still dizzy but I got up and walked over, fiddled with the little porcelain pitchers of cream and milk, the star anise and cinnamon sticks tucked into a wicker basket by the carafe of cider. I felt the stares. A middle-aged woman in a baseball cap, drenched in sweat and wearing headphones, ripped into a pack of synthetic sugar and poured it into a cardboard cup, her finger marionetting a tea bag into the hot water, practically jogging off down the hall. I poured myself some of the mulled cider and sat down with a paper. It tasted sour and dull.

The elevator bell chimed softly. Lars and Fung came out.

Upon their arrival, I sensed multiple ironies within ironies: that I was here in the Four Seasons San Francisco, a city of outsiders now overrun with insiders; the front page of *The New York Times,* paper of record of their potential undoing, staring up at me; my entrepreneur clients, whose venture, financed by a member of the Manhattan gentility, was my conundrum to solve, their fortunes hinging on my expertise and wisdom, the justification for this triage meeting. My clients normally wanted to leap the wall into the press, but now I had to solve for zero, break out, leap the back out of the media into something akin to mediated oblivion.

Lars gamely shook my hand and looked more disheveled than he had in Copenhagen. He had these disappointing splotches of facial hair, a sense of "almost" growing on his face, head shaved to a near shine, which offset the bags under his eyes. I noticed, for the first time, his incisors had never dropped properly and he had crooked front teeth—coffee stained, almost equine—although he wore a well-tailored blazer. Fung was dressed like a boy in roll-cuff jeans, white t-shirt, a flash of neon argyle sock. She had shaved her head into a partial Mohawk.

He kept his hand low on her waistline and she kept inviting it by putting her hand on his shoulder and giddily pecking at his nape. I thought I should show them to the world happily in love, debunk the violent rape mythology, yet every broadcast journalist likes to be perceived as 50/50 and it was unlikely we would be doing anything other than giving airtime to accusations.

Despite these extreme appearances, they still retained that vague, one-IPO-away-from-cultural-shaman look. A female guest in an orange visor by the coffee turned to stare.

I felt a trembling hand resting on my right shoulder. I turned and it was Alan. Lankier and shorter than I remembered, he had a big donor's handshake: quick, pulsing squeeze, and smile-nodding with his lips closed. *You sure as fuck know who I am.*

He said nothing to Lars and Fung and led us down the hallway to a conference room comically over-adorned with notepads, hotel pens, handfuls of Swiss mints in cellophane in white ramekins, and pitchers of alkaline water with slivers of cucumber and lemons. There were carafes of fresh-squeezed juices beside a "tasting bar" of different varieties of nuts.

We began to assemble plates of almonds and cashews with spoons, and this ceremony carried on for longer than it needed to and soon I realized there were nearly a thousand calories of nuts on my dish and I was still semi-nauseas. Lars fished a lemon out of the pitcher with a fork and brought it to his lips, tasting the citrus as if it were a kind of palliative. I looked around but could not locate any coffee, which seemed absurd in such a room. Alan sat down. I felt like I was frivolously wasting everyone's time and money, loitering at the nut bar. I felt Alan watching me. Lars poured a glass of honey mango pineapple something. Fung was untwisting the candies on the table. My body was buzzing from an absence of chemicals but I did my best to sustain the tension, claim the pulpit, and slowly returned to the table with a glass of alkaline water and a bread plate filled with almonds, walking at a holy pace as though I was carrying viaticum.

At the head of the table, Alan was reclined in a black leather director's chair, sporting peak lapels, crossing his legs, a hand resting on his elevated knee, ready, perhaps, to swat at the air around him Napoleonically to accentuate a point.

"Gentlemen," he said, a too-long, self-aware dramatic pause. "As Mark has explained to me, this is a complete and total crisis." I heard the cleverness in his opening sentence, an attempt to affix the diagnosis to my professional pedigree and forfeit any personal involvement in what was to come—to give it all over to me. This seemed to work; Lars and Fung turned toward me and held their stares. Lars sipped his lemon water and smiled with a boyish innocence. Fung popped an almond and gave one of those resigned, close-lipped smiles reserved for funerals, terminations, moments of dirty work.

"We don't really know what is to transpire. We don't know if the attorney general is going to press statutory rape charges against Fung. We don't know if he will also bring charges for distribution of an illegal substance. We don't know what the press will write but we know what they write will not be flattering, which is why we have all agreed to retain the services of Mr. White and his firm. We know that any whiff of scandal will spook investors and chase away billions in investment before the IPO. I am not talking here about regular order scandal. I am talking about history books type scandal, the Challenger exploding in the sky before it reaches outer space."

Alan looked at Lars and Fung an extra moment to see if the reference to the 1984 NASA disaster was lost on them, born a full decade later.

Alan's spool of facts and circumstances around OneSpeak went on like this, frame by frame, and quickly drained the room of any potential for humor or ambiguity. And just when things had been titrated perfectly, when the room seemed eager to hear me bellow forth my opinions about how to defuse this time bomb, Alan played dystopic notes.

"The sentences for these kinds of crimes are fairly meaty—several years without parole, is what I'm made to understand by counsel. While it's quite premature to flash forward to the trial and prison time, I think it's also prudent for us to develop some messaging about succession planning for the future, for continuity's sake. Investors will be wary of buying this stock if they think one of its founders will be absent from the operations soon thereafter."

Alan sat back in his chair, folded his hands, and said, "I'd now like to introduce Jackson Bellafonte."

A tall man in wire rim glasses strode in and sat beside Alan. He didn't make eye contact, just opened a folder, glanced at some scribbled notes, and said that our best and leading argument was that there was no penetration, only kissing, which, obviously, no one believed, including Alan. I was Googling him as he spoke: he was the lead defense attorney at Gibson Dunn. Jackson went on this way, unvarnished, for five minutes or so.

Lars lowered his gaze to the table, hands folded, ashen. Fung stared into her water glass. Many of the legal scenarios just presented, some of which included a guilty plea, most of which included hard jail time in a maximum-security detention prison, had frozen conversation.

"There was no penetration." said Fung. She was not smiling.

"Let's hear what Mark has to say," Alan said.

I was itchy all over. With little prepared, save for a few standard one-liners, I was unsure of how to steer this room following talk of long-term incarceration. I stood up, semi-gracefully, and walked over to the tasting bar where I poured a lemon water, tossed a few almonds on the tiny plate, performing each task more slowly than normal to try and prolong the silence.

Fung spoke suddenly, practically shouting. I also heard the angle and depth of her voice; this was a device common in Silicon Valley, the loud, obnoxious ambush question meant to rattle the subject, some cross-examination technique.

"You've never really handled anything like this before, have you?" she said.

Alan recoiled slightly, took a sip of water. Lars just looked at Fung, whether approvingly or in admonishment I could not tell.

"It's a penetrating question," I said without irony.

Alan immediately laughed, almost spitting out his water.

Lars even chuckled. Fung focused a bitter stare at me. But the joke had done its work: a swift judo kick at the aggressor, now crouched in a choke hold of chagrin from which she could not escape without my expertise.

"Mark," said Lars, "it's that she means there are no rules for this particular situation."

"Don't translate me. Don't you translate me. Who knows if he even followed along; he could have been sleeping."

"How can someone sleep through such a nightmare," I said. It was true on many levels. I heard Monica yelling at me.

I stood up and started to professorially pace the room. Standing would always shut them down. Despite my withdrawal, I felt alarmingly at ease. Adrenaline calm.

"I want you to think of the situation this way: OneSpeak has a virus. The virus is bad media, very bad. It is not infecting just the coverage of the company but the very headlines of the stories covering OneSpeak. It's really the worst type of crisis, and there are limited options, a limited array of best-case outcomes."

I saw their eyes trained on mine, probing for weaknesses in my argument, each for different reasons, then I continued to pace and pulled back the zoom lens, just slightly.

"Imagine these headlines: French Company Accused of Transporting Jews to Auschwitz; Tiger Woods Alleged to Have Sex Addiction; Man Accused of Raping Wife. Where can we go from here, legitimately? These stories cannot be erased. They cannot be radically altered without some evidentiary *deus ex machina* proving innocence. Rightly or wrongly, the headlines have calcified into perceptions."

I noticed Alan shifting in his seat.

"So that is our reality check, our assessment, if you will. Now, where do we go? We first need to realize the press will say they want to get your story but will only want to entrap you into divulging any under-looked sensational aspects of the evening, to try and eke out a little fifteen minutes for themselves, get that raise, that new position, that spot on MSNBC." I received a few smirks.

"So—therefore," said Fung. I noticed she had a miniscule tattoo under her ear, possibly Chinese calligraphy.

"Therefore, what would you do to chase a virus out of computer software?"

"Write escape code. False data to migrate the virus out of the system."

"A trap door," Alan said.

"A trap door. And in the media this is essentially a kind of 'redirect'… we know the press chases the cheese, so to speak. So, we must give them something new to chase to switch out the headlines. This bad stuff might still be in the media, but our best hope is to push it down closer to the end of the stories, where no one reads it. Honestly, does anyone here even read past the third or fourth paragraphs anymore?"

"Not me," said Lars.

"Mark what are we thinking here?" said Alan. He stood, too, showing solidarity with my perspective.

"The idea of an op-ed piece is out of the question. Editors will only accept accounts of the evening, which I'm sure Jackson will overrule without debate."

"And you would be correct," Jackson said.

"Interviews are out." I was leading them to a cul-de-sac of ideas that I could control easily enough.

"Do you love each other?" I said, looking straight at Lars.

They both looked at me, partly bewildered and partly annoyed. Alan's expression remained unchanged.

A server slipped into the room and changed out the coffee service, and when he departed I repeated the question again, hoping the brinksmanship would compel them to forfeit themselves to whatever illogical logic would flow from here.

"How is this remotely relevant to you getting my IPO on track?" Fung said.

"What do investors want?" I said, noticing Alan getting a little squirmy at my third question in a row. "Clarity. Certainty. They looked at OneSpeak and there is such a flurry of commotion that it's hard to see into the nucleus of the company, see your talents and the business that you've built. Honestly, I'm not sure if I can make that commotion vanish, but maybe we can try and change the complexion of the noise, if you will. So, do you love each other?"

"Jesus!" she said and got up and stormed out of the room.

"I definitely love her but what is your question implying—or demanding?"

"Mark, maybe we should take five, reset, etc." Alan said.

"I think you should go and buy an engagement ring today."

Lars and Alan were frozen, as if the idea needed to sink in, slow motion, for them to understand it completely.

Fung kind of stormed back in. She had forgotten her purse. The stillness immediately affected her.

"Well, what happened?" she said.

Lars stood up to approach her. Alan went a little wide-eyed, ready for the first pitch of these playoffs.

"Fung," he said, taking her by the hands, "I do love you very much. I want to build this company with you, whatever we must do for it."

"Okay…," she said with some blasé.

He reached into his pocket and pulled out a mid-sized, silver Danish Kroner. Fung looked horrified; Alan seemed bemused, still popping almonds. It was almost too painful to watch.

"I want to make the ultimate commitment to you. Will you marry me?" He handed her the Kroner.

She stared at it, head bowed.

"How is taking this coin at all part of the P.R. plan, if there even is one, which I have barely heard today?"

"It's the coin of the realm of love," said Alan. "And Mark is right: an engagement will shake things up, reframe this from a perceived crime to clandestine love."

"I thought our plan was 'no penetration'?" she said flatly.

"And of course, she is still a virgin," Jackson said with his arms folded.

"Well, of course. Then you were and remain a 'virgin' for your future husband. It's plausible," I said.

"It's fucking pathetic," she said, and she threw the Kroner across the room and knocked over an almond dish and with American haste stormed out.

★

"I HAVE her tracked," Alan said, showing me a pulsing dot on his phone. "I've been having them tracked since the rape. An insurance policy, kind of." He stood up from the conference table and we walked together to the lobby.

I gave him a long gaze when he had said 'rape,' but he said it with such fluidity, nonchalance, even, that the word lost its sting.

Alan emphatically insisted he return to my hotel with me to "cobble the strategy." I did not know yet the full strategy without Fung. He had a sedan waiting. The nausea was gone but in its place was something else, an agitation and impatience.

"Where do they usually go?" I said.

"Stimulants, stimulants, and more stimulants. Right now, Gerald says she buying cigarettes. He'll keep us apprised. I'd like to eat something. Where are you staying?"

"Hotel Huntington."

"Just fantastic. Fantastic. Say, Mark, one thing I would like to mention, your recent troubles. I know it's presumptuous and out of line to mention it, I do. But I like you and everyone is entitled to a 'non-penetration' fuckup. Do you have good counsel?"

"Good counsel…," I hesitated because I realized I was involved with so many situations where good counsel might be needed. "I pay dozens of people prime money to do subprime work, if that is what you're implying."

"Precisely," he said, stepping over the curb. "Then you're in good hands." We were nearing Nob Hill and all its charming row houses. He laughed hard. I pretended to laugh but felt aggravated and my eye sockets ached.

The hotel was just ahead and the doorman recognized me and said my name. This seemed to impress Alan. We went to the restaurant. A waiter brought menus and waters with lemons and it seemed utterly ridiculous that, only an hour ago, we'd been trying to beat back a media wildfire for twenty-first-century tech scions, and now we were commiserating beneath color lithographs of nineteenth-century locomotives and wall sconces mounted on elk tusks.

"That's a Jeroboam of Cabernet. Over there on the ledge behind the leather booths."

I turned and saw the largest bottle of wine I had ever seen, a relic of Hawthorne.

"Not pretentious in its time, at its inception, nowadays a colossal pretension. We forget this is a country strung together on pretensions. We thrive on size and daring. Revolutionary War, Louisiana Purchase. Nuclear weapons. Hiroshima. Moon shots. The Internet, smartphones and all the other encoded trinkets we make out here."

He swatted his hand at the air.

"I write my boys, I tell them, there is nothing wrong with big things. There are ideas and there are Jeroboam ideas."

"You might like my idea then," I said.

The waiter came and we ordered house salads and *croque monsieurs*. Alan was staring across the room at the dark oak walls of the bar and the colossal portraits of the Big Four, the industrialists responsible for connecting the western frontier of the continent back to the buzzing cities of the east, fierce-looking men in three piece suits who styled their moustaches in the Prussian manner.

"My idea is to use Twitter—use it today—to break news of the engagement...beat the press," I said.

"So one tweet?"

"Many, many tweets. We write an essay, kind of, and crack it up into pieces and fling them out, one by one, like bits of a stained-glass window."

"Mark, it's a radical notion. Why not. Why not."

"I think I can have things reassembled by two in the afternoon Pacific time. And Mark, listen, think about better counsel," he said again, non-specifically, and I wondered if he had someone like Gerald following me. It was half past noon.

We said goodbye and I sat for a while in the bar drinking coffee.

I tried Hawthorne four, maybe five times before I left a voicemail. He was unresponsive to my texts, so I took a deep breath and called Wendy.

"It's me," I said.

"Hey me. We got your statement out. It's like a warzone. I've turned down ten print interviews today on your behalf already."

"Yes, well, that's what statements are for. Listen, I need your help on something. A statement, something quick. It's for OneSpeak."

There was a calculating pause on the line, as if she was formulating multiple potential responses.

"Is this for the IPO next week?"

"Yes, well, it's kind of for today, in about three hours—but related to the IPO."

"Mark—"

"Yes, I know, but can someone on your media team whip it up? I'm with Alan. Something pithy; it's for Twitter."

"Twitter? Twitter!"

"Twitter, yes."

"Mark, let's be serious, for a moment. Iran uses Twitter."

"So does Tom Brady."

"To smack-talk Roger Gooddell. This isn't the right medium. Why don't you just issue an *actual* statement? Or issue a short video statement. Maybe a press conference? Why does it have to be so complicated all the time?"

"Wendy, I appreciate your point of view, and you are a vital member of the company's leadership team," I said, trying to sound authoritative, "but it's what we have discussed out here and it's been a fucking long two weeks so please get one of your robo-boys or girls to SMS this to me or whatever they do and let's get it done in ninety minutes please."

"One other thing before you go."

I had been avoiding this for several months.

"So, listen, when the time is right, maybe next week, I want to sit down with you and understand where you are taking us, me, in particular, what my role is, my long-term, and how it impacts my bottom line."

The words kind of spilled out, flat, clearly rehearsed, but an awkward presentation once the lights shone bright.

"Wendy, I promise we will discuss it when I return. Promise."

When I hung up I ordered another coffee, sat for a while, feeling dizzy and suddenly depressed. I thought again about Colin's grades. I thought about the $250,000 I had just paid back to Skadden Arps. My stomach turned. He would be home soon. My withdrawal raged. I had a splitting headache, dizziness. I signaled the waiter, paid the bill and walked outside for air.

I walked for ten minutes down California Street past Old St. Mary's Cathedral, staring at the pavement, trying to stay calm and avert a migraine. I walked down Grant Avenue and saw the Dragon Gates and walked past windows with upside-down roasted ducks, noodle bars and tea shops, places that sold ornately painted bric-a-brac, and there was a man in shaggy clothes, malarial skin, dragging his long bow across the strings of his *erhu*, that lilting, off-key melody, and as I walked another block it competed with Cher's "Believe" coming from the alley.

Empty grace. I sweat, no nerves or heat, just a nervous lust for the drugs, the drugs, prescription drugs. I am only a nervous system. Nervous, only, I am…I thought I was smelling the roasted chestnuts and the monumental rain, church bells, forsythias, and she seemed sculpted from stone driving on the tallgrass peninsula and those Taliban faces in the taxis and Fanta bottles and irradiated peaches.

I stopped, almost fainting. Here in these streets I was reduced to mar-rowless anonymity, a body, no self.

I had ninety minutes to put my experiment into motion. First, I needed calm. I walked until I came upon a tea shop with a few Westerners at the bar. I ordered chamomile, hoping to anesthetize myself. Was there a cleanse for this type of situation?

The old woman sprinkled what looked like dried herbs into my cup, until it floated. She held up five fingers.

Five dollars? Five minutes? The hand stayed there until I nodded it away.

The Westerner beside me, college-aged, was eating something petite resembling marzipan. The old woman migrated to him to swipe his card on the insertable scanner for her iPhone. I reached for my wallet and it wasn't there; I'd left my wallet in the café. I felt panic radiate from my stomach into my limbs and face, heat rushing to the surface, more sweating, and when this raw panic mixed with my withdrawal symptoms, I felt a gastric rush and vomited on the floor, splattering my shoes and even my socks. I sat up at my stool, perspiring, some vomit on my chin. In the sudden hush, I could hear every judgmental thought in the room. I had no money. I was a body, no self, an idling American engine. I stood and ran out into the dense sidewalk crowds and tried to go back to where I'd heard the Cher music, to where the entrance to this place was, the Dragon Gates, Café de la Presse. Eighty minutes. My phone almost dead. I nearly tripped over a homeless man in a soiled Hillary Clinton t-shirt. I thought I knew where I was going and then I did see some ATMs and heard Western sounds and Western faces and it was as if they were waiting for me, the waiter holding the wallet above his head when I returned, visibly stricken at my radically altered appearance from just an hour ago. I tipped him.

"Thank you, thank you, thank you." I realized I was panting.

He handed me a glass of water and I drank it down, asked for another. "I need an outlet," I said, a little buoyant that I had found my wallet.

While the phone recharged, I made a mental list of all the mishaps that had gotten me to this point, a physical and mental wreck in a prominent tourist café in the heart of San Francisco.

I smelled the cheap cotton candy of Mimi's perfume, heard the street traffic through the open window.

Sixty minutes.

I thought that if this draft was being assembled professionally, at least capably, then I could quell my disarray by venturing back into Chinatown and find someone to perform acupuncture, anything to neutralize the withdrawal. I texted Wendy and she wrote back: "on track." I unplugged my phone, drank down a glass of ice water, and walked back into Chinatown to a place near where I had gotten sick. There was a street sign in English: "Traditional Chinese Medicines." I still felt the vulture presence of my anonymity. I climbed the stairs.

A narrow flight of carpeted stairs led up to the kind of door you see on the sides of warehouses. The street noise was dimmed. I heard high-pitched Chinese voices snapping Mandarin, perhaps Cantonese, a wailing Chinese infant somewhere on the third floor. I rang a bell and the door clicked opened.

A smallish bat-eyed woman with brown teeth rose from a chair, the strands of her hair had separated from each other, filled with static. She gestured me towards a makeshift treatment room, a bamboo plant on the table. I smelled marijuana. On a shelf on the wall hung dried herbs, stacked canisters filled with unpronounceable things, skinny vials of extracts, the paraphernalia she used to light little fires to spread over the body and extinguish more pain.

Would something she concocted to drink finally do it? Or her hands, hot with fire, or the tiny glass cups from the cardboard box used for suction? There were so many potential palliatives it was hard to register them all.

Her English was threadbare.

I saw myself in this scene as if from above: He spoke slowly, first in plain English, pointed at things, his neck, but she was squinting and reverted to pidgin English and he explained his medications and he went more slowly, repeating himself with body language too, moving his hands in a circular motion around his head and slumping his shoulders. She did not appear to understand anything but he sensed that she knew he wanted help. He did not have the language to clarify anything and wondered how in any language you could describe the locus of a pain that was total and comprehensive and near permanent.

She motioned him to the table and told him to remove his shoes, socks, and shirt. He thought then, at that moment, of his son three thousand miles across the country, in school, maybe in another kind of pain. He was facedown on the table, staring at cigarette burns on the carpet. The marijuana smell was everywhere. From the corner of his eye, to the right, were glass pots with smoke burns on the rims stacked in a cardboard box. Little needles entered the fat of his back, neck, earlobes.

Her hands came back to his neck. He felt her discover the pain very quickly, pressing her thumbs into it.

She tore open a package and, then, he felt a slight pinch of the needle in his skin, the tapping of her nail against the head to drive it deeper into the surface to reach the pain. All the needles were in his neck. She kept asking if it hurt. He lay motionless while she ran her palms across his back, probing with her thumbs up and down his spine.

After a few minutes, she withdrew the needles from his neck. She returned her thumb to the places where there had been pain, and now he was reporting that there was no pain anymore in those places.

He flipped over. The fluorescent light stung his eyes. He closed them while she ran her hands over his chest, legs, and arms in examination.

She sensed something and reported that he should no longer consume spicy foods.

"Too, too hawt! No balance. Cold here, but hot here." Her hands made a kind of seesaw motion. "You need make hot less and get the balance."

He nodded.

Heavy footsteps in the hall and then the doorbell rang. She left him there to open the door. It was the next appointment. She reentered the room and pushed against his stomach in such a way that he became aware of his organs. She was smiling now, kind of giggling, and she told him not to take any more medicines, that it was very bad for him, very bad, and "no think, think too much!" play-slapping his skull in admonition as a mother would scold her grown child.

I put on my shirt, paid the sixty dollars, the next appointment already there, waiting by the half-dead fern. The infant on the third floor was still wailing.

I walked down the stairs, neutralized, into the daylight, moderately worried about OneSpeak. I turned on my phone: it lit up—twelve texts, eight voicemails, dozens of emails, everyone connected to the OneSpeak endeavor searching for me.

Fifteen minutes.

Stepping over oozing garbage bags on the sidewalk, passing the upside-down ducks in the windows, it occurred to me I was worse than absentee. There was another name for it, one I did not want to confront. It lay bare before me, undisguised. I would not name it. I felt a fear I had not felt since her death, glacial and ash, whatever came before the very end. I understood it now, what a man would do to himself when the options were stricken from his map, the detours invisible or missing altogether. Where were my angels on the banks?

I felt soft raindrops.

Where are you, where are you? Where are you, daddy? Colin was texting.

I forced myself to return to the hotel, guardedly said hello to the door-man, who did a double take, and raced to my room, less than ten minutes, fired up the laptop and looked for the most recent email from Wendy, which said she had given this "experiment" to my beloved Joel James, and then opened the most recent email from him and clicked on the attachment, the "edgy and monumental" Twitter statement he'd drafted:

We would like to acknowledge that recent events have brought unwarranted scrutiny. #onespeak #onevoice

We would like to tell the world what we know. #onespeak #onevoice

In one voice, all at once. #onespeak #onevoice

I, Lars, greatly respect and admire Fung, as a woman, a coder and a companion. #onespeak #onevoice

I, Fung, greatly respect Lars for the same reasons. #onespeak #onevoice

We have broken no laws, only the one that says you should never fall in love with your business partner. #onespeak #onevoice

We are happy to announce, today, that we are officially engaged. [photo] #onespeak #onevoice

We are continuing to preserve ourselves for our wedding night. #onespeak #onevoice

In the meantime, we are fine-tuning OneSpeak for its IPO next week. #onespeak #onevoice

We are also proceeding with our wedding plans, set for some time next year. #onespeak #onevoice

Thanks and Appreciate, Lars and Fung #onespeak #onevoice

When I was done reading it, I felt sick again.

Alan texted from downstairs in the bar. I changed my shirt and combed my hair, gargled until I was presentable, and raced downstairs, taking the stairwell.

In the bar, Alan had a table set up, more lemon waters and some olives in a dish.

It was two o'clock in the afternoon, Pacific time, well past the East Coast media filing deadlines.

"Just in time. A little last-minute fine tuning?" he said. His tie was off.

"Sorry I am late."

"Not late at all, two minutes to spare. Please sit down, you look drained, completely drained, I know these things must be tough to pull off with so little notice."

"So are they engaged? Officially?" I tried not to pant.

"Officially enough."

"So you're okay with this statement?"

"Well, obviously I've not read anything, Mark, but that's not the point here. We are derisking an investment, thanks to you. Anyway, Lars is in love, maybe not Fung, but one is all it takes to make a wedding happen."

I read it again on my phone. The statement was a bad goulash of clichés, sentimentality, and rushed, artless, cymbal crash pathos. I was glad Alan had not seen it, and I wondered if I should disclose that I was not its author, that I abhorred the statement altogether, maybe only conceived of it due to my mental state. But such disclosures would be worse than whatever I was concealing with my nondisclosure. I was checkmated from all sides.

"Bollinger, two glasses," Alan shouted to the barman, who nodded without hesitation.

I logged in, typed in the passwords to OneSpeak's account, and cut and pasted the lines on the status window, hitting send, one by one.

We waited for about thirty seconds.

As the lines of the statement, seven tweets in all, issued from my laptop, Alan was hovering over my shoulder, chewing an olive.

A blinking screed, empty declarations hollered into the cacophonous Web. Mere seconds passed in that silence, when these were just expiring, senseless tweets, like all others.

Alan paced while nothing happened. Then, the audience numbers began to climb too steeply. I knew what was happening when the retweets started to accumulate too fast to count. More and more likes and retweets and quoted tweets, some unabashedly angry, others parodistic, more retweets and likes and I watched the counter jump until we hit five thousand retweets, then twenty thousand until we were officially trending, nationally, but not in a good way.

"They're laughing at us; they are deriding the statement. It's a hoax. Mark, this was a failed scheme."

"These things fluctuate," I said a little too effortlessly. He looked at me suspiciously.

"Turn this off, recant the tweets and forget it, Mark."

"This is permanent. Irrevocable."

"Turn it off, Mark. Remove the tweets!"

"It's permanent, Alan!" I was shouting as if through airborne turbulence.

We were at fifty thousand retweets and the latest, by a prominent *New York Times* columnist read, *what to do when your PR guy falls asleep at the twitters......*

"My oh fucking my. This was a failed scheme. You've blown it."

Alan set down his wine glass so harshly that he cracked the stem. He withdrew from me some, still close enough to monitor my screen.

Sixty thousand retweets.

By now Fung was a meme; she was Photoshopped as a mail-order Chinese wife, on all fours wearing a dog collar, a Scandinavian brute trailing behind her, both headed to an altar in an Ewok forest with condoms hanging from branches.

I felt my heart racing, the perspiration returning. I was irrevocably a leper, to him and possibly to many more. *You've absolutely blown this, Mark.* My phone was ringing and so was his, a commotion of anxiety radiating from our little table to the guests around us, who were staring blatantly.

The waiter emerged from the galley behind the bar, two glasses of champagne on his tray. He waded into our orbit, then wisely retreated.

chapter six

A SUDDEN, heavy fog delayed my six-thirty flight to Washington to nine o'clock that night. I didn't walk into the house until half past seven the next morning, and Colin was waiting for me, dressed for school in mismatched socks.

"I missed you buddy!" I knelt and held out my arms.

He ran to me for a hug. Mae was at the stove and didn't look up.

"Any presents?"

"Here," I said, handing him an Alcatraz keychain I bought at NEWSWORLD in Terminal B. He dangled it like a chemical specimen. "Cool."

I noticed a crusty rash around his mouth, maybe impetigo, and his hair was growing over his ears.

"Mae, what is this?" I said, turning his head towards her with my hands on his chin to steer his head.

She was stirring something on the stove with a towel over her shoulder and didn't turn around.

"We noticed this yesterday. I made an appointment for him for today. Vaseline didn't work good."

"Very good. Great. I can take him. Text me where and when please. Colin, can we discuss your report card? I had a chance to see it. Have you?"

He looked away but Mae stopped and turned.

His head dropped and he started to play with his grits with his spoon.

"How did you see already? It's in my backpack still."

"The teacher emailed it. I saw it. All of it. Colin?"

He was pouring the grits from his spoon back onto the rim of the bowl and it was dripping down the edges. He was making that face.

"I just...it's...I can't do my homework good and then I don't know it, my work, when I do the tests I do bad. Are you mad at me, daddy?"

He had tears running down both cheeks. Mae came over to him and he put his head into her stomach and wept. She would not look at me. I said, "I will go and see your teacher and learn how I can help you better, okay?"

"You aren't mad at me?"

"I'm disappointed but I am not mad."

"Does this mean I'm stupid?"

"What? What!" I walked over to him and rubbed his back as he cried into Mae. "Stupid, of course not, Colin! Hell no. Hell no. Don't say that. Don't speak like that."

"Well, the other kids said so."

"Who?"

He looked up. His cheeks were the same color now as his rash. "Billy. And Marcus. And Gregg."

"You showed them your report card?"

"At recess."

"Why did you do that?"

"They gave him a name," Mae said, looking at me. She stood up and he gradually pulled away.

"Super D. They call me Super D."

"We are not calling you that. They are not calling you that. You hear me? Hey, listen, look up, you hear me? You are smart, very smart. Who is your teacher, what's her name again?"

"Ms. Duncan."

"I am going to see Ms. Duncan today. And we'll talk about ways to improve your grades tonight. Now, let me have that report card so I can take it with me."

He brought his backpack to the table and opened it. He reached inside and started pulling out papers, crumpled and torn, some shoved inside folders and some not. In between sheets was a worn photograph of us both on horseback from two years ago.

"Colin, is this how you keep your bag?"

His head lowered towards the grits.

I didn't want to make him cry again; I didn't want to force him to reorganize himself. I knew already, even stuck in my own condition and circumstances.

"Hey, look up, look up at me, Colin. Daddy will fix this for you, okay? Daddy can fix this." As I said it, I thought it sounded too much like a question. Mae left the room. He gave an abbreviated smile.

"Okay," he said, and he reached to me for a hug.

He kicked at the piles of leaves as we walked downhill, the eight hundred or so yard trip to school. I walked him inside the school to his classroom and signaled to the teacher. Ms. Duncan came into the hallway.

"Mr. White, thank you so much for coming in. We had called and emailed. I saw this coming, but it seems like this is where Colin ended up for the semester."

I didn't remember any calls or emails but I knew what that really meant.

"Does he need a tutor? He's not a stupid boy; you know that's what they're calling him at recess."

"Who is?" She was squinting.

"Some boys. Billy, he said and some others. Super D."

"Alright I can watch for that. I will take care of that, Mr. White, but, listen—and I must run back in shortly—Colin needs your help. I think a tutor is a good start, but he seems very distracted, very out of sorts. Now I don't know exactly what's gone on at home. I know about his mom. Maybe there are some issues there, Mr. White. The school has an excellent counselor he can speak to."

I was feeling fatigued from my flight and the episode at breakfast. There was no energy to quarrel. I buttoned my jacket and stuck out my hand.

"Ms. Duncan, you are a good teacher. I will take everything you said under advisement."

She cupped my hands in hers and emitted a pained expression that made it seem she'd cry if only she were allowed.

"He's a sweet boy, Mr. White. Such a sweet, loving boy."

I drove the parkway in silence. We hear ourselves all too well in the quiet of a car. Monica's voice was still there. I couldn't stand it, so I turned on the local FM radio and they were talking about an approaching freak winter storm, to hit by week's end. Did we have provisions? Would school be cancelled? Good, I thought. Good time to close the office. Good time for people to forget about me falling asleep on cable news and trying to help a couple reckless tech titans rehabilitate themselves. I left a message with Dr. Weller, hoping to see him today.

I tried Harry but got his voicemail.

The office called five times. I let it all go to voicemail.

Mae texted: *four o'clock today, Dr. Reginald, you take him please thanks.*

Late in the morning traffic was light and I took K Street, the spine of the city, past McPherson Square and the St. Regis and into Chinatown. It was windy and some of the newspaper machines had tipped over and there were fast-moving clouds against the face of the slate sky. Pedestrians walked behind their iPhones.

I pulled into my garage and the attendant, a cherub-faced Ethiopian, gave a wave from his booth and I descended the ramp to my reserved spot and just sat there idling, many minutes, petrified to enter my own office, the stares and whispers and all the microclimate brusqueness among my executives, vying for privilege and my favor. Now, what would they say? And Colin, that poor boy, that sweet, loving boy, he did not deserve this. Iron sharpens iron. What if he is not iron and he breaks?

I sat there in the stale yellow light of the parking garage for nearly ten minutes, engine running. The attendant knocked on the window to check on me and I pretended to be on a conference call. He smiled and backed away. I devised a plan for how to behave inside the office, found some Altoids in the glove compartment, and guzzled the rest of the tepid bottled water in the car.

I walked up the ramp instead of riding the elevator. The wind lifted my tie. It smelled like a storm, all that flinty cold in the nose.

I had my plan for entry, but I wasn't ready just yet to reemerge as... Mark White, Chairman and CEO. I took the long way, looping around the building, passing the hypodermic park the city was redesigning for the residents of the luxury condos a block away. I walked down to City Center, where the winter window displays seemed painfully misaligned with the current season, and I thought about trying a new coffee shop, one with high stools and a tiled floor, lots of light, but I decided to walk back to

Chinatown Coffee where it was cast iron dark and musty and they would start my cortado the moment I entered.

I heard the church bells ring across the street eleven times as I arrived, smelling the roasted Arabica from outside the door. If it tolled six times, it might have been us splitting the bed at the hostel near the Ponte Vecchio in Florence. Seven times we would have been at the cava bar at the foot of the Catedral de Santa Maria del Mar in Barcelona. Then I felt a deep guilt: How many bell tolls would it take for me to be home with Colin?

We are never where we are.

I drank down the cortado and walked back towards the office. Along the way, I decided to enter the CVS; I walked to the school supplies aisle and started to grab anything I thought a third grader might use and put it in the basket: folders, staple remover, yellow highlighters, felt pens, tape, sticky notes, and a binder. There were some kids' Spiderman sunglasses at the checkout and I bought those too, along with a pack of sugarless gum. At the last minute, I grabbed the matching backpack that went with it.

I stood outside my building and looked up, going over my plan of reentry. Ride the elevator and fake a jovial phone conversation. Walk onto my floor, laugh a lot. Mosey my way towards my office. Strike upbeat tones as I swung the CVS bag, waving and smiling to various employees while in imaginary phone conversation. Generally, appear sublimely unaffected by recent distress. I took two pills for just in case my mood changed.

They would never know I was walking in so late because my eight-year-old son with mixed mood disorder was nearly flunking out of public school. Margaret came by and took all the CVS bags and stashed them at her cubicle beside her purse.

"Maybe some tea?"

"That would be lovely, Margaret. Oh, and I must take Colin to the doctor's at four. Sally?"

"She's been looking for you." Her expression was politely professional; I couldn't tell if she was angry with me, chagrined, or genuinely trying to give me comfort by showing no emotion.

She came back with the chamomile tea and reached across and patted my hand, not looking at me, and left, closing the door behind her.

There was a knock and Sally came in.

"So," I said.

She started to cry, her own condition seeming to worsen as she did.

"Mark people...are calling me...they...think you are crazy now...or something...and this reporter is calling staff...and we just wired that money to Skadden...like you asked...and I am worried, Mark, very worried that you're in some trouble you're not telling me."

She reached across and took a tissue I handed her.

"Sally, shhh, Sally. Please. Look at me, Sally. We are all fine. Lots of operating capital. Lots of clients."

"I know but they're making fun of you now." She covered her mouth as if she had blasphemed.

"Saying what?"

"Calling you a P.R. junkie. Someone wrote it in the bathroom, the men's room, and Hawthorne and I have heard staff talking and laughing."

"You know I'm not a junkie."

"I know that."

"You know I was just tired, busy week, went straight to bed."

"Yes."

"So then?"

"Excuse me?"

"So, then, what the hell do we care what some kids say. They'll complain all the same."

"Mark it's more than the kids, it's pretty much all the executives as well. And they know you've been seeing Harry. So they're scared."

"How the fuck do they know these things!" I realized I had stood up and Sally leaned back as if I was going to bark at her again.

"I'm sorry. Very sorry. It's not you. I found out Colin is flunking school today."

"Oh, Mark!" She started to make the same face as Ms. Duncan.

I told her I was leaving at four because he probably had impetigo.

"Mark, you're carrying too much, too much. Monica would have said so, too. Tell me how I can help you and it's done."

I thought she was over the line but I let it go. She closed the door on the way out and I grabbed the tea and sloshed it onto the saucer cup; my hand was tremoring.

She was probably right that it was all too much. I'd be leaving the office early, for my boy, so fuck you all. They would never know they were employed because of Colin, that Monica told me she was pregnant, and I determined, right then and there, that I wanted to launch this business.

We were vacationing at the Auberge du Soleil for our anniversary, an enclave midway up Rutherford Hill with an Aix-en-Provence vibe, a sweeping vista of the valley.

"You don't have to throw touchdowns, Mark, not every time. I'm happy where we are."

She sank into the warm infinity plunge pool and then swam up to the ledge and looked at the Napa Valley.

"You were never poor. You had everything." I saw up alongside her. We were shielded from view of the spa area by some enormous azaleas and perfect, bushy yellow roses.

"Except a father."

"Both of our fathers should have shot each other in a dual at Augusta."

She pinched me and smiled. "Your son will need a father, better than ours."

"Monica, I make $65,000 per year. You sold four paintings last year. College will cost our entire household income. How will we live?"

"There is a massive inheritance sitting in the bank. Not everyone decides to start a business just to swell their manhood. You cannot stage your life this way, to please everyone else. A business is a burden. I saw it happen to my father. I saw whatever I saw of him, whatever was left over. Don't you think it might be this way for you? Why do you think you're different, Mark? Men with power must forfeit something. We have money now. I know it's my father's but it's ours."

We held each other in the water and breathed the sulfurous air of the soil down below, where cabernet grapes had been planted on the slope by the hotel to make the house wine. It was her father's money alright, and I was enjoying spending it.

The pool was even more spectacular, up the hill by the main house, and the deck was sand-colored limestone and all the sitting areas were partially canopied in Moroccan red fabric, a row of white oleander trees separating the pool deck from an upper level of chaise lounges near the bar.

That morning, so early in the day, there was no one, except for an old man wrapped in towels, sweating and sleeping in the sun, and some middle-aged man from the East Coast, on his third espresso, barking into his cell on the balcony facing the valley, hairy chest and caramel tan.

I took a lounge chair beneath the oleander trees facing the view and began to read *The Beast in the Jungle*. Édith Piaf sang out of speakers hidden in the blooming trees. A Mexican gardener tended obscure, silvery herbs in terra cotta pots, looking often at me.

We got out, rinsed off, dressed, and walked uphill to the pool and ordered Aperol spritzes. An elderly man lowered himself into the water like he was getting into a saddle, and he began to swim laps, kind of crawling across the pool, in slow motion, trying to defy his age, at war with the water. The sound was soupy. It interfered with the lyrical views of the valley.

"You are too judgmental," she said, laughing. She pressed her cold glass against my skin and it hit me like a shock.

"I am just being observant. Why is he even swimming? He is barely moving."

"At least he's moving," and I knew she was encouraging me to use the outdoor gym.

"It sounds like death stirring."

She was laughing hard now. Reaching my fingertips into the lemon water on the table I flicked some of it at her and she giggled and squealed at the sudden cold.

"I am sharing an opinion. If no one ever did that there would be no books." I regretted saying that, so I tried to divert: "So what do you think of my big plan?"

"I think it's big and nothing else. But if you must, you must. You know I could care less about the money. Just only use half of it and keep the rest for Colin."

Later that day, we made a trip to a vineyard she had carefully chosen. We took a road full of switchback turns up the mountain. We passed vineyards with "For Sale" signs and white and yellow farmhouses with porches seemingly plucked from *The Wizard of Oz*.

It was a dry, dusty day and the sun hung high over the valley. We pulled into the winery; there was a Tuscan-style farmhouse that now served as a tasting room. Cows grazed in the fields. Higher up, the vines were perfectly combed in rows across the hill, running up to the fog line where the grade was too steep to plant anything. A beat-up terrier roamed the gravel lot.

We did a vertical tasting of the '08s and '09s, years which, the vintner told us, someone preeminent had written, were *magnificent* but still needed to shed their "baby fat."

By the time we returned to the pool that afternoon, the place had become overrun with East Coast couples, an American mess of noise. Everyone seemed to be in a flux of unmade plans, smoking. A man with a crustacean sunburn relayed questions for a deposition over the phone at the edge of the pool; his wife badly dyed strawberry blonde hair. There was a couple from New Jersey telling people that they were from New Jersey; she was topless and he looked like a Catholic who skipped confession.

There was clatter coming from the main house above where there was a wedding, Koreans, I think, wearing tuxedos in the full September heat, nearly ninety-eight degrees by three o'clock, so hot that some winemakers had decided to pick their grapes early, that very day, we were told, lest the heat unleash the tannins past the point of no return.

I sat again among the oleander trees, facing south, gazing into the year's vintage still bonded to the earth. The sky was pale and a breeze shook the umbrellas beside the lounge chairs. The waiters were polite Hispanics who looked slightly bewildered at their surroundings. Little boxwoods were pruned like Christmas trees and under-planted with variegated English ivy that spilled down the sides of the pots. The plants by the pool were dark green and lush as if they had never missed a day of watering, thriving in the unrelenting California sun that could doom the vintage within an hour if a winemaker was not careful.

Someone within earshot began to carry on about vacations in northern Italian towns or wherever it was where you could drink Barbera d'Alba.

"Let's go," I said, kissing Monica on the cheek, leading her back to our room. I flung open the doors to let in the light from the valley as we undressed. Afterwards, while she slept, I logged on and wired $2 million to the new Bank of America account, set up under the name of White & Partners.

★

DR. WELLER called, sounding concerned, and urged me to come in before lunch.

I crossed town and was on his couch within thirty minutes.

After I explained all that had happened, he rested his hands on his Buddha belly, and wiping his glasses with his sweater, proceeded to ask me what I thought had happened, starting with Mimi.

I considered lying, but I was honestly tired of lying, to him, to myself, whoever else confronted me about plans, preoccupations, the level of the office music, the provenance of the art on the walls, the equity structure of my company. Harry Golucci thought I was a liar, I was sure of it. He didn't care because I had him on retainer, I said.

"This is how you evade yourself, Mark" he said, "you deviate from direct inquiry, you loop off, you entertain, but it's a deviation—from yourself primarily."

What a gut-punch thing to say. For a moment I wondered if I should try and cry, summon a high-caliber breakdown, right there in his presence; it occurred to me more than once that I was perhaps being discounted as a serious patient because my non-breakdown history, even though I came to see him right after Monica. But I wasn't sure I could cry, let alone commit to a full-fledged emotional catharsis on this dismal couch with coffee stains and a decade of other patients' tears soaked into the cushions.

I took a sip from my water bottle and switched my phone to mute.

"My college roommate, this one night, before Monica, he came in crying, right there, first week of school, like I wasn't even there. His father had been fired. He wasn't even sure if he could stay in school," I said, sitting up to show that this was not another looping evasion.

"He told me about what it was like, helping his father pack up his office. He told me the worst part was pulling all the pins from this map hung on the wall, seeing all the pushpin holes in all the places his father had been, and then rolling that map up, as if it was the end of his father's world. Professionally speaking it was—he was sixty-four. You know, honestly, I see those pushpin holes in that map all the time."

"Or maybe you're worried you won't push the pins back in the places you have been. What happened to him?"

"My roommate? Father had to sell their house. He stayed in school. Married up. Works in New York. I saw Vic two days ago."

"You are too angry with yourself, Mark. We all wage these little wars against ourselves. You're waging your own without even knowing it."

"I ask myself all the time: Am I pushing the pins in or pulling them out?"

"It's always a question of perspective. What is right for an individual at a given moment in time? You have a son, a business, how much more carousing can you keep doing, Mark?" He said that word, *carousing*, too menacingly, and I looked away to his wall of cheap tribal masks.

"I'm tired. I see holes in the map, my life, and I don't have the energy lately to try harder. I'm honestly considering selling my business, but I can't."

I said it all in the most unadorned fashion, hoping the directness would bring him back into my camp.

"You've reached out to Harry again?"

"Yes, but he says that 'recent events' make a sale challenging."

"Now or ever?"

I looked up at him and thought I detected some sympathy; his eyes were exploring every micro-movement of mine. They were glassy and wet-look-ing, some undisclosed geriatric condition, lower right lid pink and inflamed. I imagined him administering drops after his shower, feeling sick when he woke, not feeling well enough to come into this attic office in Georgetown, climb the thirty or so stairs to withstand hours of free association from divorcees, violent couples, schizophrenics, alcoholics, the bipolars, and the abject depressed. I hadn't noticed his core humanity; it was an oversight I likely had committed with Margaret, maybe Sally, others too, including myself and Colin. These were people rooting for me, even Harry.

"I assume he means ever."

"And you've exhausted all your options?"

"Not really, but I am frankly too exhausted to try."

"How much sleep?"

"Some."

"Drinking?"

"Lots. Every day, all day."

"And smoking?"

"Occasionally."

"Colin?"

"He had impetigo. And he is flunking out of school."

"Since?"

"Yesterday."

He paused and appraised me, physically.

"Are you adhering to the regimen?" That was his phrase for the cocktail of pills.

"Mostly, yeah, I would say ninety percent of the time, eighty percent maybe, no ninety, ninety-five, actually."

"Well it isn't working well, that I can tell. None of it. And we need to introduce some mechanistic interventions."

"What?"

"Things to keep you productive, things that override your resting anxiety."

"And Colin?"

"When you are well, he'll be well. Let me ask you, how many coffees per day?"

I paused. "Espresso drinker. Six, maybe eight. So no changes to his meds?"

"A mechanistic intervention is me telling you no espressos after three in the afternoon—and only three per day. When you are well, he'll be well."

"Booze?"

"I'd like to see a moratorium. Thirty days."

"And so then sex, and drugs, and rock and roll?"

"Frankly, I'd like to see you having some sex."

"Hookers?"

"Preferably consensually."

"And a vacation?"

"I don't see that as possible right now."

"Everything is impossible until we determine it's important. Take Colin to Hawaii. Go to Aruba. Go somewhere, Mark."

Now I sighed, stared out the window behind him at the Apple store nearby on Wisconsin Avenue. There was a line snaking down the street, waiting for something new. I heard Monica again but did not disclose those to Dr. Weller.

"I am only secure in my own fantasies. That's the part that hurts. I know these fantasies cannot be real."

I was shifting in my seat, trying not to make eye contact, trying on expressions with my lips. He had a Bloomingdale's bag full of psychiatric drug samples in a corner behind the La-Z-Boy. Maybe some of these would silence the voice in my head, shut the door on the whispers forever. I was loath to give him more ammunition against me; I wanted to continue, more adherence, more focus, more sessions, but no drastic changes.

"That's a very thin line, what's realistic, what's fantasy—and there exists the possibility that what is perceived as fantasy is actually something we can obtain through our own perseveration and imagination. But for now, I would like to try a new medication, to help stabilize you. I want you to taper off the other pills, eventually all the way, but for now cut the dose in half this week and call me and we'll see about running them down to zero by week three. I would encourage you to avoid making grand business plans, just let your psyche recover."

"Nothing for Colin?"

"It's a new product. You take this once a day, along with your other medications—for now." He had leaned across and handed me a prescription. "I'll wager that this medication can get you well, Mark, and that is the most important medication for Colin. I think it will help, too, with the racing thoughts, calm you, quell anxiety. Mark, these past few years, for you, have been an ordeal, to say the least. Let yourself acclimate, Mark. There are no pushpins anymore, not at your age."

He paused and waited for me, then said, "We try it and see. We talk again in a few days, you have my cell and will text with anything. We are our chemistry, Mark, pure and simple. We can make corrections. We can make progress here, Mark. But you have to buy in."

We agreed on another appointment a week from now. When I was outside, the line outside the Apple store had fattened into a crowd, even people in fancy tents and drinking steaming coffee from canteens, presumably there from the night before. I heard a girl in a pink winter coat asked her father if she was getting the pink iPhone.

I walked for a few minutes, leaving the crowd behind. I thought I needed a sanitarium, a month or so in the Hotel Savoie in the Alps, like T.S. Eliot. This would do me right, for sure, or if I could get a fat check and walk away from this business that was strapped to my left leg like a special-needs child, that would be better. I knew my cards were dealt, however, and I had no energy to try and find and play new ones. I figured that if the status quo of my life prevailed I was going to deteriorate unpleasantly in a cold climate with a finite stockpile of cash and gold. My son was just an accent on my schedule. The time I had to give him was subdivided from time spent on mammoth endeavors that my warped, fragile psyche could barely endure anymore. This is why some men buy guns, I thought. I got new pills instead. Colin got chocolate pancakes and hockey sticks and carpool rides and occasional spaghetti dinners with dad.

I got in the car and knew that Monica had been right all along.

I thought of those fall mornings in Madrid walking to the cabs for the bureau, planning to author something, something incandescent, thinking I would always have open fields of time. Your first real happiness you will always believe is unlimited. There was not one pinion of obligation in the world fastening my life to anything.

I pulled over and dredged up one of David Foster Wallace's many commencement speeches from YouTube, put it on, and started driving again.

I listened to that voice of his, satin quiet, some restrained vigor, all the pulp of his mind in that calm manner, a pitch approximating serenity. You could forget who it was and confuse him with a holy man. Hearing him talk about "American life" and "why I got rid of my TV" with such humor, it was hard to believe he was riddled with such pain, the kind the medicines couldn't touch.

I drove in stop-and-go traffic, Foster Wallace bringing me company.

"Humanity is slow motion merging with machines. Science is able to reengineer people. Soon we won't have to even drive cars, for whatever reason. Designer babies riding solo in driverless cars so their mothers can work. The father isn't even working; he's hatching profits on the market, shorting things and buying puts, essentially legalized, upscale gambling. We call all this democracy; we call all this capitalism. And now we publish our feelings minute to minute, epic cultural solipsism. I hate writing in public, the pretense of it, some Starbucks bohemian dashing off curdled doggerel to an ex, a manqué huddling over his notebook in the center of the café in Harvard Square. Good writing is hard work, not spectacle; writers require solitude, time, and great concentration, and I just cannot imagine that any real work, any good work, gets done over the sound off the milk steamer, the swoosh of traffic in the public square. Who's to blame anyway for this Left Bank conceit that great thought arose from smoky cafés over endless coffees and *fine à l'eau* on rainy days—Hemingway, Baudelaire, Rimbaud, Sartre? When the aliens eventually invade, they will most definitely turn away and rush home, scared off by the self-centeredness, the skinny jeans, the colonies of Me in every town. Maybe they won't come. Our signals cascade into space in perpetuity, maybe they know us this way already. Maybe we know each other too well and the narcissism is a kind of protective enamel. Self-love is harder than self-loathing. But we are obsessed with happiness and we are the unhappiest people maybe on this planet, perhaps ever. We assign ourselves the right to it in our constitution. Yet, rich as we are, we swallow the most antidepressants of anyone on the planet, we reek of unhappiness and whine when we don't have it, you know some cultures don't even have this word. It's not even a concept. You are however you feel. No words to describe it."

I looked down at my iPhone, and it was a close up shot of him, sipping a can of soda. He paused for too long; I raised my gaze back to the road and heard him pivot, saying, "the American Dream. I read the other day—read is not the right word—I saw a headline on a screen, somewhere in Times Square, it said that Bank of American analysts think there's a reasonable chance we live in a matrix world controlled by artificial intelligence. Completely unprovable, I guess completely possible but if that's true then what? This story spanned across the big screen for less than ten seconds, and I have been studying this possibility for several weeks. Elon Musk is a proponent of the theory. Why would he not be? It supports his hypothesis, I guess, that he's special, the chosen vessel for so much innovation. But what is a driverless car, an advancement or a senseless luxury? Most luxury is senseless, I suppose. But I don't think we live in a matrix. The world reeks of imperfection and suffering. Seems those things would be the first to go in a rebooted future. And they are worsening, worsening. And these technologies are not designed to help anyone outside the middle and upper classes but really aimed at augmenting their lifestyles, improving this existence, aid towards that elusive happiness. There's no money in mobile air conditioning in Africa. I've often felt the equatorial nations might boost economic output quickest through air conditioning. And all these poor people have cell phones, some more than one. We are dangerously over-reliant on various modes of communication, and the result is that we communicate less and that people have more information but much less knowledge. I met a man last week who declared he was moving east. Can you believe that? No one utters those words, moving east, with any pleasure anymore. East has always connoted a retrograde version of the world. The wagons rolled west, the steamships rolled west, the gold rush, the Titanic, railroads, all the world's tailspin energy of the last 150 years has been in a westerly direction. The only symbol I know for my experiment is that silly Christopher Columbus statue in Barcelona, where he's pointing east to Mallorca, entirely by accident, but it's always struck me as some sort of prescient defiance by the city planners. So, in my next life, I am headed inexorably east, all the way to Goa. I don't pretend to not want a sort of spiritual catharsis to play out. Mind you I have been a devout Christian my entire life. But there is something missing. I need space—vast, clean, beautiful space—to sit and to think and to breathe and I imagine there is a perfect spiritual center, a kind of community center, where you teach English reading and writing to the children, and there I can sort of rehabilitate my senses entirely, retreat, give up, transcend the culture cloud that seems to trail me everywhere I go. I know what you are thinking: you would move east to teach poor little Indian kids English so they can move west and become CEOs of their tech startups in San Francisco? This is the ultimate conundrum, Mark. America is the only game in town, and the game inside that game is money, money and power and technology. I view it this way, maybe some of those kids vacuum up what I teach and then they shove off for our shores and the story plays out, one more curly-cue circle of history, or maybe one of these kids is special, breaks the cycle, heads for our shores but does something with the power and money and knowledge that truly helps the world. That is my dream."

*

I RODE the elevator to my floor numb through a haze of high-wattage stares near the bathrooms and then it cleared to a partial calm by the senior executive offices until I saw Hawthorne half-jogging towards me.

"Mark!" He was panting. "We've caught wind of a story."

He followed me into my office. I saw Wendy and Hank standing and watching down the hall.

"What does this mean?"

"It's about you, I'm afraid."

"What for falling asleep on cable? Whatever."

"Mark it's sounding very much like an expansive and detailed, sources say, kind of hit piece, and we should take this very seriously. Very seriously. It's a decapitation strike, Mark."

"Christ, Hawthorne you sound totally paranoid. We get written about all the time."

"Mark this story is all about you. You only. Just you."

He said the last part with a bit of relish that gave me pause. My hand started to tremor again and I put it in my pocket. By the time Hanna called my cell, I was clear that she was writing a massive hit piece on me. Occasionally, such articles could carry a luster and catapult a subject into micro-stardom, the ordeal, in the end, a twisted blessing. But I was too well-known. We would trade skirmish for scandal. While I was quiet with my money, I had failed to keep my legend in the garage, which, in Washington, was the golden rule of keeping your fame intact in the first place. Now, the stories about me and White & Partners roamed the open field; she had a clear shot and she would be taking it, so good for her, I thought. *Maybe she'll crack my ribs. Maybe she'll hit an organ.*

Hawthorne said he had some impromptu thing at the Ecuadorian Embassy. Sally went into her office and closed the door. There were younger professional staff racing up and down the halls.

I went into my office, closed the door, wiped my brow, and exhaled. I sat down on my empty couch. I took an extra pill, hearing Dr. Weller's phantom admonishment. I scanned my email and saw one from Alan.

Dear Mr. White,

This letter is to inform you that Long Bridge Management is terminating your engagement, retroactive to the beginning date of the contract. Your failure to abide by the terms of the contract and provide material counsel and advisory services to us and our investment, OneSpeak, represents a breach of the agreement. Therefore, we not only vitiate this contract but also demand that the entirety of the shares allocated to you in conjunction with this engagement be returned to us. Our counsel at Gibson Dunn & Crutcher will be supervising this transaction to ensure that it occurs swiftly and prior to the IPO in ten days.

This letter shall also serve as a cease and desist, prohibiting you from speaking publicly, privately, or otherwise commenting upon your activities in relation to OneSpeak or your engagement with Long Bridge. Failure to abide by the terms set forth in the contract signed by our respective firms could result in damages and Long Bridge will be compelled to act against you individually, as well as your firm, White & Partners.

Sincerely,

Alan P. Newman

I had never been fired before. It had not occurred to me that Alan would fire us, I suppose, or maybe it was the fact that he hadn't done so already that surprised me. It felt like yesterday was a year ago. I read the email again. I didn't think to email it to my outside counsel for input. I didn't know what to do. I had the money, the shares, I suppose, somewhere, I could give it back. What else would I need to give back? When would the bleeding stop? Why did I do this to myself?

I threw the Matisse coffee table book at the wall. Margaret rushed in.

"Mark!" Her fingertips shielded her lips.

"I tripped," I said, gamely.

She walked over to pick up the book, closing it and putting it back on the table. She angled it back to its original position, took a tissue and wiped off some fingerprints on the table.

"I'm fine, really."

She closed the door as one does for a sick, sleeping child.

My hand was tremoring as I typed a riddle to Colin: how many pearls are in the ocean?

Then my cell rang.

"Mark," she said with faux bonhomie.

"Hanna."

"So, where should I start?"

The reply bubble appeared: "That's a trick question daddy pearls are in oysters not the ocean."

I smiled and then wondered where he was in the school that he had had immediate access to his cell phone. I imagined him wearing those Spider-Man sunglasses.

"What's the topic?" I said to Hanna.

"Where do I even start?" Her voice was empty of judgment, more interrogative than moralistic.

"Nothing champagne and strawberries can't fix?"

"Were you taking medication the night you fell asleep on MSNBC?"

"Surely you have more important topics worthy of your column, like the situation in Crimea, Republicans in Congress, the budget."

"Yes or no?" she said.

I had no idea how she knew this, stunned, and considered the choices: lie and deny; evade and no comment; or probe further at the vaporous edge of other questions and risk showing fear. Fear, for a good reporter, is a flashlight in the fog, something they'll follow until they are hovering over the dead body in the woods.

"That's an absolute lie."

"Were you on something when you tweeted the OneSpeak statement?"

"I strenuously deny the allegations against me, all of them." That came out a little too officiously, and I realized I had tilted the interview toward predator and prey dynamic.

"Are you seeing a psychiatrist?"

I was stunned, truly, not that she had uncovered so much about my personal life but that she was prepared to use the grainy bits to advance herself. I considered bribing her. I wondered how she obtained this information and then I narrowed the suspects to about two people in my office and felt an odd mix of grief, fear, and relief.

"When is this sad specimen of journalism publishing?"

"Today, probably after lunch." She sounded completely devoid of pleasure.

"Jesus, Hanna!"

"I'm sorry, Mark, it's my job. The piece is written. I need your quotes. ASAP."

Instead of the panic I should have felt at the prospect of a career-ending story on me and the company coming over the horizon, the sky going dark, I felt a rare surge of hate. It felt like a fever that would not break. I wanted to scream. I wanted to scream and turn the hose on her, this gossip stenographer, this social climber fucking over anyone to get to stories like these.

"There are dozens of people in town like me, dozens. Did you even think to investigate them? Huh?! Dozens of people doing terrible things—cheating on their wives, their clients, getting drunk on Monday night at Café Milano and snorting coke in the bathroom. Me? I go home to my kid whose mom died in a hit and run. And if I took a little medicine—and I am not saying I do— to stay focused and even keeled, so the fuck what? So, the fuck what! How is this a story? There's people fleeing dictators in Syria, all over the world, fuck, kids getting limbs chopped off. You? You're writing about some pathetic P.R. guy who was tired and fell asleep and couldn't help two goofy fucking startup assholes from tanking their IPO. How is this journalism? You are writing gossip and passing it off as news."

I was standing over the poly con, hands on the table.

"I didn't do this to you, Mark."

"No fucking shit! Some asshole hit her with his car and smashed her face and killed her and left two corpses here on earth to rot. Rot! Rot! Rot!"

I was shaking and quivering and Margaret rushed back in, seeming to grasp immediately the tenor of the situation, and she backed out and closed the door firmly.

She did not miss a step: "Mark…you didn't say off the record. I might have to use some of this."

"Fuck off use whatever you like!" I said and hung up.

It took me a few minutes to cool down. I took my calm pill. It didn't help.

I just sat there, quiet, breathing, the Catskill whateverthefuck. There wasn't any water, just a dish of broken Altoids. I stared at pictures on my window ledge. Time seemed to speed up, without texture. I looked out the window and I saw no preternaturally blue ocean, no rosemary beyond the hills in terra cotta pots, just an end to garden parties, a tide of bad press, an ebbing of millions of dollars of business, assuredly, once this piece published. I should have known long ago that this was how White & Partners might end, not a whimper, but a big fucking bang. Did I ignore the signs or was it willful delusion? I didn't need a gun. Self-delusion is the primary weapon of self-assault.

I let it all sink in. It was a quarter past two; I needed to leave soon to get Colin to the doctor's. I knew how that might look now to the staff: Mark is running scared; Mark is selling the company; Mark is suing THE BEACON.

I couldn't find Hawthorne but I told Sally and Wendy what had happened. They both looked shocked, although Wendy couldn't quite conceal her self-righteous smirk.

"This was a story waiting to be written Mark, a hanging curveball," she said.

"Wendy!" Sally said.

"We need to recognize the scale of a crisis to address it effectively. Mark, I'll draft a very crisp statement. We will distribute it out as soon as the piece hits. I'll get Harold to monitor the press. We'll see what happens. I'll take things from here. Mark, go home."

★

THE DOCTOR confirmed it was impetigo, gave us a half-used tube of the damn cream on the spot, the infection was that bad, and then we went for haircuts where the Vietnamese women shaved our necks and massaged our heads. I had my phone shut off totally. He looked handsome, save for the rash. I took the new pill Dr. Weller prescribed over dinner: baked ziti and cokes, Rocco's. On the way home, we stopped and I told Colin to wait outside while I went into the 7-Eleven to buy Marlboro Lights.

When we got home I showed him all the things from CVS.

He laid them out on the floor and inserted them all into his new bag. Atticus looked on. Then we took out the crumpled papers from his old backpack and stuffed them into his new binder. I bathed him, applied his cream again, rubbed his legs with arnica oil to ward away the aches of growing pains and tucked him in.

"Why do you smell like a fireplace?"

"I was eating some burnt toast."

"Oh, well, good thing you bought me some gum. You can have a piece."

"That's very sweet."

I gave him a bath to get the little hairs off his head, applied the cream again around his lips, and we played *NHL 17* on the Nintendo for a while, as I tried to contain my welled-up anxiety about the story.

Tonight, he fell asleep in minutes.

I tiptoed downstairs, Atticus followed.

I turned on the phone, breathing steadily. The headline read "The Fall of the House of White" and insinuated that I was a moody derelict who took pills for "an undisclosed medical reason" with multiple staff giving detailed accounts of me arriving late and departing early and popping small yellow pills in meetings. She cherry-picked one of the more salacious things I had said in anger and made it the lead quote: "And if I took a little medicine—and I am not saying I do— to stay focused and even keeled, so the fuck what! So the fuck what! How is this a story?"

"No one is really sure what Mark is doing out of the office so much and many executives are thinking of leaving since it is pretty obvious he's been trying to sell the company," said an anonymous insider, Hanna wrote. Alan Newman had declined to comment, along with Lars and Fung, other than confirming the termination notice.

It was a Richter scale eight or nine.

An alert from the *Associated Press* flashed on the home screen. The storm could morph into snow within two days.

Wendy had sent an all-staff email, linking to the story, but also appending a statement:

White & Partners strenuously objects to the tenor and substance of the baseless

THE BEACON *article by Ms. Nelson. Hers is clearly a sensationalized view of a company and man who represent some of the world's great brands and countries and employs dozens of talented people around the globe.*

I smiled, briefly, when I read this. It was a very good statement. Wendy went on in her email to outline standard protocols for crises such as this, you know, the standard no chatting, no talking, no forwarding, etc. The first reply to her email was Hawthorne, who wrote a lengthy response that panegyrized the firm and me.

There were more pieces. Hanna's article had spawned a sub-species of knock offs and retreads on other websites and blogs, but I was most worried it might jump over to print media. I lit a cigarette and smoked as I read; Atticus sat up and sniffed the air. There was something meaty on *The Huffington Post*, summarizing our work for sovereign clients and speculating on terminations. That was it for today. Not quite Pompeii. But I knew this story had more days to erupt, vaporize more revenue, encourage more of my people to flee the smoldering ruins and step forth anonymously and take their shots. I was not afraid of a fight, but, fuck you, step out of the shadows and fire your arrows with integrity. It would be an ambush, shots from all directions. I had no cover.

I ended the night in my upstairs office, sifting through old papers, smoking up to the threshold of nausea.

Every time I redirected my thoughts away from what had happened, my mind would graze back to a new aspect of my troubles, producing a new variety of panic and fear. I would try and turn away, but it was there physically, in the gut, a hostile takeover of my nervous system.

I thought I might read to divert my mind.

Atticus was watching me. He followed me downstairs where I built a fire.

I poured two thumbs of Macallan 18 and sat down in the chair. I sort of dozed off, then came back again. I recalled our first trip to Tuscany.

We were driven slowly up a winding gravel road, branches brushing the Renault, until we arrived at the villa with the deconsecrated church.

"Mark, it's perfect," she said as we pulled in through the iron gates. "It's absolutely perfect."

The property manager, Andi, his father and his mother were waiting for us when we pulled up. He was maybe twenty, working for the faraway real estate firm that owned and rented the compound. He wore shorts and a baseball cap.

They took the bags from Monica and asked us which language we preferred. I said Italian. Monica smirked and elbowed me, and they saw the gesture and began speaking their broken country English.

We walked uphill on a step stone path through olive trees and wild rosemary bushes.

"These are the figs," he said, looking up. "This, how you say, this is. You call, I think, a laurel."

"Mountain laurel," I said.

"Yes, that is it."

The villa had many entrances, each leading to something different like a courtyard, a patio, some place augmented by a broad view of the valley. There was some kind of castle across the hill, and I could see the faint blue path that was their swimming pool, although ours was obscured by more olive trees.

Monica came up behind me and took my hand.

"Come on," she said. We walked to some cushioned chairs and a table and she put down a bottle of San Pellegrino. She opened a pack of Marlboro Lights.

"Here you go," she said and handed me the first cigarette.

"Oh my God you did not!"

"Did too."

"Jesus how long has it been? Like ten years."

"Well, relax. Don't let anything disturb you here, Mark."

"I won't. There's no need. Nothing works here anyway. My signal is dead."

"Mine too. But we have Wi-Fi."

"I was afraid of that."

"Yup. Keep inhaling."

"I feel dizzy already."

"It'll wear off."

"Remember you did this to me when we went to our first keg party?"

"And you drank too much and puked on Sarah Stetson's shoes."

"She was hot."

"She was a slut."

"Still hot, but not a classy lady."

"She has five kids now. For real."

"How do you know this?"

"Magic."

I passed her the cigarette and she drew from it quickly and blew the smoke out of the right corner of her mouth towards the valley. There was a storm, a grey suede sky that filled the space far off between the hills, and there was thunder that carried towards us, some little droplets of rain.

She brushed a wet spot from her cheek and took another drag. She handed it to me. I inhaled too greedily and began spasmodically coughing.

"You are such a rookie. Still handsome, though."

"You are devious. You're giving me drugs and trying to make me pliant. Well I'm resisting your overtures. You'll need to do better than this, Monica."

"Slow down. Breathe a little and succumb to my desires." She motioned like a genie.

I drew it in better and felt the nicotine work into my mind and sedate me. She finished her cigarette and stamped it out with her shoe, then poured a little of her wine onto it. The butt made a hissing sound. There was a longer than normal silence. She was looking at me.

I was looking at the suede storm and said, "We came all the way to Tuscany to smoke."

"There was nowhere else to take you where you wouldn't use the phone."

"I know you think it means I don't care about you and Colin. But I do. I care so much. That's why I plunge into the work. I can't help it. It rings and it rings and I am needed. I am the product. I hate it and I have no choice."

It began to rain a little. I extinguished my cigarette under my sneaker and tossed the butt into some ornamental foliage. She passed me some wine. It was young chianti and it tasted sour and dry.

"I hate storms," I said. "They activate me the wrong way."

"It's passing, look. Over there." Behind the mesh of gray rain there was some expiring afternoon light.

"Is any of it helping?" she asked.

"I don't know. I just sit there and talk. And talk. And talk."

"That's the point."

"I know. He doesn't say much."

"Dr. Weller comes highly recommended. You remember Sheri's husband. He went through something. He got well. You'll get well. It just takes time."

"That's what you think? I'm going through something?"

"Well you are. You've lost thirty pounds. You don't sleep. What would you call that?"

"A good month at an ashram." She didn't laugh.

"Hand me another," I said. I lit it and began to smoke aggressively.

"You were depressed once in college. Remember? Never like this. I love you and want you to be well so you can pursue your passions and your dreams. Don't you still have those?"

I looked out at the valley for a very long time. She was right. There was light behind the storm. This far away, though, it appeared still. Suddenly saw cars in the road. No noise. We were too high up to be touched by very much.

"I just don't even know what's wrong anymore." I put my elbows on my knees and kept staring out to the horizon.

She put her hand on my shoulder. I knew she wanted good things for me, and evacuating my malignant thoughts from my mind each Tuesday to Dr. Weller, however uncomfortable and monotonous it seemed, was a bridge to somewhere, maybe. She said I seemed better, recently, thought my appetite was improving and I wasn't waking before dawn anymore and reading emails. She shot her arrows in all my sleuth arguments, and so I finally relented to seeing a psychiatrist.

The church bell was ringing. We looked behind us, startled to see Andi tugging a long rope dropped from the bell to shoulder height.

"It's time," he said, "it's time. Time is up for now."

"What does he mean?" I said. "Andi, *que dice?*"

We stood up and walked to him. When we drew near a pair of doves flew from out of the wisteria on the trellis by the door.

"He probably saw lightning. Come on."

He was squatting up and down pulling the rope. "No more time, Signore White. Come in from *la terraza*. Please. You are out of time."

chapter seven

THEY WERE saying it was the ghost of Althea, a post-tropical system
that just a few days ago had the bones of a hurricane, and now it was
racing up the coast, converging with polar air, swelling with Atlantic wind,
a massive Nor'easter, they called it, soon to suffocate the entire northeast
for the indefinite future, halting commerce, grounding flights, shuttering
government, all the schools, freezing the November homeless.

It started just after dark. We were being buried by the hour, inch by
inch, through the long night. The snowfall morphed parked cars, bushes,
and hedges into vast white hills, and looking at the floodlit belfry through
my window, where earlier that week I had seen lingering passerines on the
crucifix, the brightened snow was falling quickly, canted and hard, sharp
as coins.

The school closings were announced that day, long before the snow had
even arrived. Mass emails were sent around, copying everyone, speculating
as to the duration of the closures. Since there had been due warning, the
regional authorities had managed to amass a fleet of diesel trucks fitted
with hydraulic plows and an arsenal of magnesium chloride to melt the ice.
By midnight everything had been deployed; even my landscaping company
had entered the fray; by early morning (or was it deep in the night) my
driveway was being cleared, a narrow path being dug to the front door,

salted with pellets harvested from the Dead Sea, good for the environment, the invoice later said. But of that monumental blizzard that heaped almost two feet of snow on everything within fifty miles of Washington and kept schools closed for five days, my primary recollection is of the scraping sound of shovels outside at four in the morning, laborers chasing after the wind, as I, nesting in warm thread count, was in theoretical asleep.

Sally did not hesitate to close the office for the next two days, and, given the news stories, I wasn't going to argue with her. By the time the pack melted and the roads were passable again, it would be Monday. I used the second free day to take Colin to a Van Gogh exhibition. That I had become aware of this temporary installation was pure serendipity: while reading all the clips about me, I started to clean out my junk mail and saw a pro-motional email from The Phillips Collection. Colin was still asleep. They had thirty-five Van Goghs on loan from the Musée d'Orsay, many of them landscapes from his time in the South of France. Monica had taken a class at The Phillips; I remembered that I was a repeat donor and it occurred they had probably been sending me emails like this for two years, inviting me to private viewings.

I clicked the link and found that most of the prime visit times were already reserved but there was a slot early the next day. The roads might be icy, but I purchased the tickets. I looked outside. The backyard was a desert of white. I put on a pot of drip coffee, grabbed my copy of the collected works of Robert Frost, built a fire with birch wood and sat in the chair beside it, reading and trying to decode a few deceptive short poems, waiting for Colin to wake up so I could tell him about the outing.

He reacted to the news with no particular astonishment and asked if we were also going to go somewhere together the following day. No, I said. There is school, probably, again, and daddy must go back to work. He sighed and cast his eyes towards the fire, but he brightened up a bit when I said we could go sledding. I had him in bed early that night, as our slot was at nine o'clock in the morning.

Two days after the mega storm, the parkway was slushy in Virginia, but when we crossed Memorial Bridge and entered the city, the pavement was dry, the streets etched into tall snowbanks. Only a few stores looked open; the federal government was still closed; Washington felt mostly deserted, its inhabitants having retreated in sudden hibernation, though I knew that it was the migration of professionals from the suburbs, in and out of the city, that filled the place with life force, a vaudeville rhythm to drown out the trace pulse of residents who dwelled in pockets throughout DC. Whenever it snowed badly the city felt drained out.

The exhibition would close the following week, and that fact must have been on the minds of everyone in the metropolitan area who had anything to do with the arts: the gallery lobby was full, a horde in wet boots, checking coats and taking brochures, talking hurriedly; it was a marked counterpoint to the chapel world outside. From the gray empty streets, how had this museum been filled with so many? They must have taken cabs, I thought, or were stranded at hotels, numbing out on a third day of sights. The room held a certain anticipatory energy; even Colin grew more alert.

We checked our coats and an Indian woman took them and handed me a ticket, and I gave Colin a dollar to drop into the tip cup. I wondered if she had even been permitted to view the exhibit; when she said thank you I detected in her voice a note of that familiar assimilation, all the angularity of her accent burnished away.

She smiled at me when I handed Colin the dollar and seemed to notice my skin tone.

I unfolded the brochure, which told us to begin on the second floor, and Colin and I took the grand staircase, where a massive Alexander Calder mobile hung from the ceiling. Colin seemed amused by them and reached out to try and touch it before I moved him along wordlessly up the stairs into the exhibit room.

Even across the crowded room, I could feel the weather of the painting. The prevailing mood in any Van Gogh is of shadowy despair; it's in all the twisted cypresses, the transfigured three-dimensional space, the menace of unseen winds, the dark stars; their negative space is somehow imbued with panic. This view, possibly, is at odds with the perspective of most, who would find affinity with the surface sheen of the works and look no farther than that to see into the soul of the painting. Gazing into gardens in Arles and cypress groves and beach houses perched atop cliffs, all rendered in his unmistakable impasto brushstrokes, it was hard not to connect with the room's energy, feel that you were in some transcendental accord with the historical past. This exhibition was called Van Gogh Repetitions, and by featuring several versions of the same painting—sometimes a sketch accompanying a full-blown painting—meant to show the evolution of some of his most famous works. I had not before considered him an artist capable of such devotion. This is not to say Van Gogh was not a passionate artist, as he is well known for working with manic intensity, in rapid bursts, but this exhibition revealed that he also preplanned many of his paintings, searching for the right alchemy of color.

There were clusters of people at each painting, everyone lingering to read the title plaques. I bowed to read something: the curators had brilliantly excerpted some of Van Gogh's letters to his brother, Theo, the art dealer.

We moved in and it occurred that Colin might try and reach out to feel the paint, which up close was as thick as icing. I whispered in his ear, and I read him the first sign, "there can be no blue without yellow…and orange." It was curious phrasing, not to say that complimentary colors reach their vibrato when in each other's presence, but to suggest that one does not fully exist without the other, vice versa. But in looking at the heightened drama, the contorted dimensions in the juxtaposition of reds/greens, purples/yellows, blues/oranges, such as in *Bedroom in Arles*, 1889, it's easy to understand what he means: removing one strand of color would instantaneously deflate the intensity of the whole painting.

I would rather die of passion than of boredom, read another sign beside *Pine Trees at Sunset*, all knotted oak and wind and fear. What do you think of these paintings, I asked Colin. This one looks creamy he said, and I was immediately relieved that, at least for now, he wasn't seeing past the painter's technique; he was not feeling any of the root trauma in the work.

"I like how he paints squiggly," Colin said. We were standing before *Garden of the Asylum*.

The elegant older woman beside him was standing back, shaking her head with her hand on her chin. Colin rested his head on his chin, doing it all wrong.

"Yeah," I said, "it doesn't have to be all smooth to be good."

We moved through the room in less than fifteen minutes, faster than I would have liked, so not wanting yet to leave, I took Colin downstairs to see the museum's most famous masterpiece, Renoir's *Luncheon of the Boating Party*, whose yellows are almost incandescent. I pointed out the most unique aspect of the painting, that no one's gaze is met by another's. It is a deceptive work of surface beauty concealing private, intimate longings. We stood there for no longer than twenty seconds and Colin said he was hungry.

We passed under the Calder and exited. It was snowing outside again, coming down in mouth-sized flakes. We chased them with our tongues. There was a bakery across the street that looked open. When we walked inside it was empty and warm. We took off our coats and sat by the bay window looking out at the museum. I ordered us croissants and hot chocolates. We sat for a while, watching the snow fall; I was thinking about the fact that Van Gogh died without any fame, having sold few paintings, his impasto style lampooned by critics.

The mood of the paintings was captured perfectly in this weather, I thought, the elements summed up in a mood, or vice versa. I was starting to enjoy the feeling of being stranded in an unexpected winter, my permanent life on a temporary shelf. Colin was staring out the window, his hot chocolate untouched. I had almost forgotten everything that was happening to me outside of this moment.

"Are you okay?" I asked. He didn't respond at first, and I repeated the question.

"Are you going to work now after this?"

"Work is closed today. Daddy closed it, remember?"

"Oh," he said and sunk his chin into his hands. "Do you think you'll close it again tomorrow?"

It was not until later that evening, after drawing him a bath, that the idea came to me: we would take a trip. I didn't know when this would be, but the notion gained momentum by the minute until it held gravity and I felt myself irresistibly drawn to a prolonged escape.

I went through all the routines of putting him bed, and then warmed the leftover drip coffee in the microwave to wake myself up so I could dig into the internet to plan this trip for us. I wasn't sure where to go or when we might leave. I was by the fire, opening and closing browsers on the laptop, trying to decide between warmth and cold, near and far. For a nanosecond I was envisioning a Kenyan safari, but considered the logistics, and moved on to your standard ski trip, but winter somehow chafed at the spirit of the idea; we should fling ourselves far out into the world and see where we might land: the mountains, the desert, the sun, the coast, the sea.

Something like a whisper floated into my mind, my fingers typing before I could think of the words.

I was finding round-trip flights that would leave tomorrow, return four days later; I was relying on that same travel website to recommend a hotel, and I was buying these tickets and reserving this hotel, seeing us both there together, the past at our backs, visions unfolding of the things we would do together.

There was a momentary thrill when I clicked the PURCHASE button on the screen.

I felt lightened with excitement. I went upstairs into my bedroom and opened the big suitcase and started putting in clothes— giddy—then tiptoed back into Colin's room and pulled out his entire bottom drawer, took it back into my room, sorted out what was what, added his things to mine in the suitcase. I took my new pills and got in bed. I remembered his Spider-Man sunglasses, and before I fell asleep I remembered I needed to pack the passports.

★

FROM THE window on approach, I could see shades of soft blue edging the island, nearly incandescent, white caps further out, catamarans coming into view as we descended, and then the blur of palm trees and rooflines and monkeys running along the rusted fence parallel to the runway, the unmistakable warm vellum of the trade winds across my face, and it conjured the curry wraps at the ramshackle stands of Accra beach, the way equatorial winter sunsets felt premature though the day was always atomically bright.

Colin put on sunglasses; I had left mine at home. He took my hand as we walked down the stairs to the runway, and it felt sweaty and I saw little beads of perspiration forming around the hairline on his neck, bangs flopped rakishly across his eye.

I emailed Sally from the Uber to Dulles with the name of my hotel, underscoring that I should be contacted only if the circumstances were exceedingly dire. But they were already dire and I knew it. At the thought of phantom client crises I felt a sudden panic. Apart from Sally, only Margaret knew of my whereabouts, knew the number of the new cell phone I had purchased just for this trip in case she needed to reach me. She got the same speech: contact me only under the most apocalyptic circumstances imaginable—otherwise not at all. But when I walked into Colin's room the morning we were to depart and saw him kneeling in front of his suitcase rearranging his shirts, when I spied through the semi-closed bathroom door combing his hair into a part and spraying himself with my cologne, I decided at that moment I would leave the cell phone behind.

"Daddy," said Colin pointing up at the coconut trees, "there's a man with a knife."

"He's the fruit man," I said. "He's cutting down the coconuts for us to eat."

"I wanna try one."

He was pulling his carryon behind him, never breaking stride. He looked younger than he was in all the sunlight.

"You drink the water inside. It's very good for you."

"I want to do that. Does mommy like coconuts?"

"Mommy was never in Barbados."

From nowhere, as we crossed the tarmac, sharp cold rain began to come down, right there in the sunlight, weighty rain in the day, thunder by two. We ran towards the customs and immigration terminal; Colin, laughing, had let go of my hand, his suitcase flying around behind him. I chased after him, almost laughing myself.

The terminal had a vaulted ceiling and a tall bank of windows. We were all shivering in the air-conditioning; my linen shirt stuck to my chest. The immigration forms I had painstakingly completed aboard just an hour ago were now a runny mess. I looked around and realized that everyone was transforming their appearance with accessories, lotions, sunglasses—shedding northern climate clothing: hoodies, sweatpants, jackets—right there in the open.

"Daddy you have boobies," said Colin, pointing at my soaked, sloping chest.

The family in front of us began laughing hysterically, and I began to laugh too, took off his sunglasses, and kissed him on the forehead and tickled his stomach.

The immigration officer gave us a fleeting glance as he stamped our passports.

The baggage claim was in charming disarray: plenty of British retirees, token American couples, families herding glazed-over children dressed for sledding. Everyone was white. Yellow birds darted around overhead. The luggage carousel spun but there were no suitcases on it: they'd all been taken off already and strewn about the floor. We found our bags after ten minutes heaped in a corner with all the others from our flight. I politely waved away the valets, who seemed to sulk away until they spotted another person my age with multiple bags. We had only two suitcases: mine and the carry-on Colin had been dragging behind him.

By the time we were outside, the rain had stopped and it was very sunny. When I saw a mass of drivers holding up signs with last names, I momentarily had wished that I had booked us somewhere with such an amenity, but I had made the arrangements in a stupor and had overlooked these things; I made the reservations blind to location and luxury. I figured that if we were to spend the time truly away then it should also be away from the conventional vacation trappings—Wi-Fi, room service, steel drum brunches.

I made eye contact with an older taxi driver who motioned us to follow him down the sidewalk, past the hotel shuttle kiosks to his white minivan. He loaded the bags and we settled on a price of twenty dollars Barbados. The windows were partially down—there was no air-conditioning—and he drove down the hill, tight turns, accelerating wherever there was open road too fast. We rounded coral retaining walls, practically scraping them, passing all the barefoot men and kids on sidewalks, a breath away from the window, took blind hills by force, wound through sugar cane fields shoulder high, chattel houses in Easter hues, bushy with bougainvillea, set back from the road hardly at all. We came downhill, finally, into Holetown, then Christ Church, tourist towns where naked shanty hovels hunched in the sun amid eyefuls of raw vegetation: tamarinds, baobabs, gully shrub, ginger lily, shaggy moss of the bearded fig. They grew lushly, immune to the surrounding human noise. As we turned the hill and ascended, we came to a clearing, a panorama of the windless leeward side of the island. The water was unbelievably blue. Colin leaned against the window. That's turquoise, I said. Why is it so shiny? That's iridescence. I could have said it was flickering sapphire and it would not have been hyperbole; there may have been five million crests per second glittering in all directions, a Morse Code of light that seemed to be messaging something indecipherably grand.

I motioned the driver to stop at the next mart, some place with rotisserie chickens in the window, and I bought a six pack of Banks and some vanilla wafers for Colin using my US money. We started out again, Colin spilling crumbs on his lap on the seat, the driver not caring; the mood had seemed to hit after I handed him the beer and he flipped on the FM station to local reggae. His taxi license was taped to the dashboard; there was a Virgin Mary icon hanging from the rearview mirror, pictures of grandkids in ponytails.

Just as I formulated the question of where me might get lunch, we were driving near a beach and a cluster of huts just yards off the road caught my eye.

I asked the driver to pull over. There were picnic tables under the Banyan trees where women in head wraps sold food from the trunk of their minivans. I thought Colin might be tired and want to rest at the hotel, but when I imagined us unpacking and getting settled, driving back this way in the traffic because where we were the beach was too rocky for swimming, I figured, realistically, we wouldn't make it back here until at least three o'clock, which was dangerously close to the premature 5:25 p.m. sunset, I decided to take a chance. I offered Marshall lunch and a twenty-dollar tip, explaining that after he ate I wanted him to drive our luggage to the hotel and leave it with the concierge. He seemed perplexed at first.

"Daddy are we staying here, can we stay here please?"

Then he seemed to get it. He nodded and took the cash, speaking in dialect to the women, and fish cakes and macaroni pie, beers and an orange Fanta began to appear. The entire lunch cost six dollars Barbados. The woman was heaping a larger helping of fried fish cakes on top of yellow rice on Styrofoam plates, flashing her shock white teeth, and all of us were eating in the shade of the banyan trees in silence.

I opened the suitcase, searched for swimsuits and t-shirts, zipped them closed and handed them back to Marshall.

The beach glowed like a movie set. There were no clouds. The water was bluer than the sky. I realized we hadn't any sunscreen or hats or beach towels. Colin was running ahead into the water already. He was a strong swimmer, and although there was an undercurrent here and sizable waves I remembered it wasn't particularly strong and there were lifeguards now— something new to the place—standing and scouting the waters, surprisingly vigilant for the Caribbean. The water, up close, was still impossibly blue. The Concorde used to make its midday arrival here, over this beach, close enough to think you could reach its white belly with a bottle.

I waved to Colin and yelled to not go too far out. I walked over to a hut that sold hand-made jewelry and brand sunscreens, towels, little wooden figurines and keychains. I paid for the necessary items with the last of my American money, and I saw another hut—a true beach bar.

I found the man who rented the lounge chairs and gave him instructions about where to set us up, handed him the bag of items and the towels, tipped him exceedingly well and spied on him for a good thirty seconds until I was sure he was handling things in earnest. Colin was waving at me from the shoreline, happy and wet from swimming. I waved back and gave him a signal with my open hand that I'd be there in five minutes and he nodded. Usually in a moment like this I would have checked my phone. I felt a rising panic at the thought of what might be transpiring in my absence; what clients, by Murphy's Law, had caught an overnight virus of unhappy? My new pills were with Marshall now. I tried Dr. Weller's breathing exercises for a minute, feeling ridiculous to be doing this thirty minutes into a vacation, the only distressed person on this sunny beach amid the loud reggae and beer and rum. I became angry that work had already encroached on me, even thousands of miles away, even without a phone. Or was it that I was incapable of steeling myself, of segregating personal life from work life? The latter seemed too intertwined and so I asked myself to try and decouple the placid present from the dystopic future that I was conjuring up, a set of competing, contemporaneous mindsets. Fuck this. Fuck this anxiety. I decided to order a rum punch.

The bartender—arguably not the right term in this instance—sensing my stress, offered me a cigarette, which I accepted and lit from his, inhaling and feeling instantaneously better, noticing his silver front teeth as he smiled. I smoked furtively, looking back towards the beach at Colin who was playing in the sand with a makeshift friend. I ordered the drink and decided that when I finished this cigarette I would buy a pack of Marlboro Lights and smoke them furtively at night on the patio, if our room had one. The rum drink, he said, came strong, very strong, or *effective*, an emphatic smile and chuckle accompanying the last dosage strength, suggesting that if I were not some pussy American tourist, I would order the effective.

I was still feeling good from the cigarette and went for it. He put away the standard-sized plastic cup that the other pussy tourists drank from and pulled out a big clear plastic cup, almost beer mug height, and filled it halfway with ice and two thirds dark Mount Gay rum. He turned and ladled some homebrew fruit punch from a giant cooler, added a rum floater, then grated fresh nutmeg over the top; it looked like he'd sprinkled sand in my drink. He stood there, arms folded, teeth flashing. I took one sip and smiled back: the spice and saccharine mix masked the alcohol so all you tasted really was the dark caramel of the rum and the aromatics of the nutmeg. It could have been the cigarette, but I felt a euphoric buzz within about

twenty seconds. I took a greedy second sip and walked over to the perfectly
set up lounge chairs, screwed my drink into the sand, lit the other cigarette
that he'd given me that I had tucked behind my left ear, lay down, scanned
the blue sea, watched Colin play some more, finished the cigarette, took
another gulp of the effective drink, feeling now almost drunk, and waved
Colin over finally for sunscreen.

After I had slathered him all over with SPF 50, sprayed his armpits and
neck for good measure, I told him to wait twenty minutes until he could go
back in. West Indian sun can burn you within an hour. He sat down easily
enough and started playing with the cigarette butts with his toes, simultaneously burying them and excavating them. I didn't want him to make the
connection and think I was smoking.

"Colin," I said, "let's take a walk," channeling an overly avuncular
tone—overdone considering he seemed perfectly happy. His pills were with
Marshall too, who I figured had already reached the Coral Mist Hotel.
Worried he might convulse into some unforeseen panic attack, I tried to
hurry him up out of the chaise, finishing off the watery rum at the bottom
of my glass, tasting the ice cubes, and distracting him from seeing me gulp
it down by pointing out a large swell forming way out.

The sand was hot. We walked down to the shoreline, Colin taking my
hand, waves breaking and washing up to our feet—the water sometimes
ankle deep—and considering the tilt of the island and that we were on the
Caribbean side, we were walking, what I suspected, due north towards the
large black rocks at the end of the beach. The water was bathwater warm.
I had forgotten all about that. I had forgotten now all about the office, my
panic nullified by the nicotine and alcohol, a warm Zen buzz now, the sun
at its zenith, so bright that I was squinting through the cheap sunglasses I
had bought at the hut. There was no seaweed or trash or empty beer bottles
washing ashore; beaches in Barbados were pristine, which I supposed was
the result of some generalized genuflection to the beauty of the place.

When we got to the large rocks I had to help Colin maneuver over them
to cross to the next beach where there was a kind of boardwalk built atop
a retaining wall, passing a scattering of beach bars. The walkway stretched
out into the sea for a quarter mile. When can we see the hotel, he said. I was
looking out into the horizon as he said this, the rum fog still there, and was
reminded that we had skipped going to the hotel entirely and I had remain-
dered our possessions with Marshall, who I hoped had not made off with

everything. Why don't we stay until the sun goes down? Are you thirsty? Let me see your shoulders. Are you burning? I had left the sunscreen at the beach chairs, and I noticed that his shoulders were getting red. Up ahead was another hut that sold the same items as the last hut. I bought a SPF 50 spray and a little Rasta bead necklace that I put on him, unloading an excessive sunscreen cloud on his entire upper body as he held his arms out wide, eyes and mouth shut tight. He exhaled deeply after the cloud dissipated and we continued down the path, the waves crashing against the wall and spraying all the way up, at times, to our faces. We can go back if you want. To the hotel, I mean. Are you thirsty? He seemed engrossed by the surroundings. We kept walking all the way to the end to where a blockade of concrete slabs made it impossible to go any farther. We sat down.

"Daddy is it possible to be in two places at the same time?"

"Yes, well...I think so." I paused, suspicious of his question. "Yes, I think that's somewhat possible."

"Do you know how?"

"Well, I guess you would be standing in one place but your mind stuck in another place. Does that make sense?"

"Daddy, you don't get it! You could be, like, okay, if there's a sign, and it says, Maryland, and you're standing there, and, okay, if you are near the other state and your foot is over the line and you're standing in both states by the sign, then you would be in two places at the same time. Silly!"

We sat for a while perspiring and watched the waves. Then he started talking about the sharks; at some point on the walk, he had gotten his hands on a few brochures about sport fishing charters. Reading from the brochure, Colin was reciting to me the positives of each captain, the kinds of fish each claimed they routinely caught, whether there was a meal served or a snack, free soda and beer, or all the above. He wasn't sure if going after sailfish meant you wouldn't catch sharks and vice versa. I watched his face squint in the sun as he scrutinized both sides of at least four foldouts. The longer charters took around six hours, I said. He seemed to understand. We agreed to go with Captain Amos: from the stern of the Sea Bream, he held a marlin shoulder high, hook through the mouth, a scattering of fathers and sons off to the side, boys his age. One had on the captain's hat. Everyone appeared satisfied.

I knew the sun would set within the hour. My buzz was wearing off but I wasn't thinking about anything to do with office life, selling the firm at such and such a multiple, my pills. I felt fresh again and stripped of professional debris; I thought that I should delete my Twitter account; I decided that I would re-quit coffee. There were no clouds in the sky and it was the brightest hour of the day. Now and then a large wave would crash against the rocks and I could taste the sea spray. Had my mother been here, she would have held very still, like Colin, staring out at the water, blanking out, like me, relieved from life. Colin was not talking now, and I thought I should just let him be for a while, though I occasionally handed him the water bottle; he took quiet sips and handed it back to me, his gaze fixed on the horizon. I thought about telling him I thought the water looked like sapphire, that there was a message encoded in all the flashing crests. But I thought again, better to just let him be; perhaps he wouldn't require pills this trip, maybe me neither; perhaps each day was like a crash against the rocks, only to be repeated and improved upon the next day. Maybe I should just tell Harry to put us up for auction, take the first decent multiple, sell the house and move us south, or west, or wherever there was not something to remind him of her, someplace we could be still, like this, and think of nothing but fill up with everything. A large wave broke, soaking our legs. We moved wordlessly back a bit. The heat was leaving the air, the sun starting to slip. Wave runners were circling near Accra, and bodies porpoised in and out of the water out past the surf. The ocean became silvery the more the sun fell. Perhaps now would be a good time to ask him about her, or to tell him about her—both. He looked so calm, I thought he might be thinking of her already anyway.

"I know you miss her very much," I might say.

I felt her presence more now than ever, somewhere in the negative space between the reflections of water light. I wanted to tell him how it happened, all of it, every last detail, that they found her on a Friday after midnight, rolled down into a trench against the storm drain, face up, hair blood-mashed onto her face, ribs cracked and molars shattered, chest collapsed, probably dead on impact.

There were no clues to follow, not even skid marks. Probably across state lines by now, the sheriff said.

After fourteen years, we had learned to respect each other's boundaries without resentment. Her last morning, we did not speak: she was wrapping a commission from a Bowery dealer, some colossal sylvan showpiece, and she never liked to talk with anyone when she was nearing a painting's completion.

The week prior we'd been in Nantucket. Geraniums spilled from window boxes and old English roses climbed up clapboard to the roofline. We swapped theories of life on morning walks. The August lawns were newly fertilized and the air had a faint chemical sting. You were where you were, certain places seeped in and defined you without consent, I said. She said this was a "lovely conceit." She believed that life was a sine wave, happiness was learning to live well between the peaks and troughs.

We had an informal roster of places we planned to take you when you were old enough to appreciate their radiance—Bali, the Christmas islands, Aix-en-Provence during the mistral, seaside Nordic villages where you could eat venison under heat lamps in October on the waterfront.

He was still staring out at the sea. Did I tell him, then, that our final walk turned out to be on Hulbert at sunrise, the seven hundred or so yards after the blast of the fog horn, before three deep gusts from the lone ferry at the vanishing point of Nantucket Sound, the joggers in fleece, lot after lot of third homes, oceanfront, flags waving above the crushed white oyster-shell driveways, and the September seagulls squawked and the next ferry groaned and the brinish low tide smell floated to us? Would he understand?

We were home the next day and she was gone the day after that. He would understand that.

That last night we grilled lamb chops and drank an '07 Napa Cab. I counted four police cars. Atticus must have barked and woken her. She must have been restless and wanted to walk him around the block, I told them. I awoke in my bed and that's when I found her missing. The leash was gone. There was only the flood-lit steeple. They wrote all this down. The moon was waning gibbous. I summoned everything and they took it all down.

It was a while before I called the police. After thirty minutes I ventured into the street and searched for her face through the spray of humid streetlight—but not too far or for too long: Colin, you were only four, and sleeping inside. I sent texts—nothing. I called and got voicemail. The police were immediately suspicious about the lag between her disappearance and my call, but like anyone confronted by desperation, I held out hope that, at any moment, she would round the corner of Norton Street, the little white dog in tow.

I eavesdropped on the radio dispatch for a stray account of her whereabouts. Nothing.

Did I tell him he was sound asleep on his stomach, head sideways, cheek on the mattress and breathing through his mouth? The police lights spun red on the rails of his crib. Every few seconds his face was lit red but he did not awaken. I draped another blanket around the crib, a canopy to shield him from the light. He woke up smiling.

*

A MAN in dreadlocks was approaching from the beach, climbing over the rocks, holding pointy aloe leaves. I gave a thumbs up and Colin looked at me; I smiled back and told him it would be like an icy massage; he smiled and turned back to the water. The man seemed to read the moment, sat down beside us without a trace of noise and just started to break open the aloe spears with his machete, chopping against the rocks. He was wearing the standard paraphernalia and smelled like pot.

Maybe with that money I could buy a vineyard, launch a legacy family business, unplug a bit, or just pull out altogether and open a cheese shop in Vermont, a little petting zoo of goats in the back. The ideas were getting more ridiculous with each passing minute. I was most certainly of two minds: one discordant with reality; the other, painfully, was aware that the other was adrift, taken by some unknown current to an unknown place—but where? In this faraway setting, my senses dilated, it was clear now that the busyness that had once consecrated my life was a veneer that I could no longer pretend had any depth. After such knowledge, what decisions?

The aloe looked opaque and gooey as he squeezed it into the clear Carib bottle. He was piping the ooze through the neck with his pinky. The man motioned for a smoke, pointing to my ear. I thought that I shouldn't—but wanted to. He started on me first. He rubbed the cold viscous pulp over my back, my neck, back of arms. Near complete surface coverage. There had been sand in his hands so it felt exfoliative. Colin scooted a little bit towards him when it was his turn. It was late enough now that you could look straight into the sun.

The bottle was empty so the man hacked open another spear. He applied it direct to Colin, wiping his back with the interior flesh of the plant. He giggled a bit, held silent. There was sea foam fizzing on the rocks. I was not thinking now of anything except that my back felt sticky as the aloe dried, my skin tightening as it dried out completely. I swiped a little of the aloe still wet on Colin's back with my pinky and made quick brushstrokes with it on his cheeks. When the man was finished with us, I asked him to make Colin one of those Rasta bead necklaces, and he got out his fishing wire and threaded it through the black and red and yellow and orange beads, checking twice to see if the length would wrap around his neck. He tied it off. I gave him a wet wad of money from my pocket and then he didn't leave us. I thought about telling him to go, but it would have forced an absence onto the scene.

I looked directly into the sun and shut my eyes; in maybe three minutes it would drift beneath the water line. I saw us all, from a distance, facing the water, sandy and golden-faced with island twilight. The seagull pausing above, maybe diving down to catch the skipping fish. I took off my sunglasses, Colin removed his too. The man was smoking his joint and humming something to himself. It was now visibly sinking, a Fauvist orange. You could look right at it now. Some people on the beach rose to watch; some stopped in the water and turned to see it. When the sun had gone, he did not leave us.

I placed my hand on Colin's back, who wore his own glazed expression, then said, "I promise you she is in a better place."

★

AT THE hotel, our bags were standing behind the counter still wet with rain. A husband and wife team showed us to our room, which was sparse but clean, a tiny gecko crawling up the sliding glass door.

I felt oily after the afternoon at the beach, and told Colin to take a quick shower and change into some clean shorts and a t-shirt. He left the door ajar and soon I saw the steam pour through. There was a crude chair, something just big enough for a man, in the corner, and I sat down, shedding my fatigue from the sun and the day's travel.

It was before eight o'clock; I wondered if Captain Amos might answer a call. There was a rotary phone on the nightstand and I dialed the number on the brochure, got no answer, dialed the number below it, and a woman answered.

Is there room on tomorrow's charter for two? You are very lucky. There has been a cancellation. It's very lucky for you, you should know. We leave at seven thirty. I can pay by cash? We will send you a van, yes, where are you? Christ Church, near The Gap, Coral Mist. Yes, okay, Sheila and Philip, they send many to us. You are in good hands. We will send the van. You must be ready then, okay? Fine, we will be ready. Is there a cooler for drinks, may I bring snacks? Of course, yes, but you may not smoke, okay? And your son has done this before? He will be fine.

We hung up and when Colin came out of the bathroom I told him we were scheduled to set sail tomorrow, eight a.m.

He was wrapped in a towel trailed by shower steam. I told him the good news; he gave a fist pump, then we high-fived, then a hug.

"Come on, are you hungry?" I said.

"Yes! Will there be snacks on the boat? What kind of fish? And how long is it?"

"Yes, we will get some snacks. And it's a four-hour trip and we will hopefully get some marlin or snapper."

★

WE WALKED out into the loud music and bought two curry chicken rotis, ate them from the tinfoil on the bus stop bench, and drank orange Fanta with the rest of the locals. His cheeks were still flush from the shower, or was it that he was heat-stricken? He had devoured his roti before I had finished mine. There was no one else waiting for the bus and so we sat there for a few minutes, watching the stray cats venture in and out of shadows, licking shallow puddles, dried-out coconut husks.

I mentioned again that we needed to be up early, prepared to litigate bedtime, but he acquiesced, saying, "We need to be on our best behavior tomorrow," and so we walked back down to the Coral Mist, taking the long way around the block.

There was an unnamable bug sound, sort of like chirping, in the trees, the air. There were a few abandoned tenements in between pink condominiums, the odd two-story hotel. In between each of these we could see the moonlight stretched out on the water. A few tourists were out, mostly pairs talking in heavily accented English, eastern European, perhaps; other than that, it was mostly the barefoot locals congregated at the food carts with beers, smoking. I saw another mart and we bought more wafers, a bag of potato chips, more Fantas, Swiss chocolate for the cooler. The woman seated at the checkout had purple press-on nails and handed Colin a post-card of Crane Beach.

"Do you like it here?"

"Yeah, it's pretty cool. I like the smell," I said.

"Will it be okay on the boat tomorrow? Once we're out, we can't go back?"

"You'll be fine. I'll give you some Dramamine—it's medicine for tum-mies. I'll give you some of that; you will be fine. Question: are marlin mammals?"

"Daddy?" He let go of my hand and stopped walking. "Why do I take so many medicines?"

I had long expected this question from him, was surprised it hadn't come earlier, but standing here in Barbados in the warm night, his words seemed absurd; I felt as if this boy here with me was immune from suffering and did not warrant treatment for anything of any kind. There were no easy distractions in the night and talking intimately with anyone in the dark, it was always easier to tell the truth.

"It's like protection for you. A wall."

"Why do I need protection? From who?"

"Everyone needs protection of some kind. Our feelings sometimes crawl over the wall and make it hard to be happy people."

"So the medicine kills the feelings?"

"We cannot kill our feelings. Do you remember the man today who massaged your back with that cold stuff?" We started walking again, my gait quickening to abbreviate the conversation.

"But daddy, the feelings are real! They are scary sometimes, real scary, and I don't think the pills are helping me."

"Do you remember the man—"

"They are really scary, okay! You don't understand me at all. It's why I can't read so good. This is what I've been trying to tell you about." He was breathing heavily, and I wanted to get him back to the room to his pills.

"We can talk about this in bed, pal. Okay? We can talk about this. Let's get back to our room and we will talk about this."

He sniffled, wiped his eye with his forearm, and nodded. I thought, right then, that I should correct the record, confess that his mother had found this place, or that at least she had been here, but because he seemed so fragile and had no pill in his system, near enough to full-blown panic, I thought better of it, the imbalance of the moment its own kind of equilibrium.

But we didn't talk about it much more when we got back to the room and I did not administer a pill. He was too fast: he kicked off his sneakers, took off his shirt, and, without asking, crawled into my queen bed. I scratched his hair and brushed away some of the aloe flakes on his back he had missed in the shower. I lay awake for a while, turned off the light when it started to rain, the drops accumulating on the sliding glass door. I had forgotten to pack books, and I lay there not knowing what to do in the dark, unplugged and unburdened, as it were. The room was strangely soundproof and I thought about putting on the TV to break up the silence, read some of the Bible aloud, if there was one in the drawer. Thoughts of work encroached but I warded them away. I should have tried harder, I thought. I should have never left. We should have stayed in Madrid, attempted what everyone who flings themselves abroad attempts, and then I should have tried when I had the chance again in Boston, and, again and again, I should have done what she had suggested and reapplied for the David Foster Wallace MFA, and if he had not hanged himself and I had not attempted something else entirely, starting this company, and had I never bought that dog, it would all have been different and the three of us would be here on this magic island. I thought now maybe I was having a panic attack. For five minutes I did the breathing exercises. He was sleeping soundly, the sheets over his shoulders rising and falling. I lay awake for a little while longer, listening, trying not to think too much about anything. The gecko, backlit in street light, ran midway up the glass, darted to the right, then vanished.

★

WHEN IT was time to go the next morning it was still dark and the bug sounds were still there, echoing somewhere behind the patio in the dark, tangled vines. There was a sea wind shaking unseen things and their rustle sent creatures scattering. The van was idling by the front office, its radio faintly audible through the cracked window. Come on pal, I said. Just get in and you can sleep on the way. There was an orange blush over the hills and all the vegetation was still a black mass, and we did not hear the wild chickens that we would hear the next morning, much later, from the soccer field up high in the terraced uplands.

It was nearly an hour's drive to Bridgetown, mostly along the coast-line through morning rain. At first we rode alone, then we stopped at a turquoise motel off Highway 7 and picked up a sun-pinkened man with an elaborate camera hanging from his thick neck. He nodded at me, that innate gesture meant to relate your inability to speak in the other's lan-guage; he was maybe Bulgarian, old enough for a family. He had a ring. I wondered why he was alone as the radio hosts talked cricket, more dia-lect and totally impenetrable. The man was fiddling with camera features, adjusting the lens and aiming it out the window. We hit potholes at full speed but Colin stayed sleeping. I had forgotten the night before. I had dreamt of nothing, awoke vague as to my life and circumstances: It took a while for the facts of my life to return and resume their orbit around me; it took me a few minutes to remember the name of the charter, and when we stepped out into the windy morning, at first, I did not realize that the waiting van was meant for us.

Could this become some annual father-son trip, some scheduled communion with each other and ourselves? We needed more rituals. The thought occurred just after an image of my typewriter surfaced, after seeing a decrepit hotel and sensing a verandah. There were different versions of the same place, just as there were several versions of the same person, a palimpsest accrued over time, although I was sure Colin was too young to be burying old selves, yet I was not so sure this couldn't be true, even for a young boy. Sunsets. Charters. Bodysurfing. We were enacting the idea of Barbados rather than living in it, yet, alongside us, maybe this man and his camera, tourists and natives—maybe both—were reaching those deeper layers.

Regrets are unfinished selves.

When we pulled in bay, the crew was already loading coolers onto the boat when we came down the dock. There was a delay. We should be mov-ing out in the next twenty. I used the time to buy some Dramamine and biscuits at the only open store in the marina; I had forgotten to pack all the snacks from the night before. When we got back to the boat, a lanky girl was running, almost falling, shouting at the crew, dialect again, something about rope. Captain Amos was still not there, and his crew leapt onto the dock and began to jog after the girl, saying nothing to us as they fled. Colin looked at me and we started off after them, and soon a small crowd was gath-ering further down the marina where a fifty-footer was gradually capsizing, the mast a few degrees off center, the stern nearly at water level. Two men were emptying chum buckets filled with water over the bow, and there were some much younger Bajans aboard too, yelling out to some other crew—across the marina on a much larger yacht—for an extension cord to power the pump. It was clear all parties were concerned, on the verge of outright desperation; they worked together hurriedly but efficiently, tying the boat off to various points on the dock, in all directions, tensions from all angles meant to right the sinking vessel. The girl came running into the crowd with the end of the extension cord, irate. She wore a beaded necklace and held the pendant as if it were an amulet. *She don't let me plug this in, she heartless. We Bajans are caring people not heartless people. She don't care that his ship sink. She close the door on me. She heartless.* Some of the older men, who had been setting up the fish market, had come down the bridge and started pointing at the listing *Orpheus*, knotted to the pier. There was a general murmuring about the need to find a generator aboard another boat. She heartless, said another pointing back to the shop. Take it over there, said the Brit, that shop over there, right there, pointing to The Waterfront Café: its sliding doors, steps from our boat, were being unlatched and flung open by the poor soul on opening-shift. I heard camera clicks, looked behind me, and saw the man from our van. Standing, he seemed larger than before. It bothered me how my perspectives seemed to carousel, no uniform, immutable view of anything. Comfort is fixed horizons. A man in his sixties, wearing a Yankee cap, emerged from the hull wet from the waist down. Someone shouted over from another boat that the mast was about to hit against another sail, and some of the crew got about untying that sailboat from the dock to head off a collision. There, she heartless: the amulet girl with the extension cord was shouting back across the square to the shopkeeper who had come out to see this all for herself. The mast was a few more minutes, a few more degrees, from horizontal. Cars stopped on the bridge.

I felt the need to give Colin a running commentary on everything trans-piring. He looked worried, but I was confident, I told him, that the boat would never sink. How could it? Will this happen to our boat, he asked. But it could happen, right? Even if you say it won't happen, it might happen, just tell me that it might happen, okay? There was screaming now back by the shops and the girl, again irate, had someone by the hair, pulling her to the cobblestones. *You heartless bitch.* Some men jumped and pulled them apart. The shopkeeper was crying that she had not paid the bill and there was no electricity, no volts, no volts, for me, or for anyone, and you can plug it but it won't charge nuthin'. I had Colin by the shoulder, as if this alter-cation might trigger a street fight, but the Brits kept emptying their buckets and someone now was running, turn it on, he shouted, turn it on, nearly tripping over the ropes of the dock and falling into the marina; you could see a spray of water fluting from the hull onto the deck and then into the marina as the man in the Yankee cap walked the pump hose up from below deck, onto the deck, then let it drain into the marina. The police had come, splitting the two up, no billy clubs. The crowd unclenched.

We walked back to our boat and I dosed out the Dramamine right there, feeling a little illicit to be doing so in the open, in front of the crew, who were explaining to a laughing Captain Amos what had occurred. They all started laughing and then told us to come aboard. The Bulgarian man was checking his photos, reclined in the fighting chair at the stern. Colin hopped up onto the other seat and we pulled out of the slip.

We were headed north, as far as Speightstown, and trolled for a good hour before catching anything worthwhile. The captain said they had caught two marlins just yesterday, thirty minutes to reel in the first one; Colin seemed rapt by the story, eating the last of the chocolate and, by now, our Bulgarian companion had begun to speak a little English, all the way up the coast uttering short, malformed phrases about the sunlight, some other place he had been fishing very recently, people I assumed were his chil-dren—it was hard to tell if he was an alcoholic or simply enjoying himself a little too much as he had already consumed several beers by the time we had reached the tip of the island. From time to time the crew spoke to us, but with an infrequency that gave me the sense that the boat was ours, and it felt, by extension, that the wide blank ocean was ours too. There had not been much action until there was a sudden hard tug on the line. Colin leapt up, was handed the reel that was bending like a willow, looked at me for an approving nod, and started arching his back to give himself leverage as he reeled in something like it might overpower him. When it got near enough to the boat to see I could tell it wasn't a marlin, but a narrow flashing silver thing. I took the rod and lifted it shoulder-high to haul the fish out of the water, realizing the captain had slowed the boat. Without the chop it pulled out easily, thrashing violently as I swiveled it above the deck when one of the crew took it, using some kind of plier to remove the hook. They said it was a barracuda. It convulsed on the deck until it was tossed into the cooler, the lid was closed, and you could tell when it finally asphyxiated because the thudding stopped.

"Can we eat that one?" Colin said, making a disgusted face. The Bulgarian man was giving a thumbs-up, nodding vigorously, and one of the crew said it was delicious, like swordfish.

The boat turned and we began to head back, this time closer inland, and you could see little pink or red beach umbrellas dotting the beaches of all the luxury resorts in St. James Parish. I sat on a folding chair drinking a beer. *We go now to Batts Rock Beach, treat for the little guy*, the tallest one said; his hair was near gold from sun exposure. We slowed into a tiny cove without surf, dropped anchor, and a breeze blew across the fishing lines, a faint quartet of high-pitched notes, squealing violin sounds. Captain Amos came down the stairs without using the handrail and told Colin he could jump off the boat to swim. He was already wearing his swim trunks and I helped him undress, retied his drawstring, lifted him up to the bow and watched him jump. The water was clear enough that I could see his feet from the deck. The water here seemed to glow blue, a fleshy translucency. I took off my shirt and sandals and dove off the bow. Colin looked shocked to see me when I surfaced, smiling with wonderment, and I could hear the crew hooting and laughing from the boat. The water was pleasantly warm and we swam together towards the cove; I could see the rocks were coral, dusty white, and there was no inlet for the water but further down beside the cove was a shady beach, by the looks of it a local secret. I had the feeling that I should have known about this place, as Monica and I had hunted all over the coast for tucked away places, trying to shed the tourist aura, sampling all the rum shops in the eastern half of the island, seeking to penetrate the nucleus of the place.

"Can we go to that beach?" he asked.

"I'm not sure how we can. We'd be leaving the boat behind. All our stuff is there. All of our things." I reread his expression and he seemed to be chiding me.

"Besides," I said, "there are sharks at this beach. We'd have to get past the sharks to get to that beach."

"Dad, sharks do like it down here. They prefer cold water. They like it to be refreshing for them because they swim so hard and they get sweaty."

"Are you going to try and eat your barracuda?"

"On the boat?"

"Silly, at a restaurant. When we get back. You should try it. We can put that Bajan hot sauce on it. You should try that too." He was making a face.

"I would prefer not to."

"Come on."

"Nope!"

"What will it take?"

He spun his head around in the water, as if scanning the shelves of a toy store.

"What are you looking at?"

"I'm looking for cool boats. Ours is slow. I wanna go fast."

"So if I take you on a fast boat tomorrow will you try the fish and the sauce with me when we dock?"

He was smiling and nodding, treading water. After a day his skin had already darkened, my genetics kicking in, and his brownish hair had lightened. For a moment I noted this dichotomy, was cognizant of Van Gogh's aphorism about opposing colors, and wondered why he had never painted the ocean, having lived so close to it in Southern France.

"Dad?" he said, startling me back into the moment. "Are you thinking of mommy?"

"Am I thinking of mommy?" I wasn't sure why I had repeated his question, and thought it must have sounded ridiculous to him.

"Yeah, mommy. Like how much she liked it here?"

Now I was completely startled. How did he know this?

"You know, it's okay, dad. I know it's true. You were here on a vacation and you were skinny. Mommy looked so beautiful."

I thought about telling him we needed to swim back to the boat, invoke some unspecified urgency that would short-circuit this conversation. How could he know this?

"When we get back to the room, I will show you the pictures on my phone," he said.

"Your phone is here?"

"Well, yeah, I brought it in case you had to go and work or something. Don't be mad. Please don't be mad. It's in my sneaker. I'll try the barracuda, okay? Just don't be mad at me."

Monica took photos here, yes, and, yes, they were on an old-fashioned Nikon and now how were they possibly on Colin's phone? I began to question the rationale for getting him the phone, angrily cross-examining Dr. Weller in my mind. What else had he seen?

"You look like her," I said. He visibly relaxed. "I'm not mad. I'm just confused. Where did you see these pictures?"

"Google."

"You Googled mommy and saw these pictures?"

"She has a website, Facebook—and all these pictures are there. I'm in it too, when I was a baby in blankets, and some have you and her at a school and there are some with pandas at a zoo and there are some too, yeah, where you guys are standing in all these long sticks with vines with some horses."

He had seen his delivery photos; he had seen the Bronx Zoo and her Harvard Law School graduation; he had seen our anniversary pictures of Napa Valley. How deep and how wide was his view of the past?

A horn blew and I turned and saw Captain Amos waving at us to return to the boat. Colin looked fragile, expectantly waiting for me to scold him. Were we not shoulder deep in water, I would have hugged him. I heard all the things I wasn't supposed to say, and then I heard all the things Monica would have wanted me to say. He treaded water, looking at me. *Be gentle with him. I am being gentle with him. He is crying out for you. I know what he is doing. You can be happy. You can both be happy. I am happy, I said. He is happy now. Be careful, Mark. I hear you but I cannot see you. Where are you? I can still taste the ocean on your skin. Where did you go I cannot hear you? Tell me what to do, tell me what to do with everything I have almost destroyed.*

When I finally spoke, I made sure that I had extinguished all the shock in my voice. We were swimming back to the boat, heads up, in the current-less water, some flying fish darting along the surface.

"You know," I said, "we should look at these photos together, tonight. What do you think?"

"You're not mad?"

"I'm not mad."

"I can keep my phone?" He was breathing hard, tired from swimming.

"You can keep the phone."

We headed south, a few minor catches along the way, until we slipped back into port. The doors of The Waterfront Café were flung open, the tables filled with the sunburnt all the way out onto the dock. Captain Amos handed us our fish in a clear plastic bag, helped us off the boat, shook our hands, gave us a brochure for a catamaran snorkeling cruise that would set sail at sunrise tomorrow morning—and it would be a good price for us—and I walked into the café, to my surprise, handed the fish over without a word to the hostess, who took it from me without hesitation, appraising what was in the bag, and she guided us to a table half inside and outside, and I ordered a rum punch and a soda for Colin. Minutes later she brought out a wooden platter with the barracuda prepared three ways—fried, jerk grilled, and sautéed—and there were ramekins of rice and peas and a little green salad topped with ribbons of shaved carrots, a homemade vinaigrette. It was all delicious. Colin ate more than I did and we didn't speak until most of the fish was gone and there was only the rice left, soaking in the juices. I ordered another rum punch and proceeded with the inevitable.

"How did you find those pictures?"

"Mommy has a Facebook page."

She sometimes experimented with black and white photography when she couldn't paint, blocked, or had simply exhausted her theme, as she called it. She only sold her paintings, however; the photographs were an artistically therapeutic diversion. They were pictures of almost anything with a pulse, the major and predictable milestones in our lives and the vaporous in between. They were head-on, sometimes frightening shots of subjects, unflinching portraits that captured human personalities in transition, the shaded states of being in between absolute moods, or some winter cardinal or sleeping safari lion or Rwandan gorilla that exuded an air of humanity. She was fixated on life, the frame by frame of this and that. She would also catalogue her work with the ardor of a taxonomist, at first in files and photo albums, then, halfway into our marriage, in megabytes and pixels; I knew she had a Facebook page but seeing that I did not have one myself, I never really paid much mind to it and, until now, it had never really occurred that it would perpetuate posthumously, her life suspended in digital amber. Facebook was our client and I considered how I might use the connection to pull the page down. My hands were shaking.

"How many times have you been on her Facebook page?" I said, signaling to the waitress to refill my cocktail. My chest felt tight and something like a fog had settled into my throat, making it difficult to fully inhale. I did my breathing.

"I guess every day."

"Every day?"

"At school, in the bathroom, maybe sometimes after I go to sleep, at night, when you're sleeping, when I hear you snoring."

"Have you shown the pictures to anyone?"

"The other kids think it's weird."

"Do you think visiting the page is weird?"

"Do you think it's weird, daddy?"

"I think your mommy loved you very much and she would be taking lots of pictures of you were she here with us still."

"But do you think it's weird?"

"I'm not sure why you think it's weird, Colin."

"It's that the pictures feel real and, well, I guess sometimes they make me talk to her, just like we are talking right now, and I feel weird to talk to nobody because that's strange. That's wrong."

I drank down the refill and knew it would take a little more time for it to kick in. The *Orpheus* was reloading with new passengers, an American couple with teenage girls overdressed for fishing. The sun, soon enough, would reach its peak, though it was cool in the shaded semi-indoors.

"It's not weird and it's not wrong. You cannot think that. Okay? Look at me. You are not strange…hey, pal, look at me." He had tears streaking down his cheek, in a full fit. "Colin," I said, reaching across the table to touch his shoulder, "you are just a little boy and the things you feel can be confusing. And you don't have to tell your friends about the things you see online—or your mother. Whatever you are telling them."

He was looking up now, not wiping his eyes.

"Do you know what happens when you lose an arm or leg? You still feel it, they say, I mean you feel the part you've lost. Of course it's not there, but the point is your mother, when she died, she was a major part of you, and it's like this, you feel her even when she's not there."

"Dad…"

"Yes?"

"According to reality, mommy was hit by a car. Is this really how she died?"

Now I knew that he had been searching the web, not just Googling pictures of his mother. How could I not have seen this coming? I had equipped him with a smart phone, blanketed our home in Wi-Fi, given him nil by way of facts concerning Monica's disappearance—that's what I called it for a good while—and now he was answering all his own questions, seeing everything through the unfiltered lens of the internet while I wandered museums. Rattling the past, Colin must have been scared and curious by what he discovered. I doubted whether he could fully metabolize it and sensed he had a wellspring of more questions for me that I was afraid I might never answer.

"Do you two want dessert?" the waitress asked, though she quickly backed away when she saw Colin. "Maybe I will come back in a minute," she said, winking at me as if she knew this was over some trivial matter like buying the wrong postcard or not catching enough fish. I signaled for the check.

It didn't seem right to reenact his mother's death here, by the wharf. The *Orpheus* was slipping out again, and we both noticed, at the same time, that the sinking ship was absent from its slip. The thought crossed our minds at the same time. There was no longer a crowd, just the undulating water where, not long ago, there had been a listing vessel.

"Did it sink? Is it gone?" he said.

I scratched my head and took off my sunglasses.

There was a barefoot man squatting under Independence Bridge, the overlook for this morning's mayhem. He was strumming a duct taped guitar, in song, common Bob Marley, but *a cappella*, nearly drowned out by the street traffic. As we turned back to the empty slip, we saw, at full mast, the *Sea Nymph* pulling into port, now with a full crew, British and Bajan, an ennobling sight after its near peril that morning. She docked, emptied herself of her passengers, and more came aboard, the crew restocking her with more drinks and more passengers, and, just like that, she was sailing back out to sea.

★

ONLY WHEN I knew he was asleep, his breathing audible and patterned, did I look for and find his phone in his sneaker. I had to plug it in as the battery was nearly drained. The room held still in the perfect darkness. I checked all the open browser windows and saw multiple images of her carousel one by one before me as I drew each screen towards me with my thumb. She was all there, she was always there, all over the web, every year of her from college through her final months.

He rustled and turned over, still asleep. I went and got a cup of water from the bathroom sink, tip-toed back and opened the sliding glass door, turned on the patio light, and sat down on the damp chair, checking his search history. That he had been leading this clandestine interior life for, presumably, the entire nine months since I had gotten him the phone, was startling enough. I was even more surprised to learn that he had been surfing for hits on me. He had discovered all the major ones, a few profiles of the firm and some gossipy clips. I started to read the articles myself. They were mostly banal but a few had bite, painting a harsh portrait of White & Partners, making me feel foreign to myself. Was I really a "spin machine" and a "merciless mouthpiece" for leaders of some of the world's poorest countries? The pieces did not mention the charities we represented, the Fortune 10 clients, or the G7 countries. He would never know that unless I told him, and I had not told him anything about my work. It crossed my mind that just as I had told him very little about Monica, I had also revealed to him very little of myself. I finished my water and continued to browse through what he had seen, and then I got on Google and started to search myself, saw my biography, if that's the word, unfurl in reverse chronology, the first hit my literal bio cached from my company's website. I clicked and began to read:

Mark White is the Chairman and CEO of White & Partners, which he founded in 2003. Mr. White acts as a senior advisor to Heads of State, CEOs and global corporations, and serves as a senior consultant on many of the firm's retained accounts. He also plays an active role in special project work. His areas of expertise include crisis and litigation communications, corporate reputation, M&A, public policy, and international issues management. He resides in Virginia with his family.

I sat back in the chair and stared at the sky in appraisal, as if the words were strung up in the heavens. I felt like a real drink now, a cigarette, but there was only the tepid tap water. The bug sounds were still there, but I could no longer hear the late-night congregation of Bajans at the food stand across the street; it must have been after midnight. My bio was terrible—terribly written, terribly myopic as to who I was as a person, but mostly it was terrible because it was a sketch of an incomplete man. I obviously hadn't updated it in years and I did not feel that a revision would improve it in any way. The worst part was, perhaps, that I had no sense of how to revise myself.

I went back inside the room, which had become humid from the sliding door being slightly cracked, and fished out two Lorazepam from my dopp kit, went back outside, shutting the door all the way this time, and reread my bio. If Harry was right and I could unload what was an asset in its prime, how would this read if I were just Chairman, Senior Advisor, or Of Counsel, some term that connoted importance, maybe even stature, without binding authority. I had the instinct to call his cell right then, contemplated the hour and considered his already wary perspective on my condition, and reconsidered.

I looked back at the screen and reloaded the search results on me in the news tab; it took nearly thirty seconds to load and when the haul of stories finally appeared, I had to sit up straight in my chair. There were already four from today.

Embattled DC Powerhouse Now Calls Senator Boxer "Comfort Woman"—The Beacon

Senator Boxer Slams Consulting Firm Over Twitter Comments—Associated Press

Japanese Embassy Condemns WWII Remarks By Its Own P.R. Firm—The Washington Post

All the stories had the same captioned photo of me beside the headline; it was a completely unflattering picture from a year ago, taken at our annual "Social Media Trends 3.0" conference at The Willard: I was at the Round Robin Bar, alone but surrounded by backslapping pinstripers, drinking something in a highball, staring towards the camera with a distant zombie expression. It wouldn't be long before these articles, published midday, would proliferate, become a contagion among other clients, some of whom would see their names blister in these sensational stories. It would send reporters scurrying across the city to uncover more imbroglios—if there were any—so they could extend and inflate the news cycle, which, I'd guessed within a few seconds of reading the headlines, would sheer off another few million of revenue, at least four to six major clients, all while

I was sitting on this dimly lit patio in Barbados. All, as I would soon learn, because of something caused by a rogue intern.

I did not read any of the stories in full, but I tried to conjure the origins of this scandal and could not recollect anything on the schedule yesterday that would have provided cause for such a lethal tweet. I started to feel sick, heat rising in my skin and my stomach starting to gurgle. I thought about calling Sally or Margaret to ask why they hadn't called me—or had they checked out this week too? Hawthorne may have been trying to conjure me from my undisclosed location but I didn't know how to log on to my firm's email remotely; I did not know how to log on to my firm's Twitter account; after thinking of all this for a minute, it then occurred that I did not even know my own firm's Twitter handle, therefore I could not even dredge up the offending remark: I would have to manually enter *White & Partners* into the search tab within Twitter and personally review all the feathery specks that floated about, the rising dust of a spectacle for which the petty city had long been waiting. My throat was tightening now and it was difficult to breathe. If I was suffering a panic attack despite the Lorazepam, then it only confirmed for me how flimsy and impermanent my psyche was. Dr. Weller had told me that trauma lingers in your blood, hibernates, undetected, until it springs upon you, and the best remedy was for me to lay fallow for an extended period to let the source grief leech out. Your nervous system is fried, he said—and maybe he was right. Stress caused illnesses, phobias, other disorders, even cancers. I could read about it in all these *New England Journal of Medicine* articles, he said, handing me stapled photocopies. But I had not read them; I had not considered, until now, that my own indifference to the broader affairs of my firm was a symptom of my own incapacity to metabolize stress; my own nervous system was compromised, incapable of withstanding more trauma, so I simply evaded the circumstances and the relationships that offered the potential for more grief. My breath was labored and I did my exercises, taking heaving breaths, timing them to the sound of imaginary waves. I wondered if I might suffocate or have a heart attack—and what would become of Colin. Would he wake to find me sprawled on the hotel floor, stiff and white, my pulse missing? By what local authorities would the transfer of my corpse be arranged to return to the United States, and how would Colin be taken home, and to whom?

I had authored no will and he would be heaped into foster care, penniless until my estate was reconciled in probate after several years' time. I hadn't done much these past few years to author Colin, leaving much of the child rearing to Mae. My limits were long exceeded by now, and, like Dr. Weller said, perhaps I was abbreviating the time ahead of me by not avoiding stress—if that was ever possible, for anyone—or maybe it was that I had been steeping for so long in chronic anxiety that I was singing my telomeres, turning on all the switches that led to fatal disease. Which would strike first—and when?

Standing, I turned off the phone and walked to the bathroom, took two more Lorazepam, sat on the toilet, and waited in the dark. I did my breathing and imagined the waves.

I drank another glass of tap water, filtered and mineralized by the coral beneath the island, I remembered.

I took off all my clothes and let the sweating finish and wiped my brow with toilet paper. The lapping of the imaginary waves had stabilized my breathing, though maybe it was the tranquilizer. The tension eased. I stood up and I rummaged in the closet for the suitcases, naked.

When the suitcases were packed, I let myself be lulled to sleep by the sound of the pretend waves.

chapter eight

I WAS told that I needed to bow at least twice, that if I wanted to show true remorse they needed to see the back of my head.

I had to commit to memory a solemn phrase in Japanese, and we had some green tea brewed and ready, votive candles and yellow tulips arranged on the conference room table; I was told too that a gift, something rare, must follow the apology. Margaret had procured a bottle of small-batch Kentucky bourbon. There were only two hundred or so of its kind in existence, each one numbered with a hand-written label.

When the elevator chimed and the doors opened, I was expecting to the see Ambassador Satake, but it was Wendy in her sunglasses, a shock of wind-blown hair and a plastic CVS bad filled with Tupperware and green apples. She kind of grunted a hello as she walked past, texting and nodding her head as if in violent disagreement with some phantom captor. I saw Margaret coming to me now. Another elevator chimed: it was Hawthorne.

This meeting had been arranged hastily from the departures lounge at the airport in Barbados, and for two days since I suffered another round of bad press. There were two reasons I had to flee my trip with Colin prematurely: the Japanese, beholden to their distinct concept of shame, had a cultural need for an apology, and we could not move forward in business together ever again without it; the main reason, though, was that we had fucked up: drunk or worse, one of our interns, referring to the young Chinese women captured and enslaved for sex by the Japanese in World War II, attaching the photo of the Ambassador with Senator Boxer at a gala fundraiser for lung cancer awareness, tweeted, from the official Embassy account that we managed, AMBASSADOR SATAKE TACKLES CANCER! ONE COMFORT WOMAN AT A TIME!

"Do we have the music dialed to the right tune?" I asked Margaret.

"I'm not sure, Mark. Do you have something in mind?"

I had nothing in mind, big bold beautiful fucking nothing. I did not understand how a stray intern could unhinge this entire account, pin up the firm on the media wall for yet another public vivisection. They were both standing right there in my midst and I couldn't take a pill, although I had three in my pocket, without them seeing me. They would be arriving any second.

There was a distinct sound of a Japanese flute, the crashing of cymbals, cinematic music meant to mock. Hawthorne had not sipped his coffee and shouted at the girl at the reception desk, also an intern. "What the hell is this?" he said.

She receded into her chair, head swiveling, beseeching someone to pluck her from my orbit. Leaning back in her chair, she started to stammer and looked down the hall towards the bullpen of intern cubes near the server room; her fingernails were painted bubblegum pink. Why did we have all these interns anyway? I had said it aloud. Hawthorne shot me a glance. Why hadn't I sold this company when I had the chance, I had said to myself.

She quivered, no words, a cat in the rain. I heard the fever of strings build in the music; only later that day, after the apology, was I made aware that the intern who had sent the comfort woman tweet, fired that very night by Hawthorne, had out of revenge convinced someone inside the firm, at the appointed hour, to cue the theme from the soundtrack of *The Last Samurai*.

"Play something somber," he said to Margaret. "Chet Baker." She shooed the girl away and sat down at the desk and typed in something and then the cymbals gave way to a moody trumpet.

I rehearsed my demotic Japanese phrase, which sounded violent to me no matter how I said it. Margaret stepped away from the reception and walked down the hall towards her real desk; I felt my mind drift into other places, Accra Beach, that "effective" rum punch. I saw a boy again swimming with the current, tossing the beach ball at the waves, only realizing it was Colin seconds into the flashback; I saw him sleeping and waking alone while I received acupuncture in Chinatown or ate *fritto misto* in Manhattan or was seduced into empty sex or blacked out and awoke alone. I had forgotten the pitch of Monica's voice that day. I had my hands tied with Gordian obligations while too many regrets were accruing each week, sometimes hourly, it seemed. She would have told me to self-impose a sabbatical, stroked my hair, but I only saw a flabby man on a beach with his rum punch screwed into the sand watching the tide pull a beach ball, a boy in tow; and I had a fading head of hair that she could no longer tousle. There was something awful about me now and she would have seen it. There was this life, the one I was about to resume with an apology, but also another, one more vivid and sensate, flickering alongside this one, but if it was of the past or the future I could not discern. I could not remember which cheek held her dimple. Where did these memories go, still captive in my skull? Were we too unconscious to life as it happened when we could no longer elicit by will what we sought from a memory, or was it that we were meant to forget our memories over time? I rang the bell once more, but I could not hear her voice and only could smell Hawthorne's coffee and only hear Chet Baker singing "My Funny Valentine."

I heard the elevator chime. A slight panic set in. What if I had failed to execute the right preparations? Can we lose yet another client? Hawthorne immediately put the coffee on the floor against the wall. The Ambassador's aide was first off, dressed in a shaggy suit with an adolescent mustache. Ambassador Satake was next, looking every bit imperious and disappointed, along with the deputy chief of mission, their American translator in tow.

I gave the first of my deep bows and said, "Would you please follow me to the room. They had difficulty making eye contact, and they began to talk amongst themselves when they saw the preparations we'd made, as though they had an inkling of the substance and authenticity of the apology to come.

They uttered some quick Japanese to the translator, which he made no effort to translate. He continued untangling the wires of his earpieces, no polite smile for the delay. They watched me. I saw Hawthorne engaged in a prolonged Cheshire Cat expression meant to put them all at ease, but he looked somewhat ridiculous, hands folded and elbows propped on the table. We sat in silence waiting for the translator to set up. It felt like ten minutes had passed. Facing the glass wall, I registered the distinct feeling of being captive in a freak show display, as factions of the staff walking by the room every ten seconds, sneaking furtive glances, headed towards the kitchen to congregate and gossip about my much-discussed and amusing apology, the latest installment in the demise of Mark White.

I wanted to issue a convincing apology: I had rehearsed multiples times the day before, trying on different inflections to feign the right balance of disgrace and regal dignity.

"It's working now," the translator said finally, scratching his bald head.

Without hesitation, I stood. I cleared my throat. I felt nothing but anger and shame. This is what I had become. My vaunted consulting firm was a circus and I was its ringleader. I heard my father laughing. I saw my wife barely breathing, bloody in a ditch. I saw my son crying.

I was somewhere else as I stuttered through my memorized Japanese. Ambassador Satake had his head cocked, peering through one eye to appraise me, an impenetrable skeptic. I was conscious of how I moved, shifting in my seat or leaning into the table, my hands clasped in my lap; I had no sense of what I was saying. As I spoke the jagged words, they hardly seemed to matter. I gave up on the Japanese. It was all a jumble of syllables, chipped phrases anyway.

I began in my native tongue in Delphic tones. "First," I said, pausing as if to clear the air of Japanese, "I wish to convey deep regret for the dishonor that White & Partners has brought to you, the Embassy, the prime minister, and the people of Japan."

Then I introduced a gleaming apology in near perfect King's English, reiterated by the translator, who, moments after a sudden utterance by Ambassador Satake, told me deadpan in English that our contract was hereby terminated.

★

IT WAS windy at the cemetery.

I was still wearing my suit, the crumpled paper with the penitent Japanese in my breast pocket. We pulled up to the curb and parked in a heap of crispy leaves. Colin cradled the little bag of hyacinth bulbs and we walked up the hill to her plot. I foot-swept the sticks and thistles and acorns from the stiff dormant grass. There were wreathes on easels set against the others or bundles of spent daisies or store-dyed roses, sherbet red or purple, or plastic-potted chrysanthemums at the plot beside ours. The sun off the glassy face of her headstone, a luminescent shock. That end-of-season gust rushing through the leaves. Empty post-migration sky, hourglass daylight. I had kept her headstone simple:

Monica Karen White

In Loving Memory

1975 – 2012

"Though I Sang in My Chains Like the Sea"

We knelt and then he looked at me as if to invite some pacifying comment. My pocket vibrated. I let it go.

He had ruddy cheeks and swollen eyes. It was best not to hold back the gestures and consolation that might prevent any catharsis. It was best to let him go, expose the hidden flesh wounds to air, cry a while, maybe cry with him too, and maybe it was this kind of moment, a boy still in his father's orbit, all the kneeling and the praying and the tearing, this glimpse at the hollow past, that filtered out the grief still in the bones. Maybe it was the unrelenting stare into the future's white space, the brutal stare back at the stillborn paths and choices, the maybes and almosts, that finally releases us. But he did not cry. Show me something, his eyes said. Lick the bones clean. He did not know yet that it was stubborn devotion that exhumes the long dead. He did not need to relinquish her because he could hardly remember her.

The wind gusted again.

I tore the bag and poured the bulbs onto the grass, spreading them evenly into a single layer. I told him to dig a big hole; this was how we would entomb the coming spring in the wet November cement.

He two-handed the spade into the unyielding ground, four, maybe five times, and I took it from him and made sharp, quick-angled stabs into the grass and tore up some sod so he could widen the hole from there. We placed the bulbs in the hole. We did not drop them. I shook their flaky skins from the bottom of the bag into the ground, breaking them up with my fingertips, telling Colin to do the same.

Leave nothing behind, I said aloud, and then I spoke *The Lord's Prayer* in my head twice; when we had filled the hole and leveled the ground I said it aloud, still kneeling, as Colin mouthed the words in slight delay. He was bewildered, but not crying, and I held the silence a little longer until I knew it was too comfortable for him, but I did not know what to say next. I stood up, head bowed, and he rose with me, an overdone stoop. Our children struggle with their mimicry. He was still tan. His impetigo was almost gone. I took his overgrown hand; parts of him felt larger than his age, the knuckles and the knee caps, his nubby fingers. He still smelled like a small child, the cold milky scent behind his ears. I tousled his hair for a moment, exhaled and watched my breath dissipate. I wanted us to revel in this decay, lie down in it until we were mulched over and renewed. A plane in ascent made a brushstroke of white contrails in the sky. He looked up while I led him away back down the hill. There was still the wind but no other sounds of nature. I made a driving gesture, pointing at him with my hitchhiker's thumb, offering him the chance to drive the car around the cemetery. He looked down again, shook his head no, and looked back up at the vanishing jet noise. My pocket vibrated twice more.

It was dark when we arrived home. Mae was still off for the week, as I had expected that we would still be in Barbados, and our refrigerator was barren. I ordered a cheese pizza, went into the library and retrieved three photo albums, each one successively dating from the first three years of our marriage. I grabbed some of the white birch still in the basket and made an ambitious fire, embers smack-popping from the hearth nearly reaching Atticus' paws over by the sofa. Smoke billowed as I fanned with the burnt-out newspaper torch. Colin came over and sat down and took the torch and started fanning at the smoke. We spread out the old quilt from the guest room bed on the floor, and I opened all the photo albums to pages at random, watching him survey the polaroid stills of her freshman year when she hadn't yet fit into her body; the drug store developed shots of us on the window ledge of Shakespeare and Company bookstore in Paris, the only time we were ever there; those grainy home-printed photos of her renderings of Stonehenge that she painted from laptop images of the obelisk stones. I turned pages to things he had never seen, hoping that these concealed stages of our shared history, the chronological permutations of birthday cakes and Christmas trees and sunset mountain ranges and leathery summer lakes, these fixed points, might infiltrate him, that they might bestow some confidence in a backstory. He was not a free radical in the world. He came from a union, two people. We did not speak. I pulled apart the sticking pages, pointing at her in a few of the pictures; the rest, where it was just the two of us, didn't need my direction. He sat cross-legged, bending over when he wanted to examine a photo. It took nearly thirty minutes for me to exhaust the album. He removed a picture of her standing in front of some waterfall in a Maui jungle, made a wide-eyed expression. I nodded my assent. He put the picture beside him, starting a pile. After a while he turned the pages on his own and removed more from that Hawaii trip, adding them to his pile, turned more pages and ransacked more of our destinations and holidays until his pile was the height of a deck of cards. The pizza was half-eaten and cold in the greasy box. He neatened the pile and stood up.

"What can we do with these?" he said.

I led him into the kitchen, pulled the corkboard down off the wall, removed from it all the Chinese menus and school leaflets, pulled the nail from the wall, and found the hammer in the drawer full of mismatched pens and rubber bands. He followed me to his room where I hung it over his desk, leveling it by sight, handing him pins one at a time while he fixed each picture in some preordained position he had worked out in his mind.

"I think this looks great," he said. "I should take a picture of it, in case we lose these."

After he was asleep, I went downstairs and fixed a Coke and lemon, put on the Friday night hockey game and read emails. Ever since the snowstorm the evening temperatures had dipped down into the mid-thirties, and all the hardwood floors seemed to bear the change in their bones. The old house creaked, the floors snapping ever so often, loud enough that Atticus would sit up.

I texted Harry to call me.

I downed the drink, made another, and grabbed some pretzels and some dark chocolate, and when I came back to the hockey there was a siren and a roaring crowd: I watched Ovechkin on replay one-time a pass from the left circle to tie the game in the third period, a shotgun shot into some negative space that did not exist until he fired the puck and the goalie slid across the crease and froze, handcuffed. Just above his shoulder, grazing the cross bar and ricocheting back onto the ice. Tied at three with two minutes to go. I thought I should wake Colin and let him watch the overtime. The Rangers took a penalty with less than a minute remaining and I knew that I should wake Colin to watch the power play because I had the feeling that Ovechkin would take the same shot and end the game. I thought that this would make me a good father. You take your son places, show him things, and he absorbs your essence. Maybe he retains that essence, and he remembers you. I was waiting for some definitive decision to spark. I waited, came to no conclusion, and watched regulation time expire and the game conclude, exactly as I imagined it would: slapshot, same shot, cross-ice pass. Ovechkin. Harry texted to meet him at The Palm on Monday for lunch. I went to bed.

chapter nine

USUALLY THE place was bustling, but Congress was in recess and it was half empty, mainly septuagenarians and infrequent *CNN* contributors, a single *Washington Post* columnist hunched at the bar eating soup. We were seated at a table in the middle of the room. The waiter brusquely told us the specials.

"Did you enjoy your vacation?" Harry was tying a plastic bib around his neck in anticipation of lobster. I had taken too many pills in the bathroom before he arrived and wasn't hungry. I ordered grilled salmon.

When they brought the food, Harry lowered his head as snapped off appendages, sucking claws clean. "You don't know how to eat a lobster effectively," he said.

I picked at my fish. "It was good to get away. I wish it would snow like that more often." Harry chuckled but didn't look up. He was working on a claw.

I watched him eat. "You probably know why I texted you. Here's the thing," he said, finally looking up and wiping his mouth. "The number we discussed was two months ago. I called them this morning. The number has changed." He was squeezing lemon juice on his fingers and cleaning them with his napkin. He downed the rest of his chardonnay and looked at me.

"Mark, you've built a beautiful thing, truly. Not many guys can do it but you have."

"What's the number?"

"Mark—"

"Seriously, just blurt it out and tell me."

"Zero."

"Zero?"

"Mark, they don't wanna buy. They did two months ago and now they don't."

"Jesus."

The waiter came and Harry ordered cheesecake and a double espresso. I waved him off and started fiddling with the sugar packets. I felt nauseous.

"They read the news, and the news on White & Partners Mark has been rough, real rough."

"We have eighty clients. Well, we had eighty clients.... We represented a dozen countries. Alright fine we lost some but—"

"Mark, it's all about risk management for them. And they see your firm as a risk."

"This is ridiculous."

"'Who's in charge there?' they ask me. I said Mark runs the place, same as always. 'Not what we heard,' they said. The stuff with Lars and whoever was bad, Mark. This stuff with Japan didn't help."

"Well, goddammit Harry, what if we forget an earn out and just sell at a discount price."

"And you walk away the next day?'"

"Right, the next day.

"Why would you do that Mark? You've built such—"

"Never mind the lecture, Harry! If I want out, then I want out, and I think for my sake, for Colin's sake, I want out of this straight jacket once and for all. Can you do that for me, Harry? Can you do that? Please!"

As Harry spoke I pulled out my phone ostentatiously and began to text Colin that I would be home early.

"Mark, you really need to focus in, here, okay, that stunt on MSNBC, the drama with OneSpeak, Senator Boxer—fuck—it's got you dead in the water. No one will want to touch this. No one. Maybe we revisit things in nine months, a year. I've dealt with similar situations and time is on your side."

Harry didn't know it, but I didn't have time. I didn't completely know the financials, but could guess at them. I knew, now, without question, that my son needed me again. And maybe I had lost my fastball, my lustrous hubris, and I knew that to carry on like this was to endure, yet again, the same drained season.

"Harry—" I interrupted. He looked up from his pile of empty shells.

"Harry a year from now is..." I was alarmed by the implications of what was embedded in my own pause, and thought that I was depicting myself to my own lawyer in the worst possible light.

He dipped his fingers in the little bowl beside the plate and wiped his hands.

"Mark, you've had some troubles. That's in the past, but I realize for you maybe it's not. When Luciana died, I was a wreck, a mess, totally unhooked. You need to find yourself someone new. It's not a slight to Monica. It's not. She was your wife. But she is not your wife now. Men are like trains, women the rails. We need them."

I sat awkwardly, hands folded on my lap below the table, feeling upbraided. "Harry it's not that easy."

"Mark yes, it is. You meet someone, you go to a nice place like this, you drink wine, you live well." He had transitioned now into a jocular tone that moved the conversation into easier waters.

"You know," I said, not sure if I wanted to say what was coming next, "is it possible to regress? When your spouse dies, do you regress?"

He looked at me curiously, trying to decode the question. "You mean like drugs, women? That sort of regress?" He was looking at my plate of uneaten fish.

"Harry I'm just talking about basic needs. To be loved. One day, there is someone here on earth who loves you, then they're gone. Then you love that person you both produced, but you can barely produce the love sufficient for yourself."

He had his eyes averted, pointed at heap of cheesecake on the dessert tray the waiter held. Sometimes I thought Harry merely tolerated me. Maybe they all merely tolerated me. You can pay anyone in this world to do anything except to love you.

"Mark, the best we can do is an auction. You will be selling this thing like a piece of scrap, at best for a fraction of the enterprise value. A fraction.

Like maybe thirty percent. Maybe. But I need time. I need this all to heal and look better."

He pulled off the bib and motioned for the waiter.

If Harry was throwing pitches in the sand, I'd have to jettison him for a more capable surrogate.

I stood up, shook his hand, and said goodbye, leaving him with the huge bill.

There was a line for the valet but I was afraid to wait and be seen. I gave him a ten dollar bill to skip ahead, and when I got in the car I put on the BBC in time to hear about an overnight car bomb somewhere in northern Africa and I switched to Bluetooth and played *Prufrock*.

It wasn't until I had driven out of the city and into Virginia that I noticed the diminished snowbanks along the parkway, white patches on the grassy slopes down to the woods. I wavered between fixation on the effective rum cocktail from a few days earlier to my ridiculous Japanese apology to mentally canvassing the punch list of actions required by law to wind down White & Partners in the event I couldn't sell it. I called my accountant, Lucas, and asked him to forward along asset statements, and he rather gratuitously reminded me that I had no debt, which reminded me that Monica's intolerance of debt was the reason I had paid off the mortgage last year.

All the little tributaries of fear we hide from ourselves run deeper and longer than we know. I had to have known that, eventually, whatever tempest within would fight its way out into open view. Here it all was now, lathered up nice for every enemy to see. Clients were beginning to fire us, and employees would be quitting next. The brand wattage had dimmed—mine and the company's. A swift decline is always slow at first. I imagined many millions of dollars of revenue sheared off next year's operating budget; then there would be the tough choice of letting people go and dimming the wattage more or eating into the cash reserves, thereby cannibalizing the root of my equity. I sped the car up. I switched the Bluetooth back to the BBC and listened to a female voice report on the car bomb. Fifty killed.

I called Margaret and told her I was too ill for the staff meeting at three, then turned onto my street and parked between the snow dunes in my driveway.

The landscapers were shaking bags of Dead Sea salt again. There was another storm expected.

It was still an hour before Colin would come home from school. I sat there for ten minutes, warm in the car, staring at the icicles on the roofline and listening to the Libyan president vow revenge against the bombers and tried to jettison thoughts of Lars and Fung and Alan and Harry and the Japanese from my mind while thinking about buying tickets to tonight's Capitals game. I settled on a new stick for Colin instead. I got out, leaving the car running, and ran inside to give my bag to Mae and grab a peanut butter sandwich. Mae looked bewildered to see me home and trailed me. I told her to tell Colin I would be home right after he got there.

With school in session, the rink was half deserted. I asked the kid behind the counter for two youth-sized sticks with a thirty-five flex, Ovechkin curve. They were ninety-nine dollars each. I had him saw them down to the height of my sternum. I bought some rolls of red tape and sat down next to the fireplace when I got home and taped the sticks. When I finished the blade, I poked the fire a bit with the butt and twisted two feet of tape around the handle, candy-cane wrapping it, and then taping over it to form a grip.

Colin came in the front door after school.

"Daddy!" he looked surprised to see me.

"What do you think?" I said, holding the sticks upright.

"These are for me? I mean you bought them?"

"I figured there are at least five goals in these apiece, maybe ten."

"And you remembered the red tape, daddy!"

He put his arm around my waist and I noticed Mae smiling at us from the kitchen, drying a Bordeaux glass.

"Well, I know we had to cut our trip short so, you know."

He appraised me for a good five seconds and gave me a hug, wrapping his arms around my neck. Mae had finished the kitchen and was staring at me as though she required permission to leave.

"Mr. White," she said.

I walked into the kitchen; she had her purse slung over her shoulder.

"Mae, what is it?"

"I don't think it is working very good." She was looking at the floor.

I assume, like everyone else, it was a statement designed to extort more money. "You mean your salary?"

"Everything, I think, Mr. White. It's too hard for just me. He needs you, or somebody else."

"It's working fine, Mae." I started to feel short of breath.

"It is not. Not fine."

"No, no, no, Mae, please, no, you know he loves you, he really does." I reached in my pocket for the pills and there were none.

She began to cry softly, then sat down on the kitchen stool to weep.

I was afraid Colin would hear her, so I led her outside where she wept even louder.

It is too hard for me, he is just a little boy and I cannot be his mommy I am too old and cannot keep up and also he is so moody and you are away so much I don't know what to do.

It was twilight. I let Mae go on like this, her cold breath steaming out of her. She was probably right, on every count. She heaved and dropped her purse, all her credit cards spilling from her wallet. I knelt and handed them back to her.

"Can you give me two weeks? I will pay you for four, okay? This is okay? Tell me this is okay, please, Mae, please, we need you. Please. Please."

She nodded.

chapter ten

T HAT NIGHT it snowed again, this time lightly.
I awoke sometime before four in the morning to the scraping
sounds of the shovel on the driveway, and I walked downstairs and rummaged in the dark in the beverage fridge for a water.

All Stone Age desires surface out of nowhere during a storm. It's unnat-
ural to suppress them for long. I made a roaring crackling predawn fire in
my hearth; Atticus scampered downstairs and camped by the heat and fell
asleep. The idea of conjuring a whimsical trip to Barbados from this spot,
just over week ago, was impossible to imagine. I sat for a while in the dark,
weighing Harry's assessment.

A spray of black birds was in hysterics on the branches, buckshot on the
empty sycamore. By noon it would all be melted, and the schools would
not be closed and the office would need to be opened, even with the Dead
Sea salt all over the shorn driveway. Tomorrow would be like this, and so
on and so forth, etc. There was a near perfect arc in her voice lost now for
good, just a recording of her liquid soprano singing "Happy Birthday" on
my phone.

There were probably hundreds of her paintings in the basement, everything she'd never sold.

The dusting of snow had whitened the pool cover, and there were some unusual paw prints, possibly a fox. The fox could kill the dog; you need to get rid of the fox. And you need to get this sold, Mark. You will need to sell this all, declare bankruptcy, and uproot this poor boy—thanks to impetuosity and narcissism and expansionism.

I heard this voice as some mutant hybrid of Monica and Dr. Weller, neither male nor female, more plainspoken than moralistic. We all have an omniscient narrator prattling away in our heads if we are willing to listen.

I studied the fire, some stunted gaze. Atticus was still asleep. Colin was sleeping. Just the snap and pop of the firewood and my fear-shivering, that buckling of our defenses that precedes a catharsis. I knelt before the fire, my first show of piety of any kind, maybe in years, thinking that if this fire can obliterate the matter placed in its path, maybe, too, faith in something can singe away these earthly entanglements, free me from myself, and let me sail backward on my little skiff to what I was. As I knelt, I wept, softly, tears streaking my face and falling onto the tile floor. And then I began to cry hard, and I heard the hysterical birds and imagined being one, free to fly in and out of the human world, the sky, the land, the sea—it's not an escape if you're a better version of yourself—until I saw her visage clearly in the fire, looking at me, flickering in and out of focus, or was this a hallucination?

I asked the fire to tell me what to do. The fear was asphyxiative; I could see the merging of all the worst-case scenarios hitting the company, me, and Colin, at the same time. The face disappeared. Once vanished, it seemed like it had never been there. Was this an apparition? I heard the church bells toll in that light-perfect Mexican village; maybe her face went there, I heard Colin say.

I turned, startled, and saw him standing in the almost light by the French doors, in a pose that suggested eavesdropping.

How long have you been there? Daddy did you see something, daddy can ghosts travel?

She is a purple ghost, she smells like hyacinth, even in death, you need to go back to sleep, you do not need to worry about your test, you are prepared.

I am not prepared I am scared and are you going away again? And then I thought I should administer him a little white pill to get him to rest.

I led Colin to the couch, sat beside Atticus, and I took his little cold hand, put him on my lap, curled my fingers over his, and we stared into the fire.

School was delayed two hours.

I took Atticus around the block in my jeans and slippers, then came home again over my footprints and found Colin awake in the kitchen. I suggested to Colin we go out for breakfast. He jumped off the stool and ran up to his room, got dressed hurriedly in winter clothes, and I put on my boots and some thick socks.

We opened the front door, braced for that gust of freezer-cold air to hit, a dry burn. It was just a dusting, but the snow had crept under the portico, nearly to the doormat. Already, some was melting around the salt pellets, tiny craters all over the driveway.

The pavement felt wet under my slippers. We did not say much. We walked for about fifteen minutes. Hallihan's sold a good, cheap, quick breakfast. Because there was no traffic the snow on the road was pristine. We turned on Nolte and I smelled a fire, saw smoke floating out of a chimney. A male cardinal perched on a mailbox, luminous in the snow, flew away as we came near and Colin reached out for it. He was playing with his breathing, making O's in the cold air.

There were some people in thick jackets also peering into the windows of Hallihan's. I checked my watch: half-past eight. I assumed it was weather related. Colin didn't seem to care, but I was mad. I wanted coffee, a booth, syrup and pancakes, and a view of the snowy exterior.

"What about the fancy place?" he said.

We walked another half mile east to Balducci's, and they were open, all that corporate predictability, bright and astringent, bitter at the entrance. Maybe an anti-slip spray, organic. A woman in a white apron with silver teeth in a hair net was stocking glossy apples by a seasonal display of pomegranates. We were the first ones there.

"Can I get sushi?"

"Sushi? For breakfast?"

"Why not?"

Why not. We walked to the deli, grabbed subs, got a coffee from the bakery, grabbed some Swiss chocolate at the register, checked out, and sat down at the little café area by the newspapers and the massive recycling bins at the exit.

"Why don't you have your phone?"

I felt my breast pocket.

"Oh, well I guess I forgot it."

"Are you still worried?"

I looked at him chewing his sushi roll, and he seemed earnest.

"What do you mean? Worried?"

"The stories said you're in trouble."

"Are you reading my emails, Colin?"

"I'm reading Google."

I put down my coffee, looked outside, wiped my mouth, and opened the chocolate. I wouldn't lie to him.

"Daddy is going to be fine. Daddy is strong. Daddy is strong, okay?"

"I figured 'cause we both take some pills. You can talk to me."

I tousled his hair. He laughed, stole the rest of my chocolate.

We walked home over a wider trail of footprints. There were a few cars out now, slushing their way to wherever. I knew the city would be shut down, even amid what was only a dusting; I knew the morning radio shows were dishing on fender benders, this outbound lane shut down and that onramp closed. It was all a pattern, private sector life, a path without footprints that could be easily followed. I had another ten plus years like this, best case, until I could retire; the last two weeks.

We were nearing our house, the Bensons' stiffened pansies poking through the snowy leaves, and Colin was throwing stones at the icicles on their sycamores. I tried to pretend life was on pause, this was a permanent hiatus of snow and fire and food and merriment. And what had I stored up for this winter? When I got home, I set Colin up on his Nintendo and went into my office, loaded the emails from Lucas, lit some incense, opened a Coke Zero, found the most recent bank statements—about four months old—and concluded that my cash savings balance was just under $1.2 million. My annual expenses were about half a million dollars. I rummaged and found the 529A college fund for Colin; it had $345,000. I had no other savings.

I turned on my laptop and started to an email to my Morgan Stanley broker asking him to liquidate the position entirely and transfer the funds to my money market account. I knew the request would arouse concern and suspicion so I tried to head him off saying I wanted to "migrate my savings from bullion to cash as an investment strategy," but I knew he'd be calling me the next day no matter how the hell I said it.

I logged onto my Citibank checking account and made the first wire transfer ever to White & Partners—just over $225,000 to meet payroll obligations for this Friday. I emailed Sally that this was done, and thought about my foolish offer to Skadden Arps just a week ago to pay back our $250,000 in fees. Afterwards my balance was under $1 million; this was what was left. I would never again cull a distribution from the company. Four more payrolls and all the money was gone.

I looked outside and wind was blowing all the snow on the trees so it looked like a squall.

★

I WALKED Colin to school, and by the time I was in the Maserati the roads were asphalt again the snow nearly a mirage. I switched on the radio and toggled between all the satellite news stations because all the presidential candidates were hollering about each other and there were deadly airstrikes in Aleppo and Presidents Putin and Obama were reportedly not speaking and there was the sense that no one oversaw anything or even knew what to do about the unraveling world around us. I put on the NHL Network.

A lonely commute like this can render out your melancholy. I hit all green lights down K Street like an arrow shot through the heart of the city.

The office was half empty. Margaret had a vanilla-scented candle burning on her desk.

"Margaret," I said, close to noon, de-winterizing myself of my jacket and scarf at my desk, "I want to see Tomas Toren right away."

Tomas had a knack for reading the winds of the press coverage: when things were heating or if a story was expiring.

Tomas came in, hair wet, smelling like juniper, over-cologned. I assume he smoked. He was sheepish. Good, I thought. At least there's some semblance of order left in this banana republic.

"I'd like to know where you see the coverage going on OneSpeak," I said.

"Well," he said in that flat Scandinavian way, "it's not so easy, but there are some patterns. First, the Twitter saga—I mean campaign—kind of worked, sort of. You see there is little mention now of the activities in the woods, Lars and Fung. The talk now is about…"

"Go on, say it."

"You and the…stunt. We were doing sentiment monitoring on this, and, whereas before we were hired, seventy-six percent of pieces were negative based on references to statutory rape, now only thirty-five percent are negative. The coverage seems to have improved for them because they look... like victims."

"And? We can expect this to culminate in, what, some big hackathon thing? The IPO is next week. Surely the press is talking about the fact that their tech barely works."

"Pardon?"

I considered what I had said and realized that perhaps I had not said it aloud before.

"It didn't work," I said, "at least when I used it in Copenhagen. Spit out gibberish, Siri gone awry."

Tomas seemed unfazed by this revelation, part of his charm.

"Basically, the financial press coverage is focusing not just on the stunt but also whether Lars and Fung can co-manage an enterprise as a married couple. There was a column today in the *Wall Street Journal* about what might happen if they split up. Who, basically, would take over in such an event. I would say that the press, at least financial press, is going to try and pin them down on roles, and try and extract, pre-IPO, some clarity as to who on the actual CEO is."

"Hybrid roles can work well, look at Sergei and Larry."

"That was long ago, a different era, Mark."

"Ten years ago is long ago?"

"I still had pimples."

"You're all a lost generation, you millennials, hacking and clicking your way through a digital humanity. Someday, you'll forget what it was to be fully human."

He seemed amused, which was not my intent. "Maybe, Mark. That would make a good tweet by the way."

"Don't worry," I said. "No tweets today."

He didn't laugh and departed quietly. I yelled for Margaret. She came in too wide-eyed. Did everyone think I was coming unhinged? I spoke slowly, in a low voice, trying to connote calm. I was asking for chamomile tea. She emitted a little smile, left, came back in a few minutes with a beautiful tea service, wafer thin lemon slices and some cookies. She picked up a few stray gum wrappers and torn envelops from my desk and was gone.

I made the next call.

"Hi, it's Mark White, White & Partners. I'm calling for Ambassador Mapuri, if he's in."

"Mr. White, yes, of course, I remember you. Thank you again for the basket last month. Very thoughtful. Ambassador Mapuri is traveling. May I ask what this is in regards to?"

"It's about an urgent matter pertaining to a tariff on your exports soon to be imposed by the USTR," I lied.

"One moment," she said, and then a male voice: "Let me see if I can transfer you to his mobile." There was a brief pause and then, "Mr. White. Is there a problem?"

"Ambassador, honestly, none at all but I needed to speak with you rather urgently. You are aware of our—my—recent difficulties and—"

"You've got a lot of nerve!"

"Sir, I need a personal favor and I am calling you humbled and in total need of your assistance."

The line was silent. "Let me guess: you need money."

"Money?" I sounded surprised by the tone of my own voice, which was a blend of disgust and humor. "God no, I need Singapore's endorsement. To say publicly how we have had a good working relationship. I know you don't owe me this—you paid your bills and we provided a service, but I am trying to salvage my reputation and anything from you I can use will be so beneficial."

"I bloody can't believe we are even discussing this. Mr. White, you are under some delusion that your firm did something unique, when, in fact, I could just as easily have hired Akin Gump or whomever to lift those tariffs, and it seems to me I am the wrong phone call for you to be making now considering your troubles. Good day."

I sat quietly for less than twenty seconds before dialing other VIP clients who could vouch for the firm, me. The ambassadors explained diplomatically that it would appear unseemly in their countries to wade into domestic business affairs; our corporate clients, just like the French at Waterloo, had fled to the hillside villages in the moonlight to hide out from the scorching drama. Through my glass wall, I watched my interns preen about, hold court rather than working, likely pontificating about our demise.

Margaret saw me watching them. She stood up and walked towards them and they scattered back to their cubicles. The rest of the offices were half empty.

I speed dialed more clients, CEOs did not call me back. Everyone declined my offer. That was it. With that battery of two dozen calls I realized I had nothing left to offer Washington. It would take countless revolutions backwards around the sun to wind me back to my envied status. Now, White & Partners was a scrap heap. And I was its *jefe*.

★

WE WENT into the basement that night after dinner.

I had put her larger paintings in storage, including the triptych of the Rwandan gorillas. The rest were stacked on the floor along with some bronze sculptures she had acquired in San Miguel. There were maybe two hundred pieces of art leaned against each other, or in piles, some stacks making a teepee, held in balance with paint cans. I had not counted.

Colin tripped over a paint can at the base of a large piece leaning against the wall.

"I'm fine," he said rubbing his shin. The canvas wasn't punctured.

I started to file through some of the older paintings, a desolate mountain around Santa Fe, a sense of hibernating snakes in the twilight hills. Next were her meditations on sunrise: portraits of Cisco and Jetties Beaches in Nantucket. The perspective was away from the water, looking towards the beach as from a sand bar, no surf in sight. She tweaked the light grossly Fauvist, avoided pastels, so that you couldn't tell if it was dusk or dawn. In the largest painting, there were seagulls massed over something on the sand, implied grotesquerie, a small boy in a red swimsuit holding a pail, walking out of the scene. There were no clouds because she hated clouds, and why paint a cloud when there doesn't need to be one, Mark, you know it's all how you wish to see the world in what you paint. But this was me pantomiming her, I hadn't really heard her voice in days.

I put it down with some of the others and led him of the larger canvases. She was selling these, in the end, for over $10,000 per piece. Word of mouth, mostly. It got to a point where she was planning on opening a gallery. We had discussed it many times but she could never settle on a location that she felt would not leech out the art to corporate types, her words. I had suggested Jackson Hole and she laughed. London, Paris, New York were a no.

"Oh my God look at this one! Daddy look!"

"Yeah, that was one of her first ones. Do you see the little Indians have guns too?"

"Are they killing the buffalo? Did mommy really see this?"

"This was from her imagination. Poof." I waved my hands to signify magic.

"How come these aren't in that museum? Mommy's such a good painter."

He was running his fingertips over the canvas, outlining the brush-strokes as if they were braille.

"You know, I guess I never thought of that before, Colin. Mommy wanted a store for these but—"

"She died."

"Yes, she died."

"But she talks to me now."

"What?"

"I'm serious."

"I don't believe you. What does she say?"

"She tells me how to help you. You need some help, she says. She tells me how to comb my hair, which direction. She also tells me we should sell all these. She wants us to turn the basement into a playroom for me. Maybe you can make a store for these in Barbados?"

"That's not a bad idea, but people there can't really afford art. Which way does she say to comb your hair?"

"I make it spikey, like she likes, like in your pictures when you had spikey hair. Oh. Maybe we sell these in the bullfight place then."

"Madrid?"

"Yeah, there."

He was putting all the paintings back in a pile. I considered the idea from Monica's perspective.

He kept filing through the smaller paintings of the sleeping male lions and the baby chimpanzees and the mountain gorillas she had encountered in Rwanda and Zambia. Just sell them all in the bullfight place. Well, there's an idea. And how would I get all her paintings to Madrid? What does something like this cost, are there customs regulations and ridiculous receiving paperwork on the Spanish side and forms needing to be notarized? There would be something poetic and justifiable about leaving all her art in Madrid. And I still knew people who might be able to organize a show. That wouldn't be the challenge. I can always make a phone call. That's the point of being Mark White. I always knew what to do, even when I was jumping into the jet stream. The problem always was I didn't know when to stop.

"It's an interesting idea. If we do that, we won't have any more pictures of mommy's in the basement," I said.

He was preoccupied with the gorilla portraits; she had accentuated their human characteristics.

"Well we can just take pictures of them on our phones. We can see them anytime, daddy. You don't have to touch it for it to be real."

The paintings, as I viewed them, reminded me of nothing because she had done them so far away in her studio or on the road. I had visited San Miguel de Allende only once, got food poisoning from the water, and stayed in bed for three days. This was before Colin was born. I listened to the church bells on the hour, marking time, and she flitted in and out of the apartment, in between sessions, orange paint on her fingers and sleeves. When she left me a bottle of water or a banana and said, "Rest, I'll check on you again in an hour," I didn't say I love you or thank you or any of that. Even then, she had some sense, I think, that I was sick. She came and went and came back again, a guardian, and I just assumed it would stay that way. And when I told her that night that it was a stupid idea to invest in a studio in dirty Mexico, anywhere, asked why she had it in for corporate types, and she got up and took that walk with the fucking dog and she didn't come back again.

I tiptoed downstairs to the study, put on the hockey game, and watched the third period, kind of zoning out. I sifted the mail, separating bills from the frivolous ads. Nothing from relatives. I should write to a friend, but, in a mental list, realized my friends, like Monica, were memories.

I sat and watched Ovechkin at full speed, always three strides from full speed, blazing down the middle of the ice and cutting across the zone and almost scoring single-handedly. Truth was an unkempt thing. Many angles, different voices. My toes were cold in the half-winter in this creaky house. I started to hear all the noise from within the *pintxos* bars on the Carrer Montcada, the odd guitar player strumming his version of Las Fresas de Aranjuez in the Plaça del Pi, church bells on the hour, the humid musk of the ancient streets, that *piso* in Madrid, and the creamy texture of the *cerveza de grifo*, pushing the F1 key to file a story to the editors in London, all the false starts and the sense that there would always be more time.

chapter eleven

I T WAS odd that I had not seen or heard from Hawthorne since the apology to the Japanese ambassador—five days of absence—and the first thing I did that Wednesday morning was to summon Margaret, even as I was thinking of Colin's idea for the paintings: maybe we'd need to write up a little pamphlet about Monica White, her work and her milieu as a neo-realist. Then I remembered payroll was a week from today.

Margaret knocked and stepped in. "Is Hawthorne here?" I asked too mellifluously to mask my temperament.

"I haven't seen him. You want Sally?" She took my empty teacup and put in its place a shot glass of fizzy water. My mind drifted towards notions of checking myself into the Esalen Institute, living in a room with flowers in full bloom and staring at the Pacific.

"Mark? Do you need Sally?"

I snapped back. "I need Hawthorne. Where is he?"

"Hold on." I saw her go back to her desk and start calling.

About five minutes later she came back in and told me he was on line five.

"Hawthorne," I said, "where the hell are you?"

"I think we should talk." His voice was low and steady.

"We're talking now."

"I meant in person. Later in the week is good."

"Or now is good."

"Are you ashamed?"

"Pardon me?"

"Why are you avoiding this company?"

"I'm not ashamed of my role here, only of what this company has become. You've shipwrecked it, Mark, marooned us all in a wasteland of bad press."

"So you were you the leak to Hanna. Unreal."

"Preposterous! If I am the leak then so are you! Look at you, running all over town with reporters, swallowing pills everywhere. Mark, you left your prescription bottle in the trash last month after the Delta pitch, in the bathroom, and one of the staff got hold of it. Sally never told you, did she? You were the one who took a nod on TV, brokered a ridiculous deal with OneSpeak, and concocted an inane press strategy on Twitter. I'm sorry you think I leaked all this. I leaked nothing. If I was the leak, then why didn't the article mention the sexcapade in your hotel?"

He was shouting now and I had to pull the phone away from my ear.

"Where are you?"

"I'm at home. I've got the flu. This is hard on me too. Your name is my name in this town."

I envisioned him expatriating himself to London after this, one of the pocket square global firms, living out his professional days in a costly flat in Mayfair, enjoying whatever sobered notoriety preceded him. We would both be starting over. And you cannot start over so easily after forty. Your life stops being so portable once you find even modest success. Hawthorne was over fifty, what would he do? These were bloodstains on the résumé, garnet blotches all around his name. He needed to be exonerated. We both did.

"It's been a rough two weeks, I understand. I understand what I have done."

There was a long silence on the line. And then I cleared my throat and said, "There's another thing I have to tell you."

"Yes."

"I'm selling the company. I mean, trying to sell the company."

"Jesus, Mark!"

"I don't have a buyer. I just cannot do this anymore. I don't want to.

Can't do it. I have asked Harry to put it up for auction. He's been slow. I don't think he can get it done. I'm sorry. I'm truly sorry. I figured you'd assume this was the case."

"I assumed so, yes, just never so precipitously. What are you asking?"

"Pardon?"

"The price."

"Well, fuck, it was worth about $20 million a month ago. Now, half our clients gone and me writing checks in to make payroll, about zero."

"Obviously it's not worth zero, Mark. There's brand equity. We're still billing over $18 million per year, even after all the client departures."

"And still posting a $1 million loss—that's if no one else leaves."

"Then we cut."

"And trigger more negative media."

"The only way forward is through."

"I don't have the energy."

"Mark, right-size the company, close down some of the satellite offices, get it all to where there is a modest profit. If you did that, I'd buy it."

"What?"

"You heard me."

"Hawthorne, you don't have that kind—"

"Certainly, I do. And if I didn't, the payout could come from the cash flow in the business. I could payout a monthly stipend of some sort, say you are a chairman emeritus."

"Would I be keeping office hours?"

"Only if you wanted. We would rebrand, I suppose, something to show we are unabashedly back in action after all this and very much playing the game over here with loaded weapons, a stocked bar, and lots of pretty interns."

"The fucking interns."

"Yes, the fucking interns."

I heard church bells in the background.

"Where are you?"

"Truthfully, I'm in Paris."

"Why're you in Paris?"

"I was interviewing with Publicis to be Global EVP. I arrived Saturday and met with them yesterday. You'll be pleased to know it pays about a hundred thousand less than what you pay me."

"You'd hate the French."

"I love their wine."

"If you really want to do this we should really talk to Harry. Can you get back tomorrow?"

"It'll take some prodding to lure me out of Saint-Germain. I had planned on a long morning walk through the Tuileries, lunch at La Dôme, dinner with an old lover at The Crillon. I hear church bells, Mark. European church bells, the most underreported glory of Europe. All day they ring. I think they ring for me. I close my eyes and imagine it so."

"I'll call Harry if you're serious."

"If you're serious about selling me this company and letting me rebrand it, I'm completely serious. And I want to fire Joel James. I told the waiter last night in mediocre French that I was an archduke. I think he believed me. Instead of the Armagnac I ordered they brought me two thumbs of Louis XIII. It's what you get for dining in a two-star. You are much like where I was last night, the pinnacle of the Paris culinary scene, envied by every haggard chef to the point of loathing. Once exalted, they fire poison-tipped arrows at even your shadow. Well, you've got your infamy, Mark, now it's time to turn the tables. You're lucky they retired the Concorde long ago or I would otherwise be booking passage home on it and charging it to the firm this afternoon."

"Then we have a deal."

"Yes indeed, though it'll be hard to leave Paris, Mark. Global EVP. I would have traveled here once per month. But not for me. Too many layers of corporate bullshit. And the CEO lacks the insouciance for charm. You know my chambermaid leaves a tiny dish of petit fours and a small bottle of fizzy water on my desk each night. The little things count. Pillows are much the same at hotels the world over. It's the church bells and the pink macarons and the twisted lonely magnificent streets in nearly every arrondissement and the way you can drift into a bistro and drink a bottle of anything and no one labels you an alcoholic. I always find my abbreviated life abroad to be phosphorescent in a painful way. The bells cannot ring enough. The wine is never better at home, even in vintage crystal. The terroir shifts. No, I think it ends when you come back to the states. Instead of terroir we have food phobias. We flee the pleasures rooted in passion. It's been a while since you've been here, I know. You know how it is. You must come and see for yourself, the old Jacques Cousteau adage: *Il faut aller voir.*"

"Come see for yourself."

"That's it."

I swiveled my chair and took a long unfiltered gaze at the late November skyline, every so often a jet cutting across. He would make a great CEO. Of anyone, he could reconstruct something out of the rubble.

"I'm tired of planes, Hawthorne. I am tired of shifting time zones. I'm a late career reliever who's lost his fastball. Colin is going through life shadow boxing with himself."

"This is rot. Complete rot. Mark, you had a terrible few weeks. But you are young and talented. The world awaits. *Il faut aller voir.*"

★

We agreed to see each other this Friday. I wanted to unload the company at a fair price to Hawthorne. I called Harry and told him the plan and asked him to prepare a binding letter of intent, setting the sale price at $1.5 million to be paid in thirty-six equal installments over three years. Hawthorne would keep all accounts receivable and payable. I set my new title as Chairman Emeritus.

"Mark this is a mistake, a big huge fucking mistake. Don't do it," Harry screamed into the phone.

"I'm going outside the bounds, I know, but I have to make some new plans for myself."

"I'm shocked. You can pull through this and sell this for $20 million in two years. Rebuild and cash out."

"Harry, I know I can. It's that I don't want to anymore. I'd like to start keeping score another way. Please prepare the papers by Friday. And please increase your rate as a courtesy for your friendship and honesty."

By the time we ended up across the table for the closing, an overzealous associate shuttled around numbing stacks of paper signatures while Harry held court about his geese hunting expedition in Argentina during Labor Day last year, killed twelve with his father's Beretta, saying whatever was necessary to ensure we were rapt enough to not think ourselves out of the deal.

As I sat and signed at the x-marked line, I sipped at the tepid office coffee and noticed my stomach wasn't churning and I wasn't doing my breathing and my phone was ringing less, and I wondered if this was anti-climax or if it meant that I was happy.

I took a butterscotch from a dish on the table and sucked on it and signed my old life away to Hawthorne. He sat upright, wore the Brioni tie, had gel-combed his hair, and, with the gray streaks, acquired a poised mien of someone about to stroll the promenade at sunset in a tan blazer. The end figure was $1.575 million, half up front, which Hawthorne had the means to finance personally. It meant that, in the end, I would walk away with close to the amount of Monica's inheritance, the money I'd started the company with. It was enough to draw from for now.

When Hawthorne signed the final piece of paper, the associate placed it atop the stack of his and neatened the corners, Harry reached across the table with a little curdled bonhomie and said, "You're a free man, Mr. White."

I gave Hawthorne a two-handed shake, staring right into his eyes. I wanted to warn him, leave a pithy note like ex-presidents do for their successors, right there in the drawer of the Oval Office, give him a knowing wink and maybe Dr. Weller's cell, just in case.

"Splendid day, Mark, splendid day for us both."

"You are going to outdo me by a mile. I know it."

"Never."

I imagined all the money wire transferring itself into my life and I felt nothing.

Harry was already out of the room. The associate was stacking all the papers and mimed a faint goodbye.

Afterwards, there was an immodest champagne party with the seventy staff and one hundred plus guests—no media, I was told. A few principals from New York, Los Angeles, and Chicago had flown in and milled about, unaware their satellite offices were about to be shuttered or greatly downsized, trying to penetrate the web of inside jokes and common body language.

We were greeted off the elevators with clapping. A small crowd of mid-level types and a smattering of executives materialized. Some new hire in an argyle sweater, an ambitious beard, and conspicuous black rim glasses was absorbed into the speckled laughter. A pack of hipless interns put lips to their overfilled champagne flutes. Mine was half empty. The ritual of genuflecting to the new boss took on a liturgical cadence, nearly everyone adding themselves to the congregation that began near the elevators and ran nearly the length of the entire office.

Hawthorne looked at me; I thought I saw him give a little shoulder shrug. He smiled and I smiled back.

Sally came over and put her arm around me, took my near empty flute.

"Feel good?"

"It feels like a funeral."

"Mark, come on. Be happy for yourself. You don't mean that. Look around. You built all this! Now you are passing it on."

"Maybe. Maybe." I didn't want to get into it. I didn't want to get into anything anymore.

"You've wiped the board clean...not many people ever get to do that."

"It feels more like I wiped the china off the table. Like that. Maybe you're right. I rebooted. But it seems that all that's left to do is for Colin to wheel me into the assisted living complex."

She murmured something.

I looked indifferently at the congregation, their laughter thickening.

They were taking selfies now with Hawthorne. Reporters from *THE BEACON* and *The Washington Post* had come to take his picture. Guests were looking over at me and I tried not to look back and to maintain a smile.

There was full blown gaiety when a freshman congressman from the banking committee entered the gaggle, all loaded up with fresh PAC donations. He bellowed "Hawthorne" twice, extending his hand, a voice bigger than his frame. The commotion escalated: it was like a garden party from a Woody Allen film. The photographers began snapping away. Someone brought over the step-and-repeat sign with our logo all over it to serve as a backdrop. A line formed. The lights shone off Hawthorne's forehead. They snapped as he smiled, became pixelated for the press.

Yes, I could say goodbye to the cycles of stress, but so too could I relinquish the impossible task of decoding peers and subordinates.

I reached beside Sally for the flute on the table, took one last swig from it and drained it, closed my eyes hard to refocus, and listened to her repeat it. I felt anesthetized, possibly from the champagne.

She took her hands in mine and said, "You are still young."

She kissed me on the cheek. I felt her hands trembling.

Sally wore an anguished expression, like someone who had just read all my screeds.

I kissed her cheek. "I'm perfectly fine. I'm ready for the next chapter, Sally. Whatever the hell that means."

PART 3

chapter twelve

THE NEXT morning, by the time I awoke, it was already light out and Colin had climbed into bed with me, asleep, Atticus curled at his feet. I got up quietly, opened the balcony doors, and steam was rising in mysterious layers from the heated pool into the cool November morning.

I had been thinking about what I was about to do next for some time. I didn't hesitate: I walked into my basement and chose twelve large paintings.

Besides the oil on canvas work there were some gouache works from her studio in Mexico, a few formal abstract expressionist pieces; the rest was unmistakable Monica Karen White: the natural world improved and relit. I counted them all and there were 187 original paintings in our basement.

I readied to call Carmen, the broker in Spain we had used for her first exhibition.

I had not spoken with her in over ten years. She was half Spanish and French, ran the gallery on Calle Serrano in Madrid that exhibited Monica's work right after she had abandoned law. I went back upstairs and searched online to see if the gallery was still open. I couldn't find it, in English or Spanish, in Madrid. I typed in her full name multiple times in Google but didn't find anything.

I remembered I had kept an old-fashioned address book when I was in Spain. I returned to my office and looked around for it in some shoeboxes of photos and documents. It was underneath an old blue notebook. I snapped open the button. The pages were sticky. Carmen's number and address were there, written without the +34 country code.

I stared at the number for a while, assumed it was no longer working; I dialed the number and hung up when a female voice said hello.

I walked upstairs into the kitchen and Colin was fixing himself an overly generous plate of Oreos from the cupboard for breakfast. I sat down at the table and took one. I watched his movements. His arms swung when his legs were still. His knees bounced up and down like pistons while he sat. He had that little boy energy flowing. He chewed and talked.

"Oh, by the way," he said and walked over to his backpack hanging on the wall and placed an envelope on the table. I pulled out his photographs from picture day. In the picture, he looked pale and had the long hair from before Barbados, the trace of impetigo. In all there were about thirty-six copies in all different sizes. I felt a sag of guilt.

"Daddy, can I ask a question?"

"Of course."

"So, what did you do yesterday? You were home early."

"Me?"

"Yes!"

"Daddy has a new job."

"What job?"

"You."

"Huh?"

"You aren't going to have a nanny anymore."

He looked incredulous.

"Colin, daddy is staying home now, for a while, at least, and we're going to hang out more."

He smiled and his eyes bulged. "Do you get paid for that?"

"Well of course not!"

"'Cause I searched it up and saw you sold your job and I was wondering if we were poor now."

"Oh my gosh, I'm just making some changes. So I can spend more time with you. We aren't poor. God no. We aren't poor. Please don't think that."

"You're sure?"

"I'm completely positive."

He ran up and hugged my waist, sinking into me. I kissed the top of his head

"But what are you going to do all day, like, are we going to move? You're sure we aren't poor now?"

"Colin, we own this house. We never have to move. We are not poor. Daddy has too much money now. It's all safe in the bank."

"What?" He had a vague expression, as if he were registering my ambivalence.

"What do you think if we take another trip?"

His eyebrows arched and he clasped his hands together. "Like Barbados?"

"Well, we could go there, yes. Very possible. But I was thinking we should do something special for mommy."

His hands separated and fell to his sides.

"You gave me a great idea. You know how we took all those photos of mommy and put them in your room?"

"Yeah."

"What if we picked some of mommy's paintings and put them in a gallery?"

"Which ones?"

"We have so many of them. One hundred and eighty-seven. I counted. I don't know yet."

"Can I pick which ones?"

I stood up. "Yes. Of course, yes. You can pick them all."

"So, right now?"

"Well, that's fine but are you okay if we travel for Thanksgiving?"

"Is the gallery in America?"

"I'm still not sure. Come on." I led him to the basement.

He began perusing the inventory, hands on his hips. He settled on nine works in total: Scituate Harbor; Brant Point; Sunrise on the Ponte Vecchio; Windless Beach; In My Garden; Ringing by the Duomo; Cobblestones in Morning; Coffee Plantation at Sunrise; On Safari.

"Why did you pick these ones, Colin?" I was hoping by his response I would detect some softness in his position.

He kept his gaze on the paintings and said, "They made me feel very happy, and if we sell them they will make someone else feel very happy too."

"Then these are the ones. Here," I said, handing him my phone. "Can you take pictures of each? I will need them to send to the lady in Madrid."

I went upstairs and tried Carmen again. She answered on the third ring.

"Hola?"

"Carmen?"

"*Si, soy yo.*"

"Hola, Carmen, soy Mark...Mark White."

"Mark! Mark White! *Oye, como estas mi amor!*? How are you?"

We had not spoken since the funeral. She and her husband, Antonio, had flown in, cutting short her exhibition in East Berlin. She sounded smoky, a little weather in the voice. But all the dimensions of her personality still came through as before. She informed me that they were living in Barcelona now. Antonio had taken a new job with a multinational, as she called it, a three-year post. We spoke for a while, appointing the panoramic draft of our lives with the vital details before we reached the focal point of the conversation.

"And now you are completely free?"

"Well that is one way to put it," I said.

"Congrats to you. Monica would have been proud."

"She is, would be, I mean. She's the reason I called, Carmen."

I explained the situation with all the basement art, the 187 pieces, and the ones that Colin and I were prepared to part with if she could find a way to exhibit them appropriately in Spain.

"Mark, I don't have a gallery anymore. I am just a broker these days. But there is a very good place in Barcelona I can introduce you. It might not be an exhibition next week but maybe if you can come and show your work to Ferran, he can get an interest, and then we can try for something in the spring. He is very nice. It's a very good gallery, many international clientele. What do you think?"

I had not been to Barcelona in fifteen years. "I think it's perfect. Can you arrange it? I'll send you pictures of the pieces and bring some smaller ones to show. We can be there in two days."

"*Claro! Claro!* Of course! Leave it to me."

I explained that this Thursday was a major American holiday. We made plans to meet on Monday; I figured we would spend Thanksgiving week in Barcelona.

I told Colin our plans.

"Is it the bull fight place?"

"That's Madrid. This place has a beach. Mysterious buildings."

"Do we leave now?"

"Tomorrow, pal. We arrive Monday."

I went upstairs and checked on our supply of medications, saw that we were critically low on two prescriptions, and texted Dr. Weller to ask for refills in time for travel. Then, when Mae arrived, I told her we would be gone for her final week but asked if Atticus could board with her. She said it was fine, and I cut her a final check and added extra funds for goodwill. Then I went online and booked a room at the junior suite at the Hotel Arts and bought two economy fare tickets that I upgraded with points to Business Class. Later that day I went to the pharmacy to pick up our medicines, and then I called *The Washington Post* and cancelled my subscription for good because print was dead, and I tossed out the milk in the refrigerator and all the cheese, and I called the landscapers and reduced the frequency of the service from six times monthly to twice because we needed to be frugal, and I called the pool company and asked them to close the pool because it seemed senseless to watch the steam rise from it every morning, however beautiful. I preliminarily packed our suitcases, and then I took seven of the smaller canvases Colin chose to the FedEx nearby and had them bubble wrapped and express shipped to Ferran's gallery, scheduled to arrive by Monday morning, maybe hours before us.

chapter thirteen

W E FLEW down the toll road after lunch, took the exit for long-term parking.

We breezed through security because of priority clearance by the TSA, rode the underground train all the way to Terminal B, like a mall inside, the same downtown souvenirs sold in its kiosks and NEWSWORLD stores, all the flags of the world hanging from the ceiling.

We walked past a Chipotle and Dunkin Donuts to the Business Class lounge, passing a shiatsu station beside a shop that sold cell phone accessories and flamingo pink sleep masks.

"Can we go in?" he said, pointing to the NEWSWORLD.

It was filled mostly with gossip magazines and candies with Red 40 and Yellow 6.

"Sure, here's five dollars. I'll wait here. Remember, no Big Soda."

"No Big Soda."

For a while, I watched him inspect the candy bags and chocolate bars, scrutinizing them for sugar content, somehow already paternal in his mangled youth. I took the time to send a text to Carmen telling her that we were at the airport and we would be leaving after the lunch hour. I got an immediate response. *This is a good news. We are welcoming your arrival and will see you and Colin Tuesday.* I opened the email browser. Since changing my email address, there was very little: I was copied, mainly, on a few emails by Sally and Hawthorne. I wasn't expecting anything, but Sally had forwarded an email that had bounced back to her from my old address.

Dear Mr. White,

I am Arnaud Messier, Chairman and CEO of Publicis.

First, I want to wish you congratulations on the sale of your firm. Despite some of the recent troubles, it has enjoyed a fine reputation. I hope that you are enjoying this new phase of your life.

The reason I am writing is to reach out and ask if you might be willing to serve on our Global Advisory Board. As you well know, by now, our company lacks deep expertise in the United States, especially in Washington, where the policy discussion drives so much of the P.R. debate. Your background and achievements are valuable to us.

After careful consultation with my board, I am prepared to offer this position to you, on a consulting basis, and am willing to meet with you about it at your convenience to discuss the opportunity. I would be happy to handle arrangements for your travel to Paris.

I do hope we can meet. Hawthorne speaks of you with great fondness.

Sincerely,

Arnaud

I looked up at Colin. He was chatting up the checkout woman, maybe Vietnamese, taking the receipt and holding out his hand for change. He walked up to me holding his bag with a curious face.

"Ready?" I said, still glancing at the note on my phone.

"What's wrong, daddy?"

"Nothing. Nothing at all. Come on. Let's go to the lounge."

There were two seats free by the runway window. Colin went up to the buffet and came back with a bowl of cold cuts, a stack of saltines, and sticky white rice. Paris was an hour's flight from Barcelona. The saltines were underneath the rice and cold cuts. It could be a nice do-nothing job, lucrative, Colin could tag along, develop a rapport with the same transatlantic flight crew, the destinations might permeate into him, and we might see the world this way, he might end up with me some Tuesday in Tokyo at the Tsukiji tuna auction, sleep at the base of a volcano in Hakune, soak in the sulfur hot springs. We could travel with a tutor.

Publicis was a multi-billion-euro French advertising conglomerate with dozens of subsidiaries all over the world. The money would be good and I wouldn't have to do much. Advisory boards were the biggest sham in P.R. I was clearly referred by Hawthorne. I wasn't toxic. The idea was revelatory. I felt briefly nostalgic for corporate power; a letter like that inflames your vanity. Arnaud was a good recruiter, coming at me like this with a clean offer and restrained flattery. It was all engineered to elicit an agreement to meet, tickle my curiosity. It was a good maneuver. It's what I would have done to myself. You can hear him out. It was my own voice. Hear him out.

They called our flight early. When we boarded, there was that familiar wheezing of an aircraft at rest; that pleasing aroma of burnt Arabica; that bright cabin and those sunny flight attendants guiding us to our seats, on the second deck of the 747. Colin ran up the winding staircase.

Soon, the flight attendant, Nancy, came by with a trolley of pre-departure drinks. I allowed Colin to have one soda. She offered me champagne. I declined and ordered club soda and lime.

Colin began pressing buttons, his seat back rising and falling. When his drink arrived, I unfolded his tray and put his bag of M&Ms beside the soda and turned on the personal TV in the seat in front of him to some European soccer match.

If I wanted to see Arnaud, I had little time. I opened my email again and typed a frigid response that bordered on indifference, suggesting I was incredibly busy for a while in Barcelona for the week but would be willing to meet him there if time permitted. I mentioned I was traveling with my son.

Colin was squirting lemon juice into his Diet Coke and tapping his fingers all over the touch screen TV.

"Look—it does a massage," he said. I adjusted his chair so that he was recumbent; he just lay there for a while enjoying the mechanical shiatsu.

I checked to see if Arnaud had written back and realized it was half past nine in Paris. I shut the phone off for good, left the airline magazine alone, went to the bathroom one last time, and, from the corner of my eye, noticed the flight attendant pulling apart a cellophane package containing the dinner rolls, unfoiling the lids to the chef-inspired meals—pasta, chicken, or beef—the menu tonight larded with exegesis about the provenance of the food, how the forests of certain regions in Spain are conducive to raising pigs on hazelnuts to produce jamón serrano.

When I sat down, Colin had changed the channel, CNN without sound.

Images were flashing of jagged, shelled out buildings somewhere in the Middle East, peacekeepers in blue UN vests, maybe an errant bombing, blood-coated babies and women crying for their men. The caption said it was an emergency session at the UN. Then, Secretary Kerry appeared and stood solemn behind a podium; then they cut away to the studio and the pundits and analysts began their dissection, but I couldn't hear them without headphones. I missed where this was. I missed who these people were. I looked around. Others across the aisle were watching this too without headphones. This was my news dose of the day. Then came the Gershwin and the offer of Spanish newspapers and more champagne; I took a refill of juice and she handed me a copy of *El Pais* instead of *The Washington Post*.

I could decode less than thirty percent of what was on the page. Something about the Basque separatists wanting peace but not laying down their arms. Someone important arrested in Andorra. Something, in a separate piece, about Catalunya pushing for complete secession from Spain. But nuance was undetectable to me.

It's unbelievable that Spain is ever considered a single country; after all, there is no common language. Castellano, what is known as Spanish, is only spoken in the center of the country. Everywhere else they have their own language and dialect: Basque, Catalan, Galician, Balearic, Aragonese, Asturian, and the Gomeran whistle language. It is a country of superlatives and strife. Every fifty miles one is told the town boasts the best cheese or wine. The Valencians claim their paella is supreme due to the quality of the local water. So, too, do the grievances in various parts of Spain vary every fifty miles. In Barcelona, the heart of Catalunya, there is political friction with Madrid. Across Spain, there is friction with the Basques, who have been plagued by a homespun terrorist organization, ETA. Unlike many parts of Europe, Spain was relatively safe, even with ETA targeting Spaniards. What began as a response to Franco morphed into something worse than Franco: a group that car-bombed and assassinated its way to notoriety, unnerving all Spaniards, the work of a few radicals hiding out in the Pyrenees and detonating their way into the news because politics didn't conform to their impetuosity. And what did they want? Like everyone else in Spain—independence from Spain.

For Colin, I planned to keep it light. He didn't need his father's shade on everything. There was the Spain of the tourist and the other, the one of anguished political philosophy and shrapnel history. We were going to skip the Orwell version.

"Daddy?"

"Yeah buddy."

"Can you put up my seat?"

He reached for the newspaper.

"What are you reading about?" I said.

"I am practicing my Español. Daddy? If I can't speak Spanish can your friend understand me?"

"Of course. Carmen speaks English."

"And Jordi?" he asked, referring to Carmen's son.

"I am not sure, but I suppose yes. They all do. It's a prerequisite."

"What does that mean?"

"It's means if they don't do it they will have less opportunity."

Spanish newspapers fold open like books; Colin folded his open and he looked like a shrunken adult studying a dictionary.

I felt the plane rolling back from the gate; I pushed the LAND button and he came upright and I told him to look outside and watch the man in the neon vest motioning the great vessel backwards and left, and then we heard the engines flush, a low grade hum in the cabin, and I buckled his seatbelt and they played the CEO video, again I watched Athens, London, Vienna, unreal, and he was scissoring his legs in his seat, eating cashews and sucking the soda off the ice cubes, and I looked at the cover of *El Pais* and began sounding out common expressions in my head so that I could impress him with my sapling Spanish when we landed in Barcelona, where they spoke Catalan.

He took my hand as we turned on the runway. I could see the tail of one jet just inches off the horizon, lifting off, banking right. The captain's voice surfaced seraphically.

Flight attendants prepare for takeoff.

We lifted and parted from the tarmac. He was laughing hard. We rose into webs of clayish cloud. When the sun appeared, we were reduced to a smile. Passengers were sitting up straighter, putting down their sudoku pads and iPads and laptops and phones and headphones and all the things we believe in to make us better humans. And in all that speed how could you not shed some of the land-borne malaise and anxiety, forgot whatever catatonic highway you took so late or so early to make your flight, just giggle, slouch into youth, time away from earth, free to soar into the sky towards some unknown corner of this world.

The seatbelt light turned off. Cabin life had its rhythms. The hum of speed over the flannel Atlantic.

We skipped the meal. Soon, the lights dimmed. After giving him a melatonin, I pushed the SLEEP button on his seat and he fell out of American life for a while, somewhere long before Greenland, all the way to Spain. Just that fuselage hum and the darkness and the reading spotlight and *El Pais* and the satellite TV news with the rubble images and the white men in coral ties, talking and talking. I stayed awake until Nova Scotia, when we lost sight of the full moon.

chapter fourteen

W<small>E FLEW</small> over the Ebro River, into Aragon, and the plane seemed
to gather force on descent, and there was Barajas by the sea. We
banked gently towards the sun and I looked out my window on the left side
of the plane at the mosaic city that, from above, washed in light, looked like
shining white stones, and the taller mass of structures down Las Ramblas
towards the water seemed like something made by a playful child. And
there were the mountains that bound the city, the wrinkled hills scattered
with sparse firs, the two rivers flanking Barcelona like winding roads in a
field of dust.

To the north—or maybe it was east—I could make out the variegated
green land that stretched to Andorra and into the Ebro Valley; soon the
waters deepened into blue lakes and trees blanketed the hills.

There was a wildfire burning in the far hills and the smoke rose to
the sky like the mist of a great waterfall, spreading and reaching for what
seemed so many miles towards the horizon. I closed my eyes and tried to
hold all that living light, take it all within my heart. I felt a kindling deep
within me, the darkness burning and burning, lighting up, filling me with—
alas, I cannot say.

I opened my eyes when I heard the landing gear come down.

Colin was asleep as we landed. In the golden morning light, there was no sign of the impetigo. Through the light baby fat, he had a strong jaw-line, waning Caribbean tan, skin four shades shy of cinnamon. Our perfect, brown, chiseled baby boy.

He awoke easily and eagerly disembarked, and we eased through passport control, and I realized I hadn't taken my evening pill—nor had he—so while we waited for our bags I bought a bottle of Vichy Catalan and fished out the right doses and combinations from my carry-on and we swallowed them just as our bags came around the carousel, first off of the belt.

Even the most complex things change shape and become simple when you relocate yourself. Something about the overstimulation, the flood of new images and words, the feline sense of time. I turned on my phone, waited for it to pair with a local carrier; an email popped up from Arnaud. He said he could meet me in Barcelona if that was easiest. That seemed simple enough. Lunch at the hotel. An hour and a half only. I emailed him, suggesting tomorrow.

Outside, there was a line of black and yellow taxis at the curb. A man came out of one and took our bags, and I told him to take us to *el Hotel Arts, por favor.*

He looked at me in the rearview mirror, spent a second calculating, and started to fire true Castilian Spanish at me, which I couldn't follow, making out about every fifth word. He was my age, unshaven. It sounded thicker and more elegant than the Spanish in America.

Colin was looking at me smiling, expectant.

I said, "*Estamos de los Estados Unidos y tomamos un vacacion en Barcelona por la semana.*" Colin leaned across the seat and made a face at me like he had just seen a monkey shuffle cards.

"*Americano?*" he asked, smiling, his accent thinning, faintly American.

"Yes."

"Daddy you speak Español!"

"I am from Seville. In Barcelona ten years. You like Barcelona? Have you been to Seville?"

I tried him again in Spanish. "*A mi me encanta Sevilla.*"

"The best city in Spain. But Barcelona is nice too. This is your son? You like *el futbol?*"

"Colin *futbol* is soccer."

"Me? I like hockey. Where is Seville?"

"Ah, Sevilla! South of Spain. Andalucía, the soul of Spain." He took his right hand off the wheel and pointed down to signify south. He was wearing a red rubber band on his wrist that read "I Love Barcelona." He had a stack of brochures stuffed in beside the emergency brake.

Colin tapped me, asked how I knew Español, still holding a mild gaze of wonderment.

"Daddy lived here, you know that."

"You never talk about it."

"Amigo, you lived in Barcelona?"

"I was mainly in Madrid but I lived here for a short while when I moved to Spain."

"So, daddy, were you a bullfighter then?"

The driver and I laughed heartily. Colin seemed to catch on to the joke and began laughing too.

I looked out the window and started to experience déjà vu. It was early morning and the light had yet to spring on the city. The *La Vanguardia* newsstands, nearly every block, someone from an old building hosing off the pavement, scattering birds, balconies with French doors on every façade, and the tree-lined streets stretched on in a straight line. Barcelona was designed as a perfect grid of city blocks, except for the old city. He took us the long way, I wanted to see the heart of the Ciutat Vella. He started up to the La Plaza Cataluña, the grand center of the city at the top of Las Ramblas. The sidewalk tables at the Café Zurich were empty. There was a giant advertisement featuring Lionel Messi, Barcelona's star soccer forward, atop the building that could be seen a block away.

"Who is Messi?" Colin said.

"*Futbol, chico.* The best in Barcelona."

"He's the best player in the world. The Ovechkin of soccer. Only smaller," I said. Colin nodded and seemed to absorb that. The driver laughed and lit up a cigarette, rolling down his window with his left hand and using his smoking hand to drive.

We passed down Las Ramblas, a nearly mile-long thoroughfare that led all the way to the sea and splits the Gothic Quarter. Men were filling their flower stalls along the center promenade, bunches of sunflowers, rust chrysanthemums, tight-budded pink roses. There were a few street mimes out, enchanting a sparse crowd of tourists, no acrobats yet. But there was already a stream of people flowing up and down the great street. The plane trees had all shed their leaves but the bare branches on either side of Las

Ramblas arched and nearly touched. I was in a daze. I looked at the old buildings, recollecting the small, forgotten things, like how the street names are etched into marble slabs screwed into the corners of the buildings, how Barcelona has a distinct aroma, especially in the Barrio Gotico—mold and sea air and heat. I rolled down the window and there it was, unchanged, warm damp stones.

We passed La Boqueria, the enormous outdoor food market midway down the Ramblas and I looked at the trees, their creamy scaling bark. Originally, in 1703, they'd planted poplars. Without their leaves, the planes took on an irregular shape and reminded me of the tree branches in Van Gogh's *Garden in the Asylum*, willowy and domineering. I noticed it wasn't cold. I asked our driver about the weather. He said it was unseasonably warm, around twenty Celsius the past week. There were exhibition signs draped along the front of some historical buildings, English and Catalan, then Spanish.

Ahead, pointing east, was the vaunted Columbus statue and we completed the roundabout and rode north the Ronda Litoral, the old city to the west and the overhauled seafront to the east. They had torn much of the waterfront up for the '92 Olympics, planted palm trees where there had been *xiringuitos*, beach bars, and imported sand from Egypt to create a wide berth of beach. There were slums and the usual industrial eyesores; urban planners wisely, some say cruelly, swept it all away to build the most cosmopolitan of European seafronts. Barcelona, for a long time, was said to have its "back to the sea," but after the urban redesign of La Barceloneta, today it is said often by Catalans that Barcelona is open to the sea—and all the metaphors that this implies.

It wasn't the only way the city had been revised over the century. To stoke tourism, wealthy industrialists in the 1920s got the idea to build a Gothic Quarter in Barcelona. Historic buildings that were disassembled to make way for avenues like Via Laietana were put in storage. These stones were reused later in constructing the Barrio Gotico, from scratch, and this went on through the 1960s. It was a systematic urban improvisation, designed for aesthetics, less focused on historical fidelity. This was the way the Barcelona as we know it has been built: layer upon layer, stone by recycled stone—tear up a neighborhood and plant a cathedral. If you're from Barcelona, you're comfortable with the idea of history being perpetually revised. To be a Catalan is to be a revisionist.

We rode with the windows half open, breathing in the sea. The hotel was visible from far away. How could you miss something so spectacular? A blue tower with a white exoskeleton, the gleaming copper whale designed by Frank Gehry beside it, two icons in harmony at the very far end of the beach before the marina.

Colin climbed onto my lap to get a better look. Like the marina beside them, the hotel and sculpture were designed for the Olympics. It was now a Ritz-Carlton. We pulled up and three Anglo porters descended upon the car and doors opened. We were welcomed in English. I paid the driver, tipped him well. Colin tossed some pennies into the waterfall by the driveway.

"Come on," I said, holding out my hand for his.

"What about our suitcases?"

"They bring those up to the room."

A young British porter asked us about our flight as we rode the elevator to the lobby. He walked us to the front desk and wished us well. A French woman at reception told me we had been upgraded to a corner suite. I put down the credit card for deposit. She told us that the hotel had undergone recent renovations and that it now had a Michelin two-star restaurant on premises and if we would like she could plan for the two of us to eat there, which is hard to do if you're not a guest of this hotel. I told her this was unnecessary. She seemed put off, but I told her I had an important lunch meeting tomorrow and could she recommend another more casual place, and she said the hotel had a lovely pool terrace restaurant, La Terraza, and would I like to plan for that, and I said yes, for two, at one o'clock please. Colin was watching me and smiling, as if this was all theater.

Colin could swim within sight. Maybe I would need a sitter, just to monitor him. I said this under my breath to the woman as she typed. She looked up, made uncomfortably long eye contact, and said loudly that she would be pleased to arrange for a babysitter for this afternoon for two hours. Did I realize I was past the cancellation window? Yes, I did. It would total two hundred euro, inclusive of tax and gratuity. Colin had a squeamish expression. I explained the situation. It was just for an hour, I said.

"Daddy who is your lunch with? Why can't I come?"

"It's a work thing," I said, the elevator doors closing. "Push thirty-three."

We shot up to our floor without stopping.

"But I thought you weren't the boss anymore? Your new job is me?"

I thought about that and made some calculations. There was no clear answer. "You are my new job, and this is for you, in a way." He didn't seem satisfied. We walked out of the elevator.

"If you're good then I'll take you shopping for a present."

He held a blank stare and played some game with his feet where he tried not to touch the edges on the carpeting. It could not be medicated away. Not everything we suffer can be eradicated completely.

At the end of the long bright hall we reached a tall door. I handed him the key card. He slid it in a few times in the wrong direction. This made him giggle. I took it from him, reversed the direction, handed it back, and he slid it in again and it clicked.

Our room was overly spacious, a view of the sea from the bedroom, and from the living room a vista of the entire city, the Sagrada Familia rising, decadent and grotesque, a century plus in the making. There were two flat screens and two bathrooms, one of them the size of his bedroom at home.

"This is amazing!" he yelled from the shower, running into the sitting room and back into the bedroom, opening the minibar door, turning on the stereo, turning on all the lights and pushing every button he could reach. A recording of Spanish guitar, assuredly Antonio De Lucena, began to play. "We have a refrigerator with snacks! And look, free chocolate!"

I let him ransack the room like this for a while. What was the harm in letting a child dismantle the perfection of a five-star hotel room? Someone would invisibly appear just before dusk and put it all in order again, fluff the pillows and dial in the mood music.

"Colin, come here, buddy. Let's talk about the plan!" I was deciding between the gorgeous Gaudí cathedral, the agate silver sea, the Ciutat Vella, and Gaudí's twisting spires stretching to the sky, a city walled in by the verdant Serra de Collserola.

We showered and changed, took a taxi into the city, got out near the Liceu, and walked into the Barrio Gotico, got ourselves lost on purpose, walking for nearly half an hour. The morning air was still fresh.

I had agreed to meet Carmen and Jordi, her son, at eleven o'clock in la Placa de Catalunya. Colin and I rambled around the shops, walked with a light meal of bocadillos of jamón serrano, and when it was close to the time, we walked up Las Ramblas, which was thick with tourists, and he touched the flowers in the stalls as we walked past. I bought a *Vanguardia* and we got a nice table outside at Café Zurich and sat down, ordered a coffee and soda, and watched the people exit the metro and mosey into the city.

At eleven fifteen, when she still hadn't come, I grew nervous; I had left my phone in the hotel. It occurred to me she might not recognize me, and although our table was prominently located, I stood nonetheless for almost ten minutes so she could be sure to catch a glimpse of me. Before long I saw Carmen waving near the payphone by the metro exit. She was walking furiously, knowingly late, in high heels. Jordi was Colin's size. He waved to us too, even though he had never met us. They squeezed through the neighboring tables and, without a word, Carmen kissed both my cheeks and did the same to Colin. She was taller than I remembered. I shook Jordi's hand. He said "nice to meet you" in perfect English.

"You look *maravilloso, guapo*," she said.

"So do you. Thank you for seeing us. I'm really excited."

She was slightly overdressed, but this was Spain, and I did not mind her jasmine perfume.

"And you are feeling okay? The jetlag is not so bad? Can we walk? You are hungry, no?"

I smiled, answered none of her questions, left a heap of euro coins on the table, and we strolled back down Las Ramblas, Carmen eventually leading us down the narrow streets, through archways, along stone walls with history and minimal graffiti, and somewhere— could have been anywhere in this maze—church bells tolled. The streets at times were as tight as alleys, just a slit of sky; it was hard to make out the true time. There were swarms of tourists pouring in from the Via Laietana and Carrer dels Capellans by the Barcelona Cathedral, the horde drinking Cuba Libres in the Plaça Reial, with its palm lined arcade.

It was too easy to get lost in the Gothic Quarter. Find some place spectacular once off a main street and write it down—you may never see it again.

Finally, we reached the Plaça del Pi. We sat at one of the open tables at what Carmen said was a recommended café and ordered cortados. I looked up and saw the high walls of the Santa Maria del Pi, a fine example of Catalan Gothic, a style stripped of adornments, and there were pigeons on the rose window above the entrance, and the bells rang out again, startling the pigeons away.

The square was mainly locals and couples, a scattering of middle-aged men smoking alone; it was a place outside the tourist realm, even though it was only a brief walk from the Ramblas. It is one of my favorite spots in

Barcelona. Jordi and Colin ran to kick a stray soccer ball over by the church walls. Carmen lit a cigarette and passed it to me. We watched the boys play for a while and then she looked at me for a long time and said nothing. I asked her how Antonio was liking his new position. For some reason, she answered me in Spanish, Catalan-inflected accent. I heard her say that he preferred Madrid. I tried to answer her back and then she took the cigarette from me, put on fresh lipstick and laughed skyward, and we watched the boys chase away a freshly landed flock of pigeons, kicking the ball through the birds and laughing too. She was a woman who darted in and out of life's currents; she was hard to resist in her four fluent languages. I finished my cortado and signaled the waiter and ordered us another. I heard Colin scream in pleasure, his voice rising to the bell tower where it echoed. She lit me another cigarette and borrowed from it.

"You will like Ariadna." She was smoking, watching me, flicking ashes sideways.

"Who?"

"The sister of Ferran, the gallery owner. We will meet her this afternoon."

I did not answer. I understood now what this was, for her. I failed to conceal my unhappiness. This trip was to honor Monica. I had not planned on Carmen crop-dusting me with blind dates, especially with far away Catalan women. Colin ran over to me, sweating and smelling of wet pennies.

"Can I buy a soccer ball too, please?"

"Sure, we can grab one in a little bit." He ran back at the pigeons.

Carmen must have sensed my displeasure because she tried to change the subject with food. She told the waiter she wanted *albondigas* and *croquetas* and asked me if I'd like an order of *pa amb tomàquet*. It was nearly noon. I vaguely grunted yes. This meant we'd be staying another hour. Chances were, Ariadna looked like every other Catalan woman, slightly Anglo, skinny from all the coffee and nicotine, that one big lunch per day. I had never known a Spanish woman, or any other women since Monica. Except Mimi. At forty, I was malformed, unfit for another person. We conform to who we love, and if we love them enough no other person can conform to us, like a key fitting into a specialty lock.

The waiter left and returned quickly with utensils wrapped in paper napkins, and he spoke something to Carmen in dense Catalan that I didn't comprehend. She said something and he came back minutes later with a bottle of Priorat and some Diet Cokes for the boys. He uncorked the bottle, poured her a taste and she said something, and he smiled broadly, said something back, then began to laugh for a good thirty seconds, showing his yellow teeth, and retreated to the café.

I decided to let it go and be gracious. "I appreciate your consideration, Carmen. But I am not *soltero*. I still feel married. It's not right."

"Of course you do. You are a good man. Your heart is pure. But you have a big heart, enough love for two. She would not wish for you to live with these canvases, which is why you brought them to me. They are hers and they inhabit you. You cannot inhabit them. When one dies, it is this way. You are stuck on their canvas for a while. Then God says to us we must move on, expand the canvas. This is what you must do, Mark, expand your canvas."

"But I'm already stretched and framed," I said, hoping a little sarcasm might stall this conversation.

She leaned across the table, practically out of her seat, and said, "Then break the frame!"

"We don't even live here."

Carmen was smiling as she was inhaling the cigarette. She passed it back to me. I inhaled so heavily I broke into a fit of coughing. We both laughed.

"You Americans," she said, "always planning everything."

"It's why we are number one," I said.

"And it's why you take so many pills and your people are so miserable." She was smiling and took a deep sip of the wine. She was unaware of my own regimen, so I didn't take offense.

"It's why your unemployment rate is ten percent."

"Man plans and God laughs," she said, blowing me a kiss.

I tasted the wine. It was strong and had a concentrated flavor of plums and tar. "Well, I cannot argue with God." We clinked glasses and took another sip.

"No, you cannot." She kept her glass raised for a toast. "To the future, you handsome devil."

"*El futuro*," I said.

The waiter returned with the food, a plate of bread sliced lengthwise and covered in tomato puree and garlic, and casseroles of fried cheese croquets and lamb meatballs. Carmen was quick to mention she had made us a reservation at El Quatre Gats, to signal that this didn't constitute lunch. This being Spain, the entire day would revolve around food. The phone rang and she lifted one of the meatballs with a toothpick and held it while she spoke to Ferran, who, from what I could make out, said the paintings had arrived yesterday. I heard Colin scream again, and looked over, and Jordi was on the ground, a failed attempt at blocking a shot. Colin's arms were raised. Then a startle. The bells began to toll again. The birds lifted off the rim of the bell tower. They rang and rang, and Carmen couldn't hear any longer so she had to hang up. I drank the wine and ate the bread, dipping it in the garlicky sauce, waved Colin over to have some of the bread too. The bells rang on. I saw an elderly couple stand and waltz, laughing. It was noon.

Jordi came over too, and the kids devoured the food. The bells stopped, the birds returned. Carmen lit up another. I declined.

"Who's that?" said Jordi.

A man with a giant backpack had appeared, something mounted on his back. I held my stare. Others began to turn too. It looked heavy and tall, semi-globe-shaped at the top, the unmistakable shine of a lens. A camera encased in plastic guards. He was holding a map and walking, just a backpack and this device. Carmen called him a *gilipollas*, dickhead. We watched him trace the perimeter of the *placa*, then cross it, point to point, diagonally. Then he stood in the center, spun 360 degrees, until he caught the street view. The kids ran over and followed him. He wore a plaid shirt and gray cargo pants. He turned to them and I caught a glimpse of his face, softly bearded and unmistakably American, around twenty-five. What a gig. Get paid to walk Barcelona all day for Google Earth—I assumed it was them—so that we can beam ourselves back to Barcelona when you are home, encased in a blizzard, or wherever you wished to go, flitting to and fro around the globe, a Peter Pan visiting Anthony Bourdain places.

"They do this all the time here now," she said. "The satellites won't get the streets right. They must walk. To come in uninvited."

"He seems harmless. It's just a summer job."

"Mark, it's November. Like this all year long."

Invasion of the maps. A small crowd had gathered, gawking at the alien thing affixed to his back, a good nine feet high. The young man seemed unafraid of the stares. The pack seemed heavy. He had an empty water bottle, upside down in the side pocket. Do they ever stop? Does this go on for hours, days? Does he get health insurance from the digital barons for whom he's harvesting data? The faces were blurred at street level view to protect privacy. Carmen said *gilipollas* again.

The boys were talking to the man. He couldn't really lean over because of the pack. They shook hands. Colin ran back over to me.

"Daddy! Jerome's from America! And he's hungry! Can we give him something? Please!"

Before I could say no, he grabbed some of the *pa amb tomàquet* and scrambled back to Jerome. Carmen was primed for an outburst. She signaled the waiter. She pointed at Jerome and then the waiter began to use the word *gilipollas* too, nodding furiously, and I didn't have to eavesdrop on their rapid, heated Spanish to gleam the consensus of injustice that *los lobos de Silicon Valley* were bringing their war of information to the streets of Barcelona. They were talking, facing Jerome, who had folded the bread and was eating hastily. This seemed to inflame them further. The waiter turned, waved his hand in disgust at Jerome. Carmen looked at me and rolled her eyes.

"They are here all the time now. The last year the most. For us, it is very distressing."

Carmen was setting down euros and thick coins, hustling us out.

"It's just a camera. Haven't you ever used Google Earth?"

"So I can see the Eiffel Tower, Las Sagrada Familia, The Empire State? Do we need to know everything, own it visually? What is the point? What is the point of life if we know everything? What happens when we take away all the mystery?"

Scroll up to the see the church, down to look at the ancient cobblestones. I imagined someone like Lars or Alan, profiteering off this, not on the images but on the web traffic, eyeballs, and how they jacked up the advertising rates, the exodus of ad buys from broadsheets, the AM show on the morning commute, Alan at his sink in his silk robe.

I asked her how far to the gallery. She said twenty minutes by foot. Everyone in Spain was always on foot, and it was always twenty minutes to somewhere.

We walked down the Carrer de l'Ave Maria for less than a minute, Jerome in tow, mapping. I dropped back and told him it was nice he could see the city this way. He had a few days of stubble, bloodshot eyes; as a Google Trekker he could pay off his graduate school loans at Pepperdine. He had seen all of Europe this way for several months, alone. It was always like this: on foot, all day, sleep at youth hostels. It was a rig of fifteen cameras at five megapixels each, a frame shot every two seconds to render a panoramic view. Software pieced the fragments together, a coder drafting algorithms to improve the resolution. You stand on London Bridge, swivel and see the Thames.

Carmen wouldn't look at him. Jerome walked eventually walked ahead of me and disappeared down a side street.

Up ahead, Colin and Jordi were cupping their hands to windows, running into open shops and racing out. Carmen languished in accusatory silence for a while, mainly because I was an American too.

We passed a group of Canadians with their maple leaf flag stitched on their backpacks. A Scandinavian teetering on a rusted bike.

"What else will you do in Barcelona?" The shared silence had been a tonic that dissolved the bonds of me to Jerome, the cameras, California, the virus of digitalization writ large.

"There is no plan. I've lived inside one for too long. Only to enjoy Spain."

"That is a kind of plan, a good plan. Doing nothing is doing something."

"I suppose so."

"You know I am right. You came here for reason, a man with the money to go anywhere. You look tired, honestly. Do you remember why Monica would go to Mexico?"

I held quiet.

"She needed that nothing space. The mind must open up. It cannot open up under tension. An artist needs room, to roam, to learn, to see."

"I wish I had let her open the gallery there."

"You did not want it?"

"It seemed like an extravagance. I was jealous. She was an artist, I was not. Such a price." I said the last part under my breathe.

Carmen watched my face. I realized people were always trying to read my face. People were always trying to leap the barricades of intimacy.

We spoke more about her life with Antonio, who she loved deeply, and Jordi who had just been diagnosed with dyslexia and was struggling in school. I told her a sanitized version of Colin's challenges. To unburden yourself to another human being is necessary if you do not want those burdens to calcify and harden you. She said Jordi was taking a pill too for his anxiety.

I heard a guitarist. This area of the Barrio Gotico seemed vaguely familiar, but then again so did much of Barcelona, even though I was had mainly

262 / ERIC MICHAEL BOVIM

been a regular visitor here while I was living in Madrid. We turned down the Carrer Princesa, then quickly onto a narrow street immediately with a luxe chocolate shop at the corner. The boys peered in the window. They were begging us to go in, but the shop owner was locking up for lunch break.

"*Otro?*" She was holding a newly lit cigarette.

Why not? I smoked out in the open in what were likely unmapped streets, Colin up ahead. I thought of the effective rum from two weeks ago and wondered if the Priorat wasn't better. From what I could infer from the available sky down in the labyrinthine streets, the sun was nearing its height. Always a tyranny of blue in Spain. There wasn't any heat, but it was mild enough for me to take off my blazer and walk with it slung from my finger over my shoulder. We smoked and walked for another ten minutes until we were there.

"Okay, you need this now," Carmen said, handing me a mint. I took it. She appraised me and adjusted my collar. I put on my blazer.

There was one large window and you could see a mild commotion inside. Colin waded over in a hush. One of those rickety European mopeds came zipping by, full speed, blistering our solitude, then Ferran looked up and saw us and waved.

I could sense the paintings, perhaps already hung inside.

Carmen led me in, Ferran holding back as our presence settled into the space.

"Colin are you ready to see the paintings?" I said. He held my hand, nodded, leaned against my arm all sweaty.

We walked inside and the space had the scent of new construction; while the single entrance gave the sense of a confined space, clearly they had purchased and gutted the neighboring buildings, and it felt like SOHO with its high-ceilings and blonde hardwood, then again most everything about Barcelona was done in genuflection to autonomy and experimentation.

At first, I couldn't spot her work. I was struck by several notable pieces hung prominently: a lithograph by Frank Stella, varying abstract shapes; an original Picasso etching, female nude, limited edition; in the corner, by the old fireplace, a Victor Vasarely; and an artist I didn't know, John Opper, who, per Google, turned out to be a Chicago acolyte of Hans Hoffman from the 1950s, red and orange blocks in near primary colors, like a Rothko turned sideways. He had showed in The Betty Parsons Gallery, Ferran said, after 1947, when Peggy Guggenheim had closed her gallery doors for good and returned to Europe. And right near those large, recognizable FedEx boxes from America were two Jasper Johns', color etching and acquaint, and an abstract composition by the great Catalan painter Joan Miró, lithograph signed in pencil by the artist. The room was beautifully laid out, lit in tungsten halogen. Emptiness punctuated by color. I saw Ariadna looking at me, bent over and slicing the tape on the boxes, letting Colin and me take it in. Over the past few days I had spent time wandering the gallery's website, trying to penetrate some unseen core, but no number of keystrokes can unmask the essence of a place.

Il faut aller voir.

I couldn't see how Monica's realist oeuvre would immediately fit in among so much avant-garde work. Sensing my unease, Ferran came over and reassured me that he wanted the pieces. I played at my reluctance, as I didn't wish to leave Monica's artistic ashes somewhere she wasn't truly wanted. He was insistent, to the point of taking my hands and invoking unnecessary eye contact in that unabashed Spanish way. It was so forward I thought he might start stroking my cheek. He led me by the hand to the boxes; he had slit open the tops but had yet to remove the paintings. Carmen wandered over and tapped her hand on my back. Colin and Jordi ran over from the other Picasso litho.

"Which one is it?" he said, still breathing heavily.

I grabbed the mammoth gold leaf frame and lifted the 38x32 oil on canvas from its box: *Boy on Beach, Nantucket.* Of course, while they had seen pictures of this already, Carmen and Ferran gushed, whether for my benefit or out of genuine admiration I couldn't tell, but they audibly gasped with each canvas I slid from the box, neorealist stills of places from Monica's life. We all stood silent, as if stargazing, for a long time, letting the paintings work their way inside us, lush and nearly flood lit. They contrasted beautifully on the wall below the surrealism of Miró, a yin and yang of form.

"Daddy, it's weird. They look different. Kind of new."

"It's the light. This room has perfect light. We were looking at these in our basement. Not the same."

"They are perfect depictions of place," said Ariadna.

I was so engrossed I thought it was Monica's voice in my head, which I had not heard in a week. I looked up. She was standing behind Carmen, deep in a canvas, eyes down maybe out of respect. I had assumed she had been standing there for a while, since the first canvas had been lifted back into this world ten minutes ago. She saw me looking at her but held her gaze. She was petite. I put her around thirty-five. When she finally did look up, she made long eye contact. She seemed the type of woman with a repertoire of expressions.

"Where will you hang these?" I said, looking at Ferran.

"Over here."

He led us to a long wall behind the Opper.

"We can fit all eight here. I will hang them today. You can come to the party tomorrow?"

"I did not mention the party." Carmen turned to me. "Mark it is just cocktails, very small. To honor Monica."

"Can we go?" Colin shouted.

"Very small, nothing fancy," Ferran said.

"It sounds lovely." I looked at Ariadna. She was looking at the beach painting.

"Can Jordi come? Also, do I need a suit?"

They all laughed.

"Yes, Jordi can come and you can wear whatever you like," Carmen said.

"Hard to find a suit but maybe a new shirt, what do you say?" I said. "You don't need help hanging these?"

"My sister does them." Ferran nodded towards Ariadna. For the first time, I noted she was holding a hammer. "I buy, she sells—hangs and sells. We are a team."

"But this is your gallery, I am just a lowly Catalan girl who works here." They laughed again. They had done this before, this shtick. She had zero Spanish accent, sounded faintly British.

"It is not the truth. I am the boss man here. But we all follow Ariadna." Colin was looking up at her.

*

WHEN ALL the paintings were hung, we took a taxi back to the hotel. It was nearly six o'clock, and we were both exhausted. Carmen kissed us goodbye on both cheeks, Ferran gave me *un abrazo*, a hug, and Ariadna kissed Colin on the cheek. He was in a jetlagged daze in the hotel room, fluttering in and out of consciousness. I ordered us cheeseburgers from room service. He ate his into a half moon shape and then asked for a bath before putting on his pajamas and climbing into bed with me. I had left the curtains open and all the evening light from the city and the seaside poured in. I was still hungry and took some dark chocolate from the minibar. Carmen texted. What did I think? I knew what she was asking. I told her the paintings looked beautiful, thank you, and I would see her *mañana* after my lunch with Arnaud. She texted back immediately and said Ferran was very happy and impressed with me and Ariadna was too. The party was early tomorrow, *a las siete de la tarde*, please dress nicely.

Colin was half asleep, covered in a sheet. I switched off the nightstand light, and lay in silence for a while, near sleep. I felt him tap my arm.

Daddy

Huh

Are you happy

What

Happy. Are you

Sure I'm with you

I mean overall

Sure

But you were the boss and now

I'm tired. Go to sleep

Don't you miss being the boss

No go to sleep

Are you lonely

Jesus, Colin

But I don't see you on dates

Daddy is married

You are soltero

What

Spanish for single

So what

So you need to have fun and I like Ariadna

Colin please

She is nice and she likes you

She is soltero

She is and she has pretty eyes

Maybe you should date her

Hey

Ow don't kick me little man
Don't tease
Go to bed
I cant it's the lag
Jet lag
Yes jet lag
I am happy
Okay
And glad I'm not the boss
Okay

★

I HAD fallen asleep in my clothes beside Colin, outside the sheets. My mouth was parched. I got up, took and uncapped an orange juice from the minibar, and squinted at the Mediterranean light. I turned and Colin wasn't there, a cold indentation on the pillow.

I felt a panic. What if he'd gotten the notion to go for a walk or a swim on the beach or a stroll down the pick-pocket infested Ramblas? I thought to check the living room, and when I opened the door I was astonished: he was asleep on the couch, the TV on the Disney Channel, an order from room service set up on the coffee table. It was seven-thirty in the morning. There were half-eaten scrambled eggs and bacon; there was an order for me too, under the plate cover, semi-warm. I looked for signs of when he had woken. On the bill was an order for pastries, and the basket was untouched beside the TV. I looked at the room service menu: the kitchen opened at five-thirty a.m. On the tray was an empty orange juice, a white orchid blossom in a tiny jar, a cold espresso.

He was snoring and drooling on the pillow. Nothing but his boxers. I grabbed a blanket from the other room and covered him, switched off the TV, and sat down on the other end of the sectional and ate the lukewarm eggs and crisp bacon, watching the spires of the Sagrada Familia gradually brighten in the morning sun. This was the best and most useless time in Spain, the soft shapeless early morning, all the country still in a slumber. I went into the bedroom and made myself a hot espresso in the little machine with the capsules, Big Coffee, by the minibar and came back and watched the hues shift on the cathedral, gold to whiskey, brass to orange. The sky was already very blue, a feathering of clouds near the peak of Tibidabo, and I turned and watched a skiff ride through the harbor and eventually out to sea.

A child sees everything and knows nothing. That he read me so openly the night before was frightening. No one wants to be read: as humans, we prefer to be a mystery to each other, above all, to ourselves.

Arnaud surely knew I would get bored and would miss being the boss. Hawthorne suspected, too, that I might find emeritus life dull. But my fear and despair from home had been diminished in Barcelona. Certain places make us better. We tire, maybe, of our patterns, and so when we thrive in the microclimates of other places, rousing our dormant cells, we think it means we're better suited to live in that place. Maybe that's true. But I didn't need to dwell upon Dr. Weller for long to hear what he would say: First, we inhabit ourselves.

I suddenly felt compelled to walk back into the bedroom and grab my notebook, a hotel pen from the desk, another espresso. I thought I should shower first, instead. I skipped a shower and wrote a journal entry for a while on the sofa, by hand, Colin's feet nearly on my leg. I was back in Italy with Monica, but it didn't make sense for her to be Monica anymore in the story. I changed her name to Veronica, played Gaudi with her identity, put curls in her hair, more song in her voice. That was it. She was a first chair violinist. I placed us in Vienna. She was in the Vienna Philharmonic Orchestra. *Das Wiener Philharmoniker.* She played first chair and she was Slovak. Maybe we met on the slopes in Gstaad, where I spend a winter writing my novel. I would be *soltero*. A world-class violinist cannot ski, but she can *aprés*-ski. We met at The Alpina, she was dressed all in white and sat by the hearth drinking a Bitter Diablerets with cola. Hoof sounds in the snow, the sleigh ascending the slopes into the evergreen night, very little said, at first. There were too many languages in Europe to be completely given over to one. She tried to address me in German. It was useful to know a smattering of each, my character said, as the horses panted. I went on like this, for maybe an hour, ignoring my surroundings—forgetting it, really... more the right word. Colin barely rustled. I got so far as her invitation to me to hear her play Bruckner's seventh symphony in Wien when I felt a sense of depletion. I looked out at the sea again: the skiff was gone. There were sailboats now, bending and leaning into the wind. A man was already stretched out on a towel on the beach tanning. The sea produced no roily surf. I looked out at the city. The light had ignited Barcelona. Pedestrians and cars were mildly visible, even from the thirty-third floor. I loved this city. Maybe I was better here. First, we inhabit ourselves. Maybe the places we love are really hidden selves crying out.

I woke him close to eleven. He dressed quickly, grabbing toast from his half-eaten breakfast, eager to get going with our day. We rode the elevator down to the teeming lobby. All the floral arrangements looked brand new, canted yellow tulips in square glass bowls beside a stack of *International New York Times*.

We waited a bit in the lounge. I had my hand on his shoulder. "It's only an hour, then we can hang, okay, promise, okay?"

The girl the concierge had scheduled for the hour was blowing bubbles in spandex leggings, small pink purse slung over her shoulder. She did not smile. She couldn't have been twenty.

He sat down on the sofa nearly crying, only withholding tears because we were in a public place. I began to wonder if the lunch was a good idea at all. What was the point? I had an anemic nest egg in the low millions. It was impulse—and vanity—that led me to respond to Arnaud at Dulles. I didn't need to write back that day; I could have taken the week. Was I not learning? At best, it was a ten thousand a month gig. I had no desire to be the CEO of Publicis America.

I was angry at the concierge for such a low-grade babysitter. Even at the Ritz, I was just another American guest in a long line of needy tourist requests with their demands and mandates. The babysitter must have sensed my displeasure with the whole situation. I can take him now, if you like, maybe to the pool, she said. Yes, the pool. I would not look at her. Then I can watch him, I thought. I handed her the room key and told her where to find his suit, which I had forgotten. He walked off to the elevator bank before I could say goodbye.

I walked up to La Terraza early and requested a private table. The waiter placed me in the shade with a clear view of the pool. I sat with my back to the open kitchen; Colin was wading in the shallow end, looking back up at me. I waved. He didn't wave back. I ordered a lemonade and the waiter returned with a Tom Collins glass of large ice, a sprig of rosemary, a little carafe of lemonade he poured ceremoniously. I sipped it and watched the boats rock, Ibiza and Mallorca, mirages in the distance. I had ten minutes until our appointment. I looked at the other tables. Couples and families.

The women lunching beside me ordered banana smoothies and egg white frittatas. There was a gentle breeze.

Colin was looking up at me from the pool—he had his hand over his brow like a visor. The girl was slumped on a chaise, checking her phone. He had found a tennis ball and was throwing it into the deep end, swimming and fetching it, throwing it back. He repeated this game for a while.

The sun glinted off the pool water. Even in late fall, the Mediterranean light could burn. I realized that I had not instructed the girl to apply any sunscreen. From behind me, at the maître d' booth, I heard a man's voice, a French accent. There was no time left now to go to the pool and come back. I stood up and turned: it was Arnaud, already with his hand extended, that big chairman's smile broadcasting his good intent for our lunch and the years to come. Before I could pull away he placed his other hand on mine, a double-hander, putting me entirely in his grip. He wore a pastel pink shirt and dark blue tie, light gray suit, white pocket square—however the bankers dress in Monaco. He looked younger than the picture on his bio page, perhaps some injections. He had a perfect hairline, lustrous gray hair, offset by black rimmed glasses. I felt woefully underdressed in khakis, white linen shirt, and a navy blazer, the penny loafers I wore to walk Atticus in the summer.

"Mr. White, it is such a pleasure, a true pleasure. Hawthorne has told us so much." He smiled and had a fortress of perfectly white front veneers. His accent had suddenly vanished, sanitized away now that he was down to business.

I deepened my voice, stayed standing a touch longer as he began to sit, and, glancing at Colin, said I was eager to learn more about the position. That last word lingered like a misplayed note. He seemed to notice.

I sat and sipped the lemonade, trying to play it off. Suddenly, I recognized that I had been nervous, a sparrow flutter in the back of the throat. It felt ridiculous to be nervous. For ten years, as Mark White, I gave orders, I had vendors, people who lined up to be in my employ. I had no superior. Why was I nervous? The sun had shifted, a slant of light across our table. Colin was playing his game. I saw Arnaud watching me watch him.

"You brought your boy; you are a good man."

"Do you have any kids?"

He laughed and studied his iced tea. "I am a bachelor, no kids, the only one in Paris. I am sixty-five. In some sense, we have things in common."

"Maybe so."

"Do not worry. I won't pry. But I prefer to be direct. It saves money but also prevents mistakes, which cost money. So, you had some problems, sold to Hawthorne. It is good for you both, but it is a problem for Publicis in the sense that now we have no plan to build in America."

I glanced back at Colin and remembered the time I feel asleep in Mallorca and awoke to badly burned legs, the kind of burn that produced blisters and a fever.

"Arnaud, I'm eager to speak with you. Truly. But would you mind if I just checked in with my son—the heat, no sunscreen. Just five minutes."

I stood up so quickly it bumped the table and almost knocked over the lemonade. He had no opportunity to respond except to partially stand, an empty smile on his face.

I nearly ran down to the pool. "Throw me the ball," I said to Colin. The girl put down her phone when she saw me.

"Aren't you supposed to be at your stupid meeting?" he said.

"Toss it to me."

He walked over towards the shallow end where he could stand and pitched it to me hard. I had to leap to catch it, arm outstretched. It was an angry throw. I asked the girl in Spanish if he might want to go down to the beach just outside the pool but she responded to me that it was windy and there were too many gypsies. I tried to tell her in Spanish that I'd like her to take him down for a few minutes when my lunch started but I wasn't sure exactly what I was saying. He was studying me.

"Do you want some gelato?"

"Seriously?" he said.

"Yeah, seriously. They have a gelato bar right by the drinks area. Seriously, come on."

He pushed himself out of the pool and raced over to the gelato cart. The girl stayed seated. He ordered two scoops of chocolate and I ordered vanilla. We shared a chaise and ate the gelato in the sun, letting the negative sediment of moments ago settle and dissolve. I heard the barman turn on the blender and watched him pour two strawberry daiquiris, topped with whipped cream, and a waiter in white carried them to an Italian couple frolicking in the deep end.

"What are those?"

"Alcoholic drinks."

He was licking the inside of his cup.

"You know what? I want to try black rice with squid." His mouth was dark ringed with gelato.

"What?" I sat back and appraised him. He was standing on the pool deck, unconsciously semi-flexing.

"That's big boy food, you serious?" I thought about trying to find some wild five-table place in La Barceloneta, some not listed in Zagat's. I thought of the thin long rice, tar black from squid ink, the creamy texture from the garlic aioli mixed in. They called it fideuá.

"Completely serious. They showed it on the hotel TV this morning. I searched it up, it sounds good. So, can we?"

"Well, hard to argue with that. Let me do this one lunch, then we can go right after, okay?"

I looked at Colin's stone smooth shoulders, bronzing in the light. For a little boy, he had bulk already. For a man, to be strong and physically perfect was a gift. I wondered how he would use this as he grew older. How much more was he aware of my nuances than I was aware of myself? I told the girl to fetch the sunblock lotion from the pool reception. She got up and returned with a small tray of bottles and sprays, American brands, and I grabbed the pink one, shook it, and squirted some pasty cream on his shoulders and massaged it in.

"Is this man the boss?"

"He is." I wiped the excess lotion on his palms and told him to do his chest and arms.

"And he wants you to be a new boss for him."

"Sort of."

"Because you're bored with me."

"Colin! No. That is not true. This is a consulting thing, do you understand that? Part-time."

He spun the ball in his hand.

"It's just," he broke off, starting to cry. "It's just, well, I am bored too, always by myself."

"Well you have friends, you have Tommy!"

He was crying but not loudly yet. "I meant my parents. I'm bored being alone. I want you Dad, okay!" The barman turned and looked.

"Colin."

"What!"

"Can you be calm?"

"Why?"

"So daddy can do this meeting, this one single meeting then it's over."

"Then what?"

"Then we are together all week."

"So."

"So, I promise. I will even get you a souvenir."

"I want black rice."

"Okay, black rice."

"And a Messi hat."

"Okay, they don't make hats but you can get a jersey."

"Fine. How long?"

"Thirty minutes."

He took a taste of the melted gelato and dove in the pool, my signal to get the hell out.

Arnaud barely stood when I returned to our table. He took an extra few seconds to complete an email on his phone. I sat and waited. I drank another lemonade. I could hear the blender from up here. Once Arnaud hung up, the waiter materialized and took our orders.

Arnaud switched on his chairman's charm and dispensed with whatever animosity he harbored against me for visiting with Colin.

"Hawthorne said you were a good father."

"Well, I have my bad days." I realized I was nervous not so much because of who he was but because I didn't know exactly who I was supposed to be at this lunch. I wasn't the boss. This confused and distressed me, for the first time, sitting with the head of a $10-billion company eating American food in a Spanish restaurant watching my son play Sisyphus with a tennis ball in the pool. How many more revolutions around the sun must we journey until we learn what is best for us?

"Why did you come to Barcelona? I'm just curious."

"I needed a change of scenery. We both did. I know you're aware of my circumstances. Sometimes, a change can be bad, sometimes it can—just like this rosemary in my lemonade. Magic."

"Yes, but why here?" He was smiling, unbroken eye contact, and seemed to be relishing my little story.

"Spain is a kind of home. I don't have to learn how to do things here. I know how to do things here. That's not true if I visit Paris or London."

"Do you always have to travel so far to find home?"

I realized he was playing a game, trying to stress test my emotional well-being to see how I held up, if I might fall asleep or break down or send out some crazy Trump tweets. I would hold up. He was waiting for me to get drunk, to stammer on live TV. He summoned the waiter and ordered a glass of rosé, and I figured he wanted to see if I took one too. I demurred. He insisted. I said no. He seemed pleased and repeated his question.

"I've lived in Washington forever. I guess it feels stale. One misses the spectacle of Europe."

"And you are well known."

"So what?"

"Mr. White, I'm just trying to get to know you, the ways you think about life. It's no secret who you are and what your company—your former company—has been through. We are still attracted to it, to you. I'm am eager to get to know you to understand if you can help us."

Arnaud, by now, had put his elbows on the table, clasped his hands, rested his mouth at the peak of that triangle. One might have though he was flaunting his diamond cufflinks, but I had seen this affectation a lot from the very wealthy; it is meant to feign serious interest, their listening posture, they hold it briefly, take in what they need from you, make their sales pitch, and then they're out. At this point, I knew this would be a thirty-minute lunch. But what he wanted to know from me I did not yet know of myself.

"It's poetic, the sea. You chose an exceptional property," he said.

"This is a special city. I guess I wanted him to see it the right way."

"And he's enjoying it?"

"I think so." I held the silence to force him to scrub ahead to his point quickly.

"Well, congratulations again on your decision. I'm sure it wasn't easy. But you have handed it over to someone very capable, as I am sure you well know. We at Publicis, unfortunately, are not in a great position in America. We have made acquisitions that have not panned out. We have made big hires, still," he let go of his hands and opened them, indicating a vanishing, "nothing. We need someone experienced to counsel us. This is not a full-time assignment. I'd say...six months, $250,000. Not a lot for a man of your stature, but who knows where this can lead. We need someone to give us a roadmap, names, ideas, advise us so we don't buy yet another firm that runs through our fingers like all that sand out there."

He stopped and waited. He knew what he was doing. Make a concise and attractive pitch and see if I bite before the food is served. If I say yes, he can shade in the contours of what he is really looking for and be gone when the bill comes. The very rich are so savagely efficient with their time.

"Do you have an acquisition budget?"

"We do. You can help to steer it."

"Do you have targets in Washington?"

"Somewhat. We need your guidance there, too."

"Would you consider paying me in stock?"

For this question he sat back, took a long sip, and returned to his pose. "Perhaps."

We went on like this for a few more questions until the food arrived. The penne was over-sauced; his club sandwich looked better. We ate and made brittle small talk, knowing the real conversation would resume when the plates were cleared. Colin had stopped with the ball. The girl had moved into the shade, out of sight. I lay down my fork and signaled the waiter. He came and took the plates and asked us in English if we would like dessert. I ordered a coffee and Arnaud asked for a sherry. They came back with a French press and a bottle of Tio Pepe. Arnaud asked him to leave the bottle on the table and two glasses.

"It's fine."

"Please, join me."

"The coffee is enough. It's fine. You enjoy though."

"I surely will. Only Americans are afraid to drink alone."

"You're funny."

"It's not a joke."

"I know."

When the food was cleared, I could sense that Arnaud was in distress over my ambivalence. He was in no mood to eat. I dug in and he had his arms folded, peppering me with questions.

"What firms you would you go after if we did this deal, Mark?" The sun shifted and he was no longer sitting in the shade, squinting at me with his sparkling cufflinks.

I was thinking about Monica's canvases and how Carmen was planning to lay them out, whether the Jasper Johns would clash against her work or not, if it mattered, if it was more important that she was showing in this gallery in the uncharted wilds of the Barrio Gotico, and I thought about

AROUND THE SUN / 275

Google Trekker and when they last combed through my neighborhood, every piece of tech we used to be elsewhere, to help us to fall out of time, those oculus glasses they gave me at the Refugees International fundraiser last month, told me to wear them and press a button on the side, look around and you are in an internment camp for Muslims in Myanmar, you try and eat a crab cake and drink your pinot noir as you swivel and see blue sky and down to a ravine with free flowing sewage and to a young crippled woman in a wheelchair wailing and wailing, her father has died, and the flies just ward over him as he bakes, you hear the melancholy music and look up and see barbed wire and then you remove those glasses and you are back in American prosperity with hors d'oeuvres, sequin cocktail dresses, and men named Grant and Philip. The question was so prosaic I could not help to flash into the world of this morning, our beginnings never know our ends, the clanging of the rental bikes as we rushed through Wien towards the October countryside, following the trails along the Danube into the ruddy hills as far as Krems until the sky was pinkened. I imagined us renting a room for a night at a Heuriger, where they served us the new wine and a generous charcuterie board. We left the windows open and we could smell the crisp leaves, all night; there is nothing as wonderful as the first-time smell of a new lover, and she would giggle and murmur in German to me something private and I was careful not to damage her hands because she had her performance of Bruckner tomorrow night.

"I don't know," I said, "maybe there are two or three firms, but nothing I would invest in. Better to poach people. I'd decapitate a few agencies, strip away their top people. Kyle Sheppard at Brunswick is good. So is Annie Lerner. Marcus Chappman and Jorge Delorenzo. They are all Omnicom people."

"Great! Great! So, let's do it!"

He was leaning across the table now, the smell of blood had stirred his atavism.

I saw Colin pick up the ball again and throw it. The girl was still in the shadows, out of sight. I heard the women in tennis attire cackling about someone's fresh Manhattan divorce, nibbling their frittatas, sipping Evian. At some point, a caricature can surpass even itself, which is a sign of danger. I saw myself again on planes and trains, aloft in Colin's life. I did not wish to be even more rude, so I strung Arnaud along until the check came.

We made polite goodbyes and I vowed to give it serious consideration. Very serious consideration, I said.

He watched me go down to the pool. I turned and waved.

Then he was gone.

chapter fifteen

I TOLD him to dry off, sent the girl away, told him to get moving, that we were going to pack up because we were leaving this hotel.

"Where are we going, Daddy?"

"Some place more Spanish."

The woman at reception, same as yesterday, tensed up when I announced my precipitous early check-out. Is something wrong? I assured her the hotel was fine, but that we wanted to be closer to the heart of the city. *You have booked for a week,* she said. *You will lose your deposit.* That is fine. She picked up the phone and spoke in French to someone. An older man in a navy suit appeared and introduced himself as the general manager and said he wanted to be certain my stay had been pleasant. I tried my best to assure him but they seemed unconvinced. They watched us all the way to the elevator, not waving.

"Hotel Lloret," I told the taxi driver.

"What is that?" Colin said.

"We are going to a more special hotel. More atmosphere. Less American things."

"Why?"

"Because we came to be in Spain. This is not being in Spain."

"Oh. Is there a pool?"

"No—and there's no room service. There is the Ramblas," I said, pointing out the window.

The taxi retraced our route from yesterday morning, all the way up to the top of the Ramblas, the Messi ad visible from across the Plaça Catalunya. The hotel was still there, just as I recalled it, the neon cursive sign, the rooms with their balconies, the street noise. The driver stayed in the car as I lifted the luggage to the curb. I gave him some coins and he left us. Colin was sullen. For a moment, I thought about summoning another taxi and going right back to the Hotel Arts. No, you won't. You make this work, show this boy that you can make anything work, that there's more to Spain than a corporate hotel.

We took a room on the third floor, two balconies and a cathode-ray television with just one grainy English-language channel, CNN International. There was a bathroom and a king bed, some café chairs you presumably could take out onto the balcony. He was sullen when we entered but perked up a little at the view. I set the chairs outside and sat down to draw him out.

"Isn't this magnificent?" I said.

He read my every micro-expression and gesture before he decided to answer. "I guess. Why did we move again?"

"The other hotel was very beautiful, amazing. But did we fly here to eat chicken fingers and speak English all day? I want you to experience Barcelona. This is a special hotel."

"Why?"

"Because mommy and daddy stayed here once."

He took that in, could not conceal a widening smile, and stared out onto the Ramblas where a man had decorated himself in silver foil and metallic paint and was posing for pictures as the Tin Man.

"Really? In this room? Why were you here?"

"Not this room. One just like it. I had just moved here. Mommy came to visit me. I was poor. This was what we could afford. You know what? Of all the places in the world mommy traveled, she always talked about this hotel, it's little balconies and the view of the street at night. Mommy loved to be outside."

He was smiling: "That's so cool. Alright, fine, I understand, daddy. Now, can we go get the black rice you promised?"

His hair was matted from the chlorine.

"You take a quick shower, get ready, and we'll go for lunch. I know somewhere good where they have it, okay? We have the party tonight too, remember."

He was unusually pliant and went straight to the bathroom and took a long shower while I sat on the balcony smoking a cigarette I had stashed from Carmen's supply. I checked my phone for the time and saw a text arrive from Arnaud: "Mr. White, such a pleasure, please inform me of your decision, we are most eager to get started with you and no one else."

I took a long drag and noticed a Mexican food chain from America had settled in across the street, scarring the view. There was a breeze and some ashes flew into the room. I thought briefly of Veronica, her long auburn hair bouncing on the bike trail, the sleeping Danube winding through hills, and I opened the notes function on my phone and typed in some ideas of where that story would go, my mind was alight with ideas, bullets in the sky, and I went dreamy indulging the notion that she would invite me to her performance of Bruckner's symphony and seat me onstage, in the fifth violin chair, so I could experience the music as a virtuoso does, her hair in a bun while she sawed away on her violin, head tilted as if looking into a painting, and I thought of the way Ariadna was examining Monica's art, her solemnity and recognition that each of those paintings had a molten core, even for realism. It's not what you paint but what you omit and can the subject feel the omission. Her death was stained on us like indigo; her spirit found its way into the oddest things—the unnamable bug sounds in Christ Church—there was no billboard wisdom that could chase her out of my life; I wanted her there, and perhaps Carmen was right that my canvas could expand, her spirit enmeshed into the oddest things, this hotel, the moon—she loved squid ink rice and, of course, this boy.

"Daddy what are you doing?" He had a towel wrapped around his waist.

I had the cigarette hanging from my lip. Quickly I snuffed it out on the balcony and stomped methodically on it as if it would vanish. I closed my eyes and laughed inside. Sooner or later our children must learn that their parents are not perfect.

"Well, daddy was smoking."

His eyes widened.

"I am sorry."

"So, technically, you weren't smoking because it was in your mouth but you weren't breathing in. Right?"

"Uh...right."

"Also, cigarettes can help with stress. Did you know they contain a drug in them that relaxes people? I searched it up. It's true. Nicotine. It comes from plants."

"Why were you looking that up?"

"I saw you smoking in Barbados and I researched it."

I felt so relieved. I kissed his forehead and tasted soapy water. I wiped him off. I told him to get dressed and ready to go, the day had just started.

"We are going to have an adventure now!"

"We are going to have an adventure. We're going to La Boqueria. Then we are going for a long walk. Then we're going to a party."

I changed my shoes and locked the door behind us. We walked down the flight of stairs to the street and headed in the direction of the sea, walking on the busy promenade under the denuded trees. The sun was hot and I took off my jacket. I had given Colin a few euros that he was tossing into the hats and guitar cases of the various street performers. In ten minutes we were at the Boqueria. It was cool once inside and smelled like fish and raw meat. Skinned rabbits hung from their skulls. There were bins of exotic mollusks and *langostinos* squirming in Styrofoam containers. Every thirty feet was a food stand. At three o'clock, the place was packed, locals and very few tourists, men squeezed together at the counters with their *cañas* and *Albariños*. I bought Colin a little bag of spiced candied almonds for a euro. We negotiated the crowd and waded to the back, along the way I asked a man selling salted cod to point me towards the paellas and I kept walking towards the back, and we bought some candied apricots for another euro and almost tried the cheeses but the line was too long and Colin was hungry. There was room for us to sit down at the paella stand. They were using butane tanks to fire the burners, and had three massive paella pans going, the final one pure black rice with rings of calamari. He fixed us two plates, topped it with a dollop of aioli. It tasted of the sea. Colin was eating, not talking. Eating and smiling and not talking. I ordered un Estrella and bought him a Diet Coke. I showed him how to mix in the aioli and the garlic intensified the fish flavor.

"Daddy, this is my new favorite food!" His lips and teeth and tongue were black from the ink.

"It's incredible. That's true."

"*Es lo mejor de Barcelona,*" said the man cooking.

"*Mejor de Barcelona, si,*" said Colin.

I paid ten euros each and we took a long walk down to the waterfront. We sat down outside at a café at the Maremagnum. Colin said he was willing to try an horchata, and I ordered another Estrella, and I asked the girl to bring an American paper. I had bought some postcards on the Ramblas and gave them to Colin to fill out. She brought an *International New York Times*. I sat and looked out to the water. The view felt different from the one this morning. It was nice to enjoy some stillness. We watched the boats at sea until it began to darken and get chilly.

I heard my phone vibrate. Another text from Arnaud, petitioning for a call in two days. I didn't reply. Colin seemed tired from being sedentary so we walked back to the hotel.

I told him to get dressed fancy for the party. I put on a nicer shirt, cologne, looked at myself. Then I undressed and hopped in the shower, changed my razor and shaved, redressed and reapplied the cologne. He had on a white shirt and navy blazer, looked like he was going for First Communion. He asked for some cologne too. I splashed some on his cheeks with the back of my hand. He said he needed to shave. Maybe tomorrow, I said.

I hailed a taxi and asked him to drop us off near the Picasso Museum, so we could walk to the gallery. We were right on time, which meant very early in Spain. I thought we could kill the time by wandering the Gothic streets. I realized we had not done this yet at night. I realized we had only arrived yesterday, although it felt like a week. I realized I had no firm plans yet for Thanksgiving, that my only accomplishment, so far, was changing hotels and hiring a babysitter.

At night, the streets of the Gothic Quarter were enchantingly lit, and we drifted in and out of the side streets off the Carrer Montcada until it seemed like we had seen the same stone building with arches twice before. I assured him we were not lost. I wasn't going to use the map function on my phone, out of respect for Carmen. Somewhere on the Caller Mirallers I stepped into a dark wine bar and asked about the gallery and he point me further down the street and said it was on the left. We were now thirty minutes late, so, for Spain, more or less on time.

We walked further for a while until I saw them, a double take: Monica's paintings shone through the windows in the night because they had hung them all prominently at the entrance of the gallery. Carmen kissed us both as before and Ferran gave a bear hug. There were already forty or so people milling about, a table of tapas and cheese and some flutes of cava.

"This is so incredible, Carmen. Thank you so much," I said. Colin stuck out his hand to shake hers.

"You are most welcome. We thank you for bringing such special art into our lives. Ferran says there is a dealer here from Madrid who wants to meet you and ask about more pieces. This way, this way! Colin, look, there is Jordi, go say hi!"

Carmen escorted me through the crowd, put a cava in my hand, and took me to the dealer, an older Catalan man living in Madrid who indeed asked about more pieces. After brief discussion, he said he wanted Monica's triptych, at least what I had described to him, sight unseen. Ariadna materialized. She looked too beautiful. I put the cava in her hand, she nodded and took a sip. The dealer thanked me and handed me a card. When he left, Ariadna and I made small talk together.

"Colin is very sweet. Jordi talked about him all afternoon."

"That's good to hear. He doesn't have many friends."

"Yet."

"You are right, yet."

"You should say something, to everyone, a big toast," she said, her feline composure intact, the flute upright.

"I suppose you are right again. Carmen didn't need to do this for us. By the way, your English is superb."

"I studied in the US."

"Where?"

"NYU."

"That's a fine school. You weren't tempted to stay in New York?"

"Honestly, Spanish men are more fun."

"You are right again. Amazing."

"I was kidding."

"I know."

She tried to pass me the flute but I demurred.

"Not to drink, but to clink the glass for your speech."

"Ah, yes," I said. "Would you do it for me?"

When the group heard the crystal ringing, they quieted and turned to us. Colin was towards the back by the Miró with Jordi. I looked out and saw Ferran with his arm around Carmen. Ariadna stepped away and joined the group. I had given talks and speeches to rooms bigger than this before, but I didn't know what to say now. I started by thanking people,

Carmen and Ferran, the guests who came to view the art, and I wanted to thank many others too, Sally, Margaret, Hawthorne, even Dr. Weller, but I kept my remarks crisp and tight, only enough to say that tomorrow was Thanksgiving, and that indeed a gathering this grand and wonderful is cause for celebration. And I looked around and held the silence to acknowledge the way Monica was hung all around the room.

Colin was the first to clap. Then the room exploded with applause. Random friends of Carmen's and Ferran's came to embrace me and to tell me what I had done was a beautiful thing. Guests, the men and the women, were cupping my cheek in their hands, touching my shoulders, and I saw her canvases in the perfect tungsten light and heard her telling me to go, go and live my life again, and I saw our boy and his new friend laughing about something and I turned and looked for Ariadna.

She took my hand and said goodnight and that she would like to see us both tomorrow for lunch.

The walk back to the hotel was chilly, cold enough that I bought Colin an FC Barca windbreaker at a kiosk along the way. He said he was still hungry. We went inside the café beside the hotel where all the men were drinking sherry and watching tonight's match. I ordered us bowls of Catalan sausage and white beans. The beans were creamy and oily with the *butifarra* and Colin ate his entire plate and half of mine. We walked up the stairs to our room and as soon as I unlocked the door it flew open from the wind; I had inadvertently left the balcony doors open, and now there was street noise and a few leaves blowing around the room. I shut the doors and Colin went into the bathroom to get ready for bed.

I checked my phone one last time. There was another text from Arnaud, the same message as before, sent an hour ago. I watched the car lights circle La Plaza Catalunya and heard Colin singing in the bathroom, factored in the cost of missing out on more of this life, then wrote a very polite email declining the position and hit send.

I sat in the balcony chair for a while, not smoking, watching a man far down the promenade juggle swords, then fire, then both. In my news browser, I spotted a story on the fight for Mosul, and Trump was surging in the head to head polls with Clinton. I clicked through to the *New York Times*, but their paywall blocked me from the news. I typed the search term into Google and saw fresh stories on all the wires. The brutality of ISIS was unthinkable, medieval but worse because this was 2016. The article said the militant leader had tied eight boys to flagpoles—these were boys under twelve, allegedly from the resistance, whatever that could mean in bomb-battered Syria—and killed them with a chainsaw. I scrolled to keep reading but the story was interrupted by a mobile ad about summer barbeque grills, offered at a thirty percent discount. It was horrific. I closed out of the browser.

I thought about a sabbatical from not just the news but also my device. I had read an article recently about a man in London who'd given up his phone altogether, tossed it in the Thames for good. He was doing fine, the piece suggested. I wasn't fine so I certainly couldn't do worse. Maybe the time away from my digital life would rewire my brain, let the neurons reset, unwind me in the warm bath of life. I took a deep breath and inhaled the night. There was no sensible place to toss a cell phone. Did you burn it to fry the connections? I thought it was exceedingly unnecessary to walk all the way to the Mediterranean to dispense with a phone I could just as easily crush or throw out the window, but then it felt more like a true genuflection to the idea of abandoning the phone to turn its demise into a ritual, to summon Colin for one more round, to lead him out of the hotel late at night, through the Gothic maze of alleys, and back down to the Maremagnum, which is exactly what I did. There was just enough height due to the elevated boardwalk, enough people because of the nightclubs that it didn't look odd to see a man stooped over the rails dropping a hand-sized computer into the sea of antiquity.

It was gone as soon as it hit the water. I felt oddly neutral, disarmed and dismembered, human alas.

"Why did you throw it away, daddy?" Colin said.

"It had nothing left to say."

The moonlight across his face made him look older, hardened features that would likely emerge when he was a teenager. He was a handsome boy, indeed, every part his mother. *There lives the dearest freshness deep down things.* He was not going to be any trouble for me, this old soul. I sensed that he was trying to decode what I had said. I sensed all his formulated questions, one by one, float out of his head into the over-touristed night, unasked, as we just sauntered from the waterfront past the Cristobal Colon statue, pointing to the New World in the wrong direction, and then we strolled Las Ramblas and watched the street performers, the Moroccan acrobats, the mute wrinkled Catalans who painted silhouettes for twenty euro, and we bought FC Barca hats because we didn't really know any of the player names on the jerseys.

And we waded into the Barrio Gotico for what seemed like eternity, losing ourselves and finding new ways to get to the same place, which, tonight, was the Plaça de Santa Maria del Mar. There was a crowd in the great square as an acoustic guitarist was playing under a palm tree, sending notes up to the balconies and into the sky.

The doors were wide open. He took my hand and we walked inside; the nave was tall and wide, like something hollowed out, Catalan Gothic. Visitors were lighting votives, others kneeling in deep prayer in the back rows, some sat hands folded, gazing up at the crucifix. I could still hear the music; I looked back and the doors were still open wide.

I felt my pockets for coins. I pulled out a handful and there in the pile was something I did not expect, a coin with a perfect circle in the middle, an old twenty-five cent peseta. How did this get here? They had phased out the peseta in 2002. It fit neatly between my thumb and forefinger, had a certain ancient heft. There must be currency like this still in circulation, ending up in tourists' pockets, expatriating the country, purchases made partially with non-money. I checked to see if there were more. This was it.

Colin said he wanted to light a candle. I handed him a euro. He looked at it and made a comment, knelt at the flickering altar, and I handed him a stick that he used to steal fire from another candle and he lit his own. There were yellow tulips out of season at the base at the feet of the Virgin Mary, the only icon in her namesake church.

When he finally rose, he had that look you see in people long immersed in prayer. His cheeks were flushed. I fixed his hair and handed him his jacket. We stepped back into the cool night.

There was a little wine bar across the square, a scattering of tables outside and a dark interior, jazz playing, those big champagne bowls they use in France, so many Grand Crus and Reservas on sale by the glass.

We crossed the square and I handed Colin a fist of coins and he sprinkled some in the hat where the man was playing *Jeux Interdits*. There was a congregation of admirers, mostly locals. I found us a table and sat down and looked up at the moon.

I ordered a glass of Ribera del Duero, a *Fanta de naranja* for Colin. He poured the soda into his glass. The wine was amazing, smooth and concentrated. They gave us a little dish of chorizo and marcona almonds. We ate them quickly and the waiter brought a second dish. We sat for a while saying nothing, just the arpeggio of the guitar and the crisp night. Every time I sipped the wine it seemed to change. Like people too. We decline in the wrong climate, improve in others. I thought about Monica hanging in the La Ciutat Vella under tungsten light. She would have been proud of me. I thought about Hawthorne in Brioni commanding his new forces, and I wished him well as some stray gauzy clouds drifted across the face of the white full moon. I thought about how capturing these past few weeks on paper might anthologize a defining period of my life. I had time. The cathedral bells rang to mark the new hour from somewhere deep in the maze of Barcelona's lamp-lit magic streets.

And as I drank the last sip I thought about another but knew better. I got the bill and left a good tip of euros along with the peseta coin. Colin wandered over to the guitarist and sat down in the crowd. He turned and looked at me as if to ask if this was okay. I stood up to walk over. It was fine, I nodded. There was nowhere else to go.

about the author

Eric Michael Bovim is an American entrepreneur and writer. He began his career in journalism in 1999 as a correspondent for Dow Jones Newswires and Reuters, based Madrid. While in Spain, he covered the Basque separatist group, ETA, as well as tech and telecom companies that rose and fell during the dot com collapse. He is a graduate of College of the Holy Cross, and studied under Christopher Merrill, where he majored in English Literature with a focus on twentieth century fiction and poetry, and many of his essays and articles have been published in the *Wall Street Journal*, *Forbes*, *Fast Company*, and *Salon*. *Around the Sun* is his debut novel. He currently resides in Virginia.

CPSIA information can be obtained
at www.ICGtesting.com
Printed in the USA
LVHW020854220620
658650LV00004B/226